THE HISTORY OF POMPEY THE LITTLE;
OR THE LIFE AND ADVENTURES OF
A LAP-DOG

broadview editions
series editor: L.W. Conolly

Frontpiece of the first edition of *The History of Pompey the Little*, courtesy of the Thomas Fisher Rare Books Library, University of Toronto.

THE HISTORY OF POMPEY THE LITTLE;
OR THE LIFE AND ADVENTURES OF
A LAP-DOG

Francis Coventry

edited by
Nicholas Hudson

broadview editions

Library and Archives Canada Cataloguing in Publication

Coventry, Francis, 1725?-1759
  The history of Pompey the little, or, The life and adventures of a lap-dog / Francis Coventry ; edited by Nicholas Hudson.

(Broadview editions)
Includes bibliographical references.
ISBN 978-1-55111-734-8

  1. Dogs—Fiction. I. Hudson, Nicholas II. Title. III. Title: Life and adventures of a lap-dog. IV. Series.

PR3369.C7H5 2008   823'.5   C2008-903386-8

Broadview Editions

The Broadview Editions series represents the ever-changing canon of literature by bringing together texts long regarded as classics with valuable lesser-known works.

Advisory editor for this volume: Colleen Franklin

Broadview Press is an independent, international publishing house, incorporated in 1985. Broadview believes in shared ownership, both with its employees and with the general public; since the year 2000 Broadview shares have traded publicly on the Toronto Venture Exchange under the symbol BDP.

We welcome comments and suggestions regarding any aspect of our publications—please feel free to contact us at the addresses below or at broadview@broadviewpress.com.

North America
PO Box 1243, Peterborough, Ontario, Canada K9J 7H5
2215 Kenmore Ave., Buffalo, New York, USA 14207
Tel: (705) 743-8990; Fax: (705) 743-8353
email: customerservice@broadviewpress.com

UK, Ireland, and continental Europe
NBN International, Estover Road, Plymouth, UK PL6 7PY
Tel: 44 (0) 1752 202300; Fax: 44 (0) 1752 202330
email: enquiries@nbninternational.com

Australia and New Zealand
UNIREPS, University of New South Wales
Sydney, NSW, Australia 2052
Tel: 61 2 9664 0999; Fax: 61 2 9664 5420
email: info.press@unsw.edu.au

www.broadviewpress.com

Broadview Press gratefully acknowledges the financial support of the Government of Canada through the Book Publishing Industry Development Program (BPIDP) for our publishing activities.

PRINTED IN CANADA

Contents

Acknowledgements

Many thanks to friends and colleagues who provided encouragement and information towards the completion of this edition. These include Derek Carr, Brian Cowan, Alex Dick, Rick Gooding, Alex Hudson, Tina Lupton, Greg Morgan, Claude Rawson, Peter Sabor, and Mark Vessey. Many thanks to Colleen Franklin for her skilful and knowledgeable copy-editing of the typescript. My cat Hodge, who couldn't care less whether this book was published, nonetheless provided inspiration. This edition is dedicated to my wife Deb, who contributed happiness.

Introduction

Francis Coventry

What little we know of the short life of Francis Coventry (1725-54) suggests a man of high ambition and thwarted potential: he came from a good family, the son of a Buckinghamshire merchant and the daughter of a clergyman. His father appears to have been comfortable but not prosperous. He sent Francis to Eton College, a school designed to fashion gentlemen and the English elite, and later Magdelene College, Cambridge, though only as a "pensioner" rather than as a more privileged "fellow-commoner."[1] In *Pompey the Little*, Coventry reflects rather bitterly on the fawning of college tutors on these fellow-commoners, "who are Heirs to great Estates" (194).[2] But he did inherit noble blood from his father: the elder Coventry was the younger brother of William, fifth earl of Coventry. The Coventry family had an illustrious history in English court and political life dating back to the fifteenth century.

Coventry's noble ancestry seems to have exerted an important influence on his view of the world. *Pompey the Little*, whatever its virtues, is a novel of haughty snobbery. He viewed servants with disdain, calling "the lower Sort of Men-servants ... the most insolent, brutal, ungenerous Rascals on the Face of the Earth" (62–63). He treats the poor in general with disgust at their vulgarity and dirtiness. Book one, chapter nine, contains a remarkably vicious portrait of a rich merchant's son and his family, suggesting that he valued his father's noble links rather more than his profession. In contrast, Coventry seems at home in the world of the aristocracy, which he criticizes for its idleness and decadence, but whose accents and lifestyle he represents in knowing detail. In 1750, he published a poem, *Penshurst*, dedicated to William Perry, heir by marriage to the

---

1   At Cambridge in the eighteenth century, fellow-commoners were undergraduates of high rank or wealthy family permitted for this reason to join the college fellows at meals and other occasions. A "pensioner," or undergraduate of modest rank, was not permitted such privileges. He was nonetheless of a higher rank than the "sizars," whose fees were paid by the college but had to wait on the fellows and the other undergraduates.
2   All parenthetical references in the introduction are to the present edition.

Elizabethan poet Sir Philip Sidney's celebrated country estate. The poem, which shows Coventry sauntering with admiration around the estate, is filled with gleaming tributes to the Sidney family and the noble heroes of English history. He later wrote a poem praising Wilmot Vaughan, the future Earl of Lisburne. There is also evidence that Coventry moved, at least peripherally, in high circles in fashionable London society: Lady Mary Wortley Montagu, the leading literary lady of her day, claimed to recognize herself in the character of Mrs. Qualmsick, along with "many others of my Acquaintance."[1] This habit of privilege probably contributed to his anxiety about the loss of dignity in English life which underlies *Pompey the Little*, and which will be discussed later in this introduction.

Coventry's own life, rather like Pompey's, proceeded with perhaps rather less dignity than he had hoped. He entered Cambridge very late by eighteenth-century standards—he was over twenty—and he would not receive his M.A. until six years later, in 1752. In 1751, having been ordained an Anglican priest, his uncle the Earl of Coventry presented him with a parish in Edgware, Middlesex, but it was a small church and one wonders what Francis was doing with himself. His poem *Penshurst* bore signs of his literary and social ambition, and even of some talent, but it was a slight production in the crowded literary marketplace of the time. Then, very early in 1751, came *Pompey the Little*, which the poet Thomas Gray, who knew Coventry at Cambridge, said was a "hasty production."[2] Coventry published the novel anonymously, without a dedication, and there is evidence in the novel to suggest that he regarded it as an undignified trifle for a learned young man with a genteel pedigree. He must, therefore, have been pleasantly surprised by the favorable notice it received. His probable acquaintance, Lady Mary, read it at one sitting and called it "a real and exact representation of Life as it is now acted in London."[3] John Cleland, though he must have noticed

---

1   *The Complete Letters of Lady Mary Wortley Montagu*, ed. Robert Halsband, 3 vols. (Oxford: Clarendon, 1965–67), 3:4.

2   *Horace Walpole's Correspondence with Thomas Gray, Richard West, and Thomas Ashton*, ed. W.S. Lewis, G.L. Lam, and C.H. Bennett, 2 vols. (London: Oxford UP Geoffrey Cumberlege, 1948), 2:48.

3   *Complete Letters*, 3:4.

that Coventry twice sneers at his pornographic novel, *Memoirs of a Lady of Pleasure* (1748), applauded the author's "great humour, fancy, and wit" in the *Monthly Review*.[1] The novel was quickly reprinted by its prestigious bookseller, Robert Dodsley, who then gave Coventry what was a tidy sum in eighteenth-century terms, thirty pounds, to revise the novel as he saw fit. This was a task that Coventry undertook with more anxiety for fame than with wisdom. He added a fawning dedication to the novelist he particularly admired and emulated, Henry Fielding, who also had noble blood and a background at Eton. But Coventry also slashed and added to the novel to make it more ribald and marketable, more in the style of his racy contemporary Tobias Smollett than of the comparatively polite Fielding. *Pompey the Little* represented the high-point of Coventry's short life. He subsequently fell back into obscurity, wrote a rather despairing poem addressed to his friend Wilmot Vaughan, and died, like many of his characters, in the bloom of life, aged twenty-nine, reportedly of smallpox. He was buried in January 1754; no memorial or headstone survives.

POMPEY THE LITTLE AND THE EIGHTEENTH-CENTURY NOVEL

From his opening pages to his conclusion, Coventry seems painfully self-conscious that he has written a "little piece" (35) about a subject, "little *Pompey*" (44), whose physical smallness is matched by his moral unimportance. In Coventry's own estimation, *Pompey* is a slight production in a genre, the "novel," that his readers will contemptuously dismiss as degrading "the dignity of their understandings" (32). But the modern reader is likely to feel that Coventry has underestimated the interest and importance of *Pompey the Little* on several levels. Certainly the novel no longer suffers under the stigma of being an artistically "low" and undignified literary genre. And in the long history that led to the current status of the novel as the most popular and even the most prestigious genre, Coventry's book has an

---

1   *The Monthly Review*, 4: 316-17.

interesting place: it is the first so-called "it-narrative," a short-lived movement of novels that utilize non-human points-of-view. This fashion for "its" both facilitated certain narrative aims and reflects significant features of eighteenth-century British society at an important juncture of expanding capitalism. Finally, Coventry's use of a dog as his "hero" opens up a series of questions about the status of heroism in mid-eighteenth-century literature, the nature of property and commercial exchange in a consumer culture, and the philosophical characteristics of human beings in relation to animals.

That the novel was considered such an unworthy literary genre in the early 1750s might well surprise us. But it is important to keep in mind that the novel form was still in its early years of development. The very term "novel" was still only rarely used in its modern sense—Coventry actually being one of the first writers to use this word regularly in a modern sense. Previously, "novel" was used almost interchangeably with "romance" to mean fiction dominated by improbable and even miraculous events distant from the more mundane realities of common life. A standard assumption in modern scholarship, pioneered by Ian Watt in *The Rise of the Novel* (1956), locates the birth of the true "novel" in the fiction of Daniel Defoe and Samuel Richardson. In novels like *Robinson Crusoe* (1719), *Moll Flanders* (1721), *Pamela* (1740), and *Clarissa* (1746-7), it is said, Defoe and Richardson introduced a new "realism" characterized not only by the nature of events treated—these works dramatize the lives of ordinary eighteenth-century people—but also by a new detail in the treatment of time, place, and character. The romance typically concerned the adventures of stock characters such as noble princes and beautiful virgins in some vaguely described land over a undetermined span of time. Robinson Crusoe or Clarissa Harlowe, on the other hand, are fully rounded individuals who act in detailed settings and within a precise time-frame. It is interesting, therefore, that Coventry seems to credit the "rise of the novel" not to Defoe and Richardson, whom he never mentions, but rather to a third writer whom Watt and others have routinely excluded from the main line of this literary evolution—Henry Fielding. In a pamphlet sometimes ascribed to Coventry, *An Essay on the New*

Species of Writing founded by Mr. Fielding (1751),[1] the author applauds Fielding's *Joseph Andrews* (1742) and *Tom Jones* (1749) as showing that "pure Nature" (237) could be a source of entertainment and as divulging "the little Movements by which human Nature is actuated" (238). As the author writes:

> Sometime before this new Species of Writing appear'd, the World had been pester'd with Volumes, commonly known by the Name of Romances, or Novels, &c. fill'd with any thing which the wildest Imagination could suggest. In all these Works, Probability was not required: The more extravagant the Thought, the more exquisite the Entertainment. Diamond Palaces, flying Horses, brazen Towers, & c. were here look'd upon as proper, and in Taste. (237)

The key to Fielding's success, the author of the *Essay* indicates, was his invention of fictional "Biography," a form that spawned a small flood of imitations, including *Pompey the Little*. This "biography" of a lap-dog, like Fielding's novels, dramatizes a recognizable eighteenth-century world and its people down to the "lowest" and most banal events and characters. Coventry also adopted Fielding's belief in the moral and artistic value of comedy. In the dedication to Fielding, added in 1752 to the third edition of *Pompey the Little*, Coventry asserts that "we cannot well laugh too often" (32). And the whole is infused with the highly characteristic belief of the century, especially during its first half, that satire effectively reveals the foibles of modern life and human nature to their very core.

But Coventry also shared Fielding's virtually schizophrenic concern that this unapologetically comic treatment of daily life nonetheless lacked the "dignity" of real literary art. The writers of the early novel indeed tended to be people, often women, without formal literary training or a genteel education in the classics. The novel, it was thought, was a popular form available to writers and readers incapable of producing or appreciating prestigious literary forms such as the epic poem or tragic play. Hence in the preface to

---

1 This essay appears in this edition as Appendix C. While the attribution of the essay to Coventry is uncertain, I propose that much internal evidence links it to the author of *Pompey the Little*.

Joseph Andrews, Fielding playfully aligned his "comic Epic-Poem in Prose" with the tradition of epic writing, enlisting Homer's allegedly lost comic epic, *Margites,* as authority for his insistence on the essential dignity of comedy, at least in its classical forms. Fielding went on to describe what he called "the true Ridiculous," a species of comedy that provoked laughter by exposing the disjunction between reality and appearance in people's lives. Similarly, the eighteen "books" that comprise Fielding's *Tom Jones* each begin with a serious literary or moral essay describing the author's intentions in creating this "new Province of Writing."[1] In Coventry's dedication to Fielding, and elsewhere, he launches an analogous attack on those who think that the comic novel "degrades the dignity of their understandings." Fiction that exposes the follies of real life, he insists, surely merits even more respect than "the pride and pedantry of learned men" (32) who contribute nothing to the knowledge of truth as experienced by people in their daily routines. In innumerable other ways, Coventry flaunts his role as Fielding's disciple. Like Fielding, Coventry divides his novel into books and chapters, heading each chapter with a jocular description of its contents. Like Fielding's narrator, Coventry's narrative persona poses as the sagacious storyteller of a "History," addressing the reader with the formal and antiquated "thee" and "thou" and deploying avuncular variations on "my gentle Reader." And like *Joseph Andrews* or *Tom Jones, Pompey the Little* is replete with learned references and allusions that show off Coventry's classical education and that often stand in comic incongruity with his boisterous descriptions of banalities and low-life.

Yet there are also important differences between Coventry and Fielding. Coventry lacks Fielding's optimistic conviction in the morally redemptive power of literature. In contrast with Fielding, who seemed to believe that readers could be laughed out of their follies by recognizing the beauty and dignity of the "good Heart" and active compassion,[2] Coventry's comedy displays, despite the author's playfulness, a world that is almost unrelievedly dark,

---

1   *Tom Jones,* Bk. 2, ch.1.

2   I am referring specifically to the Fielding of *Joseph Andrews* and *Tom Jones.* There is a considerable darkening of Fielding's optimism by the time of his last novel, *Amelia* (1752).

corrupt and misguided. There is no "moral" to be learned from this book. Indeed, by making a Bologna lap-dog the "hero" of the novel, Coventry not only imitates Fielding's "biographical" method but also mocks it. While Joseph Andrews or Tom Jones are capable of genuine heroism, a lap-dog clearly is not. In his fawning good-nature and visceral randiness, Pompey converts the benevolence and sexual generosity of Fielding's heroes into blind and unthinking instinct. Pompey's identification as "hero" of the novel, in fact, points out the utter lack of heroism of the people around him. While some of Coventry's characters—Hillario, Jack Griskin, Jack Chace—strike ridiculous or degraded poses of hero-ism, Pompey's human companions are almost uniformly afflicted with foolishness, greed, and, often, malevolence. We must say "*almost* uniformly," because in Book Two, chapter three, Coventry presents a clutch of characters, the sisters Theodosia and Aurora, along with the latter's genteel lover, who are evidently meant as exemplars of upper-rank virtue. Yet, despite Coventry's intention, the noble lover comes off as priggish and superficial. Aurora, in banishing Pompey because his barking awakes her from a dream about the same prig, ends up seeming as self-centered and silly as any of our hero's other owners. Indeed, the characters' reactions to Pompey tend to regulate our evaluation of their moral worth: we will probably tend to like Lady Tempest, despite her uselessness and absurd fixation with dogs, because she treats Pompey more humanely than do her servants or the wicked children in Book One, chapter nine. It is nonetheless revealing that the most palat-able characters in the novel are not those who behave morally, but those who regard the world around them with cynical clarity and detachment. This could be said of Lady Tempest, the Milliner, or the politician Lord Danglecourt.

Pompey cannot be a real "hero" because his creator doggedly (so to speak) presents him as an animal rather than as the sort of personified beast familiar from Aesop's *Fables* or folk and fairy tales. Coventry's extensive revisions to the third edition of the novel tend to intensify Pompey's pure dogginess. Coventry deletes his most Aesopian chapter, in which the philosophical cat Mopsa schools Pompey's unthinking devotion to pleasure; he also diminishes Pompey's mock-heroic laments on the cruelty of fortune. As

Coventry repeatedly reminds us, dogs are surrounded by a richly ambivalent atmosphere of associations, both positive and negative. On the positive side, dogs are traditional symbols of fidelity. Yet Pompey displays an entirely understandable willingness to switch his allegiance to his various owners in order to survive. On the negative side, dogs have historically reminded people of the squalor, brevity, and dirtiness of human existence. It is in a "little dirty dog-hole of a tavern" where a circle of poor people make "trite observations" on the fidelity of dogs (184–85). Yet, in this and many other instances, humans tend to resemble dogs more than dogs personify human attributes. Coventry's human characters are generally dog-like in their willingness to fawn on those in power, in their inability to resist the calls of their stomachs and genitals, and in the basic degradation of their short lives. *Pompey the Little* is littered with human corpses as little lamented as dead dogs in a street. Coventry reserves some of his most bitterly sarcastic lines for the sudden and convenient demise of hated husbands and wives: Lady Tempest's "Monster" of a husband (who routinely hanged her dogs) "very seasonably died," leaving her the "*disconsolate Widow*" who joyously collects Pompey and fashionable lovers (59). "An old Gentleman turned of Seventy" (143) encourages one wife to drink herself to death, and is then happily relieved by the death of the next, who "caught cold one Night in *Vauxhall* Gardens, and after a short Illness of a Week or ten Days, retired to the peaceable Mansions of her Predecessors" (146). This sarcastic parody of elegiac convention ("the peaceable Mansions of her Predecessors") is rehearsed in the final mock-eulogy of Pompey, who similarly relieves the world of the trouble of a law-suit. Yet the elegy for Pompey is the only one with the least touch of pathos, if only because we have seen him endure hardship and narrowly escape death so often. And this satirical elegy mocks Pompey much less than the short, morally bereft, and atheistic lives of humans hardly more dignified than dogs.

Hence, Coventry's choice not to write a beast fable, but a biography of a real dog, raises some important philosophical questions, and also has significant implications for the form of this novel. The first philosophical issue implicit throughout the novel has already been suggested—the possibility that humans are, in fact, just animals. Twice in the novel, characters openly debate this possibility. In Book one, chapter seven, the fashionable female intellectual,

Lady Sophister, challenges two physicians to a debate on whether humans have souls; in Book two, chapter eleven, a free thinker in the "dirty dog-hole of a tavern" proposes that the vaunted "reason" of humans is shared by animals. Both debates reflect philosophical controversies that surrounded Coventry in Enlightenment Europe. The French philosopher René Descartes (1596-1650) had characterized the human body as a machine inhabited by a soul—a position that implied that animals are merely machines—but the possibility that all of human behavior could be explained without believing in either the soul or a special faculty became the *cause célèbre* of some radical thinkers who followed Descartes. In the article "Rorarius," in *Dictionnaire historique et critique* (*Historical and Critical Dictionary*), Pierre Bayle (1647-1706) sympathetically weighed the argument that human reason differed in no essential way from bestial instinct. The Enlightenment philosophers Julien Offray de La Mettrie (1709-51) and Claude Adrien Helvetius (1715-71) denied the existence of the soul and explained human nature as entirely mechanical, a system of values and fluids actuated by appetites. In England, David Hartley (1705-57) and Joseph Priestley (1733-1804) remained officially Christian (Priestley was indeed a Unitarian clergyman), yet defended comparably mechanistic views of human behavior.

Where did Francis Coventry stand in this controversy? Coventry was an Anglican priest, and expressed considerable annoyance with the free-thinking climate of his time. Yet it is significant that neither of the relevant debates in *Pompey the Little* reaches a clear resolution. Although the character of Lady Sophister is explicitly meant as a portrait of free-thinking vanity and female ignorance, her arguments against the existence of the soul are not effectively parried by the two physicians whom she drives, stunned and mumbling, out the door. The free-thinker who denies the existence of human reason is opposed only by an equally ridiculous and blustering parson. Most interestingly, we learn a great deal about the consciousness of Pompey, whose reactions to the world appear to differ in no fundamental way from a human's. He responds with hunger, lust, fear, longing, and even with pride and vanity, as circumstances dictate. While *Pompey the Little* does not explicitly underwrite the materialist cause, Coventry's presentation of his canine hero sustains the impression that humans and dogs resemble each other more than many people would like to believe. Never fully refuted in the novel are the physician's words to the hypochondriac Mrs. Qualmsick in Book two, chapter twelve: "we are but Machines, we are nothing but Machines, Madam!" (191).

A second issue raised by Coventry's use of a dog as his hero concerns the nature of property, currency, and exchange in the commercial marketplace. Coventry lived during a time of nascent capitalism and the resulting increase of commercialism. For the first time, shopping became a routine activity among middle-rank people, especially women, who sought not only necessities but also "luxuries," goods valued solely for their rarity and beauty. This growing economy of purchase and exchange struggled against a monetary regime that had yet to become fully systematic and secure. Money was not yet regularized, and coins—which were supposed to have intrinsic rather than merely representational value—were in critically short supply. As a result, the commercial economy relied heavily on credit: sagas of shop-keepers and lenders tracking down clients for payment, or of clients desperately avoiding "duns" or creditors, proliferate in eighteenth-century books and newspapers. London's Newgate Gaol seems to have been largely a holding place for people in arrears for debt. In turn, the notion of "property" became highly unstable and fluid. The bedrock of the eighteenth-century economy remained land: the most trustworthy measure of a person's financial worth was still his legal possession of "landed" property. (Women were increasingly disqualified from the legal possession of landed estates, and themselves became, like Miss Frippery in *Pompey the Little*, items of exchange in marriage for land.) But the rise of mercantile capitalism was threatening to displace this traditional idea of property, for a merchant's worth had to be assessed largely in terms of exchangeable commodities and money. As shown by James Thompson, Deirdre Lynch, Christopher Flint and others, all these changes had a profound impact on the century's literature.[1]

---

1   See James Thompson, *Models of Value: Eighteenth-Century Political Economy and the Novel* (Durham: Duke UP, 1996); Deirdre Lynch, *The Economy of Character: Novels, Market Culture, and the Business of Inner Meaning* (Chicago: U of Chicago P, 1998); Christopher Flint, "Speaking Objects: The Circulation Stories in Eighteenth-Century Prose Fiction," *PMLA* 113 (March 1998): 212-26.

Eighteenth-century fiction, right up to the time of Jane Austen, dwells obsessively on problematic issues of exchange, value, and property. Indeed, books themselves embodied a quintessential problem of property. The century's legal system struggled awkwardly with questions of copyright and the ownership of what we call "intellectual property."

This slow and incomplete evolution towards modern capitalism forms an important context for understanding *Pompey the Little*. The novel's hero, significantly, is himself a nebulous form of exchangeable property, and even a form of money. Spawned in Bologna, he arrives in England in the possession of Hillario, amongst a vast repertoire of foreign luxuries valued only for their rarity and beauty rather than their use-value. For Pompey is virtually useless (the only exceptions being when he is used by a blind beggar as a guide-dog, and later when an innkeeper plans to employ him as a "turn-spit" to rotate her rotisserie). He is repeatedly valued, desired, and exchanged among his upper-rank owners only because he is pretty, a useless luxury. Among the poorer sort, in search of real goods, his value seems equal only to a pint of beer or "a Pennyworth of Oysters" (99). That a dog constitutes a very queer and shifty form of property is brought explicitly to our attention in the lawyer's brief near the end of the novel, in this respect a suitable finale to Pompey's adventures. When Pompey is snatched from a lady's possession by Lady Tempest in St. James's Park, the lawyer is consulted to advise on whether this seizure constitutes theft. The lawyer muses that Pompey cannot really be owned because dogs are "Creatures of a *following* Nature" (210), liable to fall into the possession of any person who takes their fancy. As so often in the novel, Coventry's self-consciously trivial subject takes on a potentially momentous significance. Superficially, the scene seems intended to highlight the petty cavilings of the law. Yet the lawyer's testimony also indicates that Pompey falls outside the category of valuable property by dint of the very features that make him most "human." For humans, too, are willful creatures of "a *following* Nature," characteristically diverted by the attractions of, or profits to be gained from other human beings. And this characteristic raises pertinent questions about both the value of individual humans and their status in terms of property. Do human beings have any value, except as they are pretty? Insofar as they can be useful to others, does this usefulness make them categorizable as property, as suggested by the institutions of both servitude and marriage? This set of issues seems particularly significant when raised in an age when humans were being reduced to chattels or "beasts" by Europe's flourishing slave-trade.

As a queerly exchangeable piece of property, moreover, Pompey serves as a narrative device, an itinerant "it," inaugurating that interesting sub-genre of "it-narratives." In the two decades that followed *Pompey the Little*, English bookstalls would accumulate a small stockpile of novels about the adventures of wandering objects. At least one of these narratives, *The Life and Adventures of a Cat* (a segment of which appears in Appendix B), directly imitates Coventry's novel. Other it-narratives may well have been inspired by *Pompey the Little*, though they concern inanimate objects rather than animals. *Chrysal; or the Adventures of a Guinea* (1760), *The Adventures of a Bank-Note* (1770), or *The Adventures of a Rupee* (1782) made explicit the preoccupation with money and property that is largely implicit in *Pompey the Little*. Others dramatized the peregrinations of objects like hackney-carriages and corkscrews with the peculiar status of property that is repeatedly hired or easily lost. But apart from reflecting the unstable nature of property in eighteenth-century culture, how do we account for the popularity of these books?

The small body of recent scholarship on "it-narratives" has tended to focus on the changing status of *things* in modern culture. With old values eroding under the rise of commodity fetishism and materialist conceptions of human nature, eighteenth-century authors became increasingly preoccupied with the hazy division between objects and people. The work of Jonathan Lamb, for example, has focussed on modern versions of metamorphoses—a tradition linked in Western culture to ancient tales of transformation, and to a wider global tradition of magical overlaps between humans and objects. Not only in it-narratives, but in a variegated range of eighteenth-century satire by Swift, Pope, and others, things or animals speak like humans and humans dwell on their own diminishment to objects or beasts. While this scholarship offers valuable insights into the fashion for it-narratives, Coventry's lap-dog bears a problematic relationship to "things." In the novel, Pompey is treated routinely like a thing: with only rare exceptions, characters never address him or imagine what he is thinking or feeling. Yet the novel dramatizes Pompey as a sentient, even "thinking" being, a status that implies neither sentimentalism nor anthropomorphism, particularly in the revised version of the novel. Coventry's humans, in turn, behave like dogs, but their animalism implies no metamorphosis. The similarity between Coventry's characters and animals or even machines is presented as a brute, static fact of his world rather than as a transformation or even a revelation. With the minor exception of *The Life and Adventures of a Cat*, *Pompey the Little* stands as an exception, a *sui generis*, in the it-narrative fad that this novel helped to inspire. This novel belongs most compellingly not to a tradition of meditations about the imagined life of "things," but rather about beings that or who, in common perception, inhabit the boundary between people and objects. It is this problematic status that makes their well-being so tenuous, a peril experienced not only by domestic animals but also by slaves, children, women, and the physically and mentally disabled.

Another explanation for the popularity of it-narratives must take into account yet another form of change and instability—one that is nonetheless tied up with the questions of property that we have just considered. As the result of the burgeoning of mercantile capitalism, the traditional social hierarchy was breaking down. The aristocracy remained a small and highly enclosed group at the top of British society, its hold on the upper echelons of political power still strong, its doors still pressed hard against the crowds intruding from below. But the power and prestige of the nobility were no longer absolute or unchallenged. Its numbers and resources were declining and, as the result of primogeniture, concentrated into fewer and fewer hands. Britain was engaged in expensive wars for most of the eighteenth century and, to finance these wars, relied heavily on the bankers of the City of London, to whom the nation owed a growing and massive debt. The economic power of Britain had moved decisively towards the mercantile upper-middle orders that were competing with the French and Spanish to build a world-wide empire. These were the moneyed-men whose impatience with attempts to impose the arbitrary power of the monarchy and the aristocracy had precipitated a civil war in 1642 and the overthrow of the Catholic James II in 1688, known as the "Glorious Revolution." This event greatly strengthened the role of the House of Commons and placed important limitations on the power of future monarchs. Hence, for unavoidable financial and political reasons, the middle-ranks could no longer be treated as powerless underlings or ignored in decisions about Britain's national destiny.

The erosion of social boundaries had not advanced to the point where we can safely use the term "upward mobility" in describing these changes. It is true that marriages between the aristocracy and the merchant class were becoming more common—desired by the nobility to increase their wealth, and by merchants to increase their power and prestige. Yet British people remained acutely sensitive to the traditional social hierarchy. Not a sentence in *Pompey the Little* can be read well without trying to duplicate some of that class-sensitivity. Most important, however, the outward markers of social rank were becoming confused and amorphous. With the loosening of credit, for example, fine clothes and the wherewithal to attend exclusive social events became available to a broader sector of the middle-ranks, even down to shop-keepers and apprentices; the official paraphernalia of the old elite—swords, wigs, and even coats-of-arms—could now be widely purchased, making Coventry's London a "masquerade" where appearances had become detached from social realities. There is plenty of evidence of these confusing changes in *Pompey the Little*. In Book one, chapter nine, we enter the household of a wealthy merchant's son whose daughter, in a virtually symbolic act, has absconded with the lap-dog of the noble Lady Tempest in St. James's Park, once the exclusive reserve of people from the Court. Coventry's blistering satire of this vulgar and unruly family reveals his deeply conservative disgruntlement with the barging of grubby merchants into the precincts of traditional prestige. This phenomenon represents yet another dimension of his engrossing anxiety with the indignity of modern English life. This family is indeed "almost too inconsiderable for the Dignity of History" (78), and the whole chapter was cut from the third edition. At least in the first edition, however, Coventry acknowledges that money trumps birth in the new England, and that neither society nor his novel can ignore the presence of such coarse upstarts:

> For to tell the Reader a Secret, Money will procure its Owners Admittance any where; and however People may pride themselves on the Antiquity of their Families, if they have not Money to preserve a Splendor in Life, they may go a begging with their Pedigrees in their Hands; whereas lift a Grocer into a Coach-and-Six, and let him attend publick Places, and make grand Entertainments, he may be sure of having his Table filled with People of Fashion, tho' it was no longer ago than last Week that he left off selling Plumbs and Sugar. (79)

Coventry was no blind admirer of the aristocracy: like so many of his contemporaries, he deplored the vanity, decadence and uselessness of Lady Tempest, Hillario, and their noble coterie. "The young Nobleman" who courts Aurora in Book two represents an effort, if rather half-hearted and failed, to shame the aristocracy back into an attention to its traditional role as the guardians of the nation's manners and morals. But clearly more infuriating to Coventry is Count Tag, Aurora's upstart suitor, who has falsely appropriated both a title and the fashions of the elite. Coventry's fools and villains—Captain Vincent, the highwayman Jack Griskin, Sir Thomas Frippery, the Milliner, Jack Chace, Mr. Williams—routinely attempt to live above the rank that they deserve either socially or morally. They are cast as typical figures in the delusive and disruptive masquerade of modern England.

How then does this upheaval of the old class system relate to the fashion for "it-narratives" that *Pompey the Little* inaugurated? Writers of Coventry's era were partners in a project to create a new kind of social order in England, a project spurred by the rising power of mercantile capitalism. The old order had been moored to beliefs that now seemed not only philosophically suspect but also politically and economically unfeasible. According to a passing ideology, kings and aristocrats presided over society by virtue of some inherent "natural" hierarchy that it was unnatural and even sacrilegious to oppose. But the rising merchant or professional of the 1750s would by no means accept that he was excluded from influence in the halls of power, or from equitable social relations with the traditional elite, because of some mysterious mandate of "nature." The ascending middle-orders needed to eject the old idea of "nature" in order, crucially, to ascend. On the other hand, they also needed to reformulate the idea of "nature" in ways favorable to their own eventual consolidation of power over British society. Hence, "nature" became a term increasingly attached not to the old natural hierarchy, but to allegedly "human" measures of intrinsic worth—particularly virtue, beneficence, chastity, probity, and other moral qualities. Good manners, the ability to function smoothly in social situations (particularly those involving the chance for social advancement), were also increasingly valued as an attribute "naturally" belonging to those who deserved membership in the reformed ruling class. This coalescing concept of "human nature," which still underlies much that is thought in social sciences like psychology and economics, increasingly served the purposes of the aspiring middle-ranks in two closely interconnected ways. First, it justified the social advancement of those who now claimed common "humanity" with those who, previously, had claimed a natural superiority to all below them in the social hierarchy. Second, the idea of "human nature" provided a presumably objective standard for judging the worth of those who aspired to become part of the new ruling elite. Membership in this elite would now ideally embrace those who demonstrated superior virtue, honesty, good nature, good manners, and so forth.

For reasons that we have already considered, the issue of "human nature" is complicated in *Pompey the Little*. Influenced by radical ideas of the Enlightenment, the novel casts doubt on the reality of any meaningful distinction between humans and animals. Nonetheless, *Pompey the Little*, like the later "it-narratives," responded to the transformation of the class structure by inventing a narrative point-of-view that could move freely through the whole hierarchy, from top to bottom, judging all members of English society from oyster-wenches to aristocrats according to common standards of morality and manners. An object could move through the various ranks of English society with a facility and quickness unimaginable in a person. The walls of class exclusion had not simply disappeared; a poor person could not simply waltz or, in eighteenth-century terms, minuet into a salon full of nobility, any more than a (sober) aristocrat or ambitious merchant would be found in the company of porters and oyster-wenches. But a dog or a banknote or a corkscrew could move speedily through these ranks, in a sense accelerating and epitomizing the whole process of class confusion and peregrination that had begun to characterize English culture.

Coventry was not entirely without literary precedents that facilitated the exploration of this phenomenon of class movement. Much fun is had in *Pompey the Little* with the romance tradition of the fallen prince, habituated to clean clothes and soft beds but forced through cruel circumstance to dress in rags and sleep on hard floors—though he is always recognized, like Pompey, by a beauty allegedly unnatural among the denizens of huts and fields. Coventry also knew the tradition of the picaresque, so influential on Fielding: Pompey is a kind of *pícaro*, Spanish for "rogue," a lower-rank figure, a naughty animal, who infiltrates the upper-ranks in the style of Daniel Defoe's Moll Flanders or Tobias Smollett's Roderick Random. But these precedents could not entirely fulfill the novelist's quest for a socially mobile narrative. The *pícara* Moll Flanders, for example, can enter into polite society only through elaborate ruses facilitated by good fortune. Nor did the other influential narrative styles developed in the eighteenth century really lend themselves to exploration of the social hierarchy. Richardson's servant-heroine in *Pamela* is dragged, almost literally, kicking and screaming into the genteel circle of her attempted seducer, Mr. B.; Richardson's later novels, *Clarissa* and *Sir Charles Grandison*, only glance at figures from the lower orders insofar as they are useful to the main story. Like Fielding's novels *Joseph Andrews* and *Tom Jones*, these works closely tie their stories to the main characters. By contrast, *Pompey the Little* and the it-narratives are *not* really about the eponymous subject—the lap-dog, guinea, overcoat, and so forth. These objects are, above all, narrative devices that permit the author to contrive a series of character portraits that explore the entire social hierarchy in the light of abiding moral and "human" themes.

It is also worth considering, however, the severe limitations of the "it-narrative" technique for fully realizing the political needs of the modern novel. For neither Coventry's novel nor the it-narratives it influenced achieve an objective point-of-view—one that is able to judge society from a narrative position that seems neutral and "natural." Since the middle-ranks relied on the objective criteria of "nature" to legitimize their rise to power, only such presumably disinterested judgements could have real authority. It is important to keep in mind that eighteenth-century fiction still lacked the resources of a fully-fledged omniscient point-of-view. Not conceiving that God would stoop to writing novels, eighteenth-century novelists always wrote from an individualized human perspective. Scholars still hotly debate what Defoe or Richardson "really" meant in their depictions of society because the perspectives of their first-person narrators are limited, personalized, and, therefore, prejudiced. Even Fielding's story-telling narrators seem so individual—almost like "characters"—that we remain highly conscious of their subjective and, in Fielding's case, loftily genteel point-of-view. Similarly, Pompey is technically "objective" in his judgements, for he does not judge those he meets morally, socially, or politically, except as they give him pleasure or pain. On the other hand, Pompey's perspective falls far short of that of an omniscient narrator. Indeed, he cannot properly "narrate," for as a dog he is voiceless. The burden of narration therefore falls on Coventry's Fieldingesque narrative persona, who follows his subject through doors often inaccessible to first-person narrators, but who cannot pronounce judgment except from a first-person perspective tainted by the author's strong class prejudice. In addition, Pompey is very far from being able to read the minds of his various owners, and Coventry's narrative persona generally conforms to Fielding's implicit rule that mere story-tellers or "historians" do not have automatic access to the inner consciousness of their subjects.

We might note that the authors of later it-narratives made efforts to overcome these limitations. Never again, it would seem, would one of these authors attempt to separate the main narrative voice from the traveling "it." The adventures of the bank-note, hackney-carriage, and overcoat are all narrated as if these objects could actually think and write the novel at hand. While such a pretence facilitates, to some degree, the illusion that the novel casts entirely "objective" judgments on the characters, it strains probability to the point where fantastic comedy negates any claim to serious social critique. Writers of other "it-narratives," such as the histories of the guinea and corkscrew, invented a "spirit" or "genie" to reside within the traveling object. Such a spirit could not only go anywhere, it could also pronounce judgement from a perspective that was more authoritative because it was non-human, and therefore ostensibly unclouded by human prejudices. Moreover, such a spirit could penetrate the minds of the characters, much in the style of an omniscient narrator. Again, however, a modern reader disabused of an easy belief in spirits and alchemy is likely to read such a narrative as fantasy, and to attribute its judgments to the individualized and biased perspective of the human author.

Let us compare these experiments with the fully-fledged omniscient narrator developed after Jane Austen by canonical nineteenth-century novelists such as Charles Dickens and George Eliot. The narrators of these works, like "its," move at pleasure throughout society; not even the innermost thoughts and meditations of their characters are inaccessible to their God-like point of view. Also like God, such omniscient narrators seem absolutely objective and authoritative within the social and moral value system of the novel itself. While we are reading these novels, we characteristically forget that they are in fact being "told" from an individual human perspective because the narrator is not a "character" or person in the way the characters in the story are. This impression of objectivity is of course an illusion—an illusion exploded by the twentieth-century narrative technique of "meta-fiction." In the meta-fictional novels of John Barth, John Fowles, or J.M. Coetzee, the author exposes the subjectivity of the realist novel by openly admitting that it is all made up. Interestingly, modern scholars often point to eighteenth-century novels as precursors to meta-fiction, particularly Laurence Sterne's *Tristram Shandy* (1759-67). This highly self-conscious "autobiography" of the muddle-headed Tristram seems to expose the ultimate subjectivity and fictionality of the novel-form because it repeatedly draws attention to its own composition through repeated references to the act of writing itself. But Sterne was not demolishing any fully-realized model of realist fiction. Rather, *Tristram Shandy* capitalizes on the inherent subjectivity and uncertainty generally characteristic of the fiction before Sterne.

Many eighteenth-century novels play gleefully with the unstable boundary between fact and fiction. One thinks here particularly of Fielding's open admissions in *Tom Jones* that he himself is the creator of this "new Province of Writing." And we might think as well of *Pompey the Little*. For we are hardly supposed to *believe* that there was ever a lap-dog named Pompey whose life Francis Coventry the "historian" has diligently researched and recorded. This is an obviously fictional narrative containing the author's personal perspectives on the English society of his day.

In summary, *Pompey the Little* and the later it-narratives represent a phase of *transition* towards the creation of that sociopolitical desideratum, the omniscient narrator. (My meaning is not of course that eighteenth-century novelists were consciously trying to create omniscient narration; I mean rather than they were attempting to adapt their fictions to the exigencies and paradoxes of their transforming culture and its readership.) Omniscient narration served the needs of a capitalist society that required both to embrace all of society in a totalizing vision and to pronounce morally and politically on society in ways that seemed neutral and objective. Only such "objective" judgments could serve the needs of the emergent "middle-class" hegemony, for hegemonies must seem "natural," not foisted on society by a particular class or gender. While *Pompey the Little* represents only a stepping-stone towards that achievement in the novel, it is not, however, for that reason less valuable or interesting in its own right. Without at all impugning the importance and seriousness of literature for children, we should insist that Coventry's novel is aimed squarely at adults. (Coventry indeed seems to have disliked children.) An author thoroughly abreast of and engaged in the pressing social and philosophical issues of his day, he leads us to think about the status of heroism in a post-heroic culture, as well as the nature of human beings in relation to animals. He writes a comic novel nonetheless informed by a thoughtful, if rather dark, vision of modern society and the human condition. In these respects, *Pompey the Little* stands not only as an interesting specimen in the short tradition of it-narratives. It is also a work that deserves to be studied for its own virtues as a valuable example of eighteenth-century fiction and mock-heroic satire.

Francis Coventry: A Brief Chronology

[We know very little about Francis Coventry, and there is no biography. Readers may also consult the entry for "(William) Francis Walter Coventry" in the *Oxford Dictionary of National Biography* by David Oakleaf.]

1725	William Francis Walter Coventry born about July 15 at Mill End, Buckinghamshire, to the family of a reasonably well-off merchant with noble links
1735	birth of Coventry's fictional lapdog, Pompey
1742–44	Coventry attends Eton College
1742	admitted as "pensioner" to Magdelene College, Cambridge
1749	graduates B.A.; publication of Henry Fielding's *The History of Tom Jones, a Foundling*, a highly influential novel on Coventry's own fiction; death of the fictional Pompey
1750	anonymously publishes *Penshurst*, a country-house poem dedicated to William and Elizabeth Perry, heirs to the celebrated estate of the Sidney family
1751	*The History of Pompey the Little; or the Adventures of a Lap-Dog* published anonymously by London bookseller, Robert Dodsley, in February; also in February, the bookseller William Owen publishes *An Essay on the New Species of Writing founded by Mr. Fielding*, which is occasionally attributed to Coventry (see Appendix C); Coventry appointed vicar of Edgware, Middlesex
1752	publishes the heavily revised "third edition" of *Pompey the Little*, this time under his name
1753	publishes an edition of his cousin Henry Coventry's *Philemon and Hydaspes*, defending the Christian orthodoxy of this tract on pagan religions; also publishes an essay on gardening in the journal *The World* (no. 15, April 12), chastising the vulgarity of modern taste
1754	death and burial, January
1755	Robert Dodsley republishes *Penshurst*, along with "To the Hon. Wilmot Vaughan, Esq. in Wales," in Vol. 4 of *A Collection of Poems*
1758	Dodsley publishes "Ode to the Honourable ★★★★," a poem to a young MP in volume 6 of *A Collection of Poems*

A Note on the Text

Pompey the Little presents uniquely difficult problems for its editors. Rarely has a work been so extensively revised to the detriment of its artistic virtues and historical significance. The reasons for these revisions pose an interesting quandary in themselves. In the 1752 "third edition,"[1] Coventry seems to have tried to make his novel racier and more popular. For example, he replaced the cutting satire of the merchant's son in Book one, chapter nine, with the story of Captain and Lady Vincent. This is a much more conventional satire of quasi-genteel vanity and silliness, featuring passages of scatological humor aimed at the backside of readerly taste. On a rather higher side, Coventry seems to have made some effort to render his novel more religiously orthodox: Pompey's favorite owner, Lady Tempest, was made less of a libertine. Coventry added a chapter that attacked the Methodists, a populist upstart sect much despised by respectable Anglicans. And he deleted passages, like the defence of John Locke in Book one, chapter seven, that could be construed as controversial in orthodox Anglican terms. On the other hand, his portraits of Anglican priests remained uniformly negative, and he did not tamper significantly with sections that, as we have considered, could be construed as uncomfortably non-committal in relation to Enlightenment materialism and the philosophy of mechanism. Indeed, his changes make Pompey seem at once less of a mock-heroic personification (inclined to articulate yowls about the cruelties of "fortune") and more mundanely "human" in his panting for the creaturely comforts of food and sex. In addition, after a year of relative fame as a novelist, Coventry rightly judged that his stylistic forte was dialogue: the reader will notice that the dialogue in this novel is unusually sharp, funny, and realistic. So he added long tracts of dialogue, as in the enlarged section on the blind beggar and his highwayman son, Jack Griskin. In the process, regretfully, he tended to forget about his mute "hero," Pompey.

---

1   "Edition" is used here in its eighteenth-century sense. The unaltered "second edi-
    tion" was strictly speaking only a "reimpression" of the first edition, not a new edition
    in itself.

Such emendations make it difficult to rely on conventional editorial principles. In particular, the principle that we should give preference to the "last intentions" of the author—known as "Greg's Rationale," after the scholar W.W. Greg—seems of questionable use in a novel where these last intentions seem to have left the work less original and significant. I have therefore accorded with the decision of the novel's previous modern editor, Robert Adams Day, in attempting to produce what he called a "practical" edition that retains as much as possible from both the first and third editions. While using the first edition as my main text, additions from the third edition are indicated by square brackets. Guided by my preference for the first edition, a few of my editorial decisions differ from Day's. For example, Day replaced the portrait of Lord Danglecourt in Book two with the story of Pompey's short stay with Lord and Lady Marmazet, relegating the original chapter to an appendix. I have done just the opposite (see Appendix A). Like Day's edition, however, this edition represents the novel in a form that comprehends both the relevant versions of the text. Hence, what follows in this edition is *Pompey the Little* in its full, doggy glory, excepting the omission of some bridging paragraphs. It is not, however, a text that existed as such in Coventry's lifetime.

THE HISTORY OF POMPEY THE LITTLE; OR THE LIFE AND ADVENTURES OF A LAP-DOG

[DEDICATION [1]

TO

Henry Fielding, Esq.

SIR,

MY design being to speak a word or two in behalf of novel-writing, I know not to whom I can address myself with so much propriety as to yourself, who unquestionably stand foremost in this species of composition.

To convey instruction in a pleasant manner, and mix entertainment with it, is certainly a commendable undertaking, perhaps more like to be attended with success than graver precepts; and even where amusement is the chief thing consulted, there is some little merit in making people laugh, when it is done without giving offence to religion, or virtue, or good manners. If the laugh be not raised at the expence of innocence or decency, good humour bids us indulge it, and we cannot well laugh too often.

Can one help wondering therefore at the contempt, with which many people affect to talk of this sort of composition? they seem to think it degrades the dignity of their understandings, to be found with a novel in their hands, and take great pains to let you know that they never read them. They are people of too great importance, it seems, to mispend their time in so idle a manner, and much too wise to be amused.

Now, tho' many reasons may be given for this ridiculous and affected disdain, I believe a very principal one, is the pride and pedantry of learned men, who are willing to monopolize reading to themselves, and therefore fastidiously decry all books that are on a level with common understandings, as empty, trifling and impertinent.

Thus the grave metaphysician for example, who after working

---

1 As indicated in A Note on the Text, above, all interpolations from the third edition will appear between square brackets.

night and day perhaps for several years, sends forth at last a profound treatise, where *A.* and *B.* seem to contain some very deep mysterious meaning; grows indignant to think that every little paltry scribbler, who paints only the characters of the age, the manners of the times, and the working of the passions, should presume to equal him in glory.

The politician too, who shakes his head at coffee-houses, and produces now and then, and from his fund of observations, a grave, sober, political pamphlet on the good of the nation; looks down with contempt on all such idle compositions, as lives and romances, which contain no strokes of satire at the ministry, no unmannerly reflections upon *Hannover,* nor any thing concerning the balance of power on the continent.[1] These gentlemen and their readers join all to a man in depreciating works of humour: or if they ever vouchsafe to speak in their praise, the commendation never rises higher than "yes 'tis well enough for such a sort of thing;" after which the graver observator retires to his newspaper, and there, according to the general estimation, employs his time *to the best advantage.*

But besides these, there is another set, who never read any modern books at all. They, wise men, are so deep in the learned languages, that they can pay no regard to what has been published within these last thousand years. The world is grown old; mens geniuses are degenerated; the writers of this age are too contemptible for their notice, and they have no hopes of any better to succeed them. Yet these gentlemen of profound erudition will contentedly read any trash, that is disguised in a learned language, and the worst ribaldry of *Aristophanes,* shall be critiqued and commented on by men, who turn up their noses at *Gulliver* and *Joseph Andrews.*[2]

---

1 George II, who still held the post of Elector of Hanover, had been widely criticized for committing British troops to conflicts resulting from treaties between Hanover and other continental states, as most recently in the War of the Austrian Succession (1741-48).

2 Aristophanes (c. 428-380 BCE) was a Greek writer of scandalous and sometimes lewd comic plays. *Gulliver's Travels* (1726) by Jonathan Swift and *Joseph Andrews* (1742) by Henry Fielding were widely considered great works of Coventry's era. Coventry by no means denied the value of classical literature. But he was annoyed that pedants of his time neglected the finest contemporary works in favor of classics of questionable value.

But if this contempt for books of amusement be carried a little too far, as I suspect it is, even among men of science and learning, what shall be said to some of the greatest triflers of the times, who affect to talk the same language? these surely have no right to express any disdain of what is at least equal to their understandings. Scholars and men of learning have a reason to give; their application to severe studies may have destroyed their relish for works of a lighter cast, and consequently it cannot be expected that they should approve what they do not understand. But as for beaux, rakes, petit-maitres,[1] and fine ladies, whose lives are spent in doing the things which novels record, I do not see why they should be indulged in affecting a contempt of them. People, whose most earnest business is to dress and play at cards, are not so importantly employed, but that they may find leisure now and then to read a novel. Yet these are as forward as any to despise them; and I once heard a very fine lady, condemning some highly finished conversations in one of your works, sir, for this curious reason——"because," said she, "'tis such sort of stuff as passes every day between me and my own maid."

I do not pretend to apply any thing here said in behalf of books of amusement, to the following little work, of which I ask your patronage: I am sensible how very imperfect it is in all its parts, and how unworthy to be ranked in that class of writings, which I am now defending. But I desire to be understood in general, or more particularly with an eye to your works, which I take to be master-pieces and complete models of their kind. They are, I think, worthy the attention of the greatest and wisest men, and if any body is ashamed of reading them, or can read them without entertainment and instruction, I heartily pity their understandings.

The late editor of Mr. *Pope*'s work, in a very ingenious note, wherein he traces the progress of romance-writing, justly observes, that this species of composition is now brought to maturity by Mr. *De Marivaux* in *France*, and Mr. *Fielding* in *England*.[2]

---

1 "Beaux" here denotes vain and superficial men obsessed with fine dress; a "rake" is a debauched womanizer; "petit-maitre" means an effeminate and affected socialite, sometimes with the connotation of homosexuality.

2 See William Warburton's note to his edition of *The Works of Alexander Pope, Esq.*, 9 vols. (London, 1751), 4:131. Pierre Carlet de Chamblain de Marivaux (1688–1763) was a novelist and dramatist whose *La Vie de Marianne* (1731–35) appeared in installments and reached no *dénouement*, as Coventry observes in the following paragraph.

I have but one objection to make to this remark, which is, that the name of Mr. *De Marivaux* stands foremost of the two; a superiority I can by no means allow him. Mr. *Marivaux* is indeed a very amiable, elegant, witty, and penetrating writer. The reflections he scatters up and down his *Marianne* are highly judicious, *recherchées*,[1] and infinitely agreeable. But not to mention that he never finishes his works, which greatly disappoints his readers, I think, his *characters* fall infinitely short of those we find in the performances of his *English* cotemporaries. They are neither so original, so ludicrous, nor so well contrasted as your own: and as the characters of a novel principally determine its merit, I must be allowed to esteem my countryman the greater author.

There is another celebrated novel writer, of the same kingdom, now living, who in the choice and diversity of his characters, perhaps exceeds his rival Mr. *Marivaux*, and would deserve greater commendation, if the extreme libertinism of his plans, and too wanton drawings of nature, did not take off from the other merit of his works; tho' at the same time it must be confessed, that his genius and knowledge of mankind are very extensive.[2] But with all due respect for the parts of these two able *Frenchmen*, I will venture to say they have their superior, and whoever has read the works of Mr. *Fielding*, cannot be at a loss to determine who that superior is. Few books of this kind have ever been written with a spirit equal to *Joseph Andrews*, and no story that I know of, was ever invented with more happiness, or conducted with more art and management than that of *Tom Jones*.

As to the following little piece, sir, it pretends to a very small degree of merit. 'Tis the first essay of a young author, and perhaps may be the last. A very hasty and unfinished edition of it was published last winter, which meeting with a more favourable reception than its writer had any reason to expect, he has since been tempted to revise and improve it, in hopes of rendering it a little more worthy of his readers' regard. With these alterations he

---

1   Well-researched, with the ironic connotation of an affected display of learning.
2   Probably Claude Prosper Jolyot Crébillon, 1707-77, well-known as a libertine novelist. A less probable possibility is the Abbé Antoine François Prévost d'Exiles, 1697-1763, whose only really libertine novel was *Manon Lescaut* (1728).

now begs leave, sir, to desire your acceptance of it; he can hardly hope for your approbation; but whatever be its fate, he is proud in this public manner to declare himself.

Your constant reader,
And sincere admirer.]¹

---

1 We now return to the first edition.

BOOK I

CHAP. I

A PANEGYRIC UPON DOGS, TOGETHER WITH SOME OBSERVATIONS ON MODERN NOVELS AND ROMANCES.

VARIOUS and wonderful, in all Ages, have been the actions of Dogs; and if I should set myself to collect, from Poets and Historians, the many Passages that make honourable mention of them, I should compose a Work much too large and voluminous for the Patience of any modern Reader. But as the Politicians of the Age, and Men of Gravity may be apt to censure me for misspending my Time in writing the Adventures of a Lap-dog, when there are so many *modern Heroes*, whose illustrious Actions call loudly for the Pen of an Historian; it will not be amiss to detain the Reader, in the Entrance of this Work, with a short Panegyric on the *canine Race*, to justify my undertaking.

And can we, without the basest Ingratitude, think ill of an Animal, that has ever honoured Mankind with his Company and Friendship, from the Beginning of the World to the present Moment? While all other Creatures are in a State of Enmity with us, some flying into Woods and Wildernesses to escape our Tyranny, and others requiring to be restrained with Bridles and Fences in lose Confinement; Dogs alone enter into voluntary Friendship with us, and of their own accord make their Residence among us.

Nor do they trouble us only with officious Fidelity, and useless Good-will, but take care to earn their Livelihood by many meritorious Services: they guard our Houses, supply our Tables with Provision, amuse our leisure Hours, and discover Plots to the Government.[1] Nay, I have heard of a Dog's making a Syllogism; which cannot fail to endear him to our two famous Universities,

---

1   Coventry is evidently referring to an incident in 1722, when Bishop Francis Atterbury, a "Jacobite" or supporter of the deposed Stuart royal family, was convicted of treason largely on the basis of coded correspondence in which the name of a real dog, Harlequin, actually referred to the Stuart claimant to the throne (the "Pretender").

where his Brother-Logicians are so honoured and distinguished for their Skill in that *useful* science.[1]

After these extraordinary Instances of Sagacity and Merit, it may be thought too ludicrous, perhaps, to mention the Capacity they have often discovered, for playing at Cards, Fiddling, Dancing, and other polite Accomplishments; yet I cannot help relating a little Story, which formerly happened at the Play-house in *Lincolns-Inn-Fields*.

There was, at that Time, the same Emulation between the two Houses, as there is at present between the great Common-wealths of *Drury-Lane* and *Covent-Garden*;[2] each of them striving to amuse the Town[3] with various Feats of Activity, when they began to grow tired of Sense, Wit, and Action. At length, the Managers of the House of *Lincolns-Inn-Fields*, possessed with a happy Turn of Thought, introduced a Dance of Dogs; who were dressed in *French* Characters, to make the Representation more ridiculous, and acquitted themselves for several Evenings to the universal Delight and Improvement of the Town. But one unfortunate Night, a malicious Wag behind the Scenes, threw down among them the Leg of a Fowl, which he had brought thither in his Pocket for that Purpose. Instantly all was in Confusion; the Marquis shook off his Peruke,[4] Mademoiselle dropp'd her Hoop-petticoat, the Fidler threw away his Violin, and all fell to scrambling for the Prize that was thrown among them.——But let us return to graver Matter.

If we look back into ancient History, we shall find the wisest and most celebrated Nations of Antiquity, as it were, contending with one another, which should pay the greatest Honour to Dogs.

---

1   Coventry is casting a scornful glance at Oxford and Cambridge, the only two English universities of the time, where the curriculum still centered on the outdated and allegedly useless logic of the Middle Ages.

2   At the time that Coventry was writing, the Theatres Royal at Drury Lane and Covent Garden were the only theatres officially permitted to stage plays, and so were naturally rivals. The playhouse at Lincoln's Inn Field had closed in 1732, the same year that the Covent Garden Theatre opened, so the other rivalry he mentions must be between Lincoln's Inn and Drury Lane.

3   "Town" was the conventional term in the eighteenth century for the fashionable parts of London, as opposed to the "City," the eastern and original jurisdiction of Greater London, surrounding St. Paul's Cathedral, and the center of British commerce.

4   "A skullcap covered with hair so as to imitate the natural hair of the head; a wig; a periwig" (*OED*).

The old Astronomers denominated Stars after their Name; and the *Egyptians* in particular, a sapient and venerable People, worshipped a Dog among the principal of their Divinities.[1] The poets represent *Diana*,[2] as spending a great Part of her Life among a Pack of Hounds, which I mention for the Honour of the Country Gentlemen of *Great-Britain*; and we know that the illustrious *Theseus* dedicated much of his time to the same Companions.[3]

Julius Pollux informs us, that the Art of dying purple and scarlet Cloth was first found out by *Hercules*'s Dog, who roving along the Sea-coast, and accidentally eating of the Fish *Murex,* or *Purpura*,[4] his lips became tinged with that Colour; from whence the *Tyrians* first took the Hint of the purple Manufacture, and to this lucky Event our fine Gentlemen of the Army are indebted for the scarlet, with which they subdue the Hearts of so many fair Ladies.[5]

But nothing can give us a more exalted Idea of these illustrious Animals, than to consider, that formerly, in old *Greece*, they founded a Sect of Philosophy; the Members whereof took the Name of *Cynics*, and were gloriously ambitious of assimilating themselves to the Manners and Behaviour of that Animal, from whom they derived their Title.[6]

And that the Ladies of *Greece* had as great a Fondness for them as Men, may be collected from the Story which *Lucian* relates of a certain Philosopher; who in the Excess of his Complaisance to a Woman of Fashion, took up her *favourite Lap-Dog* one Day, and attempted to caress and kiss it; but the little Creature, not being used to the rude Grip of philosophic Hands, found his Loins affected in such a manner, that he was obliged to water the Sage's Beard, as he held him to his Mouth; which so discomposed that principal, if not only seat of his Wisdom, as excited Laughter in all

---

1   Sirius, the "dog-star," is in the constellation of Canis Major. The Egyptians worshipped a jackal-headed dog named Anubis.
2   Roman goddess of the hunt.
3   Theseus, king of Athens in Shakespeare's *A Midsummer Night's Dream*, boasts about his hunting dogs in 4.1.122ff.
4   A kind of mollusk used in ancient times to make purple dye.
5   Coventry is referring to a story told in the *Onomasticon* by the second-century CE rhetorician Julius Pollux.
6   The Cynics were an ancient Greek philosophical sect that, rejecting all worldly pleasure, reveled in being dirty and unkempt. For unclear reasons, their name does indeed derive from the Greek word for "dog."

the Beholders.[1]

Such was the Reverence paid to them among the Nations of Antiquity; and if we descend to later Times, we shall not want Examples in our own Days and Nation, of great Men's devoting themselves to Dogs. King *Charles* the Second, of pious and immortal Memory, came always to his Council-board accompanied with a favourite Spaniel; who propagated his Breed, and *scattered his Image though the Land,*[2] almost as extensively as his Royal Master. His Successor, king *James,* of pious and immortal Memory likewise,[3] was distinguished for the same Attachment to these four-footed Worthies: and 'tis reported of him, that being once in a dangerous Storm at Sea, and obliged to quit the Ship for his Life, he roar'd aloud with a most vehement Voice, as his principal Concern, *to Save the Dogs and the Duke of M____.*[4] But why need we multiply Examples? The greatest Heroes and Beauties have not been ashamed to erect Monuments to them in their Gardens, nor the greatest Wits and Poets to write their Epitaphs. Bishops have entrusted them with their Secrets, and Prime-Ministers deigned to receive Information from them, when Treason and Conspiracies were hatching against the Government. Islands likewise,[5] as well as Stars, have been called after their Names; so that I hope no one will dare to think me idly employed in composing the following Work: or if any should, let him own himself ignorant of ancient and modern History, let him confess himself an Enemy to his Country, and ungrateful to the Benefactors of *Great Britain.*

---

1 Coventry is referring to a story in *On the Salaried Posts in Great Houses* by the Roman satirist Lucian (c. 125–180 CE).

2 A quotation from John Dryden's poem in praise of Charles II, *Absalom and Achitophel,* 1. 10. Charles was famous for his many mistresses and illegitimate children.

3 This is highly provocative praise, if taken non-ironically. The Stuart King James II had been forced from the throne in 1688 ("The Glorious Revolution") for promoting Roman Catholicism, and his heirs still claimed that they were the legitimate rulers of Great Britain. Coventry's obeisance to James II as "of pious and immortal Memory" is nonetheless difficult to take seriously given his harsh criticism of the Stuarts in his poem *Penshurst* (1750). See the introduction to the poem in Appendix D, below.

4 The Duke of Marlborough, ancestor of Sir Winston Churchill, is one of the greatest military heroes in English history, though he gained this dukedom only after James II's reign. Coventry corrected this anachronism in the third edition, changing the name to "colonel *Churchill.*" Coventry ironically implies that James II valued his dogs as much as his best military commander.

5 The Isle of Dogs is in the River Thames, adjacent to London.

And as no Exception can reasonably be taken against the Dignity of my Hero, much less can I expect that any will arise against the Nature of this Work, which one of my Cotemporaries declares to be an *Epic Poem in Prose*;[1] and I cannot help promising myself some Encouragement, in this *Life-writing Age* especially, where no Character is thought too inconsiderable to engage the public Notice, or too abandoned to be set up as a Pattern of Imitation. The lowest and most contemptible Vagrants, Parish-Girls, Chamber-Maids, Pick-Pockets, and Highwaymen, find Historians to record their Praises, and Readers to wonder at their Exploits: Star-Gazers, superannuated Strumpets, quarrelling Lovers, all think themselves authorized to appeal to the Publick, and to *write Apologies* for their Lives. Even the Prisons and Stews[2] are ransacked to find Materials for Novels and Romances. [Thus we have seen the memoirs of a lady of pleasure, and the memoirs of a lady of quality; both written with the same public-spirited aim, of initiating the unexperienced part of the female sex into the hidden mysteries of love; only that the former work has rather a greater air of chastity, if possible than the latter.][3] Thus, I am told, that illustrious *Mimic* Mr. F____t,[4] when all other Expedients fail him, and he shall be no longer able to raise a Kind of Tax, if I may so call it, from Tea, Coffee, Chocolate, and Marriages, designs, as the last Effort of his Wit, to oblige the World with an accurate History of his own Life; with which View one may suppose he takes care to chequer it with so many extraordinary Occurrences, and selects such Adventures as will best serve hereafter to amaze and astonish his Readers.

---

1   The phrase used by Fielding, in the preface to *Joseph Andrews* (1742), to describe his own work.

2   Brothels.

3   The "lady of pleasure" refers to Fanny Hill, the main character in John Cleland's notorious pornographic novel *Memoirs of a Lady of Pleasure* (1748). Robert Adams Day suggests that "the lady of quality" may be Lady Vane in Tobias Smollett's *Peregrine Pickle* (1751).

4   Samuel Foote (1720-77), well known for his impersonations of notable people. The reference to Foote, clearly derogatory, may be intended as a sidelong bow to Henry Fielding, as Foote and Fielding were highly public enemies. F____t of course suggests another word. Foote had evaded contemporary theatrical licensing laws by staging performances at events advertised merely as occasions to drink coffee and tea.

This being the Case, I hope the very Superiority of the Character here treated of, above the Heroes of common Romances, will procure it a favourable Reception, altho' perhaps I may fall short of my great Cotemporaries in the Elegance of Style, and Graces of Language. For when such Multitudes of Lives are daily offered to the Publick, written *by the saddest Dogs*, or *of the saddest Dogs* of the Times, it may be considered as some little Merit to have chosen a Subject worthy of the Dignity of History; and in this single View I may be allowed to paragon myself with the incomparable Writer of the Life of *Cicero*,[1] in that I have deserted the beaten Track of Biographers, and chosen a Subject worthy the Attention of polite and classical Readers.

Having detained the Reader with this little necessary Introduction, I now proceed to open the Birth and Parentage of my Hero.

CHAP. II

THE BIRTH, PARENTAGE, EDUCATION, AND TRAVELS OF A LAP-DOG.

POMPEY, the son of *Julio* and *Phyllis*, was born A.D. 1735, at *Bologna* in *Italy*, a Place famous for Lapdogs and Sausages. Both his Parents were of the most illustrious Families, descended from a long Train of Ancestors, who had figured in many Parts of Europe, and lived in Intimacy with the greatest Men of the Times. They had frequented the Chambers of the proudest Beauties, and had Access to the Closets[2] of the greatest Princes; Cardinals, Kings, Popes, and Emperors, were all happy in their Acquaintance; and I am told the elder Branch of the Family now lives with his present Holiness in the papal Palace at *Rome*.[3]

But *Julio*, the Father of my Hero, being a younger Brother of a numerous Family, fell to the Share of an *Italian* Nobleman at *Bologna*; from whom I heard a Story of him, redounding so much

---

1 By Conyers Middleton (1683-1750), a learned writer ridiculed by Fielding for his pomposity.
2 Private rooms.
3 Pope Benedict XIV, who reigned 1740-58, had previously been Archbishop of Bologna.

to his Credit, that it would be an Injury to his Memory not to relate it; especially as it is the Duty of an Historian to derive his Hero from honourable Ancestors, and to introduce him into the World with all the Eclat and Renown he can.

It seems the City of *Bologna* being greatly over-stocked with Dogs, the Inhabitants of the Place are obliged at certain Seasons of the Year to scatter poisoned Sausages up and down the Streets for their Destruction; by which Means the Multitude of them is reduced to a more tolerable Number. Now *Julio* having got abroad one Morning by the Carelessness of Servants into the Streets, was unwisely tempted to eat of these pernicious Cates;[1] which immediately threw him into a violent Fit of Illness: But being seasonably relieved with Emetics, and having a good Constitution, he struggled thro' the Distemper; and ever afterwards remembering what himself had escaped, out of Pity to his Brethren, who might possibly undergo the same Fate, he was observed to employ himself during the whole Sausage-Season, in carrying these poisonous Baits away one by one in his Mouth, and throwing them into the River that runs by the City. But to return,[2]

The *Italian* Nobleman above-mentioned had an Intrigue with a celebrated Courtesan of *Bologna*, and little *Julio* often attending him when he made his Visits to her, (as it is the Nature of all Servants to imitate the Vices of their Masters,) he also commenced an Affair of Gallantry with a Favourite little Bitch named *Phyllis*, at that Time the Darling of this *Fille de Joye*.[3] For a long while she rejected his Courtship with Disdain, and received him with that Coyness, which Beauties of her Sex know very well how to counterfeit; but at Length in a little Closet devoted to *Venus*,[4] the happy Lover accomplished his Desires, and *Phyllis* soon gave Signs of Pregnancy.

I have not been able to learn whether my Hero was introduced into the World with any Prodigies[5] preceding his Birth; and tho' the Practice of most Historians might authorize me to invent them,

---

1 "Choice viands; dainties, delicacies" (*OED*).
2 The entire story of Julio and the poisoned sausages was omitted from the third edition.
3 French: "girl of joy," i.e., a prostitute.
4 Venus, the goddess of love, served at that time as a common euphemism for sex.
5 "An extraordinary thing or occurrence regarded as an omen; a sign, a portent" (*OED*).

I think it most ingenuous[1] to confess, as well as most probable to conclude, that Nature did not put herself to any miraculous Expence on this Occasion. Miracles are unquestionably ceased in this Century, whatever they might be in some former ones; there needs no Dr. *Middleton* to convince us of this; and I scarce think Dr. *Ch____n* himself would have the Hardiness to support me, if I should venture to relate one in the present Age.[2]

Be it sufficient then to say, that on the 25th of *May* N.S.[3] *1735*, *Pompey* made his first Appearance in the World at *Bologna*; on which Day, as far as I can learn, the Sun shone just as usual, and Nature wore exactly the same Aspect as upon any other Day in the Year.

About this time an *English* Gentleman, who was making the Tour of *Europe*,[4] to enrich himself in foreign Manners and foreign Cloaths, happened to be residing at *Bologna*. And as one great end of modern Travelling is the pleasure of intriguing with Women of all Nations and Languages, he was introduced to visit the Lady above-mentioned, who was at that Time the fashionable and foremost Courtesan of the Place. Little *Pompey* having now opened his Eyes and learnt the Use of his Legs, was admitted to frolic about the Room, as his Mistress sat at her Toilet[5] or presided at her Tea-Table. On these Occasions her Gallants never failed to play with him, and many pretty Dialogues often arose concerning him which perhaps might make a Figure in a modern Comedy. Every one had something to say to the little Favourite, who seemed proud to be taken Notice of, and by many significant Gestures would often make believe he understood the Compliments that were paid him.

But nobody distinguished himself more on this Subject than

---

1   In Coventry's time "ingenuous" generally meant "open; fair; candid; generous; noble" (Johnson), rather than "guileless, innocent; artless" (*OED*), its usual meaning at present.

2   Coventry is referring to debates about miracles in the eighteenth century involving Conyers Middleton, identified above page 42, note 1, and John Chapman (1704-84).

3   The abbreviation for "New Style." In the year of the novel's first publication, the calendar changed from the Julian ("Old Style") to the Gregorian. As the result of this change, the year began on January 1 rather than on March 25.

4   Sometimes called the "Grand Tour," this was a journey to courts and historic sights of Europe and was considered a necessary stage in the education of young, high-born Englishmen. It is fitting that "our hero," Pompey, will make the "tour" as well.

5   I.e., at her dressing-table.

our *English Hillario*; who had now made a considerable Progress in the Affections of his Mistress: For partly the Recommendation of his Person, but chiefly the Profusion of his Expences made her think him a very desireable Lover; and as she saw that his ruling Passion was Vanity, she was too good a Dissembler, and too much a Mistress of her Trade, not to flatter this Weakness for her own Ends. This so elevated the Spirits of *Hillario*, that he surveyed himself every Day with Increase of Pleasure at his Glass,[1] and took a Pride on all Occasions to shew how much he was distinguished, as he thought, above any of her antient[2] Admirers. Resolving therefore to out-do them all as much in Magnificence, as he imagined he did in the Success of his Love, he was continually making her the most costly Presents, and among other Things, presented Master *Pompey* with a Collar studded with Diamonds. This so tickled the little Animal's Vanity, being the first Ornament he had ever worn, that he would eat Biscuit from *Hillario*'s Hands with twice the Pleasure, with which he received it from any other Person's; and *Hillario* made him the Occasion of conveying indirect Compliments to his Mistress. Sometimes he would swear, *he believed it was in her Power to impart Beauty to her very Dogs*, and when she smiled at the Staleness of the Conceit,[3] he, imagining her charmed with his Wit, would grow transported with Gaiety, and practice all the fashionable Airs that Custom prescribes to an Intrigue.

But the Time came at length that this gay Gentleman was to quit this Scene of his Pleasures, and go in quest of Adventures in some other Part of *Italy*. Nothing delayed him but the Fear of breaking his Mistress's Heart, which his own great Love of himself, joined with the seeming Love she expressed for him, made him think a very likely Consequence. The Point therefore was to reveal his Intentions to her in the most tender Manner, and to reconcile her to this terrible Event as well as he could. They had been dining together one day in her Apartments, and *Hillario,* after Dinner, first inspiring himself with a Glass of Tokay,[4] began to curse his Stars for obliging him to leave *Bologna*, where he had been so divinely happy; but he said, he

---

1   Mirror.
2   Former.
3   "A fanciful, ingenious, or witty notion or expression" (*OED*).
4   An expensive dessert wine from the Hungarian region of Tokaj.

had received News of his Father's Death, and was obliged to go settle *cursed Accounts* with his Mother and Sisters, who were in a hurry for their *confounded Fortunes*; and after many other Flourishes, concluded his Rhapsody with requesting to take little *Pompey* with him as a Memorial of their Love. The Lady received this News with all the artificial Astonishment and counterfeited Sorrow that Ladies of her Profession can assume whenever they please; in short she played the Farce of Passions so well, that *Hillario* thought her very Life depended on his Presence: She wept, intreated, threatened, swore, but all to no Purpose; at length she was obliged to submit on Condition that *Hillario* should give her a Gold-watch in Exchange for her Favourite Dog, which he consented to without any Hesitation.

The Day was now fixed for his Departure, and having ordered his Post-Chaise to wait at her Door, he went in the Morning to take his last Farewell. He found her at her Tea-Table ready to receive him, and little *Pompey* sitting innocently on the Settee by his Mistress's Side, not once suspecting what was about to happen to him, and far from thinking himself on the Point of so long a Journey. For neither Dogs nor Men can look into Futurity, or penetrate the Designs of Fate. Nay, I have been told that he eat his Breakfast that Morning with more than usual Tranquillity; and tho' his Mistress continued to caress him, and lament his Departure, he neither understood the Meaning of her kisses, nor greatly returned her Affection. At length the accomplished *Hillario* taking out his Watch, and cursing Time for intruding on his Pleasures, signified he must be gone that Moment. Ravishing therefore an hundred Kisses from his Mistress, and taking up little *Pompey* in his Arms, he went off humming an *Italian* Tune, and with an Air of affected Concern threw himself carelessly into his Chaise. From whence looking up with a melancholy Shrug to her Window, and shewing the little Favourite to his forsaken Mistress, he was interrupted by the Voice of the Postilion,[1] desiring to be informed of the Rout he was to take; which little Particular this well-bred Gentleman had in his Hurry forgot, as thinking it perhaps of no great Consequence. But now cursing the Fellow for not knowing his Mind without putting him to the Trouble of explaining it, *Damn you*, cries he, *drive to the Devil if you will, for I shall never be happy*

---

1   The driver of the post-chaise, a small carriage.

again as long as I breathe. Recollecting himself however upon second Thoughts, and thinking it as well to defer that Journey to some future Opportunity, he gave his Orders for ____; and then looking up again at the Window, and bowing, the Post-Chaise hurried away, while his Charmer stood laughing and mimicking his Gestures.

As her Affection for him was wholly built on Interest, of course it ended the very Moment she lost sight of his Chaise; and we may conclude his for her had not a much longer Continuance; for notwithstanding the Protestations he made of keeping her Dog for ever in Remembrance of her, little *Pompey* had like to have been left behind in the very first Day's Stage. *Hillario* after Dinner had reposed himself to sleep on a Couch in the Inn; from whence being waked with Information that his Chaise was ready and waited his Pleasure at the Door, he started up, discharged his Bill, and was proceeding on his Journey without once bestowing a Thought on the neglected Favourite. His Servant however, being more considerate, brought him and delivered him at the Chaise Door to his Master; who cried indolently, *Begad that's well thought on*, called him *a little Devil for giving so much Trouble*, and then drove away with the utmost Unconcernedness. This I mention to shew how very short-lived are the Affections of protesting Lovers.

CHAP. III

OUR HERO ARRIVES IN ENGLAND.
A CONVERSATION BETWEEN TWO LADIES
CONCERNING HIS MASTER.

BUT as it is not my Design to follow this Gentleman through his Tour, we must be contented to pass over great part of the Puppyhood of little *Pompey*, till the Time of his Arrival at *London*: only it may be of Importance to remember, that in his passage from *Calais* to *Dover* he was extremely Sea-sick, and twice given over by a Physician on board; but some medicinal Applications, together with a Week's Confinement in his Chamber, after he came to Town, restored him to his perfect Health.

Hillario was no sooner landed, than he dispatched his *French* Valet to *London*, with Orders to provide him handsome Lodgings in *Pall-Mall*, or some other great Street near the Court; and himself set forwards the next Day with his whole Retinue. Let us therefore imagine him arrived and settled in his new Apartments; let us suppose the News-writers to have performed their Duty, and all the important World of Dress busy, as usual, in reporting from one to another, *that* Hillario *was returned from his Travels.*

As soon as his Chests and Baggage were arrived in Town, his Servants were all employed in setting forth to View in his Antichamber, the several valuable Curiosities he had collected; that his Visiters might be detained as they passed through it, in making Observations on the Elegance of his Taste. For tho' Dress and Gallantry were his principal Ambition, he had condescended, in Compliance with the Humour of the Times, to consult the *Ciceroni* at *Rome*, and other Places, as to what was proper to be purchased, in order to establish a Reputation for *Vertù:*[1] and they had furnished him accordingly, at a proportionable Expence, with all the necessary Ingredients of modern Taste; that is to say, with Fingers and Toes of ancient Statues, Medals bearing the Name of *Roman* Emperors on their Inscriptions, and *copied-original* Pictures of all the great Masters and Schools of *Italy*. They had likewise taught him a Set of Phrases and Observations proper to be made, whenever the Conversation should turn upon such Subjects; which, by the Help of a good Memory, he used with tolerable Propriety: he could descant in Terms of Art, on Rusts and Varnishes; and describe the Air, the Manner, the Characteristic of different Painters, in Language almost as learned as the ingenious Writer of a late Essay.[2] "Here, he would observe, the Drawing is incorrect; there the Attitude ungraceful—the *Costume* ill-preserved, the Contours harsh, the Ordonnance irregular—the Light too strong—the Shade too

---

1   "Ciceroni" were professional guides in Italy employed to direct fashionable foreigners in collecting items of elegant taste or "virtù," and hence to be esteemed "virtuosi." Pompey, presumably, has become one such item of taste.

2   While a previous editor, Robert Adams Day, suggests Jonathan Richardson's influential *Essay on the Theory of Painting* (1715), Coventry could be referring to one of innumerable more recent essays on painting designed for "virtuosi."

deep,"—with many other affected Remarks, which may be found in a very grave sententious Book of Morality.

But Dress, as we before observed, was his darling Vanity, and consequently his Rooms were more plentifully scattered with Cloaths than any other Curiosity. There all the Pride of *Paris* was exhibited to View; Suits of Velvet and Embroidery, Sword-hilts, red-heel'd Shoes, and Snuff-boxes, lay about in negligent Confusion, yet all artfully disposed to catch the Eye of his Female Visiters. Nor did he appear with less Eclat without Doors; for he had now shewn his gilt Chariot[1] and bay Horses in all the Streets of gay Resort, and was allowed to have the most splendid brilliant Equipage in *London*. The club at *White*'s[2] voted him a Member of their Fraternity, and there began a kind of Rivalry among the Ladies of Fashion, who should first engage him to their Assemblies. At all Toilettes and Parties in the Morning, who but *Hillario*? No-body came into the Side-box at a Play-house with so graceful a Negligence; and it was on all Hands confessed, that he had the most accomplished Way of talking Nonsense of any Man of Quality in *London*.

As the fashionable Part of the World are glad of any fresh Topic of Conversation, that will not much fatigue their Understandings; and the Arrival of a new Fop, the Sight of a new Chariot, or the Appearance of a new Fashion, are all Articles of the highest Importance to them; it could not be otherwise, but that the Shew and Figure, which *Hillario* made, must supply all the polite Circles with Matter for Commendation or Censure. As a little Specimen of this kind of Conversations may, perhaps, not be disagreeable, I will beg the Reader's patience a Moment, to relate what passed on this subject between *Cleanthe* and *Cleora*,[3] two Ladies of Eminence and Distinction in the Commonwealth of Vanity. The former was a young Lady of about Fifty, who had out-lived many Generations of Beauties, yet still preserved the Airs and Behaviour of Fifteen; the latter a celebrated Toast[4] now in the Meridian of her Charms, and giddy with the Admiration she excited. These two Ladies had

---

1   Carriage.
2   One of London's most fashionable coffee-houses.
3   It was conventional in the eighteenth century to use classical names for stock characters.
4   I.e., a beauty honored by being toasted (in her absence) by men at drinking parties.

been for some Time past engaged in a strict *Female Friendship*, and were now Sitting down to Supper at Twelve o'Clock at Night,[1] to talk over the important Follies of the Day. They had play'd at Cards that Evening at four different Assemblies, left their Names each of them at near Twenty Doors, and taken half a Turn round *Ranelagh*,[2] where the youngest had been engaged in a very smart Exchange of Bows, Smiles, and Compliments with *Hillario*. This had been observed by *Cleanthe*, who was at the same Place, and envied her the many Civilities she received from a Gentleman so splendidly dress'd, whose Embroidery gave a peculiar Poignancy to his Wit. Wherefore at Supper she began to vent her Spite against him, telling *Cleora*, she wondered how she could listen to the Impertinence of such a Coxcomb:[3] "Surely," said she, "you cannot admire him; for my Part, I am amazed at People for calling him handsome——do you really think him, my Dear, so agreeable as the Town generally makes him?" *Cleora* hesitating a Moment replied, "she did not well know what Beauty was in a Man: To be sure," added she, "if one examines his Features one by one, one sees nothing very extraordinary in him: but altogether he has an Air, and a Manner, and a Notion of Things, my Dear——he is lively, and airy, and engaging, and all that——and then his Dresses are quite charming." "Yes," said Cleanthe, "that may be a very good Recommendation of his Taylor, and if one designs to marry a Suit of Velvet, why No body better than *Hillario*——How could you like him for a Husband, *Cleora*?" "Faith," said *Cleora* smiling, "I never once thought seriously upon the Subject in my Life; but surely, my Dear, there is a such a thing as Fancy and Taste in Dress; in my Opinion, a Man shews his Parts[4] in nothing more than in the Choice of his Cloaths and Equipage." "Why to be sure," said *Cleanthe*, "the Man has something of a Notion of Dress, I confess it——yet methinks I could make an Alteration for the better in his

---

1 "Supper," in traditional English parlance, is a late meal, relatively light, served an hour or more before bedtime. (The main meal of the day, dinner, was served in the afternoon, normally between two and four o'clock.) That these fashionable ladies are having supper at such a late hour is indicative of their decadent lives.

2 One of London's fashionable pleasure-gardens.

3 "A superficial pretender to knowledge or accomplishments" (Johnson).

4 Intelligence.

Liveries."[1] Then began a very curious Conversation on Shoulder-knots, and they ran over all the Liveries in Town, commending one, disliking another, with great Nicety of Judgment. From Shoulder-knots they proceeded to the Colour of Coach-horses, and *Cleanthe*, resolving to dislike *Hillario*'s Equipage, asked her if she did not prefer Greys to Bays? *Cleora* answered in the Negative, and the Clock struck one before they had decided this Momentous Question; which was contested with so much Earnestness, that both of them were beginning to grow angry, and to say ill-natured Things, had not a new Topic arisen to divert the Discourse. His Chariot came next under Consideration, and then they returned to speculate his Dress; and when they had fully exhausted all the external Accomplishments of a Husband, they vouchsafed, at last, to come to the Qualities of Mind. *Cleora* preferred a Man who had travelled; "Because," she said, "he has seen the World, and must be ten thousand times more agreeable and entertaining than a dull home-bred Fellow, who has never improved himself by *seeing Things*:" But *Cleanthe* was of a different Opinion, alledging that this would only give him a greater Conceit of himself, and make him less manageable by a Wife. Then they fell to abusing Matrimony, numbered over the many unhappy Couples of their Acquaintance, and both of them for a Moment resolved to live single: But those Resolutions were soon exploded; "For though," said *Cleanthe*, "I should prefer a Friendship with an agreeable Man far beyond marrying him, yet you know, my Dear, *we Girls* are under so many Restraints, that one must wish for a Husband, if it be only for the Privilege of going into public Places, without the Protection of a married Woman along with one, to give one Countenance." *Cleora* rallied the Expression of *we Girls*, which again had like to have bred a Quarrel between them; and soon afterwards happening to say, she should like to dance with *Hillario* at the next Ridotta,[2] *Cleanthe* could not help declaring, that she should be pleased also to have him for a Partner. This stirred up a warmer Altercation than any that had yet arisen, and they contended with such Vehemence for this distant imaginary Happiness, which perhaps might happen to

---

1   The servants in any fashionable home would wear characteristic uniforms, known as "liveries" or "livery."
2   A social gathering with music and dancing.

neither of them, that they grew quite unappeaseable, and in the End, departed to Bed with as much Malice and Enmity, as if the one had made an Attempt on the other's Life.

CHAP. IV

ANOTHER CONVERSATION BETWEEN HILLARIO AND A CELEBRATED LADY OF QUALITY.

IF the foregoing Dialogue appears impertinent and foreign to this History, the ensuing one immediately concerns the Hero of it; whose Pardon I beg for having so long neglected to mention his Name. He was now perfectly recovered from the Indisposition hinted at in the Beginning of the preceding Chapter, and pretty well reconciled to the Air of *England*; but as yet he had made few Acquaintances either with Gentlemen of his own or a different Species; being seldom permitted to expatiate beyond the Anti-chamber of *Hillario*'s Lodgings; where his chief Amusement was to stand with his Fore paws up in the Window, and contemplate the Coaches that passed through the Street.

But Fortune, who had destined him to a great Variety of Adventures, no sooner observed that he was settled and began to grow established in his new Apartments, than she determined, according to her usual Inconstancy, to beat up his Quarters,[1] and provide him a new Habitation.

Among the many Visiters that favour'd *Hillario* with their Company in a Morning, a Lady of Quality, who had buried her Husband, and was thereby at liberty to pursue her own Inclinations, was one day drinking Chocolate with him. They were engaged in a very interesting Conversation on the *Italian* Opera, which they declared to be the most sublime Entertainment in Life; when on a sudden little *Pompey* came running into the room, and leapt up into his Master's Lap. Lady *Tempest* (for that was her Name) no sooner saw

---

1 I.e., pay an unwanted visit.

him, than addressing herself to *Hillario* with the Ease and Familiarity of modern Breeding; "*Hillario,*" said she, "where the devil did you get that pretty Dog?" "That Dog, Madam!" cries *Hillario,* "Oh *l'Amour*! thereby hangs a Tale[1]——That Dog, Madam, once belonged to a Nobleman's Wife in *Italy,* the finest Creature that ever my Eyes beheld——such a Shape and such an Air"——"*O quelle mine! Quelle delicatesse!*"[2] Then ran he into the most extravagant Encomiums of her Beauty, and after dropping many Hints of an Intrigue, to awaken Lady *Tempest's* Curiosity, and make her enquire into the Particulars of the Story, concluded with desiring her Ladyship to excuse him from proceeding any farther, for he thought it the highest Injury to betray a Lady's Secrets. "Nay," said Lady *Tempest,* "it can do her Reputation no hurt to tell Tales of her in *England*; and besides, *Hillario,* if you acquitted yourself with Spirit and Gallantry in the Affair, who knows but I shall like you the better after I have heard your Story?" "Well," said he, "on that Condition, my dear Countess! I will confess the Truth——I had an Affair with this Lady, and, I think, none of my Amours ever afforded me greater Transport: But the Eyes of a Husband will officiously be prying into things that do not concern them; her jealous-pated Booby[3] surprized me one Evening in a little familiar Dalliance, and sent me a Challenge[4] the next Morning." "Bless us!" said Lady *Tempest,* "and what became of it?" "Why," cries *Hillario,* "I wou'd willingly have washed my Hands of the Fellow if I could, for I thought it but a silly Business to hazard one's Life with so ridiculous an Animal; but, curse the Blockhead, he could not understand Ridicule——You must know, Madam, I sent him for Answer, with the greatest Ease imaginable——quite composed as I am at this Moment——that I had so prodigious a Cold, that it wou'd be imprudent to fight abroad in open Air; but if he wou'd have a Fire in his best Apartment, and a bottle of *Burgundy* ready for me on the Table after I had gone thro' the Fatigue of killing him, I was at his

---

1   The line "thereby hangs a tale," whose combined canine and sexual connotations ("tale" puns on "tail") are surely flaunted by the rakish Hillario, appears twice in Shakespeare's plays. See *As You Like It,* 2.8.28 and *Taming of the Shrew,* 4.1.48.
2   French: "Oh, what a face! Such delicacy!" Employing a smattering of French in one's conversation was considered fashionable. Revealingly, it is unclear whether Hillario is complimenting the Italian lady or the dog, as he views both merely as pretty objects.
3   "Pate" means "head." A "booby" is an uncouth fool.
4   I.e., a challenge to a duel.

Service as soon as he pleased——meaning, you see, to have turned the Affair off with a Joke, if the Fellow had been capable of tasting Ridicule." "But that Stratagem," replied lady *Tempest*, "I am afraid did not succeed——the Man I doubt was too dull to apprehend your Raillery." "Dull as a Beetle, Madam;" said *Hillario*, "the Monster continued obstinate, and repeated his Challenge.——When therefore I found nothing else wou'd do, I resolved to meet him according to his Appointment; and there——in short, not to trouble your Ladyship with a long, tedious Description——I ran him through the Body." Lady *Tempest* burst out laughing at this Story, which she most justly concluded to be a Lie; and after many pleasant[1] Remarks upon it, said with a smile, "But what is this to the Dog, *Hillario*?" "The Dog, madam!" answered he, "O pardon me, I am coming to the Dog immediately.——Come hither *Pompey*, and listen to your own Story.——This Dog, madam, this very little Dog, had at the time the Honour of waiting on the dear Woman I have been describing, and as the Noise of my Duel obliged me to quit *Bologna*, I sent her private Notice of my Intentions, and begged her by any means to favour me with an Interview before my Departure. The Monster her Husband, who then lay on his Death-bed, immured her so closely, that you may imagine it was very difficult to gratify my Desires; but Love, immortal Love, gave her Courage; she sent me a private Key to get Admission into her Garden, and appointed me an Assignation in an Orange-Grove at Nine in the Evening. I flew to the dear Creature's Arms, and after spending an Hour with her in the bitterest Lamentations, when it grew dangerous and impossible to stay any longer, we knelt down both of us on the cold Ground, and saluted[2] each other for the last time on our Knees——Oh how I cursed Fortune for separating us! But at length I was obliged to decamp, and she gave me this Dog, this individual little Dog, to carry with me as a Memorial of her Love. The poor, dear, tender Woman died, I hear, within three weeks of my Departure; but this Dog, this divine little Dog, will I keep everlastingly for her Sake."

When the Lady had heard him to an End, "Well," said she, "you have really told a very pretty Story, *Hillario*; but as to your Resolutions

---

1 Humorous.
2 Kissed.

of keeping the Dog, I swear you shall break them; for I had the Misfortune t'other Day to lose my favourite black Spaniel of the Mange, and I intend you shall give me this little Dog to supply his Place." "Not for the Universe, Madam," replied *Hillario*; "I should expect to see his dear injured Mistress's Ghost haunting me in my Sleep to Night, if I could be guilty of such an Act of Infidelity to her." "Pugh," said the lady, "don't tell me of such ridiculous superstitious Trumpery. ——You no more came by the dog in this manner, *Hillario*, than you will fly to the Moon to Night——but if you did, it does not signify; for I positively must and will take him home with me." "Madam," said *Hillario*, "this little Dog is sacred to Love! he was born to be the Herald of Love, and there is but one Consideration in Nature than [*sic*]¹ can possibly induce me to part with him." "And what is that?" said the Lady. "That Madam," cried *Hillario*, bowing, "is the Honour of visiting him at all Hours in his new Apartments——he must be the Herald of Love wherever he goes, and on these Conditions——if you will now and then admit me of your Retirements, little *Pompey* waits your Acceptance as soon as you please." "Well," said the Lady, smiling, "you know I am not inexorable, *Hillario*, and if you have a mind to visit your little Friend at my Ruelle,² you'll find him ready to receive you——though, faith, upon second Thoughts, I know not whether I dare to admit you or not. You are such a Killer of Husbands, *Hillario*, that 'tis quite terrible to think on; and if mine was not conveniently removed out of the Way, I should have the poor Man sacrificed for his Jealousy." "Raillery! Raillery!" returned *Hillario*; "but as you say, my dear Countess, your Monster is commodiously out of the way, and therefore we need be under no Apprehensions from that Quarter, for I hardly believe he will rise out of his Grave to interrupt our Amours."——"Amours!" cried the lady, lifting up her Voice, "pray what have I said that encourages you to talk of Amours?"——

From this time the Conversation began to grow much too loose to be reported in this Work: They congratulated each other on the Felicity of living in an Age, that allows such Indulgence to Women, and gives them leave to break loose from their Husbands,

---

1 Apparently a misprint for "that."
2 A morning reception in a fashionable lady's bedroom.

whenever they grow morose and disagreeable, or attempt to interrupt their Pleasures. They laughed at Constancy in Marriage as the most ridiculous thing in Nature, exploded the very Notion of matrimonial Happiness, and were most fashionably pleasant in decrying everything that is serious, virtuous and religious. From hence they relapsed again into a Discourse on *Italian* Opera, and thence made a quick Transition to Ladies Painting. This was no sooner started than *Hillario* begged leave to present her the lady with a Box of Rouge, which he had brought with him from *France*, assuring her that the Ladies were arrived at such an Excellency of using it at *Paris*, as to confound all Distinction of Age and Beauty. "I protest to your Ladyship," continued he, "it is impossible at any Distance to distinguish a woman of Sixty from a Girl of Sixteen; and I have seen an old Dowager in the opposite Box at their Playhouse, make as good a Figure, and look as blooming as the youngest Beauty in the Place. Nothing in Nature is there required to make a Woman handsome but Eyes.——If a Woman has but Eyes, she may be a Beauty whenever she pleases, at the Expence of a Couple of Guineas.——Teeth and Hair and Eye-brows and Complexions are all as cheap as Fans and Gloves and Ribbons."

While this ingenious Orator was pursuing his eloquent Harangue on Beauty, Lady *Tempest*, looking at her Watch, declared it was time to be going; for she had seven or eight Visits more to make that Morning, and it was then almost Three in the Afternoon. Little *Pompey*, who had absented himself during great part of the preceding Conversation, as thinking it perhaps above the Reach of his Understanding, was now ordered to be produced; and the Moment he made his Appearance, Lady *Tempest* catching him up in her Arms, was conducted by *Hillaro* into her Chair,[1] which stood at the Door waiting her Commands. Little *Pompey* cast up a wishful Eye at the Window above; but the Chairmen were now in Motion, and with three Footmen fore-running his Equipage, he set out in Triumph to his new Apartments.

---

[1] An enclosed chair, carried on poles by two "chairmen," in which one person could travel.

CHAP. V

THE CHARACTER OF LADY TEMPEST, WITH SOME PARTICULARS OF HER SERVANTS AND FAMILY.

THE sudden Appearance of this Lady, with whom our Hero is now about to take up his Residence, may perhaps excite the Reader's Curiosity to know who she is; and therefore, before we proceed any farther in our History, we shall spend a Page or two in bringing him acquainted with her Character. But let me admonish thee, my gentle Friend, whosoever thou art, that shalt vouchsafe to peruse this little Treatise, not to be too forward in making Applications, or to construe Satire into Libel. For we declare here once for all, that no Character drawn in this Work is intended for any particular Person, but meant to comprehend a great Variety; and therefore, if thy Sagacity discovers Likenesses that were never intended, and Meanings that were never meant, be so good to impute it to thy own Ill-nature, and accuse not the humble Author of these Sheets. Taking this Caution along with thee, candid Reader, we may venture to trust thee with a Character, which otherwise we should be afraid to draw.[1]

Lady *Tempest* then was originally Daughter to a private Gentleman of a moderate Fortune, which she was to share in common with a Brother and two other Sisters: But her Wit and Beauty soon distinguished her among her Acquaintance, and recompensed the Deficiencies of Fortune. She was what the Men call *a sprightly jolly Girl*, and the Women *a bold forward Creature*; very cheerful in her Conversation, and open in her Behaviour; ready to promote any Party of Pleasure, (for she was a very Rake at Heart)[2] and not displeased now and then to be assistant in a little Mischief. This made her Company courted by Men of all Sorts; among whom her Affability and Spirit, as well as her Beauty, procured her many Admirers. At length she was sollicited in Marriage by a young Lord, famous for nothing else

---

1   Coventry is echoing Fielding's famous disclaimer in Bk 3, chap. 1 of *Joseph Andrews* that he is satirizing "not Men, but Manners; not an Individual, but a Species."

2   This parenthetical comment, and much else in the description of Lady Tempest, was cut from the third edition in the apparent effort to make Pompey's favorite mistress more respectable morally.

but his great Estate, and far her Inferior in Understanding: But the Advantageousness of the Match soon prevailed with her Parents to give their Consent, and the Thoughts of a Title so dazzled her own Eyes, that she had no Leisure to ask herself whether she liked the Man or no that wore it. His Lordship married for the sake of begetting an Heir to his Estate; and married her in particular, because he had heard her toasted as a Beauty by most of his Acquaintance. She, on the contrary, married because she wanted a Husband; and married him, because he could give her a Title and a Coach and Six.

But, alas! there is this little Misfortune attending Matrimony, that People cannot live together any Time, without discovering each other's Tempers. Familiarity soon draws aside the Masque, and all that artificial Complaisance and smiling Good-humour, which make so agreeable a Part of Courtship, go off like *April* Blossoms, upon a longer Acquaintance. The Year was scarce ended before her young Ladyship was surprised to find she had married *a Fool*; which little Circumstance her Vanity had concealed from her before Marriage, and the Hurry and Transport she felt in a new Equipage did not suffer her to attend to for the first Half-year afterwards. But now she began to doubt whether she had not made a foolish Bargain for Life, and consulting with some of her Female Intimates about it (several of whom were married) she received such Documents from them, as, I am afraid, did not a little contribute to prepare her for the Steps she afterwards took.

Her Husband too, tho' not very quick of Discernment, had by this Time found out, that his Wife's Spirit and romantic Disposition were inconsistent with his own Gloom; which gave new Clouds to his Temper, and he often cursed himself in secret for marrying her.

They soon grew to reveal these Thoughts to one another, both in Words and Actions; they sat down to Meals with Indifference; they went to bed with Indifference; and the one was always sure to dislike what the other at any Time seemed to approve. Her Lady-ship had Recourse to the common Expedient in these Cases, I mean the getting a Female Companion into the House with her, as well to relieve her from the Tediousness of sitting down to Meals alone with her Husband, as chiefly to hear her Complaints, and spirit her up against her Fool and Tyrant; the Names by which she usually spoke of her Lord and Master. When no such Female Companions, or more properly *Toad-eaters*,[1] happened to be present, she chose rather to divert herself with a favourite little Dog, than to murder any of her precious Time in conversing with her Husband. This his Lordship observed, and besides many severe Reflexions and cross Speeches, at length he wreak'd his Vengeance on the little Favourite, and in a Passion put him to Death. This was an Affair so heinous in the Lady's own Esteem, and pronounced to be *so barbarous, so shocking, so inhuman* by all her Acquaintance, that she resolved no longer to keep any Terms with him,[2] and from this Moment grew desperate in all her Actions.

First then, she resolved to supply the Place of one Favourite with a great Number, and immediately procured as many Dogs into the Family as it could well hold. His Lordship, in return, would order his Servant to hang two or three of them every Week, and never failed kicking them down Stairs by Dozens, whenever they came in his Way. When this and many other Stratagems had been tried, some with good and some with bad Success, she came at last to play the great Game of Female Resentment, and by many Intimations gave him to mistrust, that a Stranger had invaded his Bed. Whether this was real, or only an Artifice of Spite, his Lordship could never discover, and therefore we shall not indulge the Reader's Curiosity, by letting him into the Secret; but the bare Apprehension of it so inflamed his Lordship's Choler, that her Company now became intolerable to him, and indeed their Meetings were dreadful to themselves, and terrible to all Beholders. The Servants used to stand at the Door to listen to their Quarrels, and then charitably disperse the Subjects of them throughout the Town; so that all Companies now rang of Lord and Lady *Tempest*. But this could not continue long; for Indifference may sometimes be borne in a married State, but Indignation and Hatred I believe never can; and 'tis impossible to say what their Quarrels might have produced, had not his Lordship very seasonably died, and left his *disconsolate Widow* to bear about the Mockery of Woe to all public Places for a Year.

She now began the World anew on her own Foundation, and set sail down the Stream of Pleasure, without the Fears of Virginity to check her, or the Influence of a Husband to controul

---

1 Boot-licker, sycophant, the origin of our modern term "toady."
2 I.e., not to obey any conditions, as in a treaty

her. Now she recover'd that Sprightliness of Conversation and Gaiety of Behaviour, which had been clouded during the latter Part of her Cohabitation with her Husband; and was soon cried up for the greatest Female Wit in *London*. Men of Gallantry, and all the World of Pleasure, had easy Access to her, and malicious Fame reports, that she was not over-hard-hearted to the Sollicitations of Love; but far be it from us to report any such improbable Scandal. What gives her a Place in this History is her Fondness for Dogs, which from Childhood she loved exceedingly, and was seldom without a little favourite to carry about in her Arms: But from the Moment that her angry Husband sacrificed one of them to his Resentment, she grew more passionately fond of them than ever, and now constantly kept Six or Eight of various Kinds in her House. About this Time, one of her greatest Favourites had the Misfortune to die of the Mange, as was above commemorated, and when she saw little *Pompey* at *Hillario*'s Lodgings, she resolved immediately to bestow the Vacancy upon him, which that well-bred Gentleman consented to on certain Conditions, as the Reader has seen in the foregoing Chapter.

She returned Home from her Visit just as the Clock was striking Four, and after surveying herself a Moment in the Glass, and a little adjusting her Hair, went directly to introduce Master *Pompey* to his Companions. These were an *Italian* Grey-hound, a *Dutch* Pug, two black Spaniels of King *Charles's* Breed, a Harlequin Grey-hound, a spotted *Dane*, and a mouse-colour'd *English* Bull-dog. They heard their Mistress's Rap at the Door, and were assembled in the Dining-room, ready to receive her: But on the Appearance of Master *Pompey*, they set up a general Bark, perhaps out of Envy; and some of them treated the little Stranger with rather more Rudeness than was consistent with Dogs of their Education. However, the Lady soon interposed her Authority, and commanded Silence among them, by ringing a little Bell, which she kept by her for that Purpose. They all obeyed the Signal instantly, and were still in a Moment; upon which she carried little *Pompey* round, and obliged them all to salute their new Acquaintance, at the same Time commanding some of them to ask Pardon for their unpolite Behaviour; which whether they understood or not, must be left to the Reader's Determination. She then summoned a Servant, and ordered a Chicken to be roasted for him; but hearing that Dinner was just ready to be served up, she was pleased to say, he must be contented with what was provided for herself that Day, but gave orders to the Cook to get ready a Chicken to his own Share against Night.

Her Ladyship now sat down to Table, and *Pompey* was placed at her Elbow, where he Received many dainty Bits from her fair Hands, and was caressed by her all Dinner-time, with more than usual Fondness. The Servants winked at one another, while they were waiting, and conveyed many Sneers across the Table with their Looks; all which had the good Luck to escape her Ladyship's Observations. But the Moment they were retired from waiting, they gave vent to their Thoughts with all the scurrilous Wit and ill-manner'd Raillery, which distinguishes the Conversation of those parti-coloured Gentlemen.[1]

And first, the Butler out of Livery served up his Remarks to the House-keeper's Table; which consisted of himself, an elderly fat Woman the House-keeper, and my Lady's Maid, a saucy, forward, affected Girl, of about Twenty. Addressing himself to these second-hand Gentlewomen, as soon as they were pleased to sit down to Dinner, he informed them, *that their Family was increased, and that his Lady had brought home a new Companion.* Their Curiosity soon led them to desire an Explanation, and then telling them that this new Companion was a new Dog, he related minutely and circumstantially all her Ladyship's Behaviour to him, during the time of his Attendance at the Sideboard, not forgetting to mention the Orders of a roasted Chicken for the Gentleman's Supper. The House-keeper launched out largely on the Sin and Wickedness of feeding *such Creatures with Christian Victuals,* declared it was flying in the Face of Heaven, and wondered how her Lady could admit them into her Apartment, for she said *they had already spoiled all the crimson Damask-chairs in the Dining-room.*

But my Lady's Maid had a great deal more to say on this Subject, and as it was her particular Office to wait on these four-footed Worthies, she complained of the Hardship done her, with great Volubility of Tongue. "Then," says she, "there's a new Plague come home, is there? he has got the Mange too, I suppose, and I

---

1 Again a reference to the bright uniforms, or "livery," worn by servants in upper-rank households.

shall have him to wash and comb To-morrow Morning. I am sure I am all over Fleas with tending nasty poisonous Vermin, and 'tis a Shame to put a Christian to such Offices.——I was in Hopes when that mangy little Devil died t'other Day, we should have had no more of them; but there is to be no End of them I find, and for my Part, I wish with all my Heart some-body would poison 'em all——I can't endure to see my Lady let them kiss her, and lick her Face all over as she does. I am sure I'd see all the Dogs in *England* at *Jericho*, before I'd suffer such Poulcat[1] Vermin to lick my Face. Fogh! 'tis enough to make one sick to see it; and I am sure, if I was a Man, I'd scorn to kiss a Face that had been licked by a Dog."

This was Part of a Speech made by this delicate, mincing Comb-brusher; and the rest we shall omit, to wait upon the inferior Servants, who were assembled at Dinner in their common Hall of Gluttony, and exercising their Talents likewise on the same Subject. *John* the Footman here reported what Mr. *William* the Butler had done before in his Department, that their Lady had brought home a new Dog. "Damn it," cries the Coachman, with a surly brutal Voice, "what signifies a new Dog? has she brought home ever a new Man?" which was seconded with a loud Laugh from all the Company. Another swore, he never knew a Kennel of Dogs kept in a Bed-chamber before; which likewise was applauded with a loud and boisterous Laugh: but as such kind of Wit is too low for the Dignity of this History, tho' much affected by many of my Cotemporaries, I fancy I shall easily have the Reader's Excuse, if I forbear to relate any more of it.

My Design in giving this short Sketch of Kitchen-Humour, is only to convey a Hint to all Masters and Mistresses, if they chuse to receive it, not to be guilty of any Actions, that will expose them to the Ridicule and Contempt of their Servants. For these ungrateful Wretches, tho' receiving ever so many Favours from you, and treated by you in general with the greatest Indulgence, will shew no Mercy to your slightest Failings, but expose and ridicule your Weakness in Alehouses, Nine-pin-alleys, Gin-shops, Cellars, and every other Place of dirty Rendezvous. The Truth is, the lower Sort of Men-servants

---

1   "A small European carnivorous mammal, *Mustela putorius* (family Mustelidae), with mainly dark-brown fur and a darker mask across the eyes, and noted for its fetid smell" (*OED*).

are the most insolent, brutal, ungenerous Rascals on the Face of the Earth: they are bred up in Idleness, Drunkenness and Debauchery, and instead of concealing any Faults they observe at home, find a Pleasure in vilifying and mangling the Reputations of their Masters.[1]

CHAP. VI

OUR HERO BECOMES A DOG OF THE TOWN,[2] AND SHINES IN HIGH-LIFE.

POMPEY was now grown up to Maturity and Dog's Estate, when he came to live with Lady *Tempest*; who soon ushered him into all the Joys and Vanities of the Town. He quickly came an Admirer of Mr. *Garrick*'s acting at the Play-house,[3] grew extremely fond of Masquerades, passed his Judgment on Operas, and was allowed to have a very nice and distinguishing Ear for *Italian* Music. Nor did he lie under the Censure which fell on many other well-bred People of a different Species, I mean the Absurdity of admiring what they did not understand; for as he had been born in *Italy*, 'tis probable he was a little acquainted with the Language of his native Country.

As he attended his Mistress to all Routs, Drums, Hurricanes Hurly-burlies and Earthquakes,[4] he soon established an Acquaintance and Friendship with all the Dogs of Quality, and of course affected a most hearty Contempt for all of inferior Station, whom he would never vouchsafe to play with, or pay them the least Regard. He pretended[5] to know at first Sight, whether a Dog had received a good Education, by his Manner of coming into a Room, and was

---

1 I have retained the final paragraph from the first edition, much shortened in the third edition.

2 In this chapter Coventry will play insistently on the term "a man of the town," meaning a fashionable man seeking pleasure at the highest levels of society.

3 David Garrick (1717-79), the greatest actor of his day and manager of the Royal Theatre at Drury Lane.

4 Different varieties of upper-rank household entertainments, usually involving cards and dancing.

5 In the third edition, Coventry changed "pretended" (in this context meaning "claimed") to "seemed," an indication of his attempt to avoid making Pompey unrealistically human.

extremely ambitious to shew *his Collar at Court*; in which again he resembled certain other Dogs, who are equally vain of their Finery, and happy to be distinguished in their *respective Orders*.

If he could have spoken, I am persuaded he would have used the Phrases so much in fashion, *Nobody one knows, Wretches dropt out of the Moon, Creatures sprung from a Dunghil*; by which are signified all those not born to a Title, or have not Impudence and Dishonesty enough to run in debt with Taylors for Laced Cloaths.

Again, had he been to write a Letter from *Bath* or *Tunbridge*,[1] he wou'd have told his Correspondent, *there was not a Soul in the Place*, tho' at the same time he knew there was above two Thousand; because perhaps none of the Men wore Stars and Garters,[2] and none of the Women were bold enough to impoverish their Families by playing at the noble and illustrious Game of Brag.[3] As to his own Part, his Lady was at the Expence of a Master, perhaps the great Mr. *H____le*,[4] to teach him to play at Cards; and so forward was his Genius, that in less than three Months he was able to sit down with her Ladyship at Piquet, whenever Sickness or the Vapours[5] confined her to her Chamber.

As he was now become a Dog of the Town, and perfectly well-bred, of course he gave himself up to Intrigue, and had seldom less than two or three Amours on his Hands at a time with *Bitches of the highest Fashion*: In which Circumstances he again lamented the Want of Speech, for by that means he was prevented the Pleasure of boasting of the Favours he received. But his Gallantries were soon divulged by the Consequences of them; and as several very pretty Puppies had been the Offspring of his Loves, it was usual for all the Acquaintance of Lady *Tempest* to solicit and cultivate his Breed. And here I shall beg leave to insert two little *Billets* of a very extraordinary Nature, as a Specimen of what it is that engages the

---

1 Spa-towns at which upper-rank people, along with many people further down the social hierarchy, would assemble to socialize, drink, and bathe in the allegedly medicinal water.

2 Royally bestowed honors such as the Order of the Garter, the highest rank of knighthood.

3 An ancestor of our modern poker.

4 Edmond Hoyle (1672-1769), a celebrated writer on games of chance, who is still referred to in the popular expression "according to Hoyle." Hoyle's *Rules* are still in print and widely used.

5 Depression of spirits, hypochondria, hysteria, and other nervous disorders often considered the imaginary or feigned foibles of women, particularly in the upper ranks.

Attention of Ladies of Quality in this refined and accomplished Age. Lady *Tempest* was sitting at her Toilette one Morning, when her Maid brought her the following little Scroll, from another Lady, whose Name [will be seen at the bottom of her Letter].

Dear Tempest,
My favourite little *Veny* is at present troubled with certain amorous Infirmities of Nature, and wou'd not be displeased with the Ad-dresses of a Lover. Be so good therefore to send little *Pompey* by my Servant who brings this Note, for I fancy it will make a very pretty Breed, and when the Lovers have transacted their Affairs, he shall be sent home incontinently. Believe me, my dear *Tempest,*

Yours affectionately [RACKET]

Lady *Tempest*, as soon as she had read this curious Epistle, called for Pen and Ink, and immediately wrote the following Answer, which likewise we beg leave to insert.

Dear ——
Infirmities of Nature we all are subject to, and therefore I have sent Master *Pompey* to wait upon Miss *Veny*, begging the Favour of you to return him as soon as his Gallantries are over. Consider, my Dear, no modern Love can, in the Nature of Things, last above three Days, and therefore I hope to see my little Friend again very soon.

Your affectionate Friend,
TEMPEST.

[In consequence of these letters, our hero was conducted to Mrs. *Racket*'s house, where he was received with the civility due to his station in life, and treated on the footing of a gentleman who came a courting in the family. Mrs. *Racket* had two daughters, who had greatly improved their natural relish for pleasure in the warm climate of a town education, and were extremely solicitous to in-form themselves of all the mysteries of love. These young ladies no sooner heard of *Pompey*'s arrival, than they went down stairs into the parlour, and undertook themselves to introduce him to miss *Veny*: for love so much engrossed their thoughts, that they could not suffer a lap-dog in the house to have an amour without their privity.[1] Here, while they were solacing themselves with innocent speculation, a young gentleman, who visited on a familiar footing in the family, was introduced somewhat abruptly to them. They no sooner found themselves surprized, than they ran tittering to a corner of the parlour, and hid their faces behind their fans; while their visiter, not happening to observe the *Hymeneal* rites[2] that were celebrating, begged to know the cause of their mirth. This redoubled their diversion, and they burst out afresh into such immoderate fits of laughter, that the poor man began to look exceedingly foolish, imagining himself to be the object of their ridicule. In vain he renewed his entreaties to be let into the secret of their laughter; the ladies had not the power of utterance, and he would still have continued ignorant, had he not accidentally cast his eye aside, and there beheld master *Pompey* with the most prevailing sollicitation making love[3] to his four-footed mistress. This at once satisfied his curiosity, and he was no longer at a loss to know the reason of that uncommon joy and rapture which the ladies had exhibited.]

Thus was our Hero permitted to indulge in all the Luxuries of Life; but in the midst of these Felicities, caressed as he was by his Mistress, and courted by her Visiters, some Misfortunes every now and then fell to his Share, which served a little to check his Pride in the midst of Prosperity. He had once a most bloody Battle with a Cat, in which terrible Rencontre he was very near losing his Right Eye: at another Time he was frightened into a Canal by a huge overgrown Turky-cock, and had like to have been drowned for want of timely Assistance to relieve him. Besides these unlucky Accidents, he was persecuted by all the Servants for being a Favourite, and particularly by the Waiting-gentle-woman abovementioned, who was pleased one Day to run the Comb into his Back; where two of the Teeth remained infixed, and his Mistress was obliged to send for a Surgeon to extract them. But Mrs. *Abagail* had good

---

1   "Private communication" (Johnson).
2   Sex, after the deity Hymen, god of marriage.
3   This term is meant in the obsolete sense of courting rather than sexual intecourse. One should nonetheless remember the behaviour of male dogs around females in heat.

Reason to repent of her Cruelty, for she was instantly discarded with the greatest Passion, and afterwards refused a Character,[1] when she applied for one to recommend her to a new Service.

Yet, notwithstanding these accidental Misfortunes, from which no Condition is free, he may be said to have led a Life of great Happiness with Lady *Tempest*. He fed upon Chicken, Partridges, Wildfowl, Ragouts, Fricassees, and all the Rarities in Season; which so pampered him up with luxurious Notions, as made some future Scenes of Life the more grievous to him, when Fortune obliged him to undergo the Hardships that will hereafter be recorded.

CHAP. VII

CONTAINING A CURIOUS DISPUTE ON THE IMMORTALITY OF THE SOUL.

IT is the Nature of all Mankind, Authors as well as others, to abuse the Patience of their Friends, and as I have already related two Conversations in this little Work, instead of supposing my Reader to be satiated with them, I am tempted to trespass farther on his Patience, and trouble him with a third; in which, moreover, the Name of our Hero will but once be mentioned.

Lady *Tempest*, being a little indisposed with some trifling Disorder, kept her Chamber, and was attended by two Physicians. As her Behaviour in Life had excluded her from all the prudent and virtuous Part of her Sex, her Visiters consisted chiefly of such Ladies, who had contracted a Stain, which placed them on a Level with her Ladyship: and to say the Truth, Ladies of this sort are so numerous in the great City of *London*, that no Woman need fear a Solitude, let her Imprudence be ever so glaring.

Her Ladyship's Physicians were now making their Morning Visit, and had just gone through the Examinations, which Custom immemorial prescribes——as, How did your Ladyship sleep last

---

1 Letter of reference.

Night?———do you find any Drowth,[1] Madam?———pray let me look at your Ladyship's Tongue———and many other Questions of a like Nature, which I have not Leisure now to record. When these were finished, and the youngest was preparing to write a Prescription, a violent Rap at the Door, and shortly afterwards the Appearance of a Visiter, interrupted his Proceeding. The Lady, who now arrived, came directly up to Lady *Tempest*, and made her Compliments; then sitting down, and addressing herself, after some little Pause, to one of the Physicians, asked him, *If he believed in the Immortality of the Soul?*———but before we answer this extraordinary Question, or relate the Conversation that ensued upon it, it will be for the Reader's Ease to receive a short Sketch of her Character.

In many respects this Lady was in similar Circumstances with Lady *Tempest*; only with this Difference, that the one had been separated from her Husband by his Death, the other divorced from hers by Act of Parliament;[2] the one was famous for Wit, and the other affected the Character of Wisdom. Lady *Sophister* (for that was her name) as soon as she was released from the Matrimonial Fetters, set out to visit foreign Parts, and displayed her Charms in most of the Courts of *Europe*. There, in many Parts of her Tour, she had kept Company with *Literati*, and particularly in *France*, where the ladies affect a Reputation of Science, and are able to discourse on the profoundest Questions of Theology and Philosophy. The Labyrinths of a Female Brain are so various and intricate, that it is difficult to say what first suggested the Opinion to her, whether Caprice or Vanity of being singular, but all on a sudden, her Ladyship took a Fancy into her Head to disbelieve the Immortality of the Soul; and never came into the Company of learned Men without displaying her Talents on this wonderful Subject. The World indeed ascribed the Rise of this Opinion in her Ladyship's Brain, to Self-interest; for, said they, *it is much better to perish than to burn;*[3] but for my Part, I chuse rather to impute it to absolute Whim

---

1   Thirstiness.

2   Divorce was difficult to obtain in the eighteenth century, especially for women, and had to be approved by Parliament. This requirement nonetheless affected the upper-ranks far more than the mass of people in the lower-ranks, who, having no land to exchange, usually cohabited and separated as they wished.

3   This is evidently a folk expression improvising on St. Paul's, "it is better to marry than to burn" (1 Corinthians 7.9). Its meaning here is that Lady Sophister has conveniently reasoned away her fears of burning in Hell.

and Caprice, or rather, an absurd and ridiculous Love of Paradox. But whatever started the Thought first in her Imagination, she had been at the Pains of great Reading to confirm her in it, and could appeal to the greatest Authorities in Defence of it. She had read *Hobbes*, *Malebranche*, *Locke*, *Shaftesbury*, *Woolaston*,[1] and many more; all of whom she obliged to give Testimony to her Paradox, and perverted Passages out of their Works with a Facility *very easy to be imagined*. But Mr. *Locke* had the Misfortune to be her principal Favourite, and consequently it rested chiefly upon him to furnish her with Quotations, whenever her Ladyship pleased to engage in Controversy. Such was the Character of Lady *Sophister*, who now arrived, and asked the surprising Question above-mentioned, concerning the Immortality of the Soul.

Doctor *Killdarby*, to whom she addressed herself, astonished at the Novelty of the Question, sat staring with Horror and Amazement on his Companion; Which Lady *Tempest* observing, and guessing that her Female Friend was going to be very absurd, resolved to promote the Conversation for her own Amusement. Turning herself therefore to the Doctor, she said with a Smile, "Don't you understand the Meaning of her Ladyship's Question, Sir? She asks you, if you believe in the Immortality of the Soul?"

"Believe in the Immortality of the Soul, Madam!" said the Doctor staring, "Bless my Soul! your Ladyships astonish me beyond measure———Believe in the Immortality of the Soul! Yes, undoubtedly, and I hope all Mankind does the same." "Be not so sure of that," said Lady *Sophister*———"Pray, Sir, have you ever read Mr. *Locke*'s Controversy with the Bishop of *Worcester*?"[2] "Mr. *Locke*'s Controversy, Madam!" replied the doctor———"I protest I am not sure———Mr. *Locke*'s Controversy with the Bishop of

---

1   Thomas Hobbes (1588-1679); Nicolas Malebranche (1638-1715); John Locke (1632-1704); Anthony Ashley Cooper, 3rd Earl of Shaftesbury (1671-1713); William Wollaston (1659-1724). These were prominent and, in intellectual circles, fashionable philosophers of the seventeenth and early eighteenth centuries. Across the spectrum of Christian thought, all five were taken, by someone, as threatening Christian orthodoxy, though Malebranche, Locke and Wollaston, in particular, also had devout Christian admirers. Accordingly, Coventry subsequently indicates that Lady Sophister distorts their ideas with impious intentions. He later defends Locke.

2   A notable exchange of pamphlets in 1697 between the powerful Edward Stillingfleet, bishop of Worcester, and the leading English philosopher of the time, John Locke, centered on Locke's speculation that pure matter could "think," and that therefore there is no philosophical reason to believe in an immaterial and immortal soul.

Worcester, did your Ladyship say? Let me see——I vow I can't recollect——My reading has been very multifarious and extensive——Yes, Madam, I think that I have read it, tho' I protest I can't be sure whether I have read it or no." "Have you ever read it, Dr. *Rhubarb*?" said she, addressing herself to the other Physician. ——"O yes, Madam, very often," answered he; "'tis that fine Piece of his, where——Yes, yes, I have read it very often; I remember it perfectly well——But, pray Madam, is there any Passage——I beg your Ladyship's Pardon, if I am mistaken——but is there any Passage, I say, in that Piece, that tends to confirm your Ladyship's Notion concerning the Immortality of the Soul?" "Why, pray Sir," said the lady, with a Smile of Triumph, "what do you esteem the Soul to be? Is it Air, or Fire, or Æther, or a kind if Quintessence, as *Aristotle* observed, and Composition of all the Elements?" Doctor *Rhubarb*, quite dumb-founded with her Learning, desired first to hear her Ladyship's Opinion of the Matter. "My Opinion," resumed she, "is exactly the same with Mr. *Locke*'s.——You know, Mr. *Locke* observes there are various kinds of Matter——well ——but first we should define *Matter*, which you know the Logicians tell us, is an extended solid Substance——Well, out of this Matter, some, you know, is made into Roses and Peach-trees ——the next Step which Matter takes is Animal Life, from whence we have Lions and Elephants, and all the Race of Brutes.——Then, the next Step, as Mr. *Locke* observes, is Thought, and Reason, and Volition, from whence are created Men, and therefore you plainly see, 'tis impossible for the Soul to be immortal."

"Pardon me, Madam," said *Rhubarb*; "Roses and Peach-trees, and Elephants and Lions! I protest I remember nothing of this nature in Mr. *Locke*."[1] "Nay, Sir," said she, "can you deny me this? If the Soul is Fire, it must be extinguished; if it is Air, it must be dispersed; if it be only a Modification of Matter, why then of course it ceases—if it be anything else, it is exactly the same Thing, and therefore you must confess—indeed Doctor, you must confess, that 'tis impossible for the Soul to be immortal."

[Doctor *Killdarby*, who had sat silent for some time, to collect his

---

1   The comically named Dr. Rhubarb is right at this point: Lady Sophister has utterly
    fabricated Locke's supposed philosophy.

thoughts, finding what a learned antagonist he had to cope with, began now to harangue in the following manner. "Madam," said he, "as to the nature of the soul, to be sure there have been such opinions as your ladyship mentions about it——many various and unaccountable opinions. Some called it *divinum cæleste*; others *quinta essentia*, as your ladyship observes; and others *inflammata anima*, that is, madam, inflamed air.[1] *Aristoxenus*, an old musician, as I remember, imagined the soul to be a musical tune;[2] and a mathematician that I have heard of, supposed it to be like an æquilaterial triangle.[3] *Descartes*, I think, makes its residence to be the pineal gland of the brain, where all the nerves terminate;[4] and *Borri*, I remember, the *Milanese* physician, in a letter to *Bartholine, de ortu celebri & usu medico*,[5] asserts, that in the brain is found a certain very subtil fragrant juice (which I conceive may be the same as the nervous juice or animal spirits) and this he takes to be the residence or seat of the soul; the subtilty or fineness of which he supposes to depend, madam, on the temperature of this liquor——but really all these opinions may very probably be false; we do but grope in the dark, madam, we do but grope in the dark, and it would be better to let the subject entirely alone. The concurrent opinions of all mankind have ever agreed in believing the immortality of the soul; and this, I confess, is to me an unanswerable argument of its truth. You see, madam, I purposely wave the topic of revelation."[6]

"Oh, Sir, as to that matter," said the lady, interrupting him, "as to revelation, Sir"——and here she ran into much common-place raillery at the expense only of Christianity and the gospel; 'till lady *Tempest* cut her short, and desired her to be silent on that head:

1   "Heavenly divine" and "fifth essence" are terms used in both classical and medieval philosophy. Cicero argues that the soul is "inflamed air," a variation of "fifth essence," in the *Tusculan Disputations*.
2   Not exactly. Aristoxenus, a fourth-century BCE follower of Aristotle, compared the relation of soul and body to the dependence between the parts of a musical instrument.
3   Probably Pythagoras (c. 569-474 BCE), though this doctrine has a long medieval tradition.
4   The conjecture of French philosopher René Descartes (1596-1650).
5   Dr. Killdarby cites an obscure controversy between the Milanese alchemist Giuseppe Francesco Borri (d. 1695) and the Dutch scientist Erasmus Bartholin (1625-98).
6   Killdarby means that he has proffered a rational argument (all people have believed in the immortality of the soul) rather than an argument from "revelation" (the New Testament).

for this good lady believed all the doctrines of religion, and was contented, like many others, with the trifling privilege only of disobeying all its precepts.

Lady *Sophister* however resolved not to quit the field of battle, but rallied her forces, and once more fell on her adversaries with an air of triumph. "You say, I think, Sir," resumed she, "that a multitude of opinions will establish a truth——Now you know all the *Indians* believe that their dogs will go to Heaven along with them;[1] and if a great many opinions can prove any thing to be true, what say you to that, Sir? *India* you know, doctor, is a prodigious large wide tract of continent, where the *Gymnosophists* lived,[2] and all that——Pray, lady *Tempest*, let us look at your globes."[3]

"My globes, madam," said lady *Tempest*, "what globes of mine does your ladyship desire to see?"

"What globes," replied the disputant; "why your celestial and terrestrial globes to be sure; I want to look out *India* in the map, and shew the doctor what a prodigious wide tract of continent it is in comparison of our *Europe*——however, come, I believe we can do without them——as I was saying therefore, Sir, the *Indians* you know believe their dogs will bear them company to heaven; and if a great many opinions can establish the truth of an hypothesis——you understand me, I hope, because I would fain speak to be understood——I say, if a great many opinions can prove any thing to be true, what say you to that, Sir? For instance now, there's lady *Tempest*'s little lap-dog"——"My dear little creature," said lady *Tempest*, catching him up in her arms, "will you go to heaven along with me? I shall be vastly glad of your company, *Pompey*, if you will." From this hint both their ladyships had many bright sallies, 'till lady *Sophister*, flushed with the hopes of this argument, recalled her adversary to the question, and desired to hear his reply.

"Come, Sir," said she, "you have not yet responded to my

---

1 Lady Sophister is probably thinking of Pope's *Essay on Man*, Bk. 1, ll. 111-12, but Pope was referring to Native Americans, not to the inhabitants of India, as she presumes.

2 "Naked philosophers," an ascetic cult first encountered by Alexander the Great during his invasion of India.

3 The obvious lesbian allusion here is significant because learned women like Lady Sophister were commonly considered "man-like."

argument, you have not answered my last syllogism——I think I have gravelled¹ you now; I think I have done for you; I think I have demolished you, doctor."

"Not at all, madam," said Dr. *Killdarby*; "really as to that matter, that is neither here nor there——Opinions madam, vague irregular opinions will spring up and float in people's brains, but we were talking of the dictates of sense and reason. Savages, madam, will be savage, but *Indians* have nothing to do with *Europeans*. The reply to what your ladyship has advanced, would be easy and obvious; but really I must beg to be excused——my profession does not oblige me to a knowledge of such subjects ——I came here to prescribe as a physician, and not to discuss topics of theology. Come, brother, I believe we only interrupt their ladyships, and I am obliged to call upon my lord____ and Sir *William*____ and Lady *Betty*, and many other people of quality this morning." Dr. *Rhubarb* declared that he likewise had as many visits to make that morning; whereupon, taking their leaves (and their fees) the two gentlemen retired with great precipitation, leaving her ladyship in possession of the field of battle; who immediately reported all over the town, that she had out-reasoned two physicians, and obliged them by dint of argument to confess that the soul is not immortal.]

Before I conclude this Chapter, I must beg the Reader not to imagine that any Ridicule was here intended of Mr. *Locke*, whose Name ought ever to be mentioned with Honour, and much less of the great Question debated in it; but, on the contrary, that it was designed to expose the Folly and Impiety of modern Wits, who dare to think Religion a proper Subject of Ridicule; and principally, to explode the Vanity of Women's pretending to Philosophy, when neither their Intellects, or Education qualify them for it. Beauty is no Excuse for Infidelity, and when they have so many other Arts to gain Admirers, one would think they need not be driven *to dispute against the Immortality of the Soul*.²

---

1 "To set fast, confound, embarrass, non-plus, perplex, puzzle" (*OED*).
2 Interestingly, this entire paragraph was cut from the third edition. Coventry may have thought better of giving John Locke a complete exoneration, as his views on the soul remained controversial.

CHAP. VIII

CONTAINING VARIOUS AND SUNDRY MATTERS.

POMPEY had now lived two Years with Lady *Tempest*, in all the Comforts and Luxuries of Life, fed every Day with the choicest, most expensive Dainties that *London* could afford, and caressed by all the People of Fashion that visited his Mistress:

————sed scilicet ultima semper
Expectanda dies————dicique beatus
Ante obitum nemo supremaque funera debet.[1]

A moral Reflection, no less applicable to Dogs than to Men! For they both alike experience the Inconstancy of Fortune, of which our Hero is a great Example, as all the following Pages of his History will very remarkably evince.[2]

Lady *Tempest* had been walking in St. *James's Park* one Morning in the Spring, with little *Pompey*, as usual, attending her, for she never went abroad without taking him in her Arms. Here she set him down on his Legs, to play with some other Dogs of Quality, that were taking the Air that Morning in the *Mall*;[3] giving him strict Orders, however, not to presume to stray out of her Sight. But in spite of this Injunction, something or other tempted his Curiosity beyond the Limits of the *Mall*; and there, while he was rolling and indulging himself on the green Grass, a Pleasure by Novelty rendered more agreeable to him, it was his Misfortune to spring a Bird; which he pursued with such Eagerness and Alacrity, that he was got as far as *Rosamond's Pond* before he thought proper to give over the Chace. His Mistress, in the mean while, was engaged in a warm and interesting Dispute on the Price of Silk, which so

---

1   Latin: "But of a surety man's last day must ever be awaited, and none be counted happy till his death, till his last funeral rites are paid." From Ovid, *Metamorphoses*, Bk. 3, ll. 135-7.
2   The opening paragraph was cut from the third edition.
3   A long tree-lined avenue for strolling in St. James's Park, situated in eighteenth-century London's most fashionable district.

engrossed her Attention, that she never missed her Favourite; nay, what is still more extraordinary, she got into her Coach, and drove home, without once bestowing a Thought upon him. But the Moment she arrived in her Dining-room, and cast her Eyes on the Rest of her four-footed Friends, her Guilt immediately flew in her Face, and she cried out with a Scream, *As I am alive, I have left little* Pompey *behind me.* Then summoning up two of her Servants in an Instant, she commanded them to go directly, and search every Corner of the Park with the great Diligence, protesting she shou'd never have any Peace of Mind, 'till her Favourite was restored to her Arms. Many Times she rang her Bell, to know if her Servants were returned, before it was possible for them to have got thither: but at length the fatal Message arrived, that *Pompey* was no where to be found. And indeed it would have been next to a Miracle, if he had; for these faithful Ambassadors had never once stirred from the Kitchen Fire, where, together with the rest of the Servants, they had been laughing at the Folly of their Mistress, and diverting themselves with the Misfortunes of her little Darling. And the Reason why they denied their Return sooner, was, because they imagined a sufficient Time had not then elapsed, to give a Probability to that Lie, which they were determined to tell. Yet this did not satisfy their Lady; she sent them a second Time to repeat their Search, and a second Time they returned with the same Story, that *Pompey* was to be found *neither high nor low.* At this again the Reader is desired not to wonder; for tho' her Ladyship saw them out of the House herself, and ordered them to bring back her Favourite, under Pain of Dismission, the farthest of their Travels was only to an Ale-house at the Corner of the Street, where they had been entertaining a large Circle of their parti-colour'd Brethren, with much Ribbaldry, at the Expence of their Mistress.

Tenderness to this Lady's Character makes me pass over much of the Sorrow she vented on this Occasion; but I cannot help relating, that she immediately dispatched Cards to all her Acquaintance, to put off a Drum which was to have been held at her House that Evening; giving as a Reason, that she had lost her darling Lap-dog, and could not see Company. She likewise sent an Advertisement to the News-Papers, of which we have procured a Copy, and beg leave to insert it.

Lost in the Mall *in* St. James's Park, *between the Hours of Two or Three* in
the Morning,[1] *a beautiful* Bologna Lap-dog, *with black and white Spots,
a mottled Breast, and several Moles upon his Nose, and answers to the Name
of* Pomp, *or,* Pompey. *Whoever will bring the same to* Mrs. La Place's, *in*
Duke-street, Westminster, *or Mrs.* Hussy's, *Mantua-maker in the* Strand,
or to St. James's *Coffee-house, shall receive two Guineas Reward.*[2]

This Advertisement was inserted in all the Papers for a Month,
with Increase of the Reward, as the Case grew more desperate;
yet neither all the Enquiries she made, nor all the Rewards she
offered, ever restored little *Pompey* to her Arms. We must leave her
therefore to receive the Consolations of her Friends on this afflict-
ing Loss, and return to examine after our Hero, of whose Fortune
the Reader, perhaps, may have a Desire to hear.

He had been pursuing a Bird, as was before described, as far as
Rosamond's Pond, and when his Diversion was over, galloped back
to the *Mall,* not in the least doubting to find his Lady there at his
Return. But alas! how great was his Disappointment! he ran up and
down, smelling to [sic] every Petticoat he met, and staring in every
female Face he saw, yet neither his Eyes, or Nose, gave him the
Information he desired. Seven Times he coursed from *Buckingham-
house* to the *Horse-guards,*[3] and back again, but all in vain: at length,
tired, and full of Despair, he sat himself down, disconsolate and
sorrowful, under a Tree, and there turning his head aside, abandoned himself to much mournful Meditation. In this evil Plight,
while he was ruminating on his Fate, and, like many People in the
Park, unable to divine where he should get a Dinner;[4] he was spied
by a little Girl, about eight Years old, who was walking by her

---

1 Here and elsewhere Coventry adopts the habit of fashionable people to refer to the
    early afternoon as the "morning." This was because fashionable people socialized long
    into the night and seldom arose from bed before noon.
2 This advertisement was cut from the third edition—oddly, as it provides information
    about Pompey's appearance that is absent elsewhere in the novel.
3 Buckingham-house, then the London residence of the Duke of Buckingham, was
    the precursor to the present Buckingham Palace, first made into a royal residence
    by Queen Victoria in 1837. "Horse-guards," the only gate into the Mall, was named
    after the mounted guards of St. James's and later Buckingham Palace. In other words,
    Pompey ran from one end of the Park to the other
4 Coventry is ridiculing the idle rich people in the Park who had nothing more on their
    minds than where to dine.

Mother's Side in the *Mall*. She no sooner perceived him, than she cried out, *La! Mamma! there's a pretty Dog!*———*I have a good Mind to call to it, Mamma! Shall I, Mamma! Shall I call to it, Mamma?* Having received her Mother's Assent, she applied herself, with much Tenderness, to sollicit him to her; which the little Unfortunate no sooner observed, than breaking off his Meditations, he ran hastily up, and saluting her with his Fore-paws (as the Wretched are glad to find a Friend) gave so many dumb Expressions of Joy, that Speech itself could hardly have been more eloquent. The young Lady, on her side, charmed with his ready Compliance; took him up in her Arms, and kissed him with great Delight; then turning again to her Mother, and asking her, if she did not think him a charming Creature, "I wonder," says she, "whose Dog it is, Mamma! I have a good mind to take him home with me, Mamma! Shall I, Mamma? Shall I take him home with me, Mamma?" To this also her Mother consented, and when they had taken two or three more Turns, they retired to their Coach, and *Pompey* was conducted to his new Lodgings.

As soon as they alighted at home, little Miss ran hastily up Stairs, to shew her Brother and Sister the prize she had found, and he was handed about from one to the other with great Delight and Admiration of his Beauty. He was then introduced to all their Favourites; which were a Dormouse, two Kittens, a *Dutch* Pug, a Squirrel, a Parrot, and a Magpye. To these he was presented with many childish Ceremonies, and all the innocent Follies, that are so important to the Happiness of this happiest Age. The Parrot was to make a Speech to him, the Squirrel to make him a Present of some Nuts, the Kittens were to dance for his Diversion, the Magpye to tell his Fortune, and all enjoined to contribute something to the Entertainment of the little Stranger. And 'tis inconceivable how busy they were in the Execution of these Trifles, with all their Spirits up in Arms, and their whole Souls laid out upon them.

In a few Days, little *Pompey* began to know his Way about the House alone, and I am sorry to say it, in less than a Week he had quite forgot his former Mistress. Here I know not how to excuse his Behaviour. Had he been a Man, one should not have wondered to find him guilty of Ingratitude, a Vice deeply rooted in the Nature of that wicked Animal; and accordingly, we see in all

the Revolutions of Court, how readily a new Minister is acknowl-
edged and embraced by all the Subalterns and dependent Flatterers,
who fawn with the same Servility on the new Favourite, as before
they practised to the old; but that a Dog——a Creature famous for
Fidelity, should so soon forget his former Friend and Benefactor, is,
I confess, quite unaccountable, and I would willingly draw a Veil
over this Part of his Conduct, if the Veracity of an Historian did
not oblige me to relate it.

CHAP. IX[1]

CONTAINING WHAT THE READER WILL KNOW,
IF HE READS IT.

ALTHOUGH the Family, into which *Pompey* now arrived, are
almost too inconsiderable for the Dignity of History, yet as they
had the Honour of entertaining our Hero for a Time, we shall
explain some few of their Characters.

The Master of it was Son of a wealthy Trader in the City, who
had amassed together an immense Heap of Riches, merely for the
Credit of leaving so much Money behind him. He had destined
his Son to the same honourable Pursuit, and very early initiated
him into all the Secrets of Business; but the young Gentleman,
marrying as soon as his Father died, was prevailed upon by his
loving Spouse, whose Head ran after the genteel Life, to quit the
dirty Scene of Business, and take a House within the Regions of
Pleasure. As neither of them had been used to the Company they
were now to keep, and both utterly unacquainted with all the Arts
of Taste, their Appearance in the polite World plainly manifested
their Original, and shewed how unworthy they were of those
Riches they so awkwardly enjoy'd. A clumsy, inelegant Magnificence prevailed in every Part of their Œconomy, in the Furniture
of their Houses, in the Disposition of their Tables, in the Choice of

---

1 This chapter, which contains searing satire of the upwardly-mobile "middle class,"
was deleted from the third edition.

their Cloaths, and in every other Action of their Lives. They knew no other Enjoyment but profuse Expence, and their Country-house was by the Road-side at *Highgate*.[1] It may be imagined such awkward Pretenders to High-Life, were treated with Ridicule by all the People of Genius and Spirit; but immoderate Wealth, and a Coach and Six, opened them a Way into Company, and few refused their Visits, tho' all laughed at their Appearance. For to tell the Reader a Secret, Money will procure its Owners Admittance any where; and however People may pride themselves on the Antiquity of their Families, if they have not Money to preserve a Splendor in Life, they may go a begging with their Pedigrees in their Hands; whereas lift a Grocer into a Coach-and-Six, and let him attend publick Places, and make grand Entertainments, he may be sure of having his Table filled with People of Fashion, tho' it was no longer ago than last Week that he left off selling Plumbs and Sugar.

The Fruits of their Marriage were three Daughters and a Son, who seemed not to promise long Life, or at least were likely to be made wretched by Distempers. For as the Father was much afflicted with the Gout, and the Mother pale, unhealthy and consumptive, the Children inherited the Diseases of their Parents, and were ricketty, scrophulous, sallow in their Complexions, and distorted in their Limbs. Nor were their Minds at all more amiable than their Bodies, being proud, selfish, obstinate and cross-humoured; and the whole Turn of their Education seemed calculated rather to improve these Vices than to eradicate them. For this Purpose, instead of sending them to Schools, where they would have been whipped out of many of their Ill-tempers, and perhaps by Conversation with other Children, might have learnt a more open generous Disposition, they were bred up under private Teachers at home, who never opposed any of their Humours, for fear of offending their Parents. Thus little Master, the Mother's Darling, was put under the Care of a domestic Tutor, partly because she cou'd not endure to have him at a Distance from her Sight, and partly because she had heard it was genteel to educate young Gentlemen at home.

The Tutor selected for this Purpose, had been dragged out of

---

1   I.e., their "country house" was right on the main road into London, an indication of their bad taste and desire to have their wealth on public display.

a College-Garret at Thirty, and just seen enough of the World to make him impertinent and a Coxcomb. For being introduced all at once into what is called *Life*, his Eyes were dazzled with the Things he beheld, and without waiting the Call of Nature, he made a quick Transition from College-reservedness to the pert Familiarity of a *London* Preacher. He soon grew to despise the Books he had read at the University, and affected a Taste for polite Literature——that is, no Literature at all; by which he endeared himself so much to the Family he lived in, by reading Plays to them, bringing home Stories from the Coffee-houses, and other Arts, that they gave him the Character of the *entertainingest, most facetious, best-humoured Creature that ever came into a House.* As his Temper led him by any Means to flatter his Benefactors, he never failed to cry up the Parts and Genius of his Pupil, as a Miracle of Nature; which the fond Mother, understanding nothing of the Matter, very easily believed. When therefore any of her female Visiters were commending little Master *for the finest Child they ever beheld*, she could not help adding something concerning his Learning, and wou'd say on such Occasions, "I assure you, Madam, his Tutor tells me he is forwarder than ever Boy was of his Age. He has got already, it seems, into his *Syntax*——I don't know what the *Syntax* is Ma'am, but I dare say 'tis some very good moral Book, otherwise Mr. *Jackson* wou'd not teach it him; for to be sure, there never was a Master that had a better Manner of teaching than Mr. *Jackson*——What is the *Syntax*, my Dear? Tell the Ladies what the *Syntax* is, Child!" "Why, Mamma," cries the Boy, "the *Syntax* is——it is the End of the *As in Præsenti*, and teaches you how to parse." "Ay, ay," said the Mother, "I thought so my dear; 'tis some very good Book I make no doubt, and will improve your Morals as well as your Understanding. Be a good Boy, Child, and mind what Mr. *Jackson* says to you, and I dare say, you'll make a great Figure in Life."

This is a little Specimen of the young Gentleman's Education, and that of the young Ladies fell short of it in no Particular: For they were taught by their Mother and Governess to be vain, affected, and foppish; to disguise every natural Inclination of the Soul, and give themselves up to Cunning, Dissimulation, and Insincerity; to be proud of Beauty they had not, and ashamed of Passions they had; to think all the Happiness of Life consisted in a new Cap or a new Gown, and no Misfortune equal to the missing a Ball.

Besides many inanimate Play-things, this little Family had likewise, as before observed, several living Favourites, whom they took Delight to vex and torture for their Diversion. Among the Number of these, little *Pompey* had the Misfortune to be enrolled; I say Misfortune, for wretched indeed are all those Animals, that become the Favourites of Children. For a good while he suffered only the Barbarity of their Kindness, and was persecuted with no other Cruelties than what arose from their extravagant Love of him; but when the Date of his Favour began to expire (and indeed it did not continue long) he was then taught to feel how much severer their Hate could be than their Fondness. Indeed he had from the first, two or three dreadful Presages of what might happen to him, for he had seen with his own Eyes the two Kittens, his Play-fellows, drowned for some Misdemeanor they had been guilty of, and the Magpy's Head chopt off with the greatest Passion, for daring to peck a Piece of Plumb-cake that laid in the Window, without Permission; which Instances of Cruelty were sufficient to warn him, if he had any Foresight, of what might afterwards happen to himself.

But he was not left long to entertain himself with Conjectures, before he felt in Person and in reality the mischievous Disposition of these little Tyrants. Sometimes they took it into their Heads that he was full of Fleas, and then he was dragged thro' a Canal till he was almost dead, in order to kill the Vermin that inhabited the Hair of his Body. At other Times he was set upon his hinder Legs with a Book before his Eyes, and ordered to read his Lesson; which not being able to perform, they whipt him with Rods till he began to exert his Voice in a lamentable Tone, and then they chastised him the more for daring to be sensible of Pain.

Much of this Treatment did he undergo, often wishing himself restored to the Arms of Lady *Tempest*, when Fortune taking pity of his Calamities, again resolved to change his Lodgings. An elderly Maiden Lady, Aunt to this little Brood and Sister to their Papa, was one Day making a Visit in the Family, and by great good Luck happened to be Witness of some of Ill-usage, which *Pompey* underwent: For having committed some imaginary Fault he was brought down to be tormented in her Presence. Her righteous Spirit immediately rose at this Treatment; she declared it was a shame to persecute poor dumb Creatures in that barbarous manner, wondered their Mamma would suffer it, and signified that she would take the Dog home with her to her own House. Tho' the little Tyrants had long been tired of him, yet Obstinacy set them a crying, when they found he was to be taken from them; but there was no contending; their Aunt was resolute, and thus *Pompey* was happily delivered from this House of Inquisition.

CHAP. X

THE GENEALOGY OF A CAT, AND OTHER ODD MATTERS, WHICH THE GREAT CRITICS OF THE AGE WILL CALL IMPROBABLE AND UNNATURAL.

A QUITE new Scene of Life now opened on our Hero, who from frequenting Drums and Assemblies with Lady *Tempest*, from shining conspicuous in the Side boxes of the Opera and Play-house, was now confined to the Chambers of an old Maid, and obliged to attend Morning and Evening Prayers. 'Tis true the Change was not altogether a sudden one, since his last Place had a good deal reduced his aspiring Notions; but still his Genius for Gallantry and High-life continued, and he found it very difficult to compose himself to the sober Hours and orderly Deportment of an ancient Virgin. Sometimes indeed he would turn up his Ear and seem attentive, while she was reading *Tillotson*'s Sermons;[1] but if the Truth were known, I believe he had rather have been listening to a Novel or a Play-book.

People who have been used to much Company, cannot easily reconcile themselves to Solitude, and the only Companion he found here, was an ancient tabby Cat, whom he despised at first with a

---

1   The sermons of John Tillotson (1630–94), Anglican clergyman and Archbishop of Canterbury, were highly popular, despite being dry and philosophical.

most fashionable Disdain, tho' she solicited his Acquaintance with much Civility, and shewed all the Respect due to a Stranger. She took every Opportunity of meeting him in her Walks, and tried to enter into Conversation with him; but he never returned any of her Compliments, and as much as possible declined her Haunts. At length, however, Time reconciled him to her, and frequent Meetings produced a strict Friendship between them.

This Cat, by name *Mopsa*, was Heiress of the most ancient Family of Cats in the World. There is a Tradition, which makes her to be descended from that memorable *Grimalkin* of Antiquity, who was converted into a Woman at the Request of her Master, and is said to have leapt out of Bed one Morning, forgetting her Transformation, in pursuit of a fugitive Mouse: From which Event all Moralists have declaimed on the Impossibility of changing fixed Habits, and *L'Estrange* in particular observes, *that Puss, tho' a Madam, will be a Mouser still.*[1]

It is very hard to fix the precise Time of her Family's first Arrival in *England*, so various and discordant are the Opinions of our Antiquaries on that Subject. Many are persuaded they came over with *Brute* the *Trojan*;[2] others conjecture they were left by *Phœnician* Merchants, who formerly traded on the Coast of *Cornwal*. The great B____n W____ll____s insists, that *Julius Cæsar*, in his second Expedition to *Britain*, brought over with him a Colony of *Roman* Cats to people the Island, at that time greatly infected with Mice and Rats. The learned and ingenious Dr. S____k____y, disliking all these Opinions, undertakes to prove, that they were not in *England* till the Conquest, but that they came over in the same Ship with the Duke of *Normandy*, afterwards *William* the First.[3] Which of their Conjectures is the truest, these ingenious Gentlemen must decide among themselves; which I apprehend will not be done without many Volumes of Controversy; but they are all unanimous in supposing the Family to be very ancient and of foreign Extraction.

Another of her great Ancestors, whose Name likewise is

---

1 Coventry refers to the fable of *Grimalkin* collected under the title "A Cat and Venus" in *Fables of Æsop and Other Eminent Mythologists: With Moral and Reflections* (1692) by Roger L'Estrange (1616–1704), better known as a leading political journalist and Tory propagandist. Fielding makes exactly the same allusion in Bk 12, ch. 2 of *Tom Jones*.

2 Legendary founder of Britain, better known to us as "Brutus."

3 Coventry refers to the renowned antiquarians Browne Willis (1682–1760) and William Stukeley (1687–1765).

considerable in History, was that immortal Cat, who made the Fortune of Mr. *Whitington*, and advanced him to the Dignity of a Lord-Mayor of *London*, according to the Prophesy of a Parish-Steeple to that effect.[1] There are likewise many others well known to Fame, as *Gridelin the Great*, and *Dina the Sober*, and *Grimalkin the Pious*, and the famous Puss that wore Boots,[2] and another that had a Legacy left her in the last Will and Testament of her deceased Mistress; of which satirical Mention is made in the Works of our *English Horace*.[3] But leaving the Deduction of her Genealogy to the great Professors of that Science, and recommending it to them as a Subject quite new, and extremely worthy of their sagacious Researches, I shall proceed to Matters of greater Consequence to this History.

'Tis observed by an old *Greek* Poet, and from thence copied into the *Spectator*, that there is a great Similitude between Cats and Women.[4] Whether the Resemblance be just in other Instances, I will not pretend to determine, but I believe it holds exactly between ancient Cats and ancient Maids; which I suppose is the Reason why Ladies of that Character are never without a grave Mouser in their Houses, and generally at their Elbows.

Mopsa had now lived near a dozen Years with her present Mistress, and being naturally of a studious, musing Temper, she had so improved her Understanding from the Conversation of this aged Virgin, that she was now deservedly reckoned the most philosophic Cat in *England*. She had the Misfortune some Years before to lose her favorite Sister *Selima*, who was unfortunately drowned in a large China Vase; which sorrowful Accident is very

---

1 Dick Whittington was a real mayor of London in the late 14th and early 15th centuries. According to a popular legend, he was originally a poor boy who made his fortune by giving his cat to a merchant, who later sold it for a huge sum overseas.

2 These mock-heroic titles refer to fairy stories involving cats.

3 Coventry refers to *The Epistle to Bathurst* (1733), l. 98, by Alexander Pope, who delighted in presenting himself as a modern version of Horace, the Roman satirist.

4 *The Spectator*, edited and largely written by Joseph Addison (1672-1719) and Sir Richard Steele (1672-1729), was among the most popular and influential periodicals of the eighteenth century, dispensing advice on good taste and social manners in a relaxed style designed for the middle ranks. It ran as a daily from 1711 to 1712, and was reprinted often throughout the century. In *Spectator* No. 209, Addison recorded a misogynistic comparison between thieving cats and dishonest women by the 6th century BCE lyric poet Simonides.

ingeniously lamented in a most elegant little Ode, which I heartily recommend to the Perusal of every Reader, who has a Taste for Lyric Numbers and poetical Fancy; and it is to be found in one of the Volumes of Mr. *Dodsley*'s Collection of *Miscellany Poems.*[1] This Misfortune added much to *Mopsa*'s Gravity, and gave her an Air of Melancholy not easily described. For a long while indeed her Grief was so great, that she neglected the Care of her Person, neither cleaning her Whiskers, nor washing her Face as usual; but Time and Reflection at length got the better of her Sorrow, and restored her to the natural Serenity of her Temper.

When little *Pompey* came into the Family, she saw he had a good Disposition at the bottom, tho' he was a *wild, thoughtless, young Dog*, and therefore resolved to try the Effects of her Philosophy upon him. If therefore at any time he began to talk in the Language of the World, and flourished upon Balls, Opera, Plays, Masquerades, and the like, she would take up the Discourse, and with much Socratical Composure prove to him the Folly and Vanity of such Pursuits. She would tell him how unworthy it was of a Dog of any Understanding to follow the trivial Gratification of his Senses, and how idle were the Pageants of Ambition compared with the sober Comforts of Philosophy. This indeed he used to ridicule with great Gaiety of Spirit (if the Reader will believe it) and tell her by way of Answer, that her Contempt of the World arose from her having never lived in it. But when he had a little wore off the Relish of Pleasure, he began to listen every Day to her Arguments with greater Attention, till at length she absolutely convinced him that Happiness is no where so perfect, as in Tranquillity and retired Life.

From this Time their Friendship grew stricter every Day; they used to go upon little Parties of innocent Amusement together, and it was very entertaining to see them walking Side by Side in the Garden, or lying couchant under a Tree to surprize some little Bird in the Branches. Malicious Fame no sooner observed this Intimacy, than with her usual Malice she published the Scandal of an Amour

---

1 In Thomas Gray's mock-eulogy "Ode on the Death of a Favourite Cat," first published in *A Collection of Poems. By Several Hands* (1748), the unfortunate feline Selima drowns in a fish bowl. The prestigious bookseller Robert Dodsley (1703-64), the editor of this *Collection,* took over the third edition of *Pompey the Little,* which lacked this chapter on the philosophical cat Mopsa.

between them; but I am persuaded it had no Foundation, for *Mopsa* was old enough to be *Pompey*'s Grand-mother, and besides he always behaved to her, rather with the Homage due to a Parent than the ardent Fondness of a Lover.

But Fortune, his constant Enemy, again set her Face against him. The two Friends one day in their Mistress's Closet, had been engaged in a very serious Dispute on the *Summum Bonum*, or chief Good of Life; and both of them had delivered their Sentiments very gravely upon it; the one contending for an absolute Exclusion of all Pleasure, the other desirous only to intermix some Diversions with his Philosophy. They were seated on two Books, which their Mistress had left open in her Study; to wit, *Mopsa* on *Nelson's Festivals*, and *Pompey* on *Baker's Chronicles*;[1] when alas——how little things determine the greatest Matters! *Pompey*, in the Earnestness of his Debate, did something on the Leaves of that sage Historian, very unworthy of his Character, and improper to be mentioned in explicit Terms. His Mistress unfortunately entered the Room at that Moment, and saw the Crime he had been guilty of; which so enraged her, that she resolved never to see his Face any more, but ordered her Footman to dispose of him without delay.

[CHAP. IX[2]

WHAT THE READER WILL KNOW IF HE READS IT.

CAPTAIN *Vincent* of the guards, was an exceeding handsome man, about thirty years old, tall and well-proportioned in his limbs; but so entirely devoted to the contemplation of his own pretty person, that he never detached his thoughts one moment from the consideration of it. Conscious of being a favourite of the ladies, among whom he

---

1 Robert Nelson's *Companion for the Festivals and Fasts of the Church of England* (1704) and Sir Richard Baker's *Chronicle of the Kings of England* (1643) were standard, if dour, works in literate English households.

2 The story of Captain and Lady Betty Vincent, which follows in the next three chapters, replaced chapters IX and X from the original edition. Captain Vincent became the father of the little girl who takes Pompey from St. James's Park in chapter VIII.

was received always with eyes of affection, he thought the charms of his figure irresistible wherever he came, and seemed to shew himself in all public places as an object of public admiration. You saw for ever in his looks a smile of assurance, complacency, and self-applause; he appeared always to be wondering at his own accomplishments, and especially when he made a survey now and then of his dress and limbs, 'twas as much to say to his company, "gentlemen and ladies, look at me if you can without admiration." The reputation of two or three affairs which fame had given him with women of fashion, still contributed to encrease his vanity, and authorized him, as he thought, to bestow more time and pains on the beautifying and adorning so successful a figure. In short, after many real or pretended amours, which made him insufferably vain, he married at last a celebrated town-beauty, a woman of quality, who was in all respects equal to, and worthy of such a husband.

Lady *Betty Vincent*, the wife of this gentleman, was one of those haughty nymphs of quality, who presume so much on the merit of a title, that they never trouble themselves to acquire any other. She was proud, expensive, insolent and unmannerly to her inferiors; vain of her rank, and still vainer of her person; full of extravagant airs, and tho' exceedingly silly, conceited of an imaginary wit and smartness. As she set out in life with a full persuasion that her prodigious beauty, merit, and accomplishments, must soon procure her the title of *her grace*,[1] she rejected several advantageous matches that offered, because they did not in all points come up to the height of her ambition. At length finding her charms begin to decay, in a fit of lust, disappointed pride, and opposition to her mother, with whom she had then a quarrel, she patched up a marriage with captain *Vincent* of the guards, contrary to the advice and remonstrances of all her friends and relations.

As the captain had no revenue beside the income of his commission, and her ladyship's fortune did not exceed seven thousand pounds, it may be concluded, when the honey-moon of love was over, this agreeable couple did not find the matrimonial fetters sit perfectly easy upon them. To retrench in any article,[2] they found

---

1 I.e. she expected finally to marry a nobleman and to win the right to be addressed as an aristocrat.
2 I.e., to cut back on any expense.

it impossible; to retire into the country, still more impossible; that was horrors, death, and despair——her ladyship could not hear of such a thing with patience——she was ready to swoon at the mention of it; and indeed the captain, who was equally attached to *London*, never made the proposal in earnest.

What then could they do in these embarrassing circumstances? Why, they took a little house in *Hedge-Lane*, near the bottom of *Hay-Market*, which being the center of public diversions, served to keep them a little in countenance;[1] and there they supported their spirits as well as they could, with reflecting that they still lived in the world, tho' their apartments were not so commodious as they could wish.

Fettered pride is sure to turn to peevishness, and spleen is the daughter of mortified vanity. Finding themselves cramped with want, they grew uneasy, discontented, jealous of each other's extravagance, and were scarce ever alone without reproaching one another on the article of expence. The lady powted at the captain for going to *White*'s, and the captain recriminated on his wife for playing at Brag; and then followed a long contention, which of them spent the most money.

To compleat their misfortunes, her ladyship took to breeding, which introduced a thousand new expences; and they must absolutely have starved in the midst of pride and vanity, had they not been seasonably relieved now and then by some handsome presents from lady *Betty*'s mother, my old lady *Harridan*, who was still alive, and in possession of a considerable jointure.[2]

The devotion which the captain paid to his beautiful figure, has already been described; nor was her ladyship one jot behind him in idolizing and adoring her own charms. She prided herself in a particular manner on the *lovely bloom* and *charming delicacy of her complexion*, which had procured her the envy of one sex, and the admiration of the other; tho' perhaps if her enviers and admirers had known the following little story, both these passions would have considerably abated in them.

It was our hero's custom, whenever he came into a new family, to gratify his curiosity as soon as possible, with a general survey of

---

1 I.e., kept them publicly cheerful.
2 Property owned jointly by a husband and wife, and then inherited by the wife upon widowhood.

the house. On his arrival here, his little owners were so fond of him the first day, that they lugged him about in their arms, and never permitted him to stray one moment out of their sights; but being left more at his own liberty the next morning, he thought it was then a convenient time for making his tour. After examining all the rooms above ground, he descended intrepidly into the kitchen, and began to look about sharp for breakfast; for to say the truth, he had hitherto met with very thin commons in his new apartments. At last a blue and white dish, which stood on the dresser, presented itself to his eye. This immediately he determined to be lawful prey, and perceiving nobody present to interrupt him, boldly made a spring at it; but happening unluckily to leap against the dish, down it came, and its contents ran about the kitchen. Scarce had this happened, when my lady's maid appeared below stairs, and began to scream out in a very shrill accent, "why who has done this now? I'll be whipped if this *owdacious* little dog has not been and thrown down my lady's backside's breakfast;" after which she fell very severely on the cook, who now entered the kitchen, and began to reprimand her in a very authoritative tone, for not taking more care of her dressers; "but let the 'pothecary," added she, "come and mix up his nastiness himself an he will, for deuce fetch me if I'll wait on her ladyship's backside in this manner: If she will have her clysters,[1] let the clyster-pipe doctor come and minister them himself, and not put me to her filthy offices.———O Lord bless us! well, rather than be at all this pains for a complexion, I'd be as brown as a berry all my lifetime. The finest flowers, I have heard, are raised from dung,[2] and perhaps it may be so———I am sure 'tis so at our house, for my lady takes physic twice a week, and treats her backside with a clyster once a fortnight, and all this to preserve a complexion."

While the waiting-gentlewoman was haranguing thus at the expence of her mistress, the captain's valet also came into the kitchen, and hearing his fellow servant very loud and vociferous, enquired what was the matter. "Matter," cries she, "matter enough o' conscience! don't you see there? This plaguy little devil of a dog

---

1 Enemas.

2 The lady's maid is apparently remembering the last two lines of Swift's scatological poem "The Lady's Dressing-room" (1732): "Such Order from Confusion sprung, / Such gaudy Tulips rais'd from Dung."

has been and flung down my lady's backside's breakfast." "Bless us, a prodigious disaster indeed!" replied the valet; "why, what shall we do now, Mrs. *Minikin*? I am afraid your lady's complexion will want its bloom to day." "Hang her complexion," said *Abagail*, "I wish her complexion was at the bottom of her own close-stool; she need not be so generous to her backside indeed——I am sure she is not so over-and-above generous to her servants, and her trades-folks." "True," cries the valet, "if she would treat us with a breakfast now and then, as well as her backside, methinks it would not be amiss, for deuce take me, if I ever saw such house-keeping in any family that I ever lived in, in my days. They dress plaguy fine both of 'em, and cut a figure abroad, while their servants are starving at home." "Yes, yes," said Mrs. *Minikin*, "'tis all shew and no substance at our house. There's your pretty master, the captain, has been smugging up his pretty face, and cleaning his teeth for this hour, before the looking-glass this morning. I wonder he does not clyster for a complexion too. Tho', thank heaven, he's coxcomb enough already, and wants no addition to his pride; he seems to think no woman can look him in the face without falling in love with him, with his black solitaire,[1] and his white teeth, and his frizzled hair, and his fopperies. O Lord have mercy upon us! well, every one to their own liking, but hang me if I would not marry a monkey as soon as such a powdered scaramouch,[2] were I a woman of quality.——Get out you little nasty devil of a dog; hang me if I won't brain you, and let the little vixens your mistresses say what they please."

Having said this, she set out full of rage in pursuit of poor *Pompey*, who took to his heels with great precipitation, and fled for his life; but not being nimble enough he was overtaken, and smarted severely for the trespass he had committed. To say the truth, he soon began to find himself very unhappily situated in this family; for wretched are all those animals that become the favourites of children.[3]

---

1 "An ornament for the neck" (Johnson).
2 "A buffoon in motly dress" (Johnson).
3 At this point, Coventry recites the litany of abuses suffered by Pompey at the hands of the children, as previously described in Chapter IX of the first edition. I have therefore omitted this section.

[CHAP. X

A MATRIMONIAL DISPUTE.

LADY Betty *Vincent* had a mother still living, as we hinted in the preceding chapter; who having worn out her life in vanity, cards, and all sorts of luxury, was now turned methodist at seventy, and thought by presenting heaven with the dregs of her age, to atone for the riot and lasciviousness of her youth.[1] For this purpose she had renounced all public diversions, put herself under the tuition of two great field-preaching apostles,[2] and was become one of the warmest votaries of that prevailing sect.

But besides the self-mortification she was pleased to undergo, her ladyship had likewise an additional stratagem to procure her pardon above, which she thought impossible to fail her; and this was to take her eldest grand-daughter out of the temptations of a wicked seducing age into her own family, and breed her up a methodist: the merit of which laudable action she hoped would compensate all her own miscarriages, and effectually restore her to the divine favour.

Having thus laid the scheme of compounding matters with heaven, and making the virtues of the grand-daughter balance as it were and set off the sins of the grand-mother, she now thought only of putting it in execution. In the first place she communicated her design to the two apostles, and the moment she was assured of their approbation, she dispatched a message to her daughter, desiring an hour's conversation with her the first time she was at leisure.

Lady *Betty*, who had great dependence on her mother, did not fail to answer the summons, and was with her very early the next morning; *so very early*, that the clock had but just struck one; which she said was an instance of *her uncommon filial obedience*. It may be imagined the two ladies soon came to agreement; lady *Betty* being as glad to get rid of a charge, as lady *Harridan* to acquire a compan-

---

1 Coventry shared Fielding's hostility towards the methodists, a populist movement then still attached to the Anglican Church that taught "the inner light" and faith over works, and that reached out to common people with inspirational preaching.

2 The two great leaders of methodism, both known for preaching at open-air gatherings, were John Wesley (1703-91) and George Whitefield (1714-70).

ion, which she represented as the motive that induced her to take her grand-daughter into her family.

Matters being thus settled, lady *Betty* returned home to dinner; where she observed a sullen silence till the cloth was removed, and the servants were carrying away the last things. Then it was that she pleased to open her mouth, and bade one of the footmen "tell *Minikin* to get *Sally*'s cloaths and linnen packed up against the evening." There happened at this time to be a *miff*[1] subsisting between her ladyship and the captain, and they had glowted[2] at one another for several days without exchanging a word. She did not therefore vouchsafe to ask her husband's consent in the step she was taking, nor even to inform him of it in direct terms, but left him to extract it as well as he could from this oblique message, which she sent to her maid. The captain, who plainly saw that some mystery was contained under these orders, had at first a mind to be revenged by affecting not to hear them; but curiosity prevailing over his resentment, he submitted at length to ask whither his daughter was going?

"Why, if you will spend all your life at *White*'s, and lose all your money in play, (replied the lady with an air of disdain) I must dispose of my children as well as I can, I think."

"But what connexion is there, in the name of God," said the captain, "between my playing at *White*'s, and your packing up your daughter's cloaths?——Unless perhaps you are going to send your daughter to the *Foundling-Hospital*."

"Yes, perhaps I am," cries she with a toss of her head; "If one can't maintain one's children at home, they must e'en come upon the parish,[3] and there's the end of it."

Still the captain remained unenlightened; not a ray of information transpired through the dark speeches, and indeed there seemed to be no likelihood of an eclaircissement;[4] for in this manner they continued to play at cross-purposes with one another for several minutes. At last, his patience being utterly exhausted, he insisted very earnestly, and some-what angrily, to know what was going to be done with his daughter. "Why, mamma has a mind to take the girl to live with her, if you must

---

1 "Fit of pique, a huff; a petty quarrel, a tiff" (*OED*).
2 "To look sullen, frown, scowl" (*OED*).
3 The parish, or local church district, took responsibility in the eighteenth century for unwanted children, along with the performance of other charitable activities.
4 Clarification.

know," replied her ladyship, "and that is going to be done with your daughter. If you will get children, without being able to maintain them, you may be thankful methinks to find there is somebody in the world that will take them off your hands." "Oh Madam!" cries the captain, "as to the article of begetting children, I apprehend your ladyship to be full as guilty as I am, and therefore that is out of the question——but as to your mamma's taking them off our hands, devil take me if I am not exceedingly obliged to her for it. Your mamma is welcome to take them all, if she pleases.——I only wanted to know what was going to be done with the girl, and now I am most perfectly satisfied;" which he uttered with the most taunting pronunciation in the world.

There is nothing so exceedingly provoking as a sneer to people enraged and inflamed with pride. The captain perceived the effect it had, and resolved to pursue his triumph, "My dear," added he, "to be sure the prudent care you are taking to provide for you children is highly commendable, but I am afraid your mamma will debauch the girl with religion.——She'll teach her perhaps to whine, and cant, and say her prayers under the godly Mr. *Whitefield*."

Lady *Betty* had never in her life shewn the least regard for her mother. She married in direct opposition to her will, and partly out of revenge, because she happened at that time to have a quarrel with her, and knew her disinclination to the match: but now so much was she galled with the captain's raillery, that she gladly seized on any thing which offered as a handle of reproach. With rage therefore sparkling in her eyes, and indignation glowing all over her face, she cried out, "How dare you ridicule my mamma? If mamma has a mind to be an old doting idiot, and change her religion, does it become you of all people to reproach her with it? You have the greatest obligations to her, sir, and you may be ashamed to give yourself such airs. You ridicule my mamma!——You of all people in the world! ——'Twould have been well for me, I am sure, if I had taken mamma's advice, and never *had you*; for you know you *brought* nothing but your little beggarly commission, and what is the income of a little beggarly commission? 'tis not sufficient to furnish one's pin-cushion with pins. And who pray *was you*, when I *had you*? You know you was *no blood* or *family*; and yet you pretend to ridicule my mamma! you of all people! you!——if it was not for mamma now, you would starve, you and all your brats would starve with want."

When a dispute is grown to the highest, especially if it be a matrimonial one, all sober argument and cool reply are nothing better than words spoken against the wind. The judicious captain therefore, instead of answering this invective of his spouse, very wisely, in my opinion, fell a singing; which so exasperated the fair lady, and so utterly over-set her patience, that she started from her chair, swept down two or three bottles and glasses with her hoop-petticoat, flounced out of the room, and rushed up stairs ready to burst with indignation.

All the while this dispute was passing in the parlour, our hero was the subject of as fierce a one among his little owners, or rather tormentors, in another room. For as the eldest girl was going to a different family, it was necessary they should make a separation of their playthings; and our hero being incapable of division, unless they had carved him out into shares, a warm debate arose concerning him, both sides obstinately refusing to wave their pretensions. This perhaps may seem a little wonderful to the reader, who has been informed that they were all long ago grown tired of him; but let him consider the tempers of this little family, begotten in spleen, peevishness, and pride, and I believe he will not think it unnatural, after the recent example he has seen of their parents, that a spirit of opposition should make them contend with the greatest vehemence for a matter of the most absolute indifference to them. This was in reality the cause of their contention, and they would soon have gone together by the ears, had not their mamma appeared to decide the question in favour of the eldest girl; whose claim she said was indisputable, from the circumstance of her finding him in the *Park*.

Lady *Betty* was hardly yet recovered from her passion, but being now told that lady *Harridan*'s coach was waiting for her at the door, she composed her face and well as she could, and mounted into it, attended by her daughter and the hero of this history.

[CHAP. XI

A STROKE AT THE METHODISTS.

THEY arrived at lady *Harridan*'s about seven o'clock in the evening, and were immediately conducted up-stairs into her lady's dining-room, where they found a large company of women assembled. On the first sight of so many ladies, I believe our hero concluded, he was got into some rout or drum, such as he had often seen at lady *Tempest*'s; yet on the other hand he knew not well how to reconcile many appearances with such a supposition. He saw no cards, he heard no laughing——the solemn faces of the servants, who now and then appeared, the sober looks of the company, every thing seemed to inform him, that pleasure never could be the cause of this assembly. It was indeed a sisterhood of the godly, met together to bewail the vanities of human life, and congratulate one another on their common good-luck, in breaking away from the enchantments of a sinful world.

The causes, which had converted them to methodism, were almost as various as the several characters of the converts. Some the ill-success of their charms had driven to despair; others a consciousness of too great success had touched with repentance; and both these terminated in superstitious melancholy. Disappointed love and criminal amour, tho' opposite in nature, here wrought the same effects: thunder and lightning, ill-omened dreams, earthquakes, vapors, small-pox, all had their converts in this religious collection: but far the most part of them, like the noble president, were women fatigued and worn out in the vanities of life, the battered and super-annuated jades of pleasure, who being sick of themselves, and weary of the world, were now fled to methodism, merely as the newest sort of folly, that had lately been invented.

——*Species non omnibus una,*
Nec diversa tamen; qualem decet esse sororum.[1]

The appearance of lady *Betty* in such a company as this, was like a wasp's invading a nest of drones. She was too spirited, too much drest, too worldly to be agreeable to them, and they in return gave as little pleasure to her. In short, she very soon found herself out of her element, and after sitting a few minutes only, rose up and began to make her departing curtsies.

"Why sure you are not going, lady *Betty*," cried the mother ——"I presumed upon your staying the evening with us."

---

1   Latin: "They have not all the same appearance, and yet not altogether different." From Ovid, *Metamorphoses*, Book II, ll. 13-14.

"No thank you," replied the daughter; "another time, if you please, mamma; but you seem to be all too religious abundantly for me at present. I can't afford to say my prayers above once a week, mamma, and 'tis not Sunday today according to my calculation."

"For shame, for shame, my dear, don't indulge such levity of discourse," said lady *Harridan*; "let me prevail on you to stay, lady *Betty*, and I am sure we shall make a convert of you. There is that tranquillity, my dear, that composure, that serenity of mind attending methodism, that I am sure no person who judges fairly, can refuse to embrace it. Pleasure, my dear, is all vanity and folly, an unquiet, empty, transient delusion——believe me, child, I have experienced it, I have proved the vanity of it, and depend upon't, sooner or later you will come to the same way of thinking."

"Very likely I may," replied lady *Betty*; "but you'll give me leave to grow a little wickeder first, won't you, mamma? I have not sins enough at present, I am not quite wicked enough as yet to turn methodist."

"Fie! Fie! don't encourage that licentiousness of conversation," cries the old lady; "you shock me, my dear, beyond measure, you make my blood run cold again to hear you——but let me beseech you to stay, and you'll have the pleasure of hearing the dear *Whitefield* talk on this subject——we expect him every minute."

"Do you?" says lady *Betty*; "then upon my honour I'll hie away this moment, for I'll promise you, mamma, I have not the least desire or curiosity to hear the dear *Whitefield*——and so your servant, ladies, your servant." Having said this, she brushed down stairs, and left the company astonished at her prophaneness.

As lady *Betty* went out, the dear *Whitefield* and his brother apostle entered, who were the only people wanting to compleat this religious collection. On their appearance the mysteries began, and they all fell to lamenting the wickedness of their former lives. The great guilt of loving cards, the exceeding sinfulness of having been fond of dancing in their youthful days, were enumerated as sins of the most atrocious quality; whilst other crimes, of a nature perhaps not inferior to these, were very prudently kept out of sight. Then Mr. *Whitefield* began to preach the history of his life, and related the many combats and desperate encounters he has had with the devil; how Satan confined him to his chamber once at college, and permitted him not to eat for several days together; with ten thousand other malicious pranks play'd by the prince of darkness on the body of that unfortunate adventurer, if we may believe his journals. He proceeded in the next place to describe the many miracles, which heaven has wrought in his favour; how it ceased to rain once, and the sun broke out on a sudden, just as he was beginning to preach on *Kennington-Common*; with a million more equally stupendous prodigies, which shew how great an interest heaven takes in all the actions of that religious mountebank.[1] When the company had enjoyed enough of this spiritual and suspirious[2] conversation, they proceeded in the last place to singing of psalms, and this concluded the superstition of the evening.

All the former part of the time, our hero sat very composed and quietly before the fire; but when they began to chant their hymns, surprized and astonished with the novelty of the proceeding, he fell to howling with the most sonorous accent, and in a key much higher than any of the screaming sisters. Nor was this all; for presently afterwards, Mr. *Whitefield* attempting to stroke him, he snarled and bit his finger: which being the self-same indignity that *Lucian* formerly offered to the hand of a similar imposter,[3] we thought it not beneath the dignity of this history to relate it. To say the truth, I believe he had taken some disgust to that exceeding pious gentleman; for besides these two instances of ill-behaviour, he was guilty of a much greater rudeness the next day to his works.

Lady *Harridan*, as soon as she arose the next morning, sent for her little grand-daughter immediately into her closet, and made her repeat some long methodistical prayers; after which she heard her read several pages out of the apostle's journal, and then they went to breakfast; but by mistake left poor *Pompey* shut up in the closet. The little prisoner scratched very impatiently to be released, and made various attempts to open the door; but not having the good fortune to succeed, he leaped upon the table, and wantonly did his occasions on the field-preacher's memoirs, which lay open upon it. Whether this was done to express his contempt of the book, or merely from an incapacity of suppressing his needs, is

1 Coventry is citing incidents recorded in *A Short Account of God's Dealings with the Reverend Mr. George Whitefield, A.B.* (1740). Now Kennington Park in south London, Kennington-Common had a long history of mass rallies for radical groups.

2 "Full of sighs, sighing" (*OED*). The *OED* cites this passage as the first use of "suspirious" in this sense.

3 Coventry is citing an incident in "Alexander, the False Prophet," by the satirist Lucian of Samosata (c. 125–80 CE).

hardly possible for us to determine; tho' we are sensible how much it would exalt him in the reader's esteem, to ascribe it to the former motive; and indeed it must be confessed, that his chusing to drop his superfluities on so particular a spot, may very well countenance such a suspicion; but unless we had the talents of *Æsop*, to interpret the sentiments of brutes, it will for ever be impossible to come at the truth of this important affair.

However that may be, lady *Harridan* unfortunately returned to her closet soon afterwards, and saw the crime he had been guilty of. Rage and indignation sparkled in her eyes; she rang her bell instantly with the greatest fury, and on the appearance of a footman, ordered him immediately to be hanged. His young mistress, whose love for him had long since cooled, and who besides feared her grand-mamma's resentment, did not think proper to oppose the sentence. He was had away therefore that moment to execution; which I dare say, courteous reader, thou art extremely glad to hear, as it would put a period to his history, and prevent thee from misspending any more of thy precious time. But alas! thy hopes are vain——thy labours are not yet at an end. The footman, who happened to have some few grains of compassion in his nature, instead of obeying his lady's orders, sold him that day for a pint of porter to an ale-house keeper's daughter in *Tyburn-Road*.[1] Here then, gentle friend, if thou art tired, let me advise thee to desist and fall asleep; or if perchance thy spirits are fresh, and thou dost not yet begin to yawn, proceed on courageously, and thou wilt in good time arrive at the end of thy journey.]

CHAP. XI[2]

THE HISTORY OF A MODISH MARRIAGE; THE DESCRIPTION OF A COFFEE-HOUSE, AND A VERY GRAVE POLITICAL DEBATE ON THE GOOD OF THE NATION.

POMPEY was sold, as we have just observed, to an Alehouse-Keeper's Daughter, for the valuable Consideration of a Pint of Porter. This

---

1   This is ironic, as Tyburn Road led to London's major site of public hangings.
2   We now return to the first edition.

amiable young Lady was then on the Point of Marriage with a Hackney-Coachman, and soon afterwards the Nuptials were consummated to the great Joy of the two ancient Families, who were by this Means sure of not being extinct. As soon as the Ceremony was over at the *Fleet*, the new-married Couple set out to celebrate their Wedding at the *Old Blue Boar* in *Tyburn* Road, and the Bride was conducted home at Night dead-drunk to her new Apartments in a Garret in *Smithfield*.[1]

This fashionable Pair had scarce been married three Days before they began to quarrel on a very fashionable Subject: For the civil well-bred Husband coming home one Night from his Station, and expecting the Cow-heels to have been ready for his Supper, found his Lodgings empty, and his darling Spouse abroad. At about eleven o'Clock she came flouncing into the Room, and telling him, with great *gaitè de coeur*,[2] that she had been at the Play, began to describe the several Scenes of *Hamlet* Prince of *Denmark*. Judge if this was not a Provocation too great for a Hackney-Coachman's Temper. He fell to exercising his Whip in a most outrageous Manner, and she applying herself no less readily to more desperate Weapons, a most bloody Fray ensued between them; in which *Automedon*[3] had like to have been stabbed with a Penknife, and his Spouse was obliged to keep her Bed near a Month with the Bruises she received in this horrid Rencounter.

Little *Pompey* now most sensibly felt the ill Effects of his former Luxury, which served only to aggravate the Miseries of his present Condition. The coarse Fare he met with in the roofless Garrets, or Cellars under Ground, were but indelicate Morsels to one who had formerly lived on *Ragouts* and *Fricasees*; and he found it very difficult to sleep on hard and naked Floors, who had been used to have his Limbs cushioned up on *Sopha's* and Couches. But luckily for him, his Favour with his Mistress procured him the Hatred of his Master, who sold him for a second Time to a Nymph of *Billingsgate*[4] for a Pennyworth of Oysters.

---

1 The paragraph stresses the low social rank of this couple. The precincts of Fleet Prison were the site of quick and shady marriages; Smithfield was one of the most rough-and-tumble regions of London's lower-class east side.

2 French: *gaîté de coeur*, light-hearted indifference.

3 The charioteer of Achilles in Homer's *Iliad* (see Bk. XVII).

4 A dockside area famous for its fishmongers and vulgar bustle.

His Situation indeed was not mended for the present by this Means, but it put him in the Way to be released the sooner from a Course of Life so ill suited to his Constitution or his Temper. For this delicate Fisherwoman, as she went her Rounds, carried him one Evening to a certain Coffee-house near the *Temple*,[1] where the Lady behind the Bar was immediately struck with his Beauty, and with no great Difficulty prevailed on the gentle Water-Nymph to surrender him for a Dram of Brandy.

His Fortunes now began to wear a little better Aspect, and he spent his Time here agreeably enough in listening to the Conversations and Disputes that arose in the Coffee-Room among People of all Denominations; for here assembled Wits, Critics, Templars,[2] Politicians, Poets, Country Squires, grave Tradesmen, and sapient Physicians.

The little Consistories of Wit claimed his first Attention, being a Dog of a natural Turn for Humour, and he took a Pleasure to hear young *Templars* criticize the Works of *Shakespear*, call Mr. *Garrick* to Account every Evening for his Action, extol the Beauty of Actresses, and the Reputation of Whores. Here the illustrious Mr. *F___t*[3] (before he was yet exalted to the Dignity of keeping a Chariot and Bay-horses, which perhaps may not be *the highest Exaltation* he has yet to undergo) used to harangue to a Club of his Admirers, and like a great Professor of Impudence, teach them the Principles of that immortal Science. Here he conceived the first Thought of *giving Tea*, and *milling Chocolate*; and here he laid the Plan of all those mighty Operations he has since atchieved. The Master of the Coffee-house himself is a great Adept in modern Literature, and, I believe reads Lectures of Wit to young *Templars* on their first Appearance in Town.

Pompey, when he was tired of the Clubs of Humour, would betake himself to another Table, and listen to a Junto of Politicians, who used to assemble here in an Evening with most publick-spirited Views; namely, to settle the Affairs of the Nation, and point out the Errors of the Ministry. Here he has heard the Government arraigned in the most abusive manner, for what the Government never performed or thought of; and the lowest Ribaldry of a dirty News-paper cried up as the highest

---

1 The Temple, consisting of the Middle Temple and the Inner Temple, contained official chambers for barristers and barristers in training.

2 A member of the Middle or Inner Temple.

3 Samuel Foote.

Touches of Attic Irony.[1] He has heard Sea-fights condemned by People who never saw the Sea even thro' a Telescope; and the General of an Army called to Account for his Disposition of a Battle, by Men whose Knowledge of War never reached beyond a Cock-match.

A curious Conversation of this kind happened one Day in his hearing, which I shall beg leave to relate as a little Specimen of Coffee-house Oratory. It happened at the End of the late Rebellion;[2] and the chief Orator of the Club began as usual with asserting, that the Rebellion was promoted by the Ministry for some private Ends of their own. "What was the Reason," said he, "of its being disbelieved so long? Why was our Army absent at such a critical Conjuncture? let any Man tell me that. I should be glad to hear any Man answer me these Questions. D—mn it, they may think perhaps they are acting all this while in secret, and applaud themselves for their Cunning; but I believe I know more than they would wish me to know. Thank God I can see a little, if I please to open my Eyes; and if I was in the House of Commons——'Zounds, old *Walpole* is behind the Curtain still, notwithstanding his Resignation, and the old Game is playing over again, whatever they may pretend——There was a Correspondence between *Walpole* and *Fleury*, to my Knowledge, and they projected between them all the Evils that have since happened to the Nation."[3]

The Company all seemed to agree with this eloquent Gentleman's Sentiments; and one of them ventured to say, he believed the Army was sent into *Flanders*, on purpose to be out of the Way at the Time of the Insurrection. "'Zounds," says the Orator, "I believe you are in the right, and the Wind blew them over against their Inclinations. Pox! What made *What-d'ye-callum*'s Army disperse as it did?[4] Don't you think they had Orders from above to run away?

1   I.e., irony of a fineness worthy of the ancient Greeks.
2   This refers to the Jacobite Rebellion of 1745-46, when supporters of the deposed Stuart royal family invaded England from Scotland in an attempt to overthrow King George II. From this date we learn that Pompey is now about eleven years old.
3   Sir Robert Walpole (1676-1745), who resigned in 1742 after serving for over twenty years as prime minister, was the bogey-man of Opposition politicians. André-Hercule Cardinal de Fleury (1653-1743) was the French foreign minister. At the time of the Rebellion, the English army was fighting France on the continent in the War of the Austrian Succession.
4   The leader of the Jacobite Rebellion, Charles James Stuart ("Bonnie Prince Charlie," 1720-88) suddenly reversed his army in December 1745, one hundred miles from London, for reasons still debated by historians.

——By G—d I do, if you don't, and I believe I could prove it too, if I was to set about it. Besides, if they have any desire of preventing future Invasions from *France*, why don't they send out and burn all their Shipping? Why don't they send out *V—m—n*[1] with a strong Fleet, and let him burn all their Shipping? I warrant him, if he had a proper Commission in his Pocket, he would not leave a Habour or a Ship in *France*——but they know they don't dare do it for fear of Discoveries; they are in League with the *French* Ministry; or else, damme, can any thing be so easy as to take and burn all the Shipping in *France*?"

A Gentleman, who had hitherto sat silent at the Table, replied, with a Sneer on his Countenance, "No, Sir, nothing in the World can be so easy, except talking about it." This drew the Eyes of the Company upon him, and every one began to wink at his Neighbour, when the Orator resumed his Discourse in the following manner. "Talk, Sir? No, By G—d, we are come to that pass, that we don't dare talk now-a-days; things are come to such a pass, that we don't dare open our Mouths." "Sir," said the Gentleman, "I think you have been talking already with great Licentiousness; and let me add too, with great Indecency on a very serious Subject." "'Zounds, Sir," said the Orator, "may not I have the liberty of speaking my Mind freely upon any Subject that I please? why, we don't live in *France*, Sir, and not a *Mahometan* Empire; tho' God knows how long we shall continue in the Way we are going on——and yet, forsooth, we must not talk; our Mouths are to be sewed up, as well as our Purses taken from us——Here we are paying four Shillings in the Pound, and yet we must not speak our Minds freely." "Sir," said the Gentleman, "undoubtedly you may speak your Mind freely; but the Laws of your Country oblige you not to speak Treason, and the Laws of Good manners should dispose you to speak with Decency and Respect of your Governors. You say, Sir, we are come to that pass, that we dare not talk——I protest, that is very extraordinary; and if I was called upon to answer this Declaration, I would rather say we are come to that pass now-a-days, that we talk with more Virulence and Ill-language than ever——we talk upon Subjects, which it is impossible we should understand, and advance Assertions, which we know to be false. Bold Affirmations against the Government are

---

1   Admiral Edward Vernon (1684-1757), naval hero of the War of Jenkins' Ear (1739-42).

believed merely from the Dint of Assurance with which they are spoken, and the idlest Jargon often passes for the soundest Reasoning. Give me leave to say, You, Sir, are a living Example of the Lenity of the Government, which you are abusing for want of Lenity, and your own Practice in the strongest manner confutes your own Assertions——but I beg we may call another Subject."

Here the Orator having nothing more to reply, was resolved to retire to a Place where he could not longer make a Figure. Wherefore, flinging down his Reckoning, and putting on his Hat with great Vehemence, he walked away muttering surlily to himself, *Things are come to a fine pass truly, if People may not have the liberty of Talking.* The rest of the Company separated soon afterward, all of them habouring no very favourable Opinion of the Gentleman, who had taken the Courage to stand up in Defence of the Government. Some imagined he was a Spy, others concluded he was a Writer of Gazettes,[1] and the most part were contented with only thinking him a Fool.

The angry Orator was no sooner got home to his Family, and seated in his Elbow-chair at Supper, than he began to give vent to the Indignation he had been collecting; "'Zounds," said he, "I have been called to account for my Words to-night. I have been told by a Jack-a-napes at the Coffee-house, that I must not say what I please against the Government. *Talk with Decency indeed*! a Fart of Decency!—— let them act with Decency, if they have a mind to stop People's Mouths——Talk with Decency! d___mn 'em all, I'll talk what I please, and no King or Minister on Earth shall controul me. Let 'em behead me, if they have a mind, as they did *Balmerino*, and t'other Fellow, that died like a Coward.[2] Must I be catechized by a little Sycophant that kisses the A___e of a Minister? What is an *Englishman*, that dares not utter his Sentiments freely?——Talk

---

1   Gazettes were official government newspapers, and became reputed in the eighteenth-century as organs of state propaganda, especially during the era of Walpole. As Johnson observed in the definition for "gazetteers" in his *Dictionary*, "It was lately a term of the utmost infamy, being usually applied to wretches who were hired to vindicate the court." "Court" here refers to the government appointed by the King. Both George I and II were widely distrusted for favoring politicians of questionable character and ability, though direct criticism of the royal family was legally precarious.

2   Arthur Elphinstone, 6th Lord Balmerino (1688–1746), was a prominent Scottish Jacobite who was executed after the Rebellion. The other is possibly William Boyd, Lord Killmarnock (1704-46), who was executed along with Balmerino.

with Decency! I wish I had kicked the Rascal out of the Coffee-house, and I will, if ever I meet him again, damme——Pox! we are come to a fine pass, if every little prating, pragmatical Jack-a-napes is to contradict a true-born *Englishman*."

While his Wife and Daughter sat trembling at the Vehemence of his Speeches, yet not daring to speak, for fear of drawing his Rage upon themselves, he began to curse them for their Silence; and addressing himself to his Wife, "Why do'st not speak?" cries he, "what, I suppose, I shall have you telling me by-an-by too, that I must talk with Decency?" "My dear," said the Wife, with great Humility, "I know nothing at all of the Matter." "No," cries he, "I believe not; but you might know to dress a Supper, tho', and be d——mn'd to you——Here's nothing that I can eat, according to Custom. Pox, a Man may starve with such a Wife at the Head of his Family."

When the Cloth was removed, and he was preparing to fill his Pipe, unfortunately he could not find his Tobacco-stopper, which again set his Choler at work. "Go up Stairs, *Moll*!" said he to one of his Daughters, "and feel in my old Breeches Pocket——Damme, I believe that Scoundrel at the Coffee-house has robbed me *with his Decency*——Why do'st not stir, Girl? What, hast got the Cramp in thy Toes?" "Why, Papa," said the Girl flippantly, "I am going as fast as I can."——Upon which, immediately he threw a Bottle at her Head, and proceeding from Invectives to Blows, he beat his Wife, kicked his Daughters, swore at his Servants; and after all this, went reeling up to Bed with Curses in his Mouth against the Tyranny of the Government.

Nothing can be more common than Examples in this way of People, who preside over their Families with the most arbitrary brutal Severity, and yet are ready on all Occasions to abuse the Government for the smallest Exertion of its Power. To say the Truth, I scarce know a Man, who is not a *Tyrant in miniature*, over the Circle of his own Dependents; and I have observed those in particular to exercise the greatest Lordship over their Inferiors, who are most forward to complain of Oppression from their Superiors. Happy is it for the World, that this Coffee-house Statesman was not born a King, for one may very justly apply to him the line of *Martial*.

Hei mihi! Si fueris tu Leo, qualis eris?[1]

---

1   Latin: "Alas! if you were a lion, what kind would you be?" (Martial, *Epigrams*, xii, 92).

CHAP. XII

A DESCRIPTION OF COUNSELLOR TANTURNIAN.

BUT among the many People, who frequented this Coffee-House, *Pompey* was delighted with no-body more than with the Person of Counsellor *Tanturnian*; who used to crawl out once a Week, to read all the public Papers from *Monday* to *Monday*, at the moderate Price of a Penny.[1] His Dress and Character were both so extraordinary, as will excuse a short Digression upon them.

He set out originally with a very humble Fortune at the *Temple*, not without Hopes, however, of arriving, some Time or other, at the Chancellor's Seat: But having tried his Abilities once or twice at the Bar, to little Purpose, Nature soon whispered in his Ear, that he was never designed for an Orator. He attended the Judges indeed, after this, through two or three Circuits, but finding his Gains by no means equivalent to his Expences, he thought it most prudent to decline the noisy *Forum*, and content himself with giving Advice to Clients in a Chamber. Either his Talents here also were deficient, or Fame had not sufficiently divulged his Merit, but his Chamber was seldom disturbed with Visiters, and he had few Occasions to envy the Tranquillity of Country Life, according to a Lawyer in *Horace*;

Argricolam laudat juris legumque peritus,
Sub Galli cantum consultor ubi ostia pulsat.[2]

His Temper grew soured and unsocial by Miscarriages, and the Narrowness of his Fortune obliging him to a strict Frugality, he soon degenerated into Avarice. The Rust of Money is very apt to infect the Soul; and People, whose Circumstances condemn them to Œconomy, in Time grow Misers from very Habit. This was the

---

1 Eighteenth-century coffeehouses were well-stocked with newspapers, which patrons could read as part of the small admission price. As the result, coffeehouses were sometimes called "penny universities." The penny-pinching Counsellor Tanturnian goes to the coffeehouse every Monday to read all the past week's newspapers at one sitting.

2 Latin: "One learned in law and statutes has praise for the farmer, when towards cockcrow a client comes knocking at his door" (Horace, *Satires* I. i. 9-10).

Case with Counsellor *Tanturian*, who having quite discarded his Relish of Pleasure, and finding his little Pittance, by that Means, more than adequate to his Expences, resolved to apply the Overplus to the laudable Purposes of Usury. This noble Occupation he followed a long Time, and by it accumulated a Sum of Ten Thousand Pounds which his Heart would not suffer him to enjoy, tho' he had neither Relation or Friend to leave it to at his Death. He lived almost constantly alone in a dirty Chamber, denying himself every Comfort of Life, and half-starved for want of Sustenance. Neither Love, nor Ambition, nor Joy, disturbed his Repose; his Passions all centered on Money, and he was a kind of Savage within Doors.

The Furniture of his Person was not less curious than his Character. At home indeed he wore nothing but a greasy Flannel Cap about his Head, and a dingy Night-gown about his Body; but when he went abroad, he arrayed himself in a Suit of Black, of full Twenty Years standing, and very like in Color to what is worn by Undertakers at a Funeral. His Peruke, which had once adorned the Head of a Judge in the Reign of Queen *Anne*, spread copiously over his Back, and down his Shoulders. By his Side hung an aged Sword, long rusted in its Scabbard; and his black Silk Stockings had been so often darned with a different Material, that, like Sir *John Cutler*'s, they were now metamorphosed into black Worsted Stockings.[1]

Such was Counsellor *Tanturnian*, who once a Week came to read the Newspapers at the Coffee-house, where *Pompey* lived. A Dog of any Talents for Humour could not help being diverted with his Appearance, and our Hero found great Pleasure in playing him Tricks, in which he was secretly encouraged by every Body in the Coffee-room. At first indeed, he never saw him without barking at him, as at a Monster just dropped out of the Moon; but when Time had a little reconciled him to his Figure, he entertained the Company every Time he came with some new Prank, at the Counsellor's Expence. Once he ran away with his Spectacles; at another Time, he laid violent Teeth on his Shirt, which hung out of his Breeches, and shook it, to the great Diversion of all Beholders: But what occasioned more Laughter than any Thing, was a Trick that follows.

---

1   Cutler, a wealthy seventeenth-century merchant, became a proverbial figure of avarice. Heavy knit worsted stockings would be usually worn by lower-rank laboring people.

Tanturnian had been tempted one Day, by two old Acquaintance, to indulge his Genius at a Tavern; where he complain'd highly of the Expensiveness of the Dinner, tho' it consisted only of a Beef-steak and two Fowls. That nothing might be lost, he took Opportunity, unobserved by the Company, to slip the Leg of a Pullet into his Pocket; intending to carry it home for his Supper at Night. In his Way he called at the Coffee-house, and little *Pompey* playing about him as usual, unfortunately happened to scent the Provision in the Counsellor's Pocket. *Tanturnian*, mean Time, was deeply engaged in his News-paper, and *Pompey* getting slily behind him, thrust his Head into his Pocket, and boldly seizing the Spoils, displayed them in Triumph to the Sight of the whole Room. The poor Counsellor could not stand the Laugh, but retired home in a melancholly Mood, vexed at the Discovery, and more vexed at the Loss of his Supper.

But these Diversions were soon interrupted by a most unlucky Accident, and our Hero, unfortunate as he has hitherto been, is now going to suffer a Turn of Fate more grievous than any he yet has known. Following the Maid one Evening into the Streets, he unluckily missed her at the Turning of an Alley, and happening to take a wrong Way, prowled out of his Knowledge before he was aware. He wandered about the Streets for many Hours, in vain endeavouring to explore his Way Home; in which Distress, his Memory brought back the cruel Chance that had separated him from his best Mistress Lady *Tempest*, and this Reflection aggravated his Misery beyond Description. At last, a Watchman picked him up, and carried him to the Watch-house. There he spent his Night in all the Agonies of Horror and De-spair. "How deplorable," thought he, "is my Condition, and what is Fortune preparing to do with me? Have I not already gone through Scenes of Wretchedness enough, and must I again be turned adrift to the Mercy of Fate? What unrelenting Tyrant shall next be my Master? Or what future Oyster-woman shall next torture me with her Caresses? Cruel, cruel Fortune! When will thy Persecutions end?"[1]

---

1   The speech was deleted from the third edition, further evidence of Coventry's effort to diminish the personification of Pompey.

CHAP. XIII

A SHORT CHAPTER, CONTAINING ALL THE WIT, AND ALL THE SPIRIT, AND ALL THE PLEASURE OF MODERN YOUNG GENTLEMEN.

AS he was thus abandoning himself to Lamentation and Despair, some other Watchman brought in two fresh Prisoners to bear him Company in his Confinement, who, I am sorry to say it, were two young Lords. They were extremely disordered, both in their Dress, and their Understanding; and Champaigne was not the only Enemy they had encountered that Evening. One of them had lost his Coat and Waist-coat; the other his Bag[1] and Peruke, all but a little circular Lock of Hair, which grew to his Forehead, and now hanging over his Eyes, added not a little to the Drollery of his Figure.

The generous God of the Grape[2] had cast such a Mist over their Understandings, that they were insensible at first of the Place they were promoted to; but at length, one of them a little recovering his Wits, cried out, "What the Devil Place is this? A Bawdy-house, or Presbyterian Meeting-house?" "Neither, Sir," answered a Watchman, "but the Roundhouse." "O P—x,"[3] said his Lordship, "I thought you had been a dissenting Parson, old Grey-beard, and was going to preach against Wh—ring,[4] for you must know, old Fellow, I confoundedly go *in for it*——But what Privilege have you, Sir, to carry a Man of Honour to the Round-house?" "Ay," said the other, "what Right has such an old Fornicator as thou art, to interrupt the Pleasures of Men of Quality? May not a Nobleman get drunk, without being disturbed by a Pack of Rascals in the Streets?" "Gentlemen," answered the Watch, "we are no Rascals, but Servants of His Majesty King *George*, and His Majesty requires us to take up all People that commit disorderly Riots in His Majesty's Streets." "You lie, you Scoundrels," said one of their Lordships, "'tis the Prerogative of Men of Fashion to do what they please, and I'll

---

1 A bag was a kind of hair-net for a peruke.
2 The Greek god Dionysus or the Roman god Bacchus, the god of wine.
3 "Pox," which here means venereal disease, was a common oath.
4 Whoring.

prosecute you for Breach of Privilege——D—mn you, my Lord, I'll hold you Fifty Pound, that old Prig there, in the great Coat, is a Cuckold, and he shall be Judge himself.——How many Eyes has your Wife got, old Fellow? One or two?" "Well, well," said the Watchman, "your Honours may abuse us as much as you please; but we know we are doing our Duty, and will perform it in the King's Name." "Your Duty, you Rascal," cried one of these Men of Honour, "is immediately to fetch us a Girl, and a Dozen of Champagne; if you'll perform that, I'll say you are as honest an old Son of a Whore, as ever lay with an Oyster-woman. My dear *Fanny*! If I had but you here, and a Dozen of *Ryan's* Claret, I should esteem this Round-house a Palace——Curse me, if I don't love to sleep in a Round-house sometimes; it gives Variety to Life, and relieves one from the Insipidness of a soft Bed." "Well-said, my Hero," answered his Companion, "and these Scoundrels shall carry us before my Lord Mayor To-morrow, for the Humour of the Thing. Pox take him, I buy all my Tallow-candles of his Lordship, and therefore I am sure he'll use me like a Man of Honour."[1]

In such kind of gay modish Conversation did these illustrious Persons consume their Night, and principally in laying Wagers, which at present is the highest Article of modern Pleasure. Every Particular of human Life is reduced by the great Calculators of Chances to the Condition of a *Bet*; but nothing is esteemed a more laudable Topic of *Wagering*, than the Lives of eminent Men; which, in the elegant Language of *Newmarket*,[2] is called *running Lives*; that is to say, a Bishop against an Alderman, a Judge against a Keeper of a Tavern, a Member of Parliament against a famous Boxer; and in this Manner all People's Lives are wager'd out, with proper Allowances for their Ages, Infirmaties, and Distempers. Happy the Nation that can produce such ingenious, accomplished Spirits!

These two honourable Peers had been spending their Evening at a Tavern, with many others, and when the rational Particle was thoroughly drowned in Claret, one of the Company leaping from his Chair, cried out, *Who will do any Thing?* upon which, a Resolu-

---

1   The Lord Mayor's jurisdiction did not extend beyond the City, the commercial hub in
    the eastern section of greater London. The fashionable lords are deriding the Mayor as
    a chandler, or candle-seller, and thus a lowly tradesman.
2   Then, as now, Newmarket was a racing town.

tion was immediately taken, to make a Sally into the Streets, and drink Champagne upon the Horse at *Charing-Cross*.[1] This was no sooner projected than executed, and they performed a great Number of heroical Exploits, too long to be mentioned in this Work, but we hope some future Historian will arise to immortalize them for the sake of Posterity. After this was over, they resolved to scour to Streets, and perceiving a Light in a Cellar under Ground, our two Heroes magnanimously descended into that subterranean Cave, in quest of Adventures. There they found some Hackney Coachmen enjoying themselves with Porter and Tobacco, whom they immediately attacked, and offered to box the two sturdiest Champions of the Company. The Challenge was accepted in a Moment, and whilst our Heroes were engaged, the rest of the Coachmen chose to make off with their Cloaths, which they thought no inconsiderable Booty. In short, these Gentlemen of Pleasure and High-life were heartily drubbed, and obliged to retreat with Shame from the *Cellar of Battle*, leaving their Cloaths behind them, as Spoils, at the Mercy of the Enemy. Soon afterwards, they were taken by the Watch, being too feeble to make Resistance, and conducted to the Round-house; where they spent the Night in the Manner already described. The next Morning, they returned Home in Chairs, new-dressed themselves, and then took their Seats in Parliament, to enact Laws for the Good of their Country.

CHAP. XIV

OUR HERO FALLS INTO GREAT MISFORTUNES.

WHEN the Watchman had discharged himself in the morning of these honourable Prisoners, he next bethought himself of little *Pompey*, who had fallen into his Hands in a more inoffensive manner. Him he presented that Day to a blind Beggar of his Acquaintance, who had lately lost his Dog, and wanted a new Guide to conduct him

---

1   A reference to the equestrian statue of Charles I, the king who was beheaded by the parliament in 1649 and revered by Tory members of the aristocracy, such as these lords are hinted to be.

about the Streets. Here *Pompey* again fell into the most desponding Meditations. "And was this Misery," thought he, "reserved in store to compleat the Series of my Misfortunes? Am I destined to lead about the dark Footsteps of a blind, decrepit, unworthy Beggar? Must I go daggled thro' the Streets with a Rope about my Neck, linking me to a Wretch that is the Scorn of human Nature? O that a Rope were fixed about my Neck indeed for a nobler Purpose, and that I were here to end a dreadful, tormenting Existence! Can I bear to hear the Sound of, *Pray remember the poor Beggar*? I who have conversed with Lords and Ladies; who have slept in the Arms of the fairest Beauties, and lived on the choicest Dainties this habitable Globe can afford! Cruel, cruel Fortune! when will thy Persecutions end?"

But when the first Emotions of his Grief were a little calmed, he began to call in the Aids of Philosophy; the many useful Lessons he had learnt from the sage *Mopsa*, inspired him with Resolution; and he fortified himself besides, with remembering a Speech in *King Lear*, which he had formerly heard at *Drury-Lane* Playhouse.——

> To be worst,
> The lowest, most dejected thing of Fortune,
> Stands still in Esperance, lives not in Fear;
> The lamentable Change is from the best,
> The worst returns to Laughter. Welcome then
> Thou unsubstantial Air, which I embrace;
> The Wretch, that thou has blown unto the worst,
> Owes nothing to thy Blasts.[1]

To say the Truth, his Condition was not so deplorable upon Trial, as it appeared in Prospect: For tho' he was condemned to travel, thro' dirty Streets all Day long in quest of Charity, yet at Night, both he and his Master fared sumptuously enough on their Gains; and many a lean Projector, or starving Poet might envy the Suppers of this blind Beggar. He seldom failed to collect four Shillings a Day, and used to sit down to his hot Meals with as much Stateliness, as a Peer could do to a regular Entertainment and Dessert.

---

1   *King Lear* 4.1 2–9.

There is a Story I have often heard of a crippled Beggar, who used constantly to apply for Alms at *Hyde-Park* Corner;[1] where a Gentleman, who was then just recovered from a dangerous Fit of Illness, never failed to give him Six-pence every Morning, as he passed by in his Chariot for the Air. A Servant of this Gentleman's going by chance one Day into a Alehouse, discovered this same Beggar sitting down to a Breast of Veal with some more of the Fraternity, and heard him raving at the Landlord, because the Bur[2] was gone, and he had no Lemon ready to squeeze over it; adding many Threats of leaving the House, if their Dinners were not served up for the future with more Regularity and Respect. The Servant informed his Master of this extraordinary Circumstance, and next Morning when the pampered Hypocrite applied for his Charity as usual, in the old lamentable Voice, the Gentleman put his Head out of the Chariot, and told him, with a Sarcasm, *No, Sir, I can eat Veal without Lemon.*[3]

[After our hero had lived in this condition some months in *London*, his blind master set out for *Bath*, whither, it seems, he always resorted in the public seasons; not for the sake of playing at EO,[4] it may be imagined, nor yet for the pleasure of being taken out by the accomplished Mr. *Nash*[5] to dance a minuet at a ball; but with the hopes of a plentiful harvest among infirm people, whom ill health disposes to charity. The science of begging is reduced to certain principles of art, as well as all other professions; and as sickness is apt to influence people with compassion, the objects of charity flock thither in great numbers; for wherever the carrion is, there will crows be also.

---

1   As Hyde-Park was a frequent venue for public entertainments in the eighteenth century, the corner near its entrance was a lucrative resort for beggars. During the nineteenth century, radicals orated to crowds at the same locale, which has since been known as "Speaker's Corner."
2   Sweetbread.
3   Complaints that undeserving beggars were living high off the proceeds of charity were commonplace at this time, as exemplified by Henry Fielding's legal pamphlets *An Enquiry into the Late Increase of Robbers* (1751) and *Proposal for Making an Effectual Provision for the Poor* (1753), the second pamphlet being the first to propose the institution of workhouses for the poor.
4   EO (an acronym for "even-odd") was a gambling game resembling roulette.
5   Richard "Beau" Nash (1674-1762) was Master of Ceremonies at Bath. He facilitated social events and introduced new arrivals to the appropriate company.

The many adventures that befel them on their journey; how terribly our hero was fatigued with travelling thro' miry highways, who had been used to ride in coaches and six; and how often he wished his blind tyrant would drop dead with an apoplexy, shall all be left to the reader's imagination. Suffice it to say, that in about three weeks or a month's time, they arrived at the end of their journey, and the beggar readily groped out his way to a certain alehouse, which he always favoured with his company; where the landlord received him with great respect, professing much satisfaction to find *his honour* so well in health. By this the reader will perceive that he was a beggar of some distinction.

If our hero made any reflexion, he could not help being surprized at such civility, paid to such a person in such a place; but how much greater reason had he for astonishment, when on the evening of their arrival, he saw a well-drest woman enter the room, and accost his master in the following terms, "Papa, how do you do? you are welcome to *Bath*." The beggar no sooner heard her voice, than he started from his chair, and gave her a paternal kiss; which the fair lady received with an air of scorn and indifference, telling him, "he had poisoned her with his bushy beard." When this ceremony was over, she threw herself into an arm-chair, and began to harangue in the following manner——"Well, papa, so you are come to *Bath* at last; I thought we should not have seen you this season, and I have immediate necessity for a sum of money. Sure no mortal ever had such luck at cards, as I have had. You must let me have five or ten pound directly."[1] "Five or ten pound!" cries the beggar in amaze; "how in devil's name should I come by five or ten pound?" "Come, come, no words," cried the daughter, "for I absolutely must and will have it in spite of your teeth. I know you are worth above a hundred pounds, and what can you do with your money better, than give it me to make a figure in life with? Deuce take the men, they are grown plaguy modest, or so plaguy stingy, that really 'tis hardly worth coming to *Bath* now in the seasons. Hang me if I have had a cull[2] this twelve-month ——but do you know, old dad, that brother *Jack*'s at the *Bath*?"

"Oh!" cries the beggar, "there's another of my plagues——I shall have him dunning me for money too soon I suppose, for the

---

1   Coventry is thinking of the period before 1745, when an act was passed that effectively ended public gambling at Bath.

2   "A dupe, silly fellow, simpleton, fool; a man, fellow, chap" (*OED*).

devil can't answer the extravagancies of that fellow. Well, he'll certainly come to be hanged at last, that's my comfort, and I think the sooner he swings, the better it will be for his poor father, and the whole kingdom."

"Hanged!" replied the lady; "no, no, *Jack* is in no danger of hanging at present, I assure you; he is now the most accomplished, modish, admired young fellow at the *Bath*; the peculiar favourite of all the ladies; and in a fair way of running off with a young heiress of considerable fortune. Let me see, old dad——If you'll bespeak a private room, and have a little elegant supper ready at eleven o'clock to morrow night (for *Jack* won't be able to get away from the rooms sooner than eleven) I'll bring him to sup with you, and you shall hear his history from his own mouth." To this the old hypocrite her father readily consented, and promised something decent for them; after which, starting from her chair, "well, papa," said she, "you must excuse me at present, for I expect company at my lodgings, and so can't afford to waste any more time with you in this miserable dog-hole of an ale-house." Having made this polite apology, she flew to her chair, which waited at the door, and was conducted home with as much importance, as if she had been a princess of the blood.

The next day, the blind imposter, attended by our hero, went out on his pilgrimage, and continued whining for charity, and profaning the name of G—d till night; after which, he returned to his ale house, put on a better coat, and got himself in readiness for the reception of his son and daughter. At the hour appointed, these illustrious personages entered the room, and the conversation was opened by the son in the following easy strain. "Old boy!" (cries he, seizing his father by the hand) "I am glad to see thee with all my heart. Well, old fellow, how does your crutch and blind eyes do? what, you continue still in the old canting hypocritical way, I perceive—Pox take you, I saw you hobbling through the streets to-day, old miserable, but you know I am ashamed to take notice of you in public——tho' I think I have thrown you down many a tester at the corner of a street, without your knowing whom you was obliged to for such a piece of generosity."

"Sir, I honour your generosity," replied the beggar; "but, pry-thee *Jack*, they tell me you are going to be married to an heiress of great fortune, is there any truth in the story?"

Here the beau-sharper took a *French* snuff-box out of his pocket, and having entertained his nose with a pinch of rappee,[1] replied as follows. "Yes, sir, my unaccountable somewhat[2] has had the good luck to make conquest of a little amorous tit, with an easy moderate fortune of about fifteen thousand pounds, who does me the honour to doat on this person[3] of mine to distraction. But prythee, old blue-beard, how didst you come by this piece of intelligence?" "From that fine lady your sister, sir," replied the beggar. "O pox! I thought so," cries the beau. "———*Bess* can never keep any thing in her but her teeth, nor them neither, can you *Bess*? You understand me———but as I was saying, concerning this match; yes, sir, I have the honour at present to be principal favourite of all women at *Bath*; they are all dying with love of me, and I may do what I please with any of them; but I, sir, neglecting the rest, have singled out a little amorous wanton, with a trifling fortune of fifteen or twenty thousand pounds only, whom I shall very soon whip into a chariot, I believe, and drive away to a parson."

"Lord!" cries the father, "if she did but know what a thief she is going to marry!"

"Why, what then? you old curmudgeon! She would be the more extravagantly fond of me on that account. 'Tis very fashionable, sir, for ladies to fall in love with highwaymen now-a-days. They think it discovers a soul, a genius, a spirit in them, above the little prejudices of education; and I believe I could not do better than let her know that I have returned from transportation.[4]———But prythee, old dim, what hast got for supper to night?" "Nothing I am afraid that a gentleman of your fashion can condescend to eat," replied the beggar; "for I have only ordered a dish of veal cutlets, and a couple of roasted fowls." "Come, come, prythee don't pretend to droll, old blinker!" cries the son, "but produce your musty supper as fast as you can, and then I'll treat you with a bottle of *French* claret. Come, let us be merry, and set in for a jovial evening. Pox! I have some little kind of sneaking regard for thee, for begetting me, notwithstanding your crutch and blind eyes, and I think I am not altogether sorry to see thee.———Here, drawer, landlord, bring up supper directly, you dog, or I'll set fire to your house."

---

1 A strong, coarse form of snuff.

2 His "je ne sais quoi" (French), or ineffable charm.

3 Physical appearance, the body.

4 "Transportation" to the Americas was a common punishment.

This extraordinary summons had the desired effect, and supper being placed on the table, the three worthy guests sat down to it with great importance. The lady took upon her to manage the ceremonies, and asked her papa in the first place, if she should help him to some veal cutlets? to which the answer was, "if you please madam!" When she had served her father, she then performed the same office to herself; after which, twirling the dish round with a familiar air, "I'll leave you," said she, "to take care of yourself, *Jack!*" Much mirth and pleasantry reigned at this peculiar meal, to the utter astonishment of the master of the house, who had never seen the like before. When supper was over, and they began to feel the inspiration of the claret, "*Jack!*" says the father, "I think I know nothing of your history, since you returned from transportation——Suppose you should begin and entertain us with an account of your exploits." "With all my heart," cries the son; "I believe I shall publish my life one of these days, if ever I am driven to necessity, for I fancy it will make a very pretty neat *duodecimo*;[1] and 'tis the fashion, you know, now-a-days for all whores and rogues to entertain the world with their memoirs.——Come, let us take another glass round to the health of my dear little charmer, and then I'll begin my adventures." Having so said, he filled out three bumpers, drank his toast on his knees,[2] and then commenced his narration in the following manner.

[CHAP. XV

THE HISTORY OF A HIGHWAYMAN.

"I THINK you have often told me, old father hypocrite, that you begat me under a hedge near *Newberry* in *Berkshire*. This, I confess, is not the most honourable way of coming into the world, but no man is answerable for his birth, and therefore what signifies prevarication? *Alexander* I have heard was the son of a flying dragon, and *Romulus* was suckled by a plaguy confounded

---

1 A small pocket-sized book.
2 Day suggests, not unreasonably, that Jack is a Jacobite, as the gesture seems extravagantly Roman Catholic. Yet, later, he asks God's blessing for the Protestant George II.

wolf, as I have read in *Hooke's Roman* history,[1] and yet in time he grew to be a very pretty young fellow, and a king——but you are ignorant of these matters, both of you, and therefore I only play the fool to talk about them in such company.

"Well, sir, as soon as I was born, my mother, I suppose, wrapped me up in the dirty rags of an old rotten petticoat, and lugged me about behind her shoulders, as an object to move compassion. In this agreeable situation, nuzzling behind the back of a lousy drab——excuse me, old fellow, for making so free with your consort——in this situation, I suppose, I visited all the towns in *England*, and 'tis amazing I was not crippled with having my feet and limbs bundled up in such close confinement. But I kicked hard for liberty, and at length came out that easy, *degagé*,[2] jaunty young fellow of fashion, which you now behold me.

"My genius very early began to shew itself, and before I was twelve years old, you know I had acquired a great reputation for slight of hand: which being reported to a great master of that science, he immediately took me under his care, and promised to initiate me into all the mysteries of the art. Thus I bade adieu to the dirty employment of begging, left father and mother, and struck into a higher sphere in life.

"At first indeed I meddled only with petty larceny, and was sent out to try my hand on execution-days at *Tyburn*; where having acquitted myself with honour, I was quickly promoted to better business, and by that time I was fifteen, began to make a great figure in the passages about the theatres. Many a gentleman's fob have I eased of the trouble of carrying a watch; and tho' it may look like vanity to say so, I believe I furnished more brokers shops and pedlars boxes, than half the pick-pockets in *London* besides. None of them all had so

---

1   Not surprisingly, Jack's history is inaccurate. Nathaniel Hooke's *The Roman History, from the Building of Rome to the Ruin of the Commonwealth* (1738), contains no story that Alexander the Great was sired by a dragon. Hooke does report that Scipio Africanus, "favouring a little too much the great *Alexander*'s vanity," claimed that his mother had admitted a dragon to her bed-chamber (vol. 2, p. 242). Hooke also denied the old legend that Romulus, the legendary founder of Rome, was suckled by a she-wolf, proposing instead that he and his brother Remus were suckled by a shepherd's wife nick-named Lupa, Latin for she-wolf (vol. 1, p. 14).

2   French: unconstrained, relaxed.

great a levee[1] of travelling *Jews* to traffick for buckles, seals,[2] watches, tweezar-cases, and the like, as I had. But my chief dexterity was in robbing the ladies——there is a particular art, a peculiar delicacy required in whipping one's hand up a lady's petticoats, and carrying off her pockets,[3] which few of them ever attain to with any success. That now was my glory——that was my delight——I performed it to admiration, and out-did them all in this branch of the craft.

"I remember once a chambermaid of my acquaintance, a flame of mine, gave me notice that her young lady would be at the play such a night, with a pair of diamond buckles in her shoes. You may be sure I watched her into her coach, marked her into her box, and waited for her coming out, with some more of the fraternity to assist me. At last, as soon as the play was over, out she came tittering and laughing with her companions, who by good luck happened to be all of her own sex. This now was my time; I had her up in my arms in a moment, while one of my comrades whipped off her shoes with prodigious expedition: but my reason for telling the story is this——while I had her in my arms, let me die if I could help giving her a kiss, which hang me, if the little trembler did not seem to return with her heart panting, and breasts heaving ——Deuce take me, if I was not almost sorry afterwards to see her walking to her coach, without any shoes upon her feet.

"Well, sir, this was my course of life for a few years. But ambition, you know, is a thing never to be satisfied, and having gained all the glory I could in this way, my next step of promotion was to the gaming-tables. Here I played with great success a long while, and shared in the fleecing many raw young cullies, who had more money than wit. But one unfortunate night, the devil or my evil genius carried me to a masquerade, and there in the ill-omen'd habit of a fryer, being fool enough to play upon an honourable footing, I lost all I had to a few shillings. This was a confounded stroke, this was a stunning blow to me——I lay a bed all the next day, raving at my ill-fortune, and beating my brains, to think I could be such an

---

1   A levee is an assembly of people given the privilege of attending the rising of a king or person of distinction from bed. Jack is boasting that he was similarly honored by Jewish pedlars eager to buy his stolen wares.

2   Stamps for impressing an emblematic design on sealing wax for letters and documents.

3   Ladies "pockets" were attached by a cord to their garments.

ass as to play upon the square. At last in a fit of despair, I started out of bed about nine or ten o'clock at night, borrowed a friend's horse, bought a second-hand pair of poppers,[1] with the little silver that was left me, and away I rode full gallop, night and rainy as it was, for *Hounslow Heath*.[2] There I wandered about half-dead with cold and fear till morning, and to say the truth, began to grow devilish sick of my business. When day broke, the first object that presented itself to my eyes, I remember, was a gallows within a hundred yards of me; this seemed plaguy ominous, and I was very near riding back to *London* without striking a stroke. At last, while I was wavering in this state of uncertainty, behold, a stage-coach comes gently, softly ambling over the *Heath*. Courage, my heart, cries I, there can be no fear of resistance here; a stage-coach is the most lucky thing in the world for a young adventurer; and so saying, I clapt on my mask, (the same I had worn the night before at the *Hay-Market*) set spurs to my horse, and presented my pistol at the coach-window. How the passengers behaved, I know not. For my own part, I was more than half blind with fear, and taking what they gave me without any expostulation, away I rode, exceedingly well satisfied to have escaped without resistance. Taking courage however at this success, I attacked another stage-coach with greater bravery, and afterwards a third with so much magnanimity, that I even ventured to search some of the passengers, who I thought defrauded me of my due. Here now I should have left off, and all had been well——but the devil avarice prompting me to get a little more, I attacked a single horse-man, and plundered him of a watch and about thirty guineas. The scoundrel seemed to pursue his journey quietly enough, but meeting afterwards with some of his friends on the road, and relating his case to them, they all agreed to pursue me. Meanwhile, sir, I was jogging on contentedly at my ease, when turning round on the sudden, I saw this tremendous grazier, and two or three more bloody-minded fellows, that seemed each as big as a giant, in full pursuit of me. Away I dashed thro' thick and thin, as if the devil drove; but being wretch-

---

1 I.e., pistols.
2 Situated west of London, and now partly covered by Heathrow Airport, Hounslow Heath was notorious for being infested by highwaymen who preyed on the busy route of westward-bound coaches.

edly mounted,[1] I was surrounded, apprehended, carried before that infernal Sir *Thomas Deveil*,[2] and he committed me.

"Now I was in a sweet condition. This was a charming revolution in my life. *Newgate* and the prospect of a gallows, furnish a man with very agreeable reflexions. O that cursed *Old-Baily*![3] I shall never forget the sentence which the hum-drum son of a whore of a judge passed upon me——*You shall hang till you are dead, dead, dead*——faith I was more than half-dead with hearing it, and in that plight I was dragged back to my prison.

"Excellent lodging in the condemned hole!——pretty music the death warrant rings in a man's ears!——but as good luck would have it, while I was expecting every hour to be tucked up, his majesty (G—d bless him) took pity on me the very day before execution, and sent me a reprieve for transportation. To describe the transport I felt at this moment, would be impossible; I was half-mad with joy, and instead of reflecting that I was going to slavery, fancied myself going to heaven. The being shipped off for *Jamaica* was so much better a voyage, I thought, than ferrying over that same river *Styx* with the old gaffar *Charon*,[4] that I never once troubled myself about what I was to suffer, when I got thither.

"Not to be tedious, (for I have a long story) to *Jamaica* I went, with a full resolution of making my escape by the first opportunity, which I very soon accomplished. After leading the life of a dog for about a year and a half, I got on board a ship which was coming for *England*, and arrived safe and sound on the coast of *Cornwal*. My dear native country! how it revived my heart to see thee again! O *London, London*! No woman of quality, after suffering the vapours for a whole summer in the country, ever sighed after thee with greater desire than I did. But as I landed without a farthing of money in my pocket, I was obliged to beg my way up to town in the habit of a sailor, telling all the way the confoundest lies——how I had been taken by pirates, and fought with the *Moors*, who were

---

1   I.e., he had a slow horse.
2   De Veil (1684-1746) preceded Henry Fielding as Chief Magistrate of Middlesex. This may be another sidelong compliment to Fielding, who was widely credited with cleaning up De Veil's corruption.
3   Newgate was London's main prison, and the Old Bailey its main court-house.
4   Charon is the ferryman who transports souls to Hades across the River Acheron, not the Styx, contrary to popular legend.

going to eat me alive, and twenty other unaccountable stories, to chouse[1] silly women of a few half-pence.

"Well, at last I entered the dear old metropolis, and went immediately in quest of a gang of sharpers, which I formerly frequented. These jovial blades were just then setting out for *New-Market* races, and very generously took me into their party. They supplied me with cloaths, lent me a little money to begin with, and in short set me up again in the world. There is nothing like courage——'tis the life, the soul of business——Accordingly on the very first day's sport, having marked out the horse that I saw was the favourite of the knowing-ones, I offered great odds, made as many bets as I could, and trusted myself to fortune; resolving to scamper off the course as hard as I could drive, if I saw her likely to declare against me. But as it happened to make amends for her former ill-usage, the jade was now decided in my favour; 'twas quite a *hollow thing*; *Goliah*[2] won the day, and I pocketted up about three-score guineas. Of this I made excellent use at the gaming-tables, and in short when the week was over, carried away from *New-Market* a cool three hundred. Now, my dear *Bess*, I was a man again; I returned immediately to *London*, equipped myself with lace-cloaths, rattled down to *Bath* in a post-chaise, gave myself out for the eldest son of Sir *Jeremy Griskin* of the kingdom of *Ireland*, and struck at once into all the joys of high-life. This is a little epitome of my history——Having been a pick-pocket, a sharper, a slave, and highwayman, I am now the peculiar favourite of all the ladies at *Bath*."

Here the beau finished his story, and sat expecting the applauses of his company, which he very soon received on the part of his sister: but as to that worthy gentleman his father, he had been fast asleep for several minutes, and did not hear the conclusion of this wonderful history. Being now waked by silence, and the cessation of his son's voice, as he had been before lulled to sleep by his talking, he cried out from the midst of a doze——"So, she's a very fine girl, is she, *Jack*?——a very fine girl?"

"Who is a very fine girl?" cries the sharper, slapping him over the shoulder; "why, zounds thou art asleep, old miserable, and dost not know a syllable of what has been said."

---

1 Trick.
2 Day identifies "a hollow thing" as a racing term for "a decisive victory." "Goliah," evidently the name of a horse, is an antiquated version of "Goliath."

"Yes, sir, I do know what has been said," returned the father, "and therefore you need not beat one so, *Jack*!——You was telling me about going to be married——and going to *Jamaica*."

"Going to *Jamaica*! Pox take thee, thou wantest to be going to bed. Why was there ever such a wretched old dotard? I have not seen thee these seven or eight years, and perhaps may never see thee again, for thou'lt be rotten in a year or two more, and yet canst not put a little life into thyself for one evening. Come *Bess*" added he, "let's take another bumper, and then bid old drowsy good night——*Silenus*[1] will snore, do what one can to prevent him. Here my girl! here's prosperity to love, and may all sleepers go to the devil."

"Nay, nay," cries the father; "consider *Jack*, 'tis past my bed-time many hours ago. You fine gentlemen of the world are able to bear these fashionable hours, but I have been used to live by the light of the sun. Besides, if you had been drudging about after charity, as I have all day long, I fancy you would not be in a much better condition than your poor father; but really you sharpers don't consider the toil and trouble of earning one's bread in an honest way. Why now I have not gathered about six or seven shillings this whole day, and that won't half pay for our supper to night."

Here the beau bestowed several curses on him for his stinginess, and contemptuously bidding him hoard his miserable pelf, generously undertook to pay the whole. The bill was then called for, the reckoning discharged, and the company separated, having made an agreement to meet there the succeeding evening. And thus ended this illustrious compotation.

[CHAP. XVI

ADVENTURES AT THE BATH.

NEXT morning the blind beggar, conducted by our hero, went out as usual, and presented himself before the beau-monde on

---

1   An old drunkard, companion to Dionysus, Greek god of wine.

the parade.[1] Some few people, afflicted with very ill health, were generous enough to throw him down a few sixpences; others only commended the beauty of his pretty dog; and the far greater number walked on without casting their eyes upon him.

As he was here howling forth the miseries of his condition in a most lamentable tone of voice, who should happened to pass by but his own accomplished son, in company with two ladies of figure, to whom he was talking with the greatest familiarity and ease? The gaiety of his laugh, the vivacity of his conversation, made him universally observed, and all the women on the parade seemed to envy the happiness of the two ladies with whom he was engaged.

As the party came very near the place, where the old hypocrite was stationed, he could not escape their notice; and the youngest of the ladies being struck with compassion at the sight of him, "bless me," says she, "I am sure that poor old man is the object of charity. Do stay a moment, lady *Marmazet*, I am resolved to give him something." "Pshaw, my dear! come along, child," cries her ladyship, "how can you be so ridiculous, miss *Newcome*? who gives any money to charity now a-days?" "True, madam, your ladyship is perfectly in the right," replied the beau (who now discovered his own father), "nothing can be more idle, I think, than throwing one's money away upon a set of thievish tatterdemallion[2] wretches, who are the burthen of the nation, and ought to be exterminated from the face of the earth." "Well, well, you may say as you please, both of you," says miss *Newcome*, "but I am resolved to be generous this morning, and therefore it does not signify laughing at me. Here, master, gaffar———, here's sixpence for you."

All this while Mr. *Griskin* was in extreme pain, for tho' he had no reason to fear any discovery, yet the consciousness that this deplorable object was his own father, hurt the gentleman's pride in the presence of his mistress, and greatly checked his vivacity. He endeavoured therefore all he could to hurry the young lady away from so unpleasant a scene; in which he was seconded by lady *Marmazet*, who kept crying out; "How can you be so monstrously preposterous, miss *Newcome*? Come along girl! as I hope to be saved

---

1   A main avenue in Bath.
2   Ragamuffin.

I am ashamed of you——we shall have all the eyes of the company upon us in a few minutes." "I don't care a farthing for the company," replied the young lady; "I am resolved to ask the old gentleman some questions, and therefore hold your tongue——What? Are you quite blind, gaffar?"

By this time 'squire *Griskin* was recovered from his first surprize, and perceiving no bad consequences likely to happen, thought he might venture to shine upon the occasion. "Sirrah," cries he, "you miserable old dog! what do you mean by shocking people of quality here with a sight of your detestable physiognomy? whence do you come? what do you do out of your own parish? I'll have you whipt from constable to constable back to your own settlement."

"No, please your noble honour," cries the beggar, "I hope your noble honour won't be so cruel to a poor blind man——a poor blind man, struck blind with lightning. Heaven preserve your honour from such calamities! I have very good friends down in *Cumberland*, please your royal worship, and I am travelling homeward as fast as I can, but it pleased heaven to strike me blind with a flash of lightning a long way from my relations, and I am reduced to beg for a little sustenance."

"Mercy upon me!" cries miss *Newcome*——"why, what a vast way the miserable wretch has to travel, Mr. *Griskin*? how will he ever be able to get home?"

"Oh, curse him, all a confounded lie from beginning to end, depend upon't madam! the dog has no relations or friends in the world, I'll answer for him," cries the beau. Then turning to his father, "here you old rascal," added he, "here's a shilling for you, and do you hear me, take yourself off this moment——If ever I see you upon the parade again, I'll have you laid by the heels, and sent to the house of correction." The blind wretch then hobbled away, pouring forth a thousand benedictions upon them, while lady *Marmazet* and the sharper rallied miss *Newcome* for her unfashionable generosity.

Leaving the reader to make his own remarks on this extraordinary occurrence; I shall pass over the intermediate space of time, in which nothing happened material to this history, and rejoin the three illustrious guests at their ale-house in the evening. The lady was the first that came, to whom her father related the adventure of the morning, which greatly delighted her: While she was laughing at this story, that sprightly knight her brother also came singing into the room, and throwing himself negligently into a chair, picked his teeth for a moment or two in silence. Then addressing himself to his father, "old fellow," cries he, "I was obliged to use you a little roughly this morning, but you'll excuse me——There was a necessity you know of treating you like a scoundrel and an imposter, to prevent any suspicion of our relationship." "Well, well *Jack!*" replied the father, "I forgive you, I forgive you with all my heart; for I supposed one of the ladies was your sweet-heart, and to be sure 'twas as well not to let her know you was my son, for fear of the worst that might happen, tho'f[1] you tell me women are so fond of marrying highwaymen now-a-days. Adad *Jack!* I wished for my eyes again, just to have had one little peep at her——what, is she a deadly fine girl?"

"A divine creature, sir," replied the beau; "young, melting, amorous and beautiful; innocent as an angel, and yet wanton as the month of *May*; and then——she doats on me to distraction. Did you mind how tenderly the little fool interested herself about your blind eyes, and pitied you for the confounded lies you told her?"

"Why yes, there was something very pretty I must confess," said the father, "very pretty indeed, in her manner of talking. How the deuce do you get acquainted with these great ladies?"

"O let me alone for that," returned Mr. *Griskin*; "I am made for the women, sir! I have the *toujours gay*,[2] which is so dear to them; I am blest with that agreeable impudence, that easy familiar way of talking nonsense, that happy insensibility of shame, which they all adore in men. And then, consider my figure, my shape, my air, my legs——all together, I find I am irresistible. How in the name of wonder, old fellow, could you and your trull strike out such a lucky hit under a country hedge?"

Here the fair lady was in raptures at her brother's wit, and asked her father, if he did not think him a most delightful, charming young fellow? to which the beggar replied with a groan, "O *Jack, Jack!* thou wilt certainly come to be hanged in the end; I see it as plain as can be; so much wit and impudence will certainly bring thee to the gallows at last."

Much more of this sort of ribaldry and licentious conversation passed between them; and as the father was more wakeful

---

1   I.e., even if.

2   French: "always gay," a sprightly air.

this night, than he had been the preceding one, they protracted their cups till very late: they roared, they sung, they danced, and practised all sorts of unruly, drunken mirth. At last however, they separated once more to their several beds, and fate had destined that they should never meet again in joy and friendship, at this or any other ale-house; the cause whereof will be seen in the following chapter.

[CHAP. XVII

MORE ADVENTURES AT BATH.

THE father of young *Jeremy Griskin* was so pleased with the advantageous match his son was concluding, that in the joy of his heart, he could not help talking of it to the alehouse-keeper where he lodged; tho' he had imprecated a thousand curses on his head, if ever he revealed it. The alehouse-keeper likewise had bound himself by an equal number of oaths, never to discover what he heard from the beggar; and perhaps at the time he made these vows, he meant to observe them: but being once in possession of a secret, he found it impossible to be long easy with so troublesome a guest in his bosom. With a very mysterious face therefore he whispered to several coach and footmen, who frequented his house, "that a very fine gentleman and lady came privately every night to visit an old blind beggar, who lodged with them; that these fine folks, by what he could learn, were the beggar's son and daughter; and that the fine gentleman lived amongst the quality, and was going to run away with a great fortune."

The story having made this progress, could not fail of proceeding farther; for being once commanded to the servants of several families, it was quickly served up to the tables of the great. The valets informed their masters, and the waiting gentlewomen their mistresses, as a new topic of conversation while they were dressing them.

From hence the rumour became public, and dispersed itself all over the *Bath*; so that the very next morning after the last rendezvous at the alehouse, when 'squire *Griskin* appeared with lady *Marmazet* and miss *Newcome* as usual in the pump-room,[1] they found themselves stared on with more than common attention by all the company. Several gentlemen laughed aloud as they passed by them; the young ladies all affected to titter under their fans; and the elder dames tossed up their noses with the most insolent air of disdain. As all this could not be done without a meaning, the two ladies his companions were greatly astonished, and even the beau himself, fortified as he was in impudence, could not stifle some unpleasant apprehensions. He affected however to turn it off with an air of raillery, imputed it to the d—mn'd censoriousness of the *Bath*; and expressed his wonder that people could not be allowed to be free and intimate, without drawing on themselves the scandalous observations of a whole public place.

While Mr. *Griskin* was supposed to be a gentleman, the whole tribe of coquettes and beauties looked on miss *Newcome* with eyes of jealousy and indignation, all of them envying her the happiness of engaging so accomplished a lover: but no sooner were they let into the secret of his parentage, than they began to triumph in their turns, and shewed their malice another way. Envy now changed into contempt; a malicious sneer was seen on all their faces, and they huddled together in little parties to feast on so agreeable a discovery. For spite is never so spiteful as among young ladies, who are rivals in love and beauty. "Really, madam," said one of them, "one must be obliged to take care of one's pockets, because you know if sharpers are allowed to come into public places, and appear like gentlemen, one can never be safe for a moment." To which another replied, "indeed I shall leave my watch at home when I go to the ball to night, for I don't think it safe to carry any thing valuable about one, while *miss Newcome's admirer* continues among us." Many such speeches were flirted about; for tho' the story hitherto was only a flying suspicion, they were all fully persuaded of its truth, and resolutely bent to believe it, without waiting for any confirmation, and indeed without once troubling themselves to enquire on what authority it was founded.

---

1   The main social gathering place in Bath, where visitors could drink, among other things, the medicinal water pumped into the room from the hot-springs.

The gay sharper manifestly perceived from all this, that some discovery had been made to his disadvantage; but not being willing to resign his hopes till affairs appeared a little more desperate, he very courageously presented himself that evening in the ballroom. He was indeed prudent enough to abstain from minuets, not chusing to encounter the eyes of people in so conspicuous an attitude; but as soon as the company stood up to country-dances, with a face of infinite assurance, he led miss *Newcome* towards the top of the room, and took his station as usual among the foremost files. A buzz immediately ran thro' the company, and when they came to dance, most of the ladies refused him their hands. This was a terrible blow to him; he knew not how to revenge the affront, nor yet how to behave under such an interdiction. Lady *Marmazet*, who saw with what scorn he was treated, very resolutely advanced and reprimanded several of her female acquaintance with much warmth for their behaviour, pretending it was an affront to miss *Newcome*, who came to *Bath* under her protection, and whose cause she was obliged to espouse. In reality, I believe there was another reason which quickened her ladyship's resentment, and made her behold with concern the indignities offered to a man, who had found the way of being agreeable to her ladyship, as well as to the young lady her companion. But however that be, 'tis certain her interfering did him little service; and after a thousand taunts and fleers, the unfortunate couple was obliged to sit down in a corner of the room. They stood up again some time afterwards to make a fresh attempt, which proved as unsuccessful as the former: in short, after repeated disgraces, they were obliged to give over all thoughts of dancing for the remaining part of the night; the poor girl trembling and wondering what could be the reason of all this behaviour; and even the beau himself looking very foolish under the consciousness of his own condition.

As it was pretty plain however that his father must have betrayed his secret, the ball no sooner broke up, than he flew with the greatest rage to the ale-house, rushed eagerly into the room, where the miserable wretch was then dozing, and fell upon him with all the bitterness of passion. "Where is the old rascal?" cries he; "what is it you mean by this, you detestable miscreant? I have a great mind to murder you, and give your carcase to the hounds!"

"Bless us! What's the matter now, *Jack*?" said the beggar. "Matter!" returned he; "you have been prating, and tattling, and chattering. You have ruined me, you old villain, you have blown me up for ever. Speak, confess that you have discovered[1] my secrets."

Here the beggar stammered and endeavoured to excuse himself, but was obliged at last to acknowledge, that he believed he might have mentioned something of the matter to the man of the house. "And how durst you mention any thing of the matter?" cries the son, seizing his father by the throat; "how durst you open your lips upon the subject? I have a great inclination to pluck your tongue out, and burn it before your face. You have told him, I suppose, that I am your son——'tis a lie; you stole me, you kidnapped me, 'tis impossible I could be the offspring of such an eyeless, shirt-less, toothless ragamuffin as thou art. Here I have been insulted by every body to-night, I have run the gauntlope[2] thro' the whole ball-room; all my hopes, all my stratagems are destroyed, and all is owing to your infamous prating. But mark what I say to you——set out directly, to-night, or to-morrow morning before sunrise, and budge off as fast as your legs can carry you. If I find you here to-morrow at seven o'clock, by hell I'll cut your throat. You have done mischief enough already——you shall do me no more, and therefore pack up your wallet, and away with you, or prepare to feed the crows." Having uttered this terrible denunciation of ven-geance, he rushed out of the room with as much impetuosity as he came into it, and left the poor offender staring and trembling with amazement.

The first thing he did after his son had quitted him, was to heave up a prodigious groan, which he accompanied with a moral reflexion on the hard fate of all fathers, who are cursed by rebel-lious unnatural children. As such usage he thought was sufficient to cancel all paternal affection, he felt in himself a strong desire to revenged, by impeaching, and bringing the villain to justice. But then considering on the other hand, that he could not well do this, without discovering his own hypocrisy and impostures

---

1   I.e., uncovered.
2   I.e., gauntlet.

at the same time, he prudently suppressed those thoughts, and resolved to quit the place. 'Twas hard, he said to himself, to obey the orders of such an abandoned profligate, but he comforted himself with the agreeable, and indeed very probable hopes, that he should see his son come to the gallows, without his being accessory to such an event.

Very early then the next morning, he set out with his unfortunate little guide, and made forced marches for *London*. Being willing to escape beyond the reach of his son's resentment as soon as possible, he travelled so very fast, that in little more than a week's time he arrived at *Reading*: from whence, after a day's resting, he again renewed his journey. But sorrow and fatigue so entirely overcame him, that he fell sick on the road, and it was with the greatest difficulty that he crawled up to the gate of a celebrated inn, not used to the entertainment of such guests, where he fainted and dropped down in a fit. Two or three ostlers,[1] who were the first that saw him, conveyed him to an apartment in a stable, where he lay for several days in a most miserable condition. His disorder soon rendered him speechless, and being able to ask for nothing, he was supplied with nothing: for tho' the good landlady of the house would have gladly done anything in the world to relieve him, had she known his condition; her servants, happening not to have the same spirit of humanity in them, never once informed her, that such an object of charity lay sick in her stable. Finding himself thus neglected and destitute of all comfort, he very prudently gave up the ghost, leaving our hero once more at the disposal of chance.

What future scenes of good and evil are next to open upon him, fate does not yet chuse to divulge, and therefore begging the reader to suspend his curiosity, till we have received a proper commission for gratifying it, we here put an end to this first book of our wonderful history.][2]

End of the FIRST BOOK.

---

1   Stablemen or grooms at an inn.
2   We now return to the first edition of the novel.

BOOK II

CHAP. I

A DISSERTATION UPON NOTHING.[1]

THAT great Master of human Nature, the ingenious Author of *Tom Jones*, who justly styles himself King of *Biographers*, published an Edict in his last Work, declaring, that no Person hereafter should presume to write a Novel, without prefixing a prefatory Chapter to every Book, under the Penalty of being deemed a Blockhead.[2] This introductory Chapter, he says, is the best Mark of Genius, and surest Criterion of an Author's Parts; for by it the most indifferent Reader may be enabled to distinguish what is true and genuine in this historic kind of Writing, from what is false and counterfeit: And he supposes the Authors of the *Spectator* were induced to prefix *Latin* and *Greek* Mottos to every Paper, from the same Consideration of guarding against the Pursuit of Scribblers; because by this Device it became impracticable for any Man to Presume to imitate the *Spectators*, without understanding at least one Sentence in the learned Languages.

In compliance therefore with the Edict of this royal *Biographer*, I shall beg Leave, in the Entrance of this second Book of our History, to detain the Reader with an introductory Chapter upon *Nothing*; being the most proper Subject I can recollect at present for such an initial Section; which I hope will testify my Loyalty to the great Lawgiver abovementioned, and also dispose the Reader to a favourable Opinion of my historical Abilities.

I do not recollect any Writer before myself, excepting the great Lord *Rochester*, who has treated this abstruse, learned

---

1 This "prefatory" chapter was excised from the third edition, perhaps to avoid the impression of fawning over Fielding, to whom the third edition is already dedicated.
2 Fielding prefaces each of the eighteen books of *Tom Jones* with an introductory essay. Coventry is perhaps thinking of Book V, chapter I, where Fielding playfully insists that these essays are "absolutely necessary to this kind of Writing" (that is, a "history"), but nowhere calls himself "King of *Biographers*" or threatens non-compliers with the title of "Blockhead."

and comprehensive Subject;[1] which is something wonderful, considering the great Number of Penmen, whose Works shew them to have been excellently qualified for it. But though none have treated it professedly, many and various have indirectly handled it in all Branches of Science, and in all human Probability will continue to do so to the End of the World. For though neither Poet, Philosopher, Divine, or Lawyer have ever been courageous enough to declare the Subject they were writing upon; yet Poems, Systems of Philosophy, Bodies of Divinity, and huge Reports of Law have in all Ages swelled themselves to the greatest Bulk upon *Nothing*.

Not to recur to those venerable Tomes of Antiquity, which have been delivered down to us from the peaceful Ages of monkish Darkness, modern Examples present themselves in great Abundance to our Choice. What is contained in all the Treatises of Mr. *William Wh____n* on the Trinity? Nothing. What is contained in the mighty and voluminous Epic Poems of Sir *Richard Blackmore*, Knight? absolute Nothing. What again can be collected from that universal Maze of Words, called the Universal History of all Nations, Languages, Customs, Manners, Empires, Governments, Men, Monsters, Land-Fights, Sea-Fights, and a Million more of inexhaustible Topics?[2] What, I say, can be comprehended in the tedious Pages of that ostentatious History? every Reader will be ready to answer, Nothing. The Works of *Dennis*, *Descartes*, Lord *Sh____f____ry*, and the mighty Mr. *W____rb____n*, all treat of the immortal Subject, however the ingenious Authors, out of pure Modesty, may have been contented to let them pass under the

---

1 Coventry has in mind the satiric ode "Upon Nothing" by John Wilmot, Earl of Rochester (1647-80). Curiously, he does not mention Fielding's essay "On Nothing" or the introductory chapter to Book IV of *Tom Jones*, "Containing little or nothing."

2 William Whiston (1667-1752), priest and follower of Sir Isaac Newton's physics, defended controversial positions on the Trinity and other doctrinal issues that finally drove him from the Anglican Church; Sir Richard Blackmore (1653- 1729), author of the epics *King Arthur* (1695) and *Creation* (1712), was widely mocked as a failed poet; the *Universal History* (1681) by the French theologian Jacques-Benigne Bossuet (1627-1704) inspired an English eighteenth-century work of the same title by numerous authors, and finally spanning twenty-three volumes.

fictitious Names of Plays, Systems of Philosophy, miscellaneous Reflections, and Divine Legations.[1]

That Nothing can arise out of Nothing, *ex nihilio nil fieri*, has long reigned an incontrovertible Maxim of Philosophy, and been a first Principle of the Schools: But Novelty, and a modish Love of Paradox carry me to endeavour its Confutation; and this I hope to do on the general Testimony and verbal Confession of all Mankind.

For let us attend carefully to what passes around us, and we shall find *Nothing* to have the greatest Sway in all human Actions. Does any one ask his Friend or a Stranger, *What is the News at Court to Day*? he receives constantly and universally for answer, *Nothing, Sir.*——*What was done yesterday in the House?*[2] Nothing at all, Sir.——*Any News in the City, or upon Change?*[3]——Nothing in the world——*Are our Armies in Motion, and have they atchieved any thing lately against the Enemy*? Nothing in nature, Sir, is the sure and invariable Answer, which may for ever be expected to all Questions of this kind. Yet notwithstanding this universal Declaration, if we look abroad, and trust rather to the Information of our Eyes than our Ears, we shall really find a great deal done in the World, considering how People have been employed, and that Mankind are by no means idle, tho' they are always *doing Nothing*.

Let us first cast our Eyes upon the Court, where tho' Nothing is said to be done, every thing is in reality performed. There we see Feuds, Animosities, Divisions, Jealousies, Revolutions, and Re-revolutions; Ministers deposed and again restored; Peace and War decreed, contending Nations reconciled, and the Interests of *Europe* adjusted. Yet all this is Nothing.

From the Court let us turn to the Change and City, and there also admire the infinite Productions of *Nothing*. There we see

---

1   John Dennis (1657-1734), attacked by Pope as a bad literary critic; Anthony Ashley Cooper, third Earl of Shaftesbury (1671-1713), reviled by orthodox Christians as a freethinker, and author of the miscellaneous collection of essays *Characteristics of Men, Manners, Opinions, Times etc.* (1711); while Descartes is now considered the founder of modern philosophy, he was then often regarded as the paradigmatic spinner of false philosophical systems; Warburton, earlier cited for his edition of Pope (see page 32, note 2), is here remembered for his voluminous and turgid theological treatise *The Divine Legation of Moses* (1738-41).

2   Either the House of Commons or the House of Lords.

3   I.e., at the London Stock Exchange

Avarice, Usury, Extortion, Back-biting, Fraud, Hypocrisy, Stock-jobbing,[1] and every Evil that can arise from the Circulation of Money. Thousands were there ruined Yesterday, thousands are ruining To-day, and thousands will be ruined To-morrow: Yet all this *is Nothing.*

Again, let us take a second Survey of it, and we shall see little Politicians hatching Scandal against the Government, and propagating malicious Stories, which they know to be false: We shall see Lies circulating from Coffee-house to Coffee-house, and gathering additional Strength in every Minute of their Conveyance: We shall see the turbulent Offspring of Wealth, restless in Peace, and dissatisfied in War; compelling their Sovereign to take up Arms in one Year, and almost wresting them from his Hands in another: Yet all this is Nothing.

Once more let us direct our Views to the Camp, and there again admire the Productions of *Nothing.* For tho' Nothing was said to be done during the late War,[2] and the little Politicians above-mentioned took a Pleasure to talk of the Inactivity of our Armies, yet in reality every thing was performed, that could reasonably be expected from them. 'Tis true, they did not over-run the Kingdom of *France*, besiege its Capital, and take its King Prisoner; all which I believe many People thought easy and practicable; but they kept the most numerous Armies of the most formidable Monarchy in *Europe* at bay, and often contended hard with them for the Victory, in spite of the Treachery of Allies, and the almost infinite Superiority of their Enemies. If any body chuses to call this Nothing, he has my full Consent, because it confirms the Doctrine I want to establish, that Nothing produces every Thing.

Lastly, let us examine what passes in private Life, and that will likewise furnish us with the same Reflections. Do not Quarrels of all sorts arise from Nothing? Do not matrimonial Jealousies spring from Nothing? What occasions Law-suits, Dissentions among Neighbours, improbable Suspicions, ill-founded Conjectures, and

---

1   An earlier version of stock-broking. The lowly reputation of this trade is suggested by Samuel Johnson's definition of "stock-jobber" in his *Dictionary*: "A low wretch who gets money by buying and selling shares in the funds."

2   The War of the Austrian Succession (1741-48), which was widely considered to be a waste of money and troops.

the like? What is it that fills the Brains of Projectors,[1] exercises the Fancy of Poets, employs the Machinations of Women, and draws the Swords of young coxcomb Officers in the Army, when they are strutting with the first Raptures of sudden Elevation? To all these Interrogations we may answer, *Nothing*. And not to multiply foreign Examples, what is it that I am now writing? undoubtedly the Reader will esteem it Nothing. In short, whatever we see around us,

Quicquid agunt hominess, votum, timor, ira, voluptas,
Gaudia, discursus.[2]

All these are the genuine Productions of Nothing.

I would therefore humbly recommend it to the Consideration of the two great Seminaries of *Oxford* and *Cambridge*, whether their Wisdoms shall not think fit to make an Alteration in that old erroneous Maxim of *Ex nihilo fit*, and say rather *Ex nihilo omnia fiunt;*[3] which I take to be more consistent with Truth and the Reality of Things.

Having thus discharged the Duty imposed upon me, of writing an introductory Chapter, I hope I am now at liberty to pursue the Fortunes of my Hero, without incurring the grievous Imputation of Dullness, denounced on all those, who shall disobey the royal Edict issued out for that Purpose.

CHAP. II

FORTUNE GROWS FAVOURABLE TO OUR HERO, AND RESTORES HIM TO HIGH-LIFE.

THE blind Beggar, to whose Tyranny Fortune had committed our Hero, groaned out his Soul, as the Reader has already seen, in a Stable at a public Inn. *Pompey*, standing by, had the *Pleasure of seeing*

---

1 Those who form absurd philosophical or scientific schemes.
2 Latin: "What folks have done ... their hopes and fears and anger, their pleasures, joys, and toing and froing" (Juvenal, *Satires* I. 85-86).
3 Latin: the first maxim may be translated as "from nothing comes nothing"; Coventry's "alteration" may be translated as "from nothing comes everything."

the Tyrant fall as he deserved, and exulted over him, like *Cicero* in the Senate-house over the dying *Cæsar*.[1] [This misfortune was first discovered by an ostler, who coming accidentally into the stable, and perceiving the miserable creature stretched out on the straw, began at first to holla in his ear, imagining him to be asleep: but finding him insensible to three or four hearty kicks, which he bestowed upon him, "odrabbet un,"[2] cries he, "why sure a can't be dead, can a? by gar he is—pillgarlick[3] is certainly dead." Then he called together two or three of his brethren, to divert themselves with this agreeable spectacle, and many stable jokes passed upon the occasion. When their diversion was over, one of them ran in doors to inform their mistress;] but the good Woman was not immediately at leisure to hear his Intelligence, being taken up in her Civilities to a Coach-and-Six, which was just then arrived, and very busy in conducting the Ladies to their Apartments. However, when Dinner was over, she bethought herself of what had happened, and went into the Stable, attended by two of her Chamber-maids, to survey the Corpse, and give Orders for its Burial. There little *Pompey*, for the first Time, presented himself to her View; but Sorrow and Ill-usage had so impaired his Beauty, and his Coat too was in such a Dishabille[4] of Dirt and Mire, that he bespake no favourable Opinion in his Beholders. We must not therefore think Mrs. *Wilkins*[5] of a cruel Nature, because she ordered him to be hanged, for, in reality, she is a very humane and friendly Woman; but perceiving no Beauty in the Dog to incline her to Compassion, and concluding him to be a Thief, from the Company he was found with, it was natural for her to shew no Mercy. A Consultation therefore

---

1   The Roman orator and politician Marcus Tullius Cicero (106-43 BCE) was a strong republican who opposed the dictatorial ambitions of Julius Caesar (100?-44 BCE). Cicero supported the failed military campaign to oust Caesar, led, significantly, by Pompey the Great (106-48 BCE). When conspirators finally assassinated Caesar in the senate-house, Cicero was exultant, although there is no record that he was actually there for the event.

2   The ostler is speaking in west-country dialect, as famously used by Fielding's rural characters. "Odrabbet un," possibly meaning "God rot him," is one of Squire Western's favorite curses in *Tom Jones*.

3   A bald person.

4   "The state of being partly undressed, or dressed in a negligent or careless style; undress" (*OED*).

5   Changed to "Mrs. Windmill" in the third edition.

was held in the Yard, and Sentence of Death pronounced upon him; which had been executed as soon as commanded (for the Ostler was instantly preparing a Rope with great Delight) had not one of the Chamber-maids interposed, saying, *She believed he was a sweet pretty Creature, if he was washed*, and desired her Mistress to save him. A Word of this Kind was enough to Mrs. *Wilkins*, who immediately granted him a Reprieve, and ordered him into the Kitchen for a Turn-spit.[1] But when he had gone thro' the Ceremony of Lustration, and was thoroughly cleaned, every Body was struck with his Beauty, and Mrs. *Wilkins* in particular; who had now changed her Resolutions, and, instead of condemning him to the Drudgery of a Turn-spit, made him her Companion, and taught him to follow her about the House. He soon grew to be a Favourite with the whole Family, as indeed he always was wherever he came; and the Chamber-maids used to quarrel with one another, who should take him to their Beds at Night. He likewise got acquainted with *Captain*, the great House-dog, who, like *Cerberus*,[2] terrified the Regions round-about with his Barking: yet would he often condescend to be pleased with the Frolicks of little *Pompey*, and vouchsafe now and then to unbend his Majesty with a Game of Play.

After he had lived here near a Fortnight, a Post-chaise stopt one Day at the Door, out of which alighted two Ladies, just arrived from *Bath*. They ran directly to the Fire, declaring they were almost frozen to Death with Cold; whereupon Mrs. *Wilkins* began to thunder for Wood, and assisted in making up an excellent Fire: After which, she begged the Favour to know what their Ladyships would please to have for Dinner. "If you please, Madam," said the Eldest, "I'll look into your Lardery." "With all my Heart, Madam," answered the good Landlady; "I have Fish and Fowls of all Kind, and Rabbits and Hares, and a Variety of Butcher's Meat——but your Ladyship says you will be so good to accommodate yourself on the Spot——I am ready to attend your Ladyship, whenever your Ladyship pleases."

While the Eldest was gone to examine the Lardery, the Youngest of these Ladies, having seized little *Pompey*, who followed his Mistress into the Room, was infinitely charmed with his Beauty,

1   I.e., Pompey is given the job of running on a treadmill to turn the spit in the oven.
2   In Greek mythology, the ferocious three-headed dog that guards the entrance to Hades.

and caressed him during the whole Time of her Sister's Absence. *Pompey*, in return, seemed pleased to be taken Notice of by so fair a Lady; for tho' he had long been disused to the Company of People of Fashion, he had not yet forgot how to behave himself with Complaisance and Good-manners. He felt a kind of Pride return-ing, which all his Misfortunes had not yet been able to extinguish, and began to hope the Time was come, which should restore him to the Beau-monde.[1] With these Hopes he continued in the Room all the Time the Ladies were at Dinner, paying great Court to them both, and receiving what they were pleased to bestow upon him with much Fawning, and officious Civility.

As soon as the Ladies had dined, Mrs. *Wilkins* came in to make her Compliments, as usual, hoping the Dinner was dressed to their Ladyships Minds, and that the Journey had not destroyed their Ap-petites. She received very courteous Answers to all she said, and after some other Conversation on indifferent Topics, little *Pompey* came at last upon the Carpet. "Pray Madam," said the youngest of the Ladies, "how long have you had this very pretty Dog?" Mrs. *Wilkins*, who never was deficient, when she had an Opportunity of talking, having started on so fair a Subject, began to display her Eloquence in the following Manner. "Madam," says she, "the little Creature fell into my Hands by the strangest Accident in Life, and it is a Mercy he was not hanged——An old blind Beggar, Ladies, died in my Stable about a Fortnight ago, and it seems, this little Animal used to lead him about the Country. 'Tis amazing how they come by the Instinct they have in them——and such a little Creature too——But as I as telling you, Ladies, the old blind Beggar was just returned from *Bath*, as your Ladyships may be now, and the poor miserable Wretch perished in my Stable. There he left his little Dog, and, Will you believe it, Ladies? As I am alive, I ordered him to be hanged, not once dreaming he was such a Beauty; for indeed he was quite covered over with Mire and Nastiness, as to be sure he could not be otherwise, after leading the old blind Man so long a Journey; but a Maid servant of mine took a Fancy to the little Wretch, and begged his Life; and would you think it, Ladies? I am now grown as fond of the little Fool, as if he was my own Child."

---

1 The world of the rich and fashionable.

The two Sisters, diverted with Mrs. *Wilkins*'s Oration, could not help smiling on one another; but disguising their Laughter as well as they could, "I do not wonder," said the youngest, "at your Fondness for him, Madam! he is so remarkably handsome; and that being the Case, I can't find it in my Heart to rob you of him, otherwise I was just going to ask you if you should be willing to part with him." "Bless me, Madam," said the obliging Hostess, "I am sure there is nothing I would not do to oblige your Ladyship, and if your Ladyship has such an Affection for the little Wretch——Not part with him indeed!" "Nay, Madam," said the Lady interrupting her, "I would willingly make you any Amends, and if you will please to name your Price, I'll purchase him of you." "Alack-a-day, Madam," replied the Landlady, "I am sorry your Ladyship suspects me to be of such a mercenary Disposition; purchase him indeed! He is extremely at your Ladyship's Service, if you please to accept of him."——With these Words she took him up, and delivered him into the Lady's Arms, who received him with many Acknowledgements of the Favour done her; all which Mrs. *Wilkins* repaid with abundant Interest.

Word was now brought, that the Chaise was ready, and waited at the Door; whereupon, the two Ladies were obliged to break off their Conversation, and Mrs. *Wilkins* to refrain from her Eloquence. She attended them, with a Million civil Speeches, to their Equipage, and handing little *Pompey* to them, when they were seated in it, took Leave with a great Profusion of Smiles and Curtsies. The Postillion blew his Horn; the Ladies bowed; and our Hero's Heart exulted with Transport, to think of the Amendment of his Fate.

CHAP. III

A LONG CHAPTER OF CHARACTERS.

THE Post-chaise stopped in a genteel Street in *London*, and *Pompey* was introduced into decent Lodgings, where every Thing had an Air of Politeness, yet nothing was expensive. The Rooms were hung with *Indian* Paper; the Beds were *Chinese*; and the whole Furniture seemed to shew how elegant Simplicity can be under the Direction of Taste. Tea was immediately ordered, and the two Ladies sat down to refresh themselves after the Fatigue of their Journey, and began to talk over the Adventures they had met with at the *Bath*. They remembered many agreeable Incidents, which had happened in that great Rendezvous of Pleasure, and ventured to laugh at some of the Follies of their Acquaintance, without Severity, or Ill-nature.

These two Ladies were born of a good Family, and had received a genteel Education. Their Father indeed left them no more than Six Thousand Pounds each; but as they united their Fortunes, and managed their Affairs with Frugality, they made a credible Figure in the World, and lived in Intimacy with People of the greatest Fashion. It will be necessary, for the sake of Distinction, to give them Names, and the Reader, if he pleases, may call them *Theodosia* and *Aurora*.

Theodosia, the eldest, was advancing towards Forty, an Age when personal Charms begin to fade, and Women grow indifferent at least, who have nothing better to supply the Place of them. But *Theodosia* was largely possessed of all those good Qualities, which render Women agreeable without Beauty: She was affable and easy in her Behaviour; well-bred without Falshood; cheerful without Levity; polite and obliging to her Friends, civil and generous to her Domestics. Nature had given her a good Temper, and Education had made it an agreeable one. She had lived much in the World, without growing vain or insolent; improved her Understanding by Books, without any Affectation of Wit or Science, and loved public Places, without being a Slave to Pleasure. Her Conversation was always engaging, and often entertaining. Her long Commerce with the World had supplied her with a fund of diverting Remarks on Life, and her good Sense enabled her to deliver them with Grace and Propriety.

Aurora, the youngest Sister, was in her Four and Twentieth Year, and Imagination cannot possibly form a finer Figure than she was, in every Respect. Her Beauty, now at its highest Lustre, gave that full Satisfaction to the Eye, which younger Charms rarely inspire. She was tall and full-formed, but with the utmost Elegance and Symmetry in all her Limbs; and a certain Majesty, which resulted from her Shape, was accompanied with a peculiar Sweetness of Face: For tho' she had all the Charms, she had none of the Insolence of Beauty. As if these uncommon Perfections of Nature were not sufficient to procure her Admirers enough, she had added to them the most winning Accomplishments of Art: She danced and sung, and played like an Angel; her Voice naturally clear, full, and melodious, had been improved under the best *Italian* Masters; and she was ready to oblige People with her Music, on the slightest Intimation, that it would be agreeable, without any Airs of Shyness and unseasonable Modesty. Indeed, Affectation never entered into any one of her Gestures, and whatsoever she did, was with that generous Freedom of Manner, which denotes a good Understanding, as well as an honest Heart. Her Temper was chearful in the highest Degree, and she had a most uncommon Flow of Spirits and Good-humour, which seldom deserted her in any Place, or Company. At a Ball she was extremely joyous and spirited, and the Pleasure she gave to her Beholders, could only be exceeded by that unbounded Happiness with which she inspired her Partner. Yet tho' her Genius led her to be lively, and a little romantic, whoever conversed with her in private, admired her good Sense, and heard Reflexions from her, which plainly shewed she had often exercised her Understanding on the most serious Subjects.

A Woman so beautiful in her Person, and excellent in her Accomplishments, could not fail of attracting Lovers in great Abundance; and accordingly she had refused a Variety of Offers from People of all Characters, who could scarcely believe she was in earnest in rejecting them, because she accompanied her Refusals with unusual Politeness and Good-humour. She did not grow vain, or insolent, from the Triumphs of her Beauty, nor long to spit in a Man's Face, because she could not approve his Addresses (which I believe is the Case with many young Ladies) but sweetened her Denials with great Civility, and always asked the Advice of her Sister, of whom she was passionately fond. Such was *Aurora*, the present Mistress of our Hero; and as the Characters of some of her Admirers may, perhaps, not be unentertaining, I will give a Description of two or three out of many.

And first, let us pay our Compliments to *Count Tag*,[1] who had merited a Title by his Exploits; which perhaps is the most usual Step to Honour, but always most respectable whenever it happens. 'Tis

---

1 "Tag" could denote "Any thing paltry and mean" (Johnson).

true, he had no Patent to shew for his Nobility, which depended entirely on the *arbitrium popularis aurae*, the Fickleness of popular Applause;[1] but he seems likely to enjoy it as long as he lives, there being no Probability of any Alteration in his Behaviour. His Father raised a Fortune by a Profession, and from him he inherited a competent Estate of about three hundred Pounds *per annum*. His Education began at *Westminster* School,[2] and was finished at *Oxford*; from whence he transported himself to *London*, on News of his Father's Death, and made a bold Push, as it is called, to introduce himself *into Life*. He had a strong Ambition of becoming a fine Gentleman, and cultivating an Acquaintance with People of Fashion, which he esteemed the most consummate Character attainable by Man, and to that he resolved to dedicate his Days. As his first Essay therefore, he presented himself every Evening in a Sidebox at one of the Play-houses, where he was ready to enter into Conversation with any body that would afford him an Audience, and was particularly assiduous in applying himself to young Noblemen and Men of Fortune, whom he had formerly known at School, or at the University. By degrees he got footing in two or three Families of Quality, where he was sometimes invited to Dinner; and having learnt the fashionable Topics of Discourse, he studied to make himself agreeable, by entertaining them with the current News of the Town. He had the first Intelligence of a Marriage or an Intrigue, knew to a Moment when the Breath went out of a Nobleman's Body, and published the Scandal of a Masquerade, or a Ridotta, sooner by half an Hour at least, than any other public Talker in *London*. He had a copious Fluency of Language, which made him embellish every Subject he undertook, and a certain Art of Talking as minutely and circumstantially on the most trivial Subjects, as on those of the highest Importance. He would describe a Straw, or a Pimple on a Lady's Face, with all the Figures of Rhetoric; by which he persuaded many People to believe him a Man of great Parts; and surely no Man's Impertinence ever turned to better Account. As he constantly attended *Bath* and *Tunbridge*, and all the public Places, he got easier Access to the Tables of the Great, and by degrees insinuated

---

1   Latin: Horace, *Odes*, III.ii.20.

2   One of England's most prestigious public schools (in the English sense of boarding schools largely designed for the education of gentlemen).

himself into all the Parties of the Ladies; among whom he began to be received as a considerable Genius, and quickly became necessary in all their Drums and Assemblies.

Finding his Schemes thus succeed almost beyond his Hopes, he now assumed a higher Behaviour, and began to fancy himself a Man of Quality from the Company he kept. With this View he thought proper to forget all his old Acquaintance, whose low Geniuses left them groveling in Obscurity, while his superior Talents had raised him to a Familiarity with Lords and Ladies. If therefore any old Friend, presuming on their former Intimacy, ventured to accost him in the Park, he made a formal Bow, and begged Pardon for leaving him; *but really, Lady* Betty, *or Lady* Mary *was just entering the Mall.* In short, he always proportioned his Respect to the Rank and Fortunes of his Company; he would desert a Commoner for a Lord, a Lord for an Earl, an Earl for a Marquiss, and a Marquiss for a Duke. Having thus enrolled himself in his own Imagination among the Nobility, it was not without Reason that People gave him the Style and Title of *Count Tag*, thinking it a Pity that such a Genius should be called by the ordinary Name of his Family.

[To say this gentleman was in love, would be too great an abuse of language, for he was in reality incapable of loving any body but himself. But vanity and the mode,[1] often made him affect attachments to women of celebrated beauty, from whose acquaintance he thought he could derive credit to himself. This was his motive for appearing one of the admirers of *Aurora*, whose charms were conspicuous enough to excite his pride, and that was the only passion which the count ever thought of gratifying. He knew how to counterfeit raptures which he never felt, and had all the *language* of love, without any of its *sentiment*.]

The second Cavalier, who made his Addresses in the same Place, was an old Gentleman turned of Seventy, whose Chearfulness and Vivacity might have tempted People to forget his Age, if he had not recalled it to their Remembrance, by unseasonable Attempts of Gallantry.[2] The Passions of Youth are always ridiculous in old Age; and tho' many fine Women have sacrificed their Charms to

---

1 The current fashion.
2 The entire description of the "old gentleman" that follows was deleted from the third edition.

superannuated Husbands, this Union is so unnatural, that we must suppose their Affections were fixed on Title or Estate, or something else besides the Persons of their Lovers. This old Gentleman had led a Life of constant Gallantry almost from his Cradle, and now could not divest himself of the Passion of Love, tho' he was deserted by the Abilities of it. He had already buried three Wives, and was ambitious of a fourth; tho' his Constitution was extremely shattered by Debauchery and high-living, and it seemed as if a Fit of Coughing would at any time have shook him to Pieces. Besides this, he kept several Mistresses, and all the Villages round his Country-seat were in a manner peopled with the Fruits of his stolen Embraces.

At his first Entrance into Life, he was a younger Brother, and married an ugly old Woman of Fortune for the sake of her Money, who quickly departed to his Wishes, and left him possessed of the only desireable thing belonging to her. Soon afterwards, his elder Brother also went the same Road to Mortality, and left him Heir of three thousand Pounds a Year; which enabled his Genius to display itself, and supplied him with all the Essentials of Pleasure. From this Moment he began his Career, and being a gay young Fellow, handsome in his Person, and genteel in his Address, he resolved to indulge himself in every Gratification that Money could purchase, or Luxury invent. He set up all Nights in Taverns, where he was the Wit and Genius of the Company; travelled and intrigued with Women of all Nations and Languages; made a Figure at the Gaming-Tables, and was not silent in Parliament. In short, whatever Character he undertook to appear in, he supported it always with a Spirit and Vivacity peculiar to himself. His Health of course received many Shocks from his dissolute Course of Life, but he trusted to the Vigour of a good Constitution, and despised all the distant Consequences of Pleasure, as the dull Apprehensions of Cowards in Luxury. As to Marriage, he resolved never more to wear the Fetters of that Slavery, while his Passions had so free a Range in a way more agreeable to his Inclinations: But having a long while solicited a fine Woman of but slender Fortune to comply with his Desires, and finding her deaf to any but honourable Offers, he was drawn in before he was aware, and married a second time with no other view than to have the present Possession of a Mistress. Yet he discharged the matrimonial Duties for a time with tolerable Decency, and contrived to keep his Amours as secret from his Wife as possible. But the Eyes of Jealousy could not long be deceived; and the Moment she began to expostulate with him on his Behaviour, he grew more bare-faced in his Pleasures, and less careful to conceal them from her Observation. The Lady, disappointed in her Views of Happiness, had Recourse to the common Consolation of Female Sorrows, and tried to drown them in Citron Waters;[1] which pernicious Custom grew upon her so much by Habit and Indulgence, that she often came down exceedingly disordered to Dinner, and sometimes was disqualified from performing the Offices of her Table. This extremely piqued the Pride of her Husband, who could not bear to see the Mistress of his Family in such disgraceful Circumstances, and began to wish her fairly in the other World. Enquiring how she came supplied with these cordial Draughts of Sorrow, he found they were secretly conveyed to her by her Mantua-maker,[2] who attended her three or four times a Week, pretending to bring Caps and Gowns. This again piqued his Pride, to think she should expose her foible to the Knowledge of her Inferiors, and resolving to supply her Wishes at an easier Rate, he ordered his Butler to carry up a certain Number of Bottles every Week into her Dressing-Room. The Stratagem took Effect; and the good Lady having frequent Recourse to the fatal Opiate, in a short time bade adieu to the World and its Cares.

He was now again left to the unrestrained Indulgence of his Pleasures, and had Mistresses of all Characters, from the Woman of Quality down to the Farmer's Daughter and Milk-maid. But as he advanced in Years, a Fit of Dotage insensibly stole upon him; and in an unlucky Moment he married a vain spirited young Girl of twenty, who seemed born to punish him for his Sins. Full of herself and Family, she took Possession of his House with a certain conscious Authority, and began to shew the Pleasure she found in Government and Sway. She regarded her Husband only as an Object that was to give her Command of Servants, Equipage, and the like; and her Head was giddy with Notions of domineering and Power. Her Insolence soon became intolerable to a young Lady of the Family, Daughter of his

---

1   An alcoholic drink or "cordial" flavored with lemon.
2   Dress-maker.

former Wife, who could not endure to be governed by a Mother of her own Age, and therefore with great Spirit left her Father's House. In short, the old Gentleman himself began to curse the Choice he had made, finding himself in a manner quite disregarded by his accomplished Spouse, whose Thoughts ran wholly after Drums, Assemblies, Operas, Masquerades, Ridottas, and the like; all which she pursued with the most ardent Assiduity, and seldom could find one quarter of an Hour's leisure to converse with her Husband. He found her besides, more cold in her Constitution, and less sensible of his Embraces, than he had imagined; for indeed, she was a Thing purely made up of Vanity, and provided she *made a Figure in Life*, she cared not who *enjoyed its Pleasure*. The old Gentleman groan'd severely under this Scourge of his Iniquities, and I question whether he would not have died himself of pure Spite, had not his obliging Wife saved him that Necessity, by kindly dying in his stead. She caught cold one Night in *Vauxhall* Gardens,[1] and after a short Illness of a Week or ten Days, retired to the peaceable Mansions of her Predecessors.

One would think he should now have been tired of Matrimonial Blessings; yet notwithstanding the Ill-luck he had hitherto met with, notwithstanding the natural Decay arising from his Age, and the acquired Infirmities of Intemperance, he was once more engaged in Courtship, and made one of the most gallant Admirers of *Aurora*.

She had many other Lovers, but I shall forbear the mention of them at present, to give a Description of one, who was every way worthy of her Affections, and to whom, in Reality, she had devoted her Heart. Neither *Count Tag*, nor the aged Gallant last described, had any Share in her Regard; for tho' she received them with Civility, she gave them little Encouragement to hope for Success.

The fortunate Lover was a young Nobleman, about her own Age, who conducted himself by Rules so very different from the Generality of the Nobility, that it will be a kind of Justice to his Memory to preserve his Character. He had an excellent Understanding, improved by competent Reading; and the most uncommon Uprightness of Heart, joined with the greatest Candour[2] and

---

1 One of London's popular pleasure gardens, where entrants were regaled with music and other entertainments.

2 In Coventry's time, "candour" meant "Sweetness of temper; purity of mind; openness; ingenuity; kindness" (Johnson).

Benevolence of Temper. His Soul was passionately devoted to the Love of Truth, and he never spoke or acted but with the clearest Simplicity and Ingenuity of Mind. Falshood of any Kind, even in the common Forms of Intercourse and Civility, wherein Custom licenses some Degrees of Dissimulation, he held to be a Crime; and if ever he made a Promise, there was not the least Room to doubt of his performing it. Tho' he frequently mixed in Parties of Diversion, made by other young Noblemen of his Acquaintance, yet he never joined in the Riots, that falsely challenge to themselves the Name of Pleasure, and superior Enjoyment of Life. He did not spend his Mornings in Levity, or his Nights at the Gaming-table. Nor was he ashamed of the Religion of his Country, or deterred from the Worship of his Maker, by the idle Sneers of Infidelity, and the ridiculous Laughter of profane Wits: but, on the contrary, gloried in the Profession of Christianity, and always reprimanded the wanton Sallies of those, who tried to be witty at the Expence of their Conscience. Added to these excellent Endowments, he had the greatest filial Obedience to his Father, the sincerest Loyalty to his Prince, the truest Respect for his Relations, and the most charitable Liberality to all those, whom Poverty, or Distress of any kind, recommended as Objects of Compassion. In short, whoever he has read Lord *Clarendon*'s celebrated Character of Lord Viscount *Falkland*,[1] cannot be at a Loss to form an Idea of this amiable young Nobleman; who resembled him exactly in the private social Duties of Life; and we may conclude, he would have acted the same Part in publick, had he been engaged in similar Circumstances.

Being inspired with a Passion for an agreeable Woman, he was neither ashamed to own it, nor yet did he use the ridiculous Elogiums, with which Coxcombs talk of their Mistresses, when their Imaginations are heated with Wine. He did not compare her to the *Venus of Medicis*[2] or run into any of those artificial Raptures, which are almost always counterfeited: But whenever he mentioned her Name,

---

1 Memorialized in *The History of the Rebellion and Civil Wars in England* (1671; published 1702) by Edward Hyde, Lord Clarendon (1609-74), Lucius Cary, Viscount Falkland (1610-43) died on the Royalist side fighting against the Parliamentarians in the Civil Wars.

2 The Roman statue called the Venus de Medicis (or more commonly Medici) was unearthed near Tivoli, Italy, around 1580 and was widely reputed in the eighteenth century to embody the ideal of female beauty.

he spoke of her always with a Manliness, that testified the Reality and Sincerity of his Passion. It was impossible for a Woman not to return the Affections of so deserving a Lover: *Aurora* was happy to be the Object of his Addresses, and met them with becoming Zeal.

CHAP. IV

THE CHARACTERS OF THE FOREGOING CHAPTER EXEMPLIFIED. AN IRREPARABLE MISFORTUNE BEFALLS OUR HERO.

THE two Sisters had lain longer abed than usual the Morning after their Arrival in Town, which was owing to the Fatigue of their Journey. They had but just finished their Breakfast by Twelve o'Clock; *Aurora* was then sitting down to her Harpsichord, and *Theodosia* reading Play-bills for the Evening; when the Door opened, and *Count Tag* was ushered by a Servant into the Room.

When the first Ceremonies were a little over, and the Count had expressed the *prodigious Satisfaction* he felt in seeing them returned to Town; he began to enquire what kind of Season they had had at *Bath*? "Why really," said *Theodosia*, "a very good one upon the whole; there were many agreeable People there, and all of them easy and sociable; which made our Time pass away cheerfully and pleasantly enough." "You amaze me," cries the Count; "Impossible, Madam! how can it be, Ladies!——I had Letters from Lord *Monkeyman*[1] and Lady *Betty Scornful*, assuring me, that, except yourselves, there were not three human Creatures in the Place. ——Let me see, I have Lady *Betty*'s Letter in my Pocket, I believe, at this Moment——Oh no, upon Recollection, I put it this Morning into my Cabinet, where I preserve all my Letters of Quality."

Aurora, smothering a Laugh as well as she could, said she was much obliged to Lord *Monkeyman* and Lady *Betty*, for vouchsafing to rank her and her Sister in the Catalogue of human Beings; "But surely," added she, "they must have been asleep both of them,

---

1 Changed to "Lord Marmazet" in the third edition.

when they wrote their Letters, for the *Bath* was extremely full." "Full!" cries the Count, interrupting her; "Oh, Madam, that is very possible, and yet there might be no Company——that is, none of us; No-body that one knows——for as to all the Tramontanes that come by the cross Post,[1] we never reckon them as any thing but Monsters in human Shape, that serve to fill up the Stage of Life, like Cyphers[2] in a Play. For Instance, you often see an awkward Girl, who has sewed a Tail to a Gown, and pinned two Lappets[3] to a Nightcap, come running headlong into the Rooms with a wild frosty Face, as if she was just come from feeding Poultry in her Father's Chicken-yard——Or you will see a Booby 'Squire,[4] with a Head resembling a Stone-ball over a Gate-post.——Now it would be the most ridiculous Thing in Life, to call such People Company. 'Tis the Want of Titles, and not the Want of Faces, that makes a Place empty; for if there is No-body one knows——if there are *none of us* in a Place, we esteem all the rest as Mob and Rabble."

[Here it was impossible for the two ladies any longer to contain their laughter. "Hold, hold, for heaven's sake," said *Theodosia*, interrupting him, "have a little mercy, *Count*, on us poor mortals who are born without titles, and don't banish us quite from all public places. Consider, sir, tho' you have been so happy as to acquire a title, all of us have not the same good fortune, and must we then be reckoned among the mob and rabble of life?"

"Oh, by no means," cries the *Count*, "you misunderstand me entirely——you are in the polite circle, ladies; we reckon you among the quality. Whoever belongs to the polite circle, is of the quality. I was only talking of the wretched figures, who know nobody, and are known of nobody; they are the mob and rabble I was speaking of.——You indeed! No, pardon me——but pray ladies, who was miss *Newcome*, this great beauty, that made such a figure among you at *Bath*? Was she ever in any of our drums and assemblies?"

"No, sir," replied *Theodosia*; "it was the first time of her appearing,

---

1   "Tramontanes" ("across the mountains") is a derisive Italian term for uncouth outsiders. Riding "cross post" meant coming from the opposite direction of London—that is, from the rural outposts of the west country or Wales.

2   Speechless extras on stage.

3   Streamers, here attached to a nightcap, in an attempt to approximate a proper head-dress.

4   An uncouth country gentleman.

I believe, in any public place; she came under the protection of lady *Marmazet*. She is a very agreeable girl, and really exceedingly pretty. I often conversed with her, and indeed she promises to make a very fine woman, if she does not play the fool, and throw her self away upon that odious, detestable *Griskin*."

"Ay, that *Griskin* too!" cries the *Count*, "who is that detestable *Griskin*? I think I am acquainted with all the families of any note in *England*, and yet in my days I never heard of Sir Jeremy *Griskin*."

"No, sir," said *Aurora*, with a smile, "'tis impossible you should know any such *English* family, for he gave out that he came from *Ireland*; and even there, I fancy, one should be pretty much puzzled to find it; for I am very apt to suspect that Mr. *Griskin* is nothing better than a notorious sharper. We had a report at *Bath*, that he was the son of a blind beggar. The truth of this indeed never came perfectly to light, but sure lady *Marmazet*, if she has any friendship for the girl, must be mad to encourage such a match."

"Absolutely distracted," cries the *Count*, "I can't imagine what she means by it; and indeed when she comes to town, I shall railly her ladyship for having such a beauty in *petto*,[1] without letting me know any thing of the matter."]

While this imaginary Man of Quality was thus settling the Orders and Ranks of Life, the Door opened a second Time, and a Servant introduced the amorous old Gentleman, whose Character was drawn in the foregoing Chapter. The Ceremonies that ensued on his Appearance interrupted the Count's Harangue, and fortunately gave the Conversation another Turn, before the pretty Gentleman had Time to finish his ingenious Dissertation on polite Company.

Our aged Gallant, putting on an unusual Air of Gaiety, and bustling himself up, as if his Soul intended to walk out of his Body, approached the two Ladies, and saluted them both——then sitting down, and addressing himself to *Aurora*, told her, he should for ever afterwards think the better of the *Bath* Waters, for sending her back with such a charming Bloom in her Complexion. "Madam," added he, "you out-do your usual Outdoings: I protest you look more divinely than ever; and not contented with excelling all other People, I see you have taken a Resolution at last, to excell yourself."

1　An Italianism, meaning "in secret."

"Sir," said *Aurora* laughing, "there is no Possibility of making any Reply to such extravagant Compliments.——But I thought, Sir, you intended us the Favour of your Company at *Bath* this Season." "Yes, Madam," answered he, "I did so, but my d—mn'd ignorant Physicians would banish me to *Scarborough*,[1] tho' I knew it was impossible for me to have my Health in any Place, at such a Distance from your Ladyship. I protest," added he, "you inspire me with a Youthfulness, which I have not felt this Half-year in your Absence."

While this superannuated Man of Gallantry was thus affecting the Raptures and Fire of Youth, the Door opened a third Time, and the young Lord appeared, whose Character concluded the preceding Chapter. He approached the Ladies with a respectful Bow, and enquired tenderly concerning their Health, but addressed himself rather in a more peculiar manner to *Aurora*. Her Face immediately changed in his entering the Room, and a certain Air of affectionate Languor, took Possession of her Features, which before were a little expressive of Scorn and Ridicule: in short, she received him with something more than Complaisance, and a Tone of Voice only calculated to convey the Sentiments of Love. The Conversation that ensued between them was easy, natural, and unaffected; and tho' sometimes his Lordship's Eyes would stray involuntarily to *Aurora*, yet he strove to direct his Discourse indifferently to the two Sisters, and likewise to the other Gentlemen that were present: For the Delicacy of his Passion was unwilling to reveal itself in a mixed Company. So very differently did these three Lovers express their Affection.

[But as the delicacy of *Aurora*'s passion chose to reveal itself as little as possible before witnesses, she soon recovered the gaiety of her features, and addressing herself with a smile to her beloved peer, "my lord," said she, "you are come in excellent time——the *Count* is entertaining us here with a very ingenious lecture on what is we are to call the *world*."

Count *Tag* was no stranger to his lordship, who perfectly knew, and heartily despised him for his foppery and affectation. Yet he was obliged now and then to submit to a visit from him; for being in possession of a title, the *Count*, who *haunted* all people of quality,

---

1   A minor spa town in the north of England, and a considerable journey from London.

would obtrude himself on his acquaintance contrary to his inclination; and good manners, as well as the natural candour of his temper, restrained him from expressing his detestation in too explicit terms. He had however no great desire at present to hear him upon such a topic, where his impertinence would have so great a scope, and therefore endeavoured to turn the conversation to some other subject: but the *Count*, whose eyes sparkled (as they always did) on the appearance of a man of quality, no sooner saw him seated in his chair, than he fastened immediately upon him, and began to appeal to his lordship for a confirmation of his sentiments. "My lord," said he, "I was endeavouring to convince the ladies, that if there is *no-body one knows, none of us*, in a public place, all the rest are to be considered in the light of porters and oyster-women. I dare say your lordship is of the same opinion."

"Indeed, sir, but I am not," replied his lordship, "and therefore I must desire you would not draw me into a participation of any such sentiments. The language of *people one knows*, and people *one does not know*, is what I very often hear in the world; but it seems to me the most contemptible jargon that ever was invented. Indeed for my own part, I don't understand it, and therefore I confess I am not qualified to talk about it. Who pray are we to call the *people one knows*?"

"*O mon dieu!*" cries the *Count*, "your lordship surely can't ask such a question. The people one knows, my lord, are the people who are in the round of assemblies and public diversions, people who have the *scavoir vivre*, the *ton de bonne compaigne*,[1] as the *French* call it——in short, people who frize[2] their hair in the newest fashion, and have their cloaths made at *Paris*."

"And are these the only people worth one's regard in life?" said his lordship.

"Absolutely, my lord!" cries the *Count*, "I have no manner of idea or conception of any body else."

"Then I am most heartily sorry for you," cries his lordship. "I can readily allow that people of quality must in general live with one another; the customs of the world in good measure require it; but surely our station gives us no right to behave with insolence to people

1 French: the knowledge of how to live and the air of good company.
2 Curl.

below us, because they have not their cloaths from *Paris*, or do not *frize* their hair in the newest fashion. And I am sure if people of quality have no such right, it much less becomes the fops and coxcombs in fashion, who are but the retainers of people of quality, who are themselves only in public by permission, and can pretend to no merit, but what they derive from an acquaintance with their betters. This surely is the most contemptible of all modern follies. For instance, because a man is permitted to whisper nonsense in lady *Betty*'s or lady *Mary*'s ear, in the side-box at a play-house, shall he therefore fancy himself privileged to behave with impertinence to people infinitely his superiors in merit, who perhaps have not thought it worth their while to *riggle*¹ themselves into a great acquaintance?——What say you, madam," added he, addressing himself to *Theodosia*.

"Your observation," she replied, "is exceedingly just, my lord! but why do you confine it to your own sex? pray let ours come in for a share of the satire——For my part, I could name a great many trumpery insignificant girls about town, who having *riggled* themselves, as you say, into a polite acquaintance, give themselves ten times more airs, and are fifty thousand times more conceited, than the people to whose company they owe their pride. I have one now in my thoughts, who is throughout a composition of vanity and folly, and has been for several years the public jest and ridicule of the town for her behaviour."

All this while the *Count* sat in some confusion. For tho' he had a wonderful talent, as indeed most people have, at warding off scandal from himself, and applying the satire he met with to his neighbours, he was here so plainly described, that it was hardly possible for him to be mistaken. *Aurora* saw this, and resolving to compleat his confusion, "*Count*," said she, "I have had it in my head this many a day to ask you a question——will you be so obliging as to tell me how you came by your title?" "O pardon me, I have no title, madam," cries the *Count*——"mere *badinage*² and ridicule, a nick-name given to me by some of my friends, that's all——but another time for that. At present I am obliged to call upon my lord

---

1 "Riggle" is italicized because the young lord is derisively using the term in the new and fashionable sense that subsequently became its usual meaning in modern English. In his *Dictionary*, Samuel Johnson defined "riggle" (or "wriggle") in its older sense: "To move backward and forward, as shrinking from pain."

2 Raillery.

Monkeyman, who desires my opinion of some pictures he is going to buy, after which I shall look in upon *Betty Vincent*, whom I positively have not seen for these three days." Here he rose up, and made all the haste he could away, being exceedingly glad to escape the persecution, which he saw was preparing for him.]

Little *Pompey* was witness of many of these Interviews, and began to think himself happily situated for Life. He was a great Favourite with *Aurora*, who caressed him with the fondest Tenderness, and permitted him to sleep every Night in a Chair by her Bed-side. When she awoke in a Morning, she would embrace him with an Ardour superior to his Deserts, and which the happiest Lover might have envied: Our Hero's Vanity, perhaps, made him fancy himself the genuine Object of these Caresses, but, in Reality, he was only the Representative of a much nobler Object. In this manner he lived with his new Mistress the greatest Part of a Winter, and might have still continued in the same happy Situation, if he had not ruined himself by his own Imprudence, and defeated his own Happiness by an unguarded Act of Folly.

Aurora had been dancing one Night at a Ridotta with her beloved Peer, and retired home late to her Lodgings, with Vivacity in her Looks, and Transport in her Thoughts, which Love and Pleasure always inspire. Animated with delightful Presages of future Happiness, she sat herself down in a Chair, to recollect the Conversation that had passed between them. After this, she went to-bed and abandoned herself to the purest Slumbers. She slept longer than usual the next Morning, and it seemed as if some golden Dream was pictured in her Fancy; for her Cheek glowed with unusual Beauty, and her Voice spontaneously pronounced, *My Lord, I am wholly yours.*——While her Imagination was presenting her with these delicious Ideas, little *Pompey*, who heard the Sound, and thought she over-slept herself, leaped eagerly upon the Bed, and waked her with his Barking. She darted a most enraged Look at him for interrupting her Dream, and could never be prevailed upon to see him afterwards; but disposed of him the next Morning to her Milliner,[1] who attended her with a new Head-dress.

---

1   "A seller of fancy wares, accessories, and articles of (female) apparel, esp. such as were originally made in Milan" (*OED*).

Thus was he again removed to new Lodgings, and condemned to future Adventures.

CHAP. V

RELATING THE HISTORY OF A MILLINER.

THE fair Princess of Lace and Ribbands, who took Possession of our Hero, had gone thro' a great Variety of Fortunes before she fell into her present Way of Life; some of which perhaps may be worth relating. She was originally Daughter of a Country Gentleman, who had lived, as it is called, *up to his Income*; by which Means he obtained the Character of a generous hospitable Man in his Neighbourhood, and died without making the least Provision for his Family. His Widow soon afterwards married a wealthy Lawyer in a large Market town, who like a great Vulture prey'd at large over the Country, and suffered no other Attorney to thrive within the Regions of his Plunder. The Gentlemen round-about made him Court-keeper-general of their Estates; and the poor People flocked to him with a kind of superstitious Opinion, that he could model the Laws according to his Pleasure. The Mayor and Aldermen too resorted to him for Advice in all dubious Cases, and he was a kind of petty Viceroy in the Town where he lived. Success had made him insolent and overbearing, and when he flaunted thro' the Streets on a Market-day in his Night-gown,[1] he looked prouder than a Grandee of *Spain*.

The young Lady, who was now to class him Father-in-Law, was not at all pleased with her new Situation, thinking herself much degraded by her Mother's Marriage. When therefore the Wives and Daughters of the Town came to visit her in their best Gowns, she received them very coldly, disdained to be present at any of their public Tea-drinkings, and always affected to confound their Names. She was as little pleased with the Company of her new Father, and excepting the small Time spent at Meals, used to lock

---

1 "A loose gown usually worn over nightclothes; a loose informal robe worn by men" (*OED*). The attorney is imitating a mode of negligent behavior suitable to princes.

herself up all the rest of the Day in a little Closet, to read *Cowley's* Poems, and the History of *Pamela Andrews.*[1] *Gripe* the Attorney soon observed and resented this Behaviour; and her Mother too, thinking it a Reflexion on the Choice she had made, began to take her roundly to Task about it. She told her, she wondered what she meant by giving herself such Airs, for she had no Fortune to support them: "And pray, Madam," said she, "what is your Birth, that you are so proud of, without Money?" To this the young Lady answer'd, "that if some People could demean themselves, she saw no Reason why other People should be obliged to do the same; and for her Part, she found no Charms in the Company of Tradesmen and stinking Shop-keepers." Many Altercations of this kind happened between them, till at length her Mother fairly told her, that if she disliked her present Condition, she might e'en seek for a better wherever she could. It was not long before she followed this Advice, and married a young Officer, who was quartered in the Town, without consulting any body's Inclinations but her own. This was a fair Pretence for her Parents to get rid of her; they complained loudly of her Disobedience in not asking their Advice, represented her as a forward Hussy, and renounced all Correspondence with her for the future. The young Officer swaggered a little at first, talked much of his Honour, and threatened to cane her Father-in-law; but finding the Attorney despise his Menaces, he prudently suffered his Anger to cool, and proceded no farther than Words.

The Regiment, to which this Gentleman belonged, was soon afterwards ordered into *Flanders*; and as the young Couple were then in the Honey-moon of their Love, the Bride prevailed to make a Campaign with her Husband. He consented, and fixed her in Lodgings at *Brussels*; near to which City the Army was at that Time quartered. There she had Leisure to observe the Lace Manufacture, and learnt the first Rudiments of Millinery, which afterwards became her Profession. In a little Time the News of a Battle arrived, and with it a Piece of News more terrible to the Ears of a young Bride, that her

---

1 Some eighteenth-century moralists condemned the poems of Abraham Cowley (1618-67) as lascivious, particularly *The Mistress* (1647), though Samuel Johnson dismissed this concern as ridiculous. Complaints against the novel *Pamela* (1740-41), by Fielding's bitter rival Samuel Richardson (1689-1761), concerned its evocative descriptions of sexual desire and its alleged promotion of social ambition in the lower-ranks.

Husband was among the number slain. This broke all her Measures and Hopes of Life, and she was obliged to return into *England*, with scarce Money enough to pay for her Voyage, or maintain her on the Road. On her Arrival she began to consider, whether she should not proceed to her Mother, and endeavour to obtain a Reconciliation; but Pride soon banished that Thought; her high Spirit would not suffer her to sue for Pardon, and she resolved, as a better Expedient, to go to Service. Accordingly, she procured herself the Office of a Waiting-Gentlewoman, in an agreeable Family, but unluckily there was no Table for upper Servants, and her Pride could not endure to sit down to Dinner with Menials. Preferably to this she would dine upon a Plate of cold Victuals in her Bed-chamber; thus gratifying her Vanity at the Expence of her Appetite.

From this Place she removed to another more agreeable to her Wishes, where there was a separate Apartment, for higher Servants, and her own Dominion was pretty considerable. In this Family all was Pleasure. The Lady of it having a Husband she despised, filled his House with eternal Parties of Company, studied to be expensive, and seemed resolved to see the End of his Estate before she died, without regarding what became of her Children after her Death. The Husband himself was almost an Idiot, and could hardly be said to live, for he spent his Days chiefly in dozing, and constantly fell asleep in his Chair after Dinner. His Wife treated him always with the highest Superiority, would sometimes spit in his Face, sometimes fling his Wig into the Fire, and never scrupled calling him Fool and Block-head before all Companies. This would now and then provoke him to mutter a surly Oath or two, but he had not Spirit or Courage to resent it in a proper manner. For her Part, she gave herself up to all the Luxuries of Life, and her House was a general Rendezvous of Pleasure, while her slumbering Spouse was considered both by herself and Servants as nothing better than a Cypher.

Our Milliner having lived a few Years in this Family, in which Time she saved some Money, resolved now to execute a Project she had long been forming. She had always been a great Reader of Plays, Novels, Romances, and the like; and when she saw Tragedy-Queens sweeping the Stage with their Trains at the Play-house, her Imagination would be fired with Envy at the Sight: She longed to sit in a flowered Elbow-chair, surrounded with Guards and Attendants; and was quite wild to give herself Airs of High-life in the superior Parts of a Comedy. With these Hopes she offered herself to the Stage, and was received by the Managers of *Drury-Lane*: But her Genius did not make so quick a Progress as she imagined; her Ambition every Day was mortified with Refusals; and tho' she desired only to play the Part of Lady *Townly*,[1] as a Specimen at first, the ignorant Managers could not be brought to comply with her Sollicitations. In short, she trod the Stage near two Years without once wearing a Crown, or wielding a Scepter: The Parts alloted to her, were always of the most trifling kind, and she had little else to do, than to appear on the Stage as a Mute, to make up the Retinue of a Princess, or sympathize in Silence with the Sorrows of a dying Heroine, by applying a white Handkerchief to her Eyes.

But tho' she could not make a Fortune by her Genius, her Beauty was more successful, and she had the Luck to make a Conquest of one of those pretty Gentlemen, who appear in laced Frocks behind the Scenes, or more properly on the middle of the Stage. He attended her in the Green-Room[2] every Evening, and at last made her the Offer of a Settlement, if she could be contented to sacrifice her Ambition to Love.[3] She was at first a little unwilling to leave the Theatre, where she foresaw such Advantages from her Genius; but thinking her Merit not enough regarded, and despairing of better Treatment (for she had not yet been permitted to play Lady *Townly*) she resigned herself to the Proposals of her Gallant, and set out with him immediately for the Country. There they lived in Solitude and Retirement for a Year, and probably might have done longer, had not Death spitefully interrupted their Amour, and snatched away the fond Keeper from the Arms of his theatrical Mistress. In his Will she found herself rewarded for her Constancy with a Legacy of seventy Pounds *per Annum*; with which she returned to *London*, and set up a Milliner's Shop. She had a good Fancy at new Fashions, and soon recommended herself to the Notice of People of Quality;

---

1   A witty, fashionable character in Sir John Vanbrugh's unfinished *The Provoked Husband*, which was completed and made popular by Colley Cibber in 1728.

2   "A room in a theatre provided for the accommodation of actors and actresses when not required on the stage, probably so called because it was originally painted green." (*OED*)

3   I.e., he expects her to sacrifice her stage ambitions for marriage. A "settlement" is a contractual financial arrangement upon marriage.

by which means in time she became a Milliner of Vogue, and had the Art to raise a considerable Fortune from Lace and Ribbands. The best Part of her House she let out for Lodgings, reserving to herself only a Shop, a Kitchen, and a little Parlour, which at Night served for a Bed-chamber.

Such was *Pompey*'s present Mistress, who now lived in great Ease and Comfort, after a Life of much Vexation and Disappointment.

CHAP. VI

ANOTHER CHAPTER OF CHARACTERS.

[THREE or four days after he was settled in these apartments, as he was frisking and sporting one morning about the shop, a young lady, who lodged in the house, came down stairs, and accosted his mistress in the following terms: "I want to see some ribbands if you please, madam, to match my blue gown; for lady *Bab Frightful* is to call upon mamma this evening, to carry us to the play, to see *Othellor whore of Venus*, which they say is one of the finest plays that ever was acted." "Yes really, mem, 'tis a very engaging play to be sure," replied the milliner; "indeed I think it one of the master-pieces of the *English* stage———but you mistake a little, I fancy miss, in the naming of it, for *Shakespear* I believe wrote it *Othello* moor of *Venice*. *Venice*, mem, is a famous town or city somewhere or other, where *Othello* runs away with a rich heiress in the night-time, and marries her privately at the fleet. By very odd luck he was created lord high-admiral that very night, and goes out to fight the *Turks*, and takes his wife along with him to the wars; and there, mem, he grows jealous of her, only because she happens to have lost a handkerchief, which he gave her when he came a courting to her. It was a muslin handkerchief, mem, spotted with strawberries; and because she can't find it, he beats her in the most unmerciful manner, and last smothers her between two feather-beds." "Does he indeed?" cries the young lady; "well, I hate a jealous man of all things in nature; a jealous man is my particular aversion———but however, no matter what the play is, you know, ma'am, so we do but see it; for the pleasure of a play is to shew one's self in the boxes, and see the company, and all that——Yes, ma'am, this here is the sort of ribbands I want, only if you please let me see some of a paler blue."

While the milliner was taking down some fresh ban-boxes, the young lady turning round, happened to spy *Pompey* in a corner of the shop. "O heavens!" cries she, as soon as she cast her eyes upon him, "what a delightful little dog is there! Pray, dear Mrs. *Pincushion*, do tell me how long you have been in possession of that charming little beauty?" Mrs. *Pincushion* replied that he had been in her possession about a week, and was given her by a lady of celebrated beauty, whom she had the honour of serving. "Well, if I am not amazed to think how she could part with him!" cries the young lady ——"Sure, ma'am, she must be a woman of no manner of taste in the world, for I never saw any thing so charmingly handsome since the hour I was born. Pray, dear Mrs. *Pincushion*, what is his name?"

Being informed that he was called *Pompey*,[1] she snatched him up in her arms, kissed him with great transport, and poured forth the following torrent of nonsense upon him: "O you sweet little *Pompey*! you most delightful little *Pompey*! you dear heavenly jewel! you most charming little perroquet![2] I will kiss you, you little beauty! I will——I will——I'll kiss you, and hug you, and kiss you to death." Then turning again to the milliner, "dear Mrs. *Pincushion*," added she, "you must give me leave to carry him up stairs, to shew him to papa and mamma, for in all my days I never beheld so divine a creature." Being now served with her blue ribbands, and having received the milliner's consent to her request, she flew up stairs in all imaginable haste, with the dog in her arms: but before we relate the reception she met with, let us prepare the reader with a short description of her parents.

Sir *Thomas Frippery*,[3] the father of this young lady,] formerly enjoyed a little Post in Queen *Anne*'s Court, which entituled him to a Knighthood in Consequence of his Office, tho' the Salary of it was

---

1   Coventry has evidently overlooked the fact that Pompey's name could not possibly have passed down since he was discovered in St. James's Park. On the other hand, "Pompey" was a common name for a dog.

2   Parrot.

3   While "frippery" is now usually understood as meaning "Finery in dress, *esp.* tawdry finery" (*OED*), Johnson's definition is helpful: "Old cloaths; cast dresses; tattered rags." Sir Thomas Frippery, a "cast-off" man, is dressed in the clothes of a former era.

inconsiderable, and his own Family-Estate very small. At the Death of the Queen he lost his Employment, and was obliged to retire into the Country; where he gave himself the Airs of a Minister of State, and amused his Country-Neighbours with such Stories of Courts and Intrigues of Government, that he was esteemed an Oracle of Politicks, and many of them were weak enough to believe from his Discourse, that he had constituted a kind of Triumvirate with Lord *Oxford* and Lord *B.* in the Management of public Affairs.[1] The same ridiculous Vanity pursued him thro' every Article of his Life, and tho' his Estate was known hardly to amount to Three hundred Pounds a Year, he laboured to persuade People, that it exceeded as many Thousands. For this Purpose, whatever he was obliged to do out of Frugality, he was sure to put off with a Pretence of Taste; and always mask'd his Œconomy under some pretended Reason very remote from the Truth. For Instance, when he laid down his Coach, he boasted every where how much better it was to hire Job-horses, as Occasion required, than to run the hazard of Accidents by keeping them——that Coachmen were such villainous Rascals, it was impossible to put any Confidence in them——that going into dirty Stables to overlook their Management, and treading up to one's Knees in Horse-dung was extremely disagreeable to People of Fashion——and therefore for his Part, he had laid down his Coach, to avoid the Trouble and Anxiety of keeping Horses.

When his Country Neighbours dined with him, whose Igno-rance he thought he could impose on, he would give them Alder-Wine, and swear it was Hermitage,[2] called a Gammon of Bacon a *Bayonne* Ham, and the commonest home-made Cheese he put off for the best *Parmasan* that ever came into *England*, which he said had been sent him by a young Nobleman of his Acquaintance then on his Travels.

About once in three Years he brought his Wife and Family to Town, which served for Matter of Conversation to them during the two intermediate Years, that were spent in the Country; and

---

1 Robert Harley, Lord Oxford (1678-1724) and Henry St. John, Lord Bolingbroke (1678-1751), formed the mainstay of the Tory ministry of Queen Anne (reigned 1702-14). Bolingbroke's name was eliminated from the third edition, perhaps because of posthumous revelations that he was anti-Christian.
2 A fine French wine from the Rhone Valley region.

they looked forward to the *Annus mirabilis*[1] or Winter of Pleasure, with as much Rapture and Expectation, as some Christians do their *Millennium*.[2]

During the Time of his Continuance in *London*, Sir *Thomas* every Morning attended the Levees of Ministers, to beg Restitution of his old Place, or an Appointment to a new one; which he said he would receive with the humblest Acknowledgments, and discharge in any manner they should please to prescribe. Yet whether it was that his Majesty's Ministers were insensible of his Merits, or could find no Place suitable to his Abilities, the unhappy Knight profited little by his Court-Attendance, and might as well have saved himself the Expence of a triennial Journey to *London*.

But tho' these Expeditions did not encrease his Fortune, they added much to his Vanity, and he returned into the Country new-laden with Stories to amuse his Country Neighbours. He talked with the greatest Familiarity of *his old Friend my good Lord*____, and related Conversations that passed at the Duke of ____'s Table, with as much Circumstance and Particularity as if he had been present at them.

The last Article of Vanity we shall mention, were his Cloaths, which gives the finishing Stroke to his Character: For he chose rather to wear the Rags of old Finery, which had been made up in the Reign of Queen *Anne*, than to submit to plain Cloaths of a modern make and Fashion. He fancied the poor People in his Neighbourhood were to be awed with the Sight of tarnished Lace, and the Gold-Fringe fell from his Person so plentifully, that you might at any Time trace his Foot-steps by the Relicks of Finery he left behind him.

Lady *Frippery*, his accomplished Spouse, did not fall short of her Husband in any of these Perfections, but rather improved them with some new Graces of her own; for having been something of a Beauty in her Youth, she now retained all the scornful Airs and languishing Disdain, which she had formerly practised to her dying Lovers.

They had one only Daughter, who having been educated all her Life at Home under her Parents, was now become a Master-piece

---

1 Latin: year of miracles.
2 A thousand year period that, according to some sects, would mark the end of the world and the salvation of true believers in the New Jerusalem.

of Folly, Vanity and Impertinence. She had not one Gesture or Motion that was natural; her Mouth never opened without some ridiculous Grimace; her Voice had learnt a Tone and Accent foreign to itself; her Eyes squinted with endeavouring to look alluring, and all her Limbs were distorted with Affectation. Her Conversation turned always upon Politeness, and she fancied herself so very beautiful, well-bred, genteel and engaging, that it was impossible for a Man to look upon her without Admiration.

It happened now to be the *London*-Winter with this amiable Family, and they were crowded into scanty Lodgings on a first Floor, consisting only of a Dining-room, a Bed-chamber, and a Closet; for they could not afford to take any other Part of the House to enlarge their Apartments. The Dining-room was set apart for the Reception of Company; Sir *Thomas* and my Lady took Possession of the Bed-chamber; and Miss slept in a little Tent-bed, occasionally stufft into the Closet.

[There is nothing more droll and diverting than the morning dresses of people, who being exceedingly poor, and yet exceedingly proud, affect to make a great figure with a very little fortune. The expence they are at abroad obliges them to double their frugality at home; and as their chief happiness consists in displaying themselves to the eye of the world, consequently when they are out of its eye, nothing is too dirty or too ragged for them to wear. Now as nobody ever had the vanity of appearance more than the family we have been describing, it will easily be believed, that in their own private apartments, behind the scenes of the world, they did not appear to the greatest advantage. And indeed there was something so singularly odd in their dress and employments, at the moment our hero was presented to them, that we cannot help endeavouring to set their image before the reader.

Sir *Thomas* was shaving himself before a looking-glass in his bed-chamber, habited in the rags of an old night-gown, which about thirty years before had been red damask. All his face, and more than half his head were covered with soap-suds; only on his crown hung a flimsy green silk night-cap, made in the shape of a sugar-loaf. He had on a very dirty night-shirt, richly tinctured with perspiration, for he had slept in it a fortnight; and over this, a much dirtier ribb'd dimitty wastecoat, which had not visited the wash-tub for a whole twelve-month past. To finish his picture, he wore on his feet a pair of darned blue satten slippers, made out of the remnants of one of his wife's old petticoats.

So much for Sir *Thomas*. Close by him sat his lady, combing her hoary locks before the same looking-glass, and drest in a short bed-gown, which hardly reached down to her middle. A night-shift, which likewise had almost forgot the washing-tub, shrouded the hidden beauties of her person. She was without stays,[1] without a hoop, without ruffles, and without any linen about her neck, to hide those redundant charms, which age had a little embrowned.

This was their dress and attitude, when their daughter burst into the room, and earnestly called upon them to admire the beauties of a lap-dog. Her sudden entrance alarming them with the expectation of some mighty matter, Sir *Thomas* in turning himself hastily around, had the misfortune to cut himself with his razor; which put him in a passion, when he came to know the ridiculous occasion of all this hurry. "Pox take the girl," cries he, "get away child, and don't inter-rupt me with your lapdogs. I am in a hurry here to go to court this morning, and you take up my time with silly tittle-tattle about a lap-dog. Do you see here, foolish girl? you have made me cut myself with your ridiculous nonsense——Get away I tell you——what figure do you think I shall make at the levees with such a scar upon my face?"

"Bless me, papa!" cries the young lady, "I protest I am vastly sorry for your misfortune, but I'm sure you'll forgive, if you will but look on this delightful heavenly little jewel of a dog."

"D—mn your little jewel of a dog," replies the knight; "prythee stand out of my way——I tell you I am in a hurry to go to court, and therefore prythee don't trouble me with your whelps and your puppy-dogs."

"O monstrous! how can you call him such cruel names?" cries the daughter. "I am amazed at you, papa, for your *want of taste*. How can any living creature be so utterly void of *taste*, as not to admire such a beautiful little monkey? do, dear mamma! look at him——I am sure you must admire him, tho' papa is so shamefully blind, and so utterly void of all manner of taste."

---

1 "A laced underbodice, stiffened by the insertion of strips of whale-bone (sometimes of metal or wood) worn by women (sometimes by men) to give shape and support to the figure" (*OED*).

"Why sure, my dear, you are mad to-day," replied the mother, "one would think you was absolutely fuddled this morning. Taste, indeed! I declare you are void of all manner of understanding, whatever your taste may be, to interrupt us thus, when you see we are both in a hurry to be drest. Prythee, girl! learn a little decency and good manners, before you pretend to talk of taste."

The young girl being reprimanded thus on both sides, began to look extremely foolish, when a servant entered to inform them that Mr. *Chace* was in the dining-room. "Ay, ay, go," cries Sir *Thomas*, "go and entertain him with your taste, till I am able to wait on him; tell Mr. *Chace* I happen unfortunately to be dressing, but I'll be with him in a moment of time."

Miss *Frippery* then, muttering some little scorn, hurried into the next room with the dog in her arms, to see if she could not persuade her lover, (for so he was) to discover more taste than her parents. And here indeed she had better success; for this gentleman, who was a great sportsman and fox-hunter, was consequently a great connoisseur in dogs; he was likewise what is called a *very pretty fellow about town*, and had a taste so exactly correspondent with that of the lady, that it is no wonder they agreed in the same objects of admiration. Here follows his character.]

This young Gentleman, usually called *Jack Chace* among his Intimates, possessed an Estate of Fifteen hundred Pounds a Year; which was just sufficient to furnish him with a variety of Riding-frocks, *Khevenhullar* Hats,[1] Jockey-boots, and Coach-whips. His great Ambition was to be deemed a *jemmy Fellow*; which Term perhaps some of my Readers may not understand, and therefore we must explain it by Circumstances. He always appeared in the Morning in a *Newmarket* frock, decorated with a great Number of red, green or blue Capes; he wore a short Bob Wig, neat Buckskin Breeches, white Silk Stockings, and carried a Cane-Switch in his Hand. He kept a high Phaeton Chaise,[2] and four *Bay Cattle*;[3] a Stable of Hunters,[4] and a Pack of Hounds in the Country. The

---

1   A fashionable style of hat named after the sixteenth-century Austrian aristocrat Georg Khevenhüller.

2   A light, fast two-seated carriage.

3   I.e., horses, "cattle" being the fashionable equestrian term.

4   Hunting dogs.

Reputation of driving a Set of Horses with Skill, he esteemed the greatest Character in human Life, and thought himself seated on the very Pinnacle of Glory, when he was mounted on a Coach-box at a Horse-race. He was one of the most active Spirits at *Newmarket*, and always boasted as a most singular Accomplishment, *that he did not ride above eight Stone and a Half.*[1] Tho' a little Man, and not very healthy in his Constitution, he desired to be thought capable of going through any Fatigue, and was continually laying Wagers of the Journeys he could perform in a Day. He had likewise an Ambition to be thought a Man of consummate Debauch, and endeavoured to perswade you, that he never went to Bed without first drinking Half a dozen Bottles of Claret, laying with as many Whores, and knocking down as many Watchmen. In the Mornings he attended Mr. *Broughton*'s Amphitheatre,[2] and in the Evenings, if he was drunk in Time (which indeed he seldom failed to be) he came behind the Scenes of the Play-house in the middle of the third Act, and there heroically exposed himself to the Hisses of the Gallery.[3] Whenever he met you, he constantly began with describing his last Night's Debauch, or related the arrival of a new Wh——re upon the Town, or entertained you with the Exploits of his Bay Cattle; and if you declined conversing with him on these illustrious Subjects, he swore you was a Fellow of no Soul or Genius, and for ever afterwards shunned your Company.

By living in the same House this *jemmy young Gentleman* had got acquainted with Sir *Thomas*'s Family, and seemed to be commencing a Courtship with the Daughter; which her Parents encouraged from a knowledge of his Estate. Sir *Thomas* indeed could have wished for a Son-in-Law more after his own Heart, having no great Idea of Horsemanship and the Heroes of *Newmarket*; but on the other hand, he thought it imprudent to let his Daughter slip so advantageous a Match, and therefore studied to promote it by all the Stratagems, which Parents think it lawful to practice in the disposal of their Daughters; for it must be confessed, this sage Knight had a very laudable Regard for Mr. *Chace*'s Estate.

---

1 I.e., he never weighed above eight and a half stone (112 pounds or 54 kilograms) when he rode his horse. Coventry's subsequent comment effectively deflates this boast.

2 A boxing venue set up by John Broughton (1705-89).

3 I.e., he wandered boldly onto the stage.

CHAP. VII

A SAD DISASTER BEFALLS SIR THOMAS FRIPPERY IN THE NIGHT, AND A WORSE IN THE DAY.

AND now that we have drawn the Characters of so many People, let us look a little into their Actions; for Characters alone afford a very barren Entertainment to the Reader.

Our Hero was grown a great Favourite with the Milliner, who presented him with a laced Ruff,[1] made in the newest Fashion, worn by Women of Quality, and suffered him to play about the Shop, where he was taken Notice of by all the Ladies, who came to traffic in Fans and Lace, and was often stroked by the fairest Hands in *London*. In Requital for these Favours, he one Night preserved the Honour of his Mistress from the Attacks of a desperate Ravisher, who came with a Design of Invading her Bed.

The ancient Knight, described in the last Chapter, had, in his Youth, been a Man of some Amour, and still retained a certain liquorish Inclination, tho' he was narrowly watched by the Jealousy of his Wife. From the Time of his last Arrival in Town, he had cast the languishing Eyes of Adoration on the fair Milliner with whom he lodged, and had been projecting many Stratagems to accomplish his Desires. He used frequently to call in at the Shop, whenever he found the Coast clear, under Pretence of buying little Presents for his Wife or Daughter, and there indulged himself in certain amorous Freedoms, such as Kisses, and the like, which would provoke her to cry out, *Pray Sir*——*Don't, Sir* Thomas——*I vow I'll call out, if you offer to be rude.* Inflamed with these little Preliminaries, he once attempted a bolder Deed; tho' she repulsed him with great Disdain, still he nourished Hopes of Success, and watched for a fair Opportunity of making a second Attempt.

One Midnight, therefore, when his Wife was fast asleep, he stole gently out of her Bed, and with great Softness proceeded down Stairs, to find his Way to that of her Rival. But when he came to the Door, unfortunately it was locked, and the Noise he

---

1   Ornamental scarf.

made against it awakened little *Pompey*, who lay watchful by his Mistress's Bed-side. Instantly the Dog took the Alarm, and fell to barking with so much Vehemence, that he roused his Mistress, who started, and cried out, *Who is there?* To this a gentle whispering Voice replied, *One——Pray let me in.* The Milliner, now no longer doubting but that her House was broke open by Thieves, rang her Bell with all her Might, to summon People to her Assistance, and *Pompey* seconded her with such outrageous Fits of Barking, that the amorous Knight thought it high Time to sheer off to his own Bed. As he was groping his Way up Stairs in the Dark, he ran against *Jack Chace*, who having heard the Noise, was descending intrepidly in his Shirt, to find out the Cause of it. They were both exceedingly alarm'd, and as Sir *Thomas* had some Reasons for not speaking, *Jack* was obliged to begin the Conference, which he did in the following Words, *What the Devil have we got here?* Sir *Thomas* now finding himself under a Necessity of replying, to prevent any farther Discoveries, answered with a gentle Voice, *Hush, hush Sir!——I have only been walking in my Sleep, that's all——You'll alarm the Family, Mr.* Chace! *Hush, for God's sake, and let me return to my Bed again.* This brought them to an Eclaircissement, and Sir *Thomas* repeating a Desire of returning to Bed with as little Noise as possible, *Jack Chace* lent him his Hand, and they were almost arrived at the Chamber-door, when the Maid, who had risen at the Sound of her Mistress's Bell, and with her Tinder-box struck a Light, met the noble Pair in their Shirts, on the Top of the Stair-case. She immediately screamed out, dropped her Candle, and ran back to her Garret with the utmost Precipitation. Miss *Frippery*, who had long ago heard the Noise, and lay trembling in her little Bed, expecting every Moment some House-breaker to appear and cut her Throat, now began to be revived a little at the Sound of her Father's Voice, whom she heard talking with Mr. *Chace*, and took Courage to call out from her Cabin, *Heavens, Papa! What is the Matter, Papa?* By this Time, the worthy Knight was arrived at his Bed-side, and finding his Wife asleep, blessed his Stars for being so favourable to him; and then putting his Head into the Closet where his Daughter lay, desired her not to wake her Mother with any Noise, adding, *I have only been walking in my Sleep, my Dear! that's all; and Mr.* Chace *has been so kind to conduct me back to my Bed.* So saying, he deposited himself once more by the Side of his sleeping Spouse, whose *gentle* Slumbers not all the Noise in the House had been able to disturb.

'Tis well observed, that Misfortunes never come single, and what happened to Sir *Thomas Frippery* will confirm this ancient Maxim; for the Disgrace he suffered in the Night, was followed by a more disastrous Accident the ensuing Day.

Out of Compliment to *Jack Chace*, who was then laying close Siege to his Daughter, our Knight had consented to make a Party to *Ruckolt-house*,[1] which was at that Time the fashionable Resort of all idle People, who thought it worth while to travel ten Miles for a Breakfast. Sir *Thomas*, and his Lady, went in a hired Chariot, and the Lovers shone forth in a most exalted *Phaeton*, which looked down with Scorn on all inferior Equipages, and seemed like to the triumphal Carr of Folly. But alas! the Expedition set out under the Influence of some evil Star, and Fortune seemed to take Pleasure in persecuting them with Mischances all the Day long. Sir *Thomas* had not been long landed at *Ruckolt*, before he found himself afflicted with a most violent fit of Cholic; and the Agitation of his Bowels so distorted the Features of his Face, that his Companions began to think him angry with them, and begged Pardon if they had offended him. "Zounds," cries he, "I have got the Cholic to such a Degree, that I am ready to die; and 'tis so long since I have been at any of these youthful Places of Gaiety, that I know not where to go for Relief." *Jack Chace* could not help laughing at the Distresses of his future Father-in-law, but conducted him, however, to one of the Temples of Goddess *Cloacina*,[2] whose Altars are more constantly and universally attended, than those of any other Deity. Here he was entering with great Rapidity, when, to his Surprize, he found two female Votaries already in Possession of the Temple; and 'tis an inviolable Law in the Alcoran[3] of this Goddess, as it was formerly in the Ceremonies of the *Bona Dea*,[4] that the two Sexes shall never communicate in Worship at the same Time. This put the Knight into the strangest Confusion, and he was obliged to

---

1 I.e., Ruckholt House, a park in Leyton, Essex, north-east of London.
2 I.e., an outhouse, Cloacina being the Roman goddess of sewers and filth.
3 I.e., the Koran, the Holy Book of Islam.
4 The Roman "good goddess" Fauna, whose rites were celebrated by women only.

retire, muttering to himself, *that Women were always in the Way*. The Consequences of this Disappointment I forbear to mention; only I cannot help lamenting, that Statesmen should be as subject to the Gripes as inferior Mortals; for I make no doubt, but the greatest Politicians have sometimes invaded with this Disease in the most critical Junctures, and the Business of the Nation suspended, 'till a Minister could return from his Close-stool.[1]

As the Party was returning home, *Jack Chace*, desirous of shewing his Coachmanship to the young Lady, whirled so rapidly round the Corner of a Street, that he overturned the Chaise, and it was next to a Miracle that they escaped with their Lives. But luckily the future Bride received no other Damage, than spoiling her best Silk Night gown[2] (which I mention as a Warning to all young Ladies, how they trust themselves with Gentlemen in high Chaises) and little *Pompey*, who was in her Lap, came with great Dexterity upon his Feet. The Driver himself indeed lost his Ear, which was torn off by the Wheel in his Fall; but this he esteemed a Wound of Honour, and boasted of it as much as disabled Soldiers do of the Loss of their Legs and Arms. As for Sir *Thomas*, he entirely disclaimed *Ruckolt* for the remaining Part of his Life, which he swore abounded with Perils and Dangers, and declared with much Importance, that there was no such Place in being, when he and Lord *Oxford* were at the Helm of Affairs.

CHAP. VIII

A DESCRIPTION OF A DRUM.

BUT I hasten to describe an Event, which engrossed the Attention of this accomplished Family for a Fortnight, and was Matter of Conversation to them for a Year afterwards. Lady *Frippery*, in Imitation of other Ladies of her Rank and Quality, was ambitious of having a Drum; tho' the Smallness of her Lodgings might well have excused her from attempting that modish Piece of Vanity.

---

1   Chamber-pot.
2   "A loose gown usually worn over nightclothes" (*OED*).

A Drum is at present the highest Object of Female Vain-glory; the End whereof is to assemble as large a Mob of Quality as can possibly be contained in one House; and great are the Honours paid to that Lady, who can boast of the largest Crowd. For this Purpose, a Woman of superior Rank calculates how many People all the Rooms in her House laid open can possibly hold, and then sends about two Months beforehand *among the People one knows*, to bespeak such a Number as she thinks will fill them. Hence great Emulations arise among them, and the Candidates for this Honour sue as eagerly for Visiters, as Candidates for Parliament do for Votes at an Election: For as it sometimes happens that two Ladies pitch upon the same Evening for raising a Riot, 'tis necessary they should beat up in time for Voluntiers; otherwise they may chance to be defrauded of their Numbers, and one of them lie under the Ignominy of Collecting a Mob of a hundred only, while the other has the Honour of assembling a well-drest Rabble of three or four hundred; which of course breaks the Heart of that unfortunate Lady, who comes off with this immortal Disgrace.

Now as the Actions of People of Quality are sure of being copied, hence it comes to pass that Ladies of inferior Rank, resolving to be in the Fashion, take upon them likewise to have Drums in Imitation of their Superiors: Only there is this Difference between the two Orders, that the Higher call nothing but a *Crowd* a *Drum*, whereas the Lower often give that Name to the commonest Parties, and for the sake of Honour call an ordinary Visit an Assembly.

From the Moment this great Event was resolved on, all their Conversations turned upon it, and it was pleasant to hear the Schemes and Contrivances they had about it. The first and principal Care was to secure Lady *Bab Frightful*, the chief of Lady *Frippery*'s Acquaintance, and whose Name was to give a Lustre to the Assembly. Now Lady *Bab* being one of the Quality, it was possible she might have a previous Engagement, unless she was taken in time; and therefore a Card was dispatched to her in the first Place, to bespeak her for such an Evening; and it was resolved, that if any cross Accident prevented her coming, new Measures should be taken, and the Drum be deferred till another Night. Lady *Bab* returned for Answer, *that she would wait on Lady* Frippery, *if her Health permitted*. This dubious kind of Message puzzled them in the strangest manner, and was worse than a Denial; for without Lady *Bab* the Assembly would make no Figure, and yet they were obliged to run the Hazard of her not coming in Consequence of her Answer. Every Day therefore, they sent to enquire after her Health, and their Hopes rose or fell according to the Word that was brought them; till on that Day before the Drum was to be held, a most calamitous Piece of News arrived, *that Lady* Bab *was disabled by her Surgeon,* who in cutting her Toenail had made an Incision in her Flesh; yet still she promised to be with them, *if it was possible for her to hobble Abroad.* 'Tis impossible to describe the Damp which this fatal Message struck into the whole Family; a general Consternation at once overspread their Faces, and they looked as if an Earthquake was going to swallow them up: But they were obliged to submit with Patience, and as a Glimpse of Hope still remained, they had nothing left but to put up their Prayers for Lady *Bab*'s Recovery.

At length the important Evening arrived, that was to decide all their Expectations and Fears. Many Consultations had been held every Day, and almost every Hour of the Day, that Things might be perfect and in Order, when the Time came: Yet notwithstanding all their Precautions, a Dispute arose almost at the last Moment, *whether Lady* Frippery *was to receive her Company at the Top or Bottom of the Stairs?* This momentous Question begat a warm Debate. Her Ladyship and Miss[1] contended resolutely for the Top of the Stairs, Sir *Thomas* for the Bottom, and Mr. *Chace* observed a Neutrality; till at length, after a long Altercation, the Knight was obliged to submit to a Majority of Voices; tho' not without condemning his Wife and Daughter for want of Politeness. "My Dear," said he, taking a Pinch of Snuff with great Vehemence, "I am amazed that you can be guilty of such a Solecism in Breeding: It surprizes me, that you are not sensible of the Impropriety of it——Will it not shew much greater Respect and Complaisance to meet your Company at the Bottom of the Stairs, than to stand like an *Indian* Queen receiving Homage at the Top of them?" "Yes, my Dear!" answered her Ladyship; "but you know my Territories do not commence till the Top of the Stairs; our Territories do not begin below Stairs; and it would be very improper for me to go out of my own Dominions——Don't

---

1   I.e., Miss Frippery.

you see that, my Dear? I am surprized at your want of Comprehen-
sion to-day, Sir *Thomas*!" "Well, well, I have given it up," answered
he; "have it your own Way, Child; have your own Way, my Lady,
and then you'll be pleased, I hope——but I am sure, in my Days,
People would have met their Company at the Bottom of the Stairs.
When I and Lord *Oxford* were in the Ministry together, Affairs
would have been very different——but the Age has lost its Civility,
and People are not half so well-bred as they were formerly."

This Reflexion on modern Times piqued the Daughter's Vanity,
who now began to play her Part in the Debate. "Yes, Papa," said
she, "but what signifies what People did formerly? that is nothing at
all to us at present, you know; for to be sure all People were Fools
formerly: I always think People were Fools in former Days. They
never did any thing as we do now-a-days, and therefore it stands to
Reason they were all Fools and Idiots. 'Tis very manifest they had no
Breeding, and all the World must allow, that the World never was so
wise, and polite, and sensible, and clever as it is at this Moment; and,
for my Part, I would not have lived in former Days for all the world."
"Pugh!" said the Knight, interrupting her, "you are a little illiterate
Monkey; you talk without Book, Child! the World is nothing to
what it was in my Days. Every thing is altered for the worse. The
Women are not near so handsome. None of you are comparable to
your Mothers." "Nay, there ——" said Lady *Frippery*, interposing,
"there, Sir *Thomas*, I entirely agree with you——there you have
my Consent, with all my Heart. To be sure, all the celebrated Girls
about the Town are mere Dowdies, in Comparison of their Mothers;
and if there could be a Resurrection of Beauties, they would shine
only like *Bristol* Stones[1] in the Company of Diamonds." "Bless me,
Mamma!" cried the young Lady, with Tears standing in her Eyes,
"how can you talk so? There never were so many fine Women in the
whole World, as there are now in *London*; and 'tis enough to make
one burst out a crying, to hear you talk——Come, Mr. *Chace*, why
don't you stand up for us modern Beauties?"

In the midst of this Conversation, there was a violent Rap at the
Street-door; whereupon they all flew to the Window, crying out
eagerly, *There——there is Lady* Bab——*I am sure 'tis Lady* Bab; *for I*

---

1   I.e., rhinestones.

know her Footman's rap. Yet, in spite of this Knowledge, Lady *Bab* did not arrive according to their Hopes; and it seemed as if her Ladyship had laid a scheme to keep them in Suspence; for of all the People, who composed this illustrious Assembly, Lady *Bab* came the last. They took care, however, to inform the Company from time to time, that she was expected, by making the same Observation on the Arrival of every fresh Coach, and still persisting, that they knew her Footman's rap, tho' they had give so many Proofs to the contrary. At length, however, Lady *Bab Frightful* came; and it is impossible to express the Joy they felt on her Appearance; which revived them on a sudden from the Depth of Despair to the highest Exaltation of Happiness.

Her Ladyship's great Toe engrossed the Conversation for the first Hour, whose Misfortune was lamented in very pathetic Terms by all the Company, and many wise Reflexions were made upon the Accident which had happened; some condemning the Ignorance, and others the Carelessness of the Surgeon, who had been guilty of such a Trespass on her Ladyship's Flesh. Some advised her to be very careful how she walked upon it; others recommended a larger Shoe to her Ladyship, and Lady *Frippery*, in particular, continued the whole Evening to protest the vast Obligations she had to her, for favouring her with Company under such an Affliction. But had I an hundred Hands, and as many Pens, it would be impossible to describe the Folly of that Night: Wherefore, begging the Reader to supply it by Help of his own Imagination, I proceed to other Parts of this History.

CHAP. IX

IN WHICH SEVERAL THINGS ARE TOUCHED UPON.

WHEN this great Affair was over, the Marriage came next upon the Carpet; the Celebration of which was fixed for *Easter* Week; but Mr. *Chace* recollecting in Time that it would interfere with *Newmarket* Races, procured a Reprieve till the Week following. At his Return from those *Olympic* Games, the Nuptials were celebrated before a general Assembly of their Relations, and the happy Couple were conducted to Bed in Publick with great Demonstrations of

Joy. The Bridegroom took Possession of the Bride, and Sir *Thomas* took Possession of Mr. *Chace*'s Estate.

When they had shewn their new Cloaths a little in *London*, they set out in a Body for the Country; and in a few Days afterwards, the Lodgings on the first Floor were taken by a Lady, who passed under the fictitious Name of Mrs. *Caryl*. The hasty Manner, in which she made her Agreement, infused a Suspicion into our Milliner from the very Beginning; and many Circumstances soon concurred to persuade her, that her new Lodger was a Wife eloped from her Husband. For besides that she came into her Lodgings late in the Evening, she seemed to affect a Privacy in all her Actions, which plainly evidenced, that she was afraid of some Discovery; and this encreased our Milliner's Curiosity the more in proportion as the other seemed less inclined to gratify it. But an Event soon happened to confirm her Conjectures; for three Days after the Lady's Arrival, a Chair stopped at the Door one Evening near Ten o'Clock, from whence alighted a well-drest Man about Fifty Years old, who wrapping himself up in a red Cloak, proceeded hastily up Stairs, as if desirous to conceal himself from Observation. This Adventure savoured so strongly of Intrigue, that it was no wonder our Milliner contrived to meet him in the Passage, to satisfy her Curiosity with a survey of his Features; for People, in whom that Passion predominates, often find the greatest Consolation from knowing the smallest Trifles. *Pompey* was still more inquisitive than his Mistress, and took Courage to follow the Gentleman into the Dining-Room, with a Desire, I suppose, of hearing of what passed in so fashionable an Interview.

The Lady rose from her Chair to receive this Man of Fashion, who saluted her with great Complaisance, and hoped she was pleased with her new Apartments. "Yes, my Lord," answered she, "the People are civilized People enough, and I believe have no Suspicion about me——but did they see your Lordship come up Stairs?" "'Pon my Honour, Madam," said the Peer, "I can't tell; there was a female Figure glided by me in the Passage, but whether the Creature made Remarks or not, I did not stay to observe——Well, Madam, I hope now I may give you Joy of your Escape, and I dare say you will find yourself much happier than you was under the Ill-usage of a Tyrant you despised." The Lady then related, with great Pleasantry, the Manner of her Escape, and the Difficulties that attended the

Execution of it; after which she concluded with saying, "I wonder, my Lord, what my Husband is now thinking on?" "Thinking on!" answered the Peer "—— that he's a Fool and a Blockhead, I hope, Madam, and deserves to be hanged for abusing the Charms of so divine a Creature——Good God! was it possible for him to harbour an ill-natured Thought, while he had the Pleasure of looking in that angelic Face?" "My Lord," said the Lady, "I know I have taken a very ill Step in the Eye of the World; but I have too much Spirit to bear Ill-usage with Patience, and let the Consequences be what they will, I am determined to submit to them, rather than be a Slave to the Ill-humours of a Man I despised, hated and detested." "Forbear, Madam," said his Lordship, "to think of him; my Fortune, my Interest, my Sword, are all devoted to your Service, and I am ready to execute any Command you please to impose upon me——but let us call a more agreeable Topic of Conversation."

Soon after this a light, but elegant Supper was placed upon the Table, and the Servants were ordered to retire; for there are certain Seasons, when even the Great desire to banish Ostentation. The absent Husband furnished them with much Raillery, and they pictured to themselves continually the Surprize he would be in, when he discovered his Wife's Elopement; nor did this Man of Gallantry and Fashion finish his amorous Visit till past Two o'Clock in the Morning. As he was going down Stairs, he found himself again encountered by the barking of little *Pompey*, whom he snatched up in his Arms, and getting hastily into the Chair, that waited for him at the Door, carried him off with him to his own House.[1]

The next Morning, when our Hero waked, and took a Survey of his new Apartments, he had great Reason to rejoice in the Change he had made: The Magnificence of the Furniture evidently shewed that he was in a House of a Man of Quality; and the Importance which discovered itself in the Faces of all the Domestics, seemed likewise to prove that their Master belonged to the Court. The Porter in particular appeared to be a Politician of many Years standing , for he never deliver'd the most ordinary Message but in the Voice of a Whisper, accompanied by so many Nods, Winks, and other

---

1   The portrait that follows of the statesman Lord Danglecourt was replaced in the third
     edition by the less amusing and thematically redundant activities of Lord Marmazet.
     The reader will find this section of the third edition in Appendix A.

mysterious Grimaces, that he passed among his Acquaintance for a Statesman of no common Capacity.

About Nine o'Clock in the Morning Lord *Danglecourt* was pleased to raise himself up in his Bed, and summoned his Valets to assist him in putting on his Cloaths. As soon as it was reported through the House that his Lordship was stirring, the Multitudes who were waiting to attend his Levee, put themselves in Order in his Antichamber to pay their Morning Homage, as soon as he pleased to appear. Several of them, however, who came on particular Business, or were necessary Agents under his Lordship, were selected from the common Groupe, and introduced into the Bedchamber; where they had the inexpressible Honour and Pleasure to see his Lordship wash his Hands and buckle his Shoes in private.

But his Lordship was condemned this Morning to give private Audience to the chief Inhabitants of a Borough-Town, of which (to use the common Phrase) he *made the Members*,[1] and consequently was obliged to treat them with that ceremonious Respect, which *Free-Britons* always demand in exchange for their Liberty. These Gentlemen were ambitious of having their Town erected into a Corporation,[2] and now waited on Lord *Danglecourt* with a Petition, setting forth the Nature of their Request, and begging his Lordship's Interest to obtain a Charter for them. They were conducted into a private Room, where his Lordship soon presented himself to them, and after saluting them all round, begged to know if he could have the Honour of serving them in any thing, making many Protestations of his particular Regard for them and eternal Devotion to their Interest. This seemed to answer their Wishes; whereupon one of them taking a Packet out of his Breast, began to read what might be called the History of their Town with more Propriety than a Petition, for it contained the Names of all the Blacksmiths, Barbers, and Attornies, that had flourished in it for many Centuries backwards. His Lordship took great Pains to

---

1 Members of Parliament for this borough would have been elected as allies of Lord Danglewood, who would have a mutual interest to maintain (through bribes and other favors) the loyalty of the town's electors. Coventry is making fun of the highly patronized electoral system in England, and its characteristic jargon of British "liberty."

2 Incorporated towns would enjoy certain benefits from the state, such as the right to appoint an official governing council, though in exchange for certain regulations such as the restriction of dissenting (non-Anglican) religious groups.

suppress his Inclination to Laughter, and for a while seemed to listen with great Attention; but at length his Patience being quite exhausted, he was obliged to interrupt the Orator of the Company, saying, "Well, Gentlemen, I won't give you the trouble to read any more; I see the Nature of your Petition extremely well, and you may depend upon my Interest; Please to leave your Petition with me, Sir, and I'll look over the remaining Part at my Leisure ———Depend upon it, Gentlemen, you shall soon be in Possession of your Desires." His Lordship then began to enquire after their Wives and Daughters, and having ordered a Salver of Sack[1] and Biscuits, he drank Prosperity to their new Corporation, representing in the strongest Terms the Honour they did him, in making him Instrumental to the Completion of their Desires, and hoped he should very soon be able to compliment them on their Success. He then conducted them to the Door, and they departed from him with the most grateful Acknowledgements of his Goodness, and the highest inward Satisfaction to think they had so gracious a Patron.

They were no sooner gone, than his Lordship returned into his Closet, and fell a laughing at the Folly and Impertinence of his Petitioners. "Curse the Boobies," cries he, "do they think I have nothing to do but to make Mayors and Aldermen?" and so saying, he threw down the Petition to the Dog, and began to make him *fetch and carry* for his Diversion. *Pompey* very readily entered into the Humour of this Pastime, and made such good use of his Teeth, that the Hopes of a new Corporation were soon demolished, and the Lord knows how many Mayors and Aldermen in a Moment perished by the unmerciful Jaws of a *Bologna* Lap-dog. But his Lordship soon grew tired of this Entertainment, and when he thought the Petition had been severely enough handled by the Dog, he snatched it from him, and flung it into the Fire, saying, with a contemptuous Sneer, *So much for our new Corporation*: After which, he called for his Hat and Sword, and went Abroad; nor did *Pompey* see anything more of him during the remaining Part of the Day.

---

1   "A general name for a class of white wines formerly imported from Spain and the Canaries" (*OED*).

CHAP. X

DESCRIBING THE MISERIES OF A GARRETEER POET.

THE next Morning his Lordship was sitting in his Study, and reading some Papers of State, his Gentleman Usher came into the Room,
and informed him, *that Mr.* Rhymer *the Poet was below.* "Curse Mr.
Rhymer the Poet," cries his Lordship, "and you too for an egregious
Blockhead——why the Devil did you let the Fellow in? Tell him
that his last Political Pamphlet is execrable Nonsense and unintelligible Jargon, and I am not at Leisure to see him this Morning."
"My Lord," said the Valet, "he desired me to acquaint you, that he
has a Plan for writing the History of your Lordship's Family, which
he wants to communicate to your Lordship for your Approbation."
"Turn the Scoundrel out of Doors this Moment," answered the
Peer, "I won't have the Honour of my Ancestors besmeared with
his *Grubstreet*[1] Ink——Stay, hold *Dickson*! let the Fellow send up his
execrable Specimen however; it will furnish me, perhaps, with a
little Diversion this Morning, if it be very absurd, and that I have
no doubt of——Go, bring the Plan." Mr. *Dickson* then went down
Stairs, and soon returned with the unfortunate Proposals, which
being ordered to read, he pronounced in the following Manner;
*Proposals for printing by Subscription Historical Memoirs of the illustrious
and noble Family of* John *Earl of* Danglecourt, *in which it will be proved
that the Virtues of all his divine Ancestors center in his present Lordship,
and that he is the Mecænas of Letters, the* Richelieu *of Politics, and the*
Hampden *of the* English *Constitution.*[2] "Very well," cries his Lordship, "this is a Sycophant, that would deify me for a Crust of Bread;
however, let him proceed in his Work, and when he has finished
it, perhaps I may give him——a Dinner." "My Lord," answered
the Valet, "unless your Lordship bestows that Favour upon him

---

1 "Grubstreet" was the proverbial home of bad London authors. Coventry's satire of
this starving writer is highly conventional, though rather dated by 1751.
2 Caius Mæcenas (b. 8 BCE), statesman and patron of letters in the reign of Augustus,
was proverbial in the eighteenth century for noble patronage; Cardinal Armand Jean
du Plessis de Richelieu (1585-1642) was the architect of French power under Louis
XIII; John Hampden (1594-1643) helped to lead Parliamentary opposition against the
allegedly arbitrary power of Charles I.

beforehand, I am afraid he will never live to finish it, for really the poor Gentleman seems a little out of Case, and I believe he is seldom guilty of Intemperance at his Meals——He begs me to present his humble Duty to your Lordship, and to inform your Lordship, that a small Gratuity would be very acceptable at present, for it seems his Wife is ready to lie-in,[1] and he says, he has not Six-pence to defray the Expences of her Groaning." "How," cried his Lordship, "has that Fellow the Impudence to beget Children? The Dog pretends here to be starving, and yet has the Assurance to deal in Procreation——Prythee, *Dickson*, what sort of a Woman is his Wife? have you ever seen her?" "Yes, my Lord," answered the trusty Valet; "but I am afraid she would have no great Temptations for your Lordship; for the poor Gentlewoman has the Misfortune to squint a little, which does not give a very bewitching Air to her Countenance, and has the Accomplishment of red Hair into the bargain." "Well then," cries the Peer, "turn the Hound out of Doors, and bid him go to the Devil. Pox take him, if he had a handsome Wife, I might be tempted to encourage him a little; but how can he expect my Favour without doing any thing to deserve it?" "Then your Lordship won't be pleased to send him a small Acknowledgement," said the Valet de Chambre. "No," replied the Peer, "I have no Money to fling away on Poets and Hackney-writers; let the Fellow eat his own Works, if he is hungry.——Hold, stay, I have thought better of it; here *Dickson*, carry him this Dog which I brought home the other Night, and bid him keep the Creature for my Sake."

Dickson was a man of some little Humour, which had promoted him to the Dignity of first Pimp in ordinary[2] to his Lordship, and perceiving that his Master had a mind to divert himself this Morning with the Miseries of an unhappy Poet, he resolved that the Joke should not be lost in passing through his Hands. Taking the Dog therefore from his Lordship, he made haste down Stairs, and accosted the expecting Bard in the following Manner: "Sir! his Lordship is very busy this Morning, and not at Leisure to speak with you, but he recommends it to you to proceed in the

---

1 "To be brought to bed of a child" (*OED*).
2 I.e., in regular service.

Execution of your Work, and begs you would do him the Favour to accept of this beautiful little *Bologna* Lap-dog." "Accept of a Lap-dog," cries the Poet with Astonishment; "bless me! what is the Matter? Surely there must be some Mistake, Mr. *Dickson*! for I cannot readily conceive of what Use a *Bologna* Lap-dog can be to me." "Sir," replied the Valet-de-chambre, "you may depend upon it, his Lordship had some Reason for making you this Present, which it does not become us to guess at." "No," said the Bard, "I would not presume to dive into his Lordship's Councils, which, to be sure, are always wise and unscrutable; but really now, Mr. *Dickson*, a few Guineas in present Cash would be rather more serviceable to me than a *Bologna* Lap-dog——Even a few *Bologna* Sausages, to carry home in my Pocket, would have been more comfortable to my poor Wife and Children." "Sir," said the Valet, "you must not distrust his Lordship's Generosity: Great Statesmen, Mr. *Rhymer*, always do Things in a different manner from the rest of the World: There is usually, as you observe, something a little mysterious in their Conduct; but assure yourself, Sir, this Dog will be the Fore-runner of a handsome Annuity, and it would be the greatest Affront imaginable not to receive him.——You must never refuse any Thing, which the Great esteem a Favour, Mr. *Rhymer*, on any Account; even tho' it should involve you and your Family in everlasting Ruin. His Lordship desired that you would keep the Dog for his Sake, Sir, and therefore you may be sure he has a particular Regard for you, when he sends you such a Memorial of his Affection."

The unhappy Poet finding he could extort nothing from the unfeeling Hands of his Patron, was obliged to retire with the Dog under his Arms, and climbed up in a disconsolate Mood to his Garret, where he found his Wife cooking the Scrag End of a Neck of Mutton for Dinner. The Mansions of this Son of *Apollo* were very contracted, and one would have thought it impossible for one single Room to have served so many domestic Purposes; but good Housewifery knows no Difficulties, and Penury has a Thousand Inventions, which are unknown to Ease and Wealth. In one Corner of these poetical Apartments stood a Flock-bed,[1] and underneath it,

---

1 A cheap mattress stuffed with cloth.

a green Jordan[1] presented itself to the Eye, which had the nocturnal Urine of the whole Family, consisting of Mr. *Rhymer*, his Wife and two Daughters. Three rotten Chairs and a half seemed to stand like Traps in various Parts of the Room, threatening Downfals to unwary Strangers; and one solitary Table in the Middle of this aerial Garret, served to hold the different Treasures of the whole Family. There were now lying upon it the first Act of a Comedy, a Pair of yellow Stays, two political Pamphlets, a Plate of Bread-and-butter, three dirty Night-caps, and a Volume of Miscellany Poems. The Lady of the House was drowning a Neck of Mutton, as we before observed, in a meagre Soup, and two Daughters sat in the Window, mending their Father's brown Stockings with blue Worsted. Such were the Mansions of Mr. *Rhymer*, the Poet, which I heartily recommend to the repeated Perusal of all those unhappy Gentlemen, who feel in themselves a growing Inclination to that mischievous, damnable, and destructive Science.

As soon as Mr. *Rhymer* entered the Chamber, his Wife deserted her Cookery, to enquire the Success of his Visit, on which the Comforts of her Lying-in so much depended; and seeing a Dog under her Husband's Arm, "Bless me, my Dear!" said she, "why do you bring home that filthy Creature, to eat our Victuals? Thank Heaven, we have got more Mouths already, than we can satisfy, and I am sure we want no Addition to our Family." "Why, my Dear," answered the Poet, "his Lordship did me the Favour to present me this Morning with this beautiful little *Bologna* Lap-dog." "Present you with a Lap-dog," cried the Wife interrupting him, "what is it you mean, Mr. *Rhymer*? but, however, I am glad his Lordship was in so bountiful a Humour, for I am sure then he has given you a Purse of Guineas, to maintain the Dog.——Well, I vow it was a very genteel Way of making a Present, and I shall love the little Fool for his Master's Sake.——Great Men do Things with so much Address always, that one is transported as much with their Politeness as their Generosity." Here the unhappy Bard shook his Head, and soon undeceived his Wife, by informing her of all that had passed in his Morning's Visit. "How," said she, "no Money with the Dog? Mr. *Rhymer*, I am amazed that you will submit to

---

1 A chamber-pot.

such a Usage. Don't you see that they make a Fool, and an Ass, and a Laughing-stock of you? Why did you take their filthy Dog? I'll have its Brains dashed out this Moment.——Mr. *Rhymer*, if you had kept on your Tallow-chandler's Shop, I and mine should have had wherewithal to live; but you must court the draggle-tail Muses forsooth, and a fine Provision they have made for you.——Here I expect to be brought to Bed every Day, and you have not Money to buy Pap and Caudle.[1]——O curse your Lords and your Political Pamphlets! I am sure I have Reason to repent the Day that ever I married a Poet." "Madam," said *Rhymer*, exasperated at his Wife's Conversation, "you ought rather to bless the Day, that married you to a Gentleman, whose Soul despises mechanical Trades, and is devoted to the noblest Science in the Universe. Poetry, Madam, like Virtue, is its own Reward; but you have a vulgar Notion of Things, you have an illiberal Attachment to Money, and had rather be frying Grease in a Tallow-chandler's Shop, than listening to the divine Rhapsodies of the *Heliconian* Maids.[2] 'Tis true, Madam, his Lordship has not recompensed my Labours according to Expecta-tion this Morning, but what of that? he bid me proceed in the Execution of my Design, and undoubtedly means to reward me. Lords are often destitute of Cash, as well as Poets, and perhaps I came upon him a little unseasonably, when his Coffers were empty; but I auspicate great Things from his Present of a Dog.——A Dog, Madam, is the Emblem of Fidelity, and that encourages me to hope his Lordship will be true to my Interest." "The Emblem of a Fiddle-stick!" cried the Wife, interrupting him, "I tell you, Mr. *Rhymer*, you are a Fool, and have ruined your Family by your sense-less Whims and Projects.——A Gentleman, quotha! Yes, forsooth, a very fine Gentleman truly, that has hardly a Shirt to his Back, or a Pair of Shoes to his Feet.——Look at your Daughters there in the Window, and see whether they appear like a Gentleman's Daughters; and for my Part, I have not an Under-petticoat that I can wear.——You have had three Plays damned, Mr. *Rhymer*, and one would think that might have taught you a little Prudence; but, Deuce fetch me, if you shall write any more, for I'll burn all

---

1 A warm gruel for babies.
2 The nine Muses, who supposedly resided on Mount Helicon in Greece.

this Nonsense that lies upon the Table." So saying, she flew like a Bacchanal Fury[1] at his Works, and with savage Hands was going to commit them to the Flames, but her Husband's Voice interrupted her, crying out with Impatience, "See, see, see, my Dear! the Pot boils over, and the Broth is all running away into the Fire." This luckily put an end to their Altercation, and postponed the Sacrifice that was going to be made; they then sat down to Dinner without a Table-cloth, and made a wretched Meal, envying one another every Morsel that escaped their own Mouths.

[CHAPTER XI[2]

A POETICAL FEAST, AND SQUABBLE OF AUTHORS.

AFTER dinner was over, Mr. *Rhymer* sat himself down to an epic poem, which was then on the anvil, and his head not being clouded with any fumes of indigestion, he worked at it very laboriously till eight or nine o'clock in the evening. Then he took his hat, and went out to meet a club of authors, who assembled every *Monday* night, at a little dirty dog-hole of a tavern in *Shire-lane*, to eat tripe, drink porter, and pass their judgments on the books of the preceding week. *Pompey* waited on his master; for as Mrs. *Rhymer* had resolutely vowed his destruction, the good-natured bard did not chuse to leave him at her mercy.

On their arrival in the club-room, they found there assembled a free-thinking writer[3] of moral essays, a no-thinking scribler of magazines, a *Scotch* translator of *Greek* and *Latin* authors, a *Grub-street* bookseller, and a *Fleet* parson. These worthy gentlemen immediately surrounded Mr. *Rhymer* with great vociferation, and began to curse him for staying so long, declaring it would be entirely his fault, if the tripe was spoilt, which they very much feared. To prevent which however, they

---

1 Coventry has conflated two myths. In Greek mythology, the "Furies" were female personifications of vengeance. "Bacchanal fury" was the madness inflicted by Bacchus on his followers, traditionally portrayed as women.
2 This chapter was added to the third edition.
3 I.e., a writer of ideas disapproved of by the church and the state.

now ordered it to be served up with all possible expedition, and on its appearance, fell to work with the quickest dispatch. The reader will believe that little or no conversation passed among them at table, their mouths being much too busily employed to have any leisure for discourse; but when the tripe was quite consumed, and innumerable slices of toasted cheese at the end of it, they then began to exercise their tongues as readily as they had before done their teeth.

By odd luck, every one of these great advancers of modern literature, happened to have a dog attending him; and as the gentlemen drew round the fire after supper in a ring, the dogs likewise made an interior semi-circle, sitting between the legs of their respective masters. This could not escape the observation of the company, and many trite observations began to be made on their fidelity, their attachment to man, and above all, on the felicity of their condition; for a dog sleeping before a fire, is by all people esteemed an emblem of complete happiness. At length, they struck into higher conversation. "Gentlemen!" says the free-thinker, "I should be glad to hear your sentiments concerning reason and instinct. I have a curious treatise now by me, which I design very soon to astonish the world with. 'Tis upon a subject perfectly new, and those dogs there put me in the head of it. The clergy I know will be up in arms against me, but no matter; I'll publish my opinions in spite of all the priests in *Europe*."

Here the *Fleet* parson, thinking himself concerned, took his pipe from his mouth with great deliberation, and said, "I don't know what your opinions may be, but I hope you don't design to publish any thing to the disadvantage of that sacred order to which I belong: if you do sir, I believe you'll find pens enow ready to answer you."

"Yes, sir, no doubt I shall," replied the free-thinker, "and who cares for that? perhaps you, sir, may do me the honour to be my antagonist, but I defy you all!——I defy the whole body of the priesthood. Sir, I love to advance a paradox;[1] I love a paradox at my heart, sir! and I'll——I'll shew you some sport very shortly."

"What do you mean by sport, sir?" cries the doctor——"If you write as you talk, I hope you'll be set in the pillory for your sport."

"You are bloody complaisant, sir," returned the free-thinker;

---

1 Among apologists for orthodox ideas, a standard allegation was that free-thinkers indulged in deliberately paradoxical arguments.

"but I'd have you to know we are not come to such a pass yet in this country, as to persecute people for searching after truth. You priests I know would be glad to keep us all in ignorance, but the age won't be priest-ridden any longer. There is a noble spirit and freedom of enquiry now subsisting in the nation; people are determined to canvass things freely, and go to the bottom of all subjects, without regarding base prejudices of education. The shops abound with a number of fine treatises written every day against religion, to the honour and glory of the nation."

"To the shame and damnation, rather," cries the *Fleet* parson; "but what is your paradox, sir?"

"Why this is my paradox, sir," replied the free-thinker; "I undertake to prove that brutes think and have intellectual faculties. That perhaps you'll say is no novelty, because many others have asserted the same thing before me; but I go farther sir, and maintain that they are reasonable creatures, and moral agents."

"And I will maintain that they are mere machines," cries the parson, "against you and all the atheists in the world.[1] Sir, you may be ashamed to prostitute the noble faculty of reason to the beasts of the field."

"Don't tell me of reason," said the free-thinker; "I don't care one half-penny for reason——what is reason, sir?"

"What is reason, sir?" resumed the doctor; "why reason sir, is a most noble faculty of the soul, the noblest of all the faculties. It discerns and abstracts, and compares and compounds, and all that."——

"And roasts eggs too, does it not? you forget one of its noble faculties," cries the other: "but I will maintain that brutes are capable of reason, and they have given manifest proofs of it. Did you never hear of Mr. *Locke*'s parrot, sir, that held a very rational conversation with prince *Maurice* for half an hour together?[2] what say you to that, sir?"

"By my faith, gentlemen!" said the *Scotch* translator interrupting them, "upon my word you are got here into a very deep mysterious

---

1   The free-thinker and the priest take extreme positions on this question. While Christian apologists opposed the idea that animals could think, for this position implied that they had eternal souls like humans, the argument that animals were mere machines, usually identified with the philosophy of René Descartes, was equally condemned by many orthodox writers as promoting unnatural cruelty. See Appendix E.

2   The free-thinker alludes to a story told by John Locke in *An Essay on Human Understanding* (1690), Bk II, ch. xxvii.

question, which I do not very well understond what to make of; but by my faith I have always thought brutes to have something particular in the intellectual faculties of their souls, ever since I read what-d'ye-callum there——the *Roman* historian; for why? you know he tells us how the geese discovered to the *Romans* that the *Gauls* were coming to plunder the capitol.[1] Now by my soul, they must have been a d—mn'd sensible flock of geese, and very great lovers of their country too, which let me tell you, is the greatest virtue under heaven. Besides, doth not *Homer* teach us, that *Ulysses*'s dog *Argus* knew his old master at his return home, after he had been absent ten or twelve years at the siege of *Troy*?[2] now by *Jove* he was a plaguy cunning dog, and had a devilish good memory, otherwise he could not have remembered his old chrony so long."

Before the *Scotchman* had finished his speech, the two other disputants, whose spirits were kindled with controversy, resumed their argument, and fell upon one another again with so much impetuosity, that no voices could be heard but their own. The scene which now ensued, consisted chiefly of noise and scolding, equal to any thing that passes among the orators at *Robin-Hood*'s ale-house.[3] In short, there was not a scurrilous term in the *English* language, which was not vented on this occasion; till at length, the *Fleet* parson heated with rage and beer, flung his pipe at his antagonist, and was proceeding to blows, had he not been restrained by the rest of the company. The festivity of the evening being by this means destroyed, the club soon afterwards broke up, and the several members of it retired to their several garrets.

As Mr. *Rhymer* was walking home in a pensive solitary mood, wrapped up in contemplation on the stars of heaven, and perhaps forgetting for a few moments that he had but three-pence half-penny in his pocket, two young gentlemen of the town, who were upon the hunt after amorous game, followed close at his heels. They quickly smoked[4] him for *a queer fish*, as the phrase is, and began to hope for

---

1   In a story told by Livy (Titus Livius, 64 BCE?-17 CE) in his *History of Rome*, a nighttime invasion of Gauls awoke Rome's geese, the squawking of which in turn roused the city.

2   See the *Odyssey*, Bk XVII.

3   A London ale-house where a large debating circle gathered.

4   I.e., detected.

some diversion at his expence. The moon now shone very bright, and Mr. *Rhymer*, whose eyes were fixed with rapture on that glorious luminary, began to apostrophize her in some poetical strains from *Milton*, which he repeated with great emphasis aloud. In midst of this, the two gentlemen broke out in a profuse fit of laughter, at which the bard turned round in surprize, but soon recovering himself, he cast a most contemptuous look at them for their ignorance and want of taste. However, as the chain of ideas in his mind was by this means disturbed, he thought it most adviseable to make the best of his way home, and for this purpose called *Pompey* to follow him. *Pompey* indeed made many efforts, and seemed desirous to obey; but in vain the poet called, in vain the dog endeavoured to follow; and it was a long while before Mr. *Rhymer*, whose thoughts were a little muddled with contemplation and porter, found out that the two gentlemen had tied a handkerchief round his neck. He then stopt to demand his property, but finding himself pretty roughly handled, he began to think his own person in danger. Taking to his heels therefore, he ran away with the utmost precipitation, and left his dog behind him; who on his part was not at all sorry to be delivered from such a master.]

CHAP. XII

SHEWING THE ILL EFFECTS OF LADIES HAVING
THE VAPOURS.

OUR Hero wandered about the Streets for two or three Hours, 'till being tired of his Peregrination, he took Shelter in a handsome House, where the Door stood hospitably open to receive him. Here he was soon found by the Servants, and the Waiting-gentlewoman carried him up Stairs, as a Beauty, to her Mistress, whom she found in a Fit, and consequently was obliged to defer the Introduction of *Pompey*, to assist her Lady with Hartshorn,[1] and other physical Restoratives, with which her Chamber was plentifully stored.

---

1   "The aqueous solution of ammonia (whether obtained from harts' horns or otherwise). *Salt of hartshorn*: carbonate of ammonia; smelling salts" (*OED*).

This Lady, by Name Mrs. *Qualmsick*,[1] had the Misfortune to be afflicted with that most terrible Sickness, which arises only from the Imagination of the Patient, and which it is no Wonder Physicians find such a Difficulty to cure, as it has neither Name, Symptoms, or Existence. She was, in reality, eaten up with the Vapours; by which Means her whole Life became an uninterrupted Series of Miseries, which she had been ingenious enough to invent for herself, because neither Nature nor Fortune had bestowed any upon her. Her Constitution originally was very good and healthy, but she had so many years been endeavouring to destroy it, by the Advice and Assistance of Physicians, that she had now physicked herself into all kinds of imaginary Disorders, and was unhealthy from the very Pains she took to preserve her Health. Her meek-spirited Husband possessed an Estate of Two Thousand Pounds a Year, the far greater Part whereof his indulgent Wife lavished away on Physicians and Apothecaries Bills; and tho' she took all Pains to render herself unlovely in the Eyes of a Husband, the good-natured simple Man was so enamoured of her sickly Charms, that he still adored her as a Goddess, and paid a blind Obedience to her Will in every Thing. As her *weak Nerves* seldom permitted her to go abroad herself, she kept her obsequious Spouse almost constantly confined in her Bed-chamber, as a Companion to her in her Afflictions: and besides the Confinement he underwent, he was obliged likewise, at all Seasons, to conform himself to the present State of her Nerves. For, sometimes, the Sound of a Voice was Death to her, and then he was enjoined inviolable Silence: At other Times, she chose to be diverted with a Book, and then he was to read *Hervey*'s Meditations among the Tombs:[2] Again, at other Times, when her Imagination was a little more chearful than usual, she would amuse herself with conjugal Dalliances, toy with her Husband, stroke his Face, and provoke him to treat her with little amorous Endearments.

As a Reward for this Humility, and Readiness to comply with her Humours, she would do him the Favour, every now and then, to take him abroad in her Coach, when her Physicians prescribed

---

1   "A (sudden) feeling or fit of faintness, illness, or sickness" (*OED*).

2   *Meditations among the Tombs* (1746) by James Hervey (1714-58), typical of the popular "graveyard" school in the eighteenth century. Often set in graveyards, these poems dwelled on themes of mortality and were filled with gloomy imagery.

her an Airing: Tho' it may be doubted whether he received any great Enjoyment of this uncommon Favour, as the Glasses and Canvasses[1] were constantly drawn up, while the sick Lady lay along it like a fat Corpse, on one whole Seat of the Coach, gasping for Air, and complaining of the uneasy Motion.

As these kinds of Distempers are very fantastical, she was often seized with the strangest Whims, and would imagine herself converted into all kinds of living Creatures; nay, when her Phrenzy was at the highest, it was not unusual for her to fancy herself a Glass-bottle, a Tea-pot, a Hay-rick, or a Field of Turnips.[2] The Furniture of her Rooms was likewise altered once a Month, to comply with the present Fit of Vapours: For, sometimes, Red was too glaring for her Eyes; Green put her in mind of Willows,[3] and made her melancholic; Blue remembered her of her dear Sister, who had unfortunately died ten Years before in a blue Bed; and some such Reason was constantly found for banishing every Colour in its Turn. But a little Specimen of her Conversation one Day with her Doctor, and the Consequences of it afterwards on her Husband, will give the best Description of her Character.

The Gentlemen of the *Esculapian* Art[4] came to attend her one morning, and she began as usual, with informing him of the deplorable State in which he found her. "O, Doctor," said she, "my Nerves are so low to-day, that I can hardly fetch my Breath. There is such a Damp and Oppression upon my Spirits, that 'tis impossible for me to live a Week longer. Do you think, Sir, I can possibly live a Week longer?" "A Week longer, Madam!" answered the Physician, "Oh, bless me! yes, yes, many Years, I hope——Come, come, Madam, you must not give way of such Imaginations. 'Tis the Nature of your Disorder to be attended with a Dejection of Spirits——Perhaps some external Object may have presented itself, that has excited a little Fume of Melancholy; or perhaps your Ladyship may have heard a disagreeable Piece of News; or perhaps the Haziness of the Weather may have cast a kind of a——a kind

---

1   The windows and curtains of a coach.
2   This satire of the supposedly imaginary ailments and fantasies of "vapourish" women is highly conventional, and comparable to Pope's *Rape of the Lock*, Canto IV.
3   Symbolic of death and mourning.
4   From Æsculapius, son of Apollo, miraculous healer and the patron of medicine.

of a Lethargy over the animal Spirits, or perhaps mere want of Sleep may have left a *Tedium* on the Brain; or a thousand Things may have contributed——but you must not be alarmed, you must not be alarmed, Madam! we shall remedy all that; we shall brace up your Nerves, and give a new Flow to the Blood." "O Doctor," said she, interrupting him, "I am afraid you comfort with vain Hopes. My Blood is quite in a State of Stagnation, Doctor; and I believe it will never flow any more——Do feel my Pulse, Doctor!" "Let us see, let us see," answered the Physician, taking hold of her Hand, "Stagnation! bless us, Madam! No, no, your Pulse beats very regularly and floridly, I protest, and your Ladyship will do very well again in time, Madam!——but you must take time, Madam! That Plexus of Nerves upon the Stomach, which I have often described to you as the Seat of your Disorder, wants some corroborating Help to give them a new Springiness and Elasticity; and when Things are relaxed, you know, Madam, they will be out of Order. You see it is the Case in all mechanical Machines, and of course it must be the same in the human Œconomy; for we are but Machines, we are nothing but Machines, Madam!" "O, Sir," replied the Lady, "I care not what we are; but do, for Heaven's sake, redeem me for the Miseries I suffer." "I will, Madam," returned the Doctor; "I'll pawn my Honour on your Recovery; but you must take time, Madam, your Ladyship must have Patience, and not expect Miracles to be wrought in a Day. Time, Madam, conquers every thing, and you need not doubt but we shall set you up again——in time. How do you find your Appetite? Do you eat, Madam?" "Not at all, Sir," answered the Lady, "not at all; I have neither Stomach, nor Appetite, nor Strength, nor any thing in the World; and I believe verily, I can't live a Week longer——I drank a little Chocolate yesterday Morning, Sir, and got down a little Bason of Broth at Noon, and eat a Pigeon for my Dinner, and made a shift to get down another little Bason of Broth at Night——but I can't eat at all, Sir; my Appetite fails me more and more every Day, and I live upon mere nothing."

Much more of this kind of Conversation passed between them, which we will not now stay to relate. When the Doctor had taken his Leave, the good-natured Husband met him at the Bottom of the Stairs, and very tenderly enquired how he had left his Spouse? To this, the Son of *Esculapius* answered, *Quite brave, Sir*; and assured him there was no doubt to be made of her Recovery; adding at the same time, "If you can persuade her to believe herself well, Sir, you will be her best Physician." "Do you think so, Doctor?" said *Qualmsick*, with a silly Smile. "Sir, I am sure of it," answered the Physician: After which Words he flew to his Coach, and drove away to the Destruction of other Patients.

Qualmsick immediately posted up Stairs to his Wife's Apartment to try the Effect of his Persuasions upon her, little thinking what a dangerous Office he was about to undertake. He began with congratulating her on the Amendment of her Health, and said he was very glad to find from the Account her Physician had been giving, that she was in a very fair way of Recovery. This extremely surprized her, and weak as she was, she began to put much Resentment into her Countenance; which *Qualmsick* observing, proceeded in the following manner. "Come, come, my Dear, you must not deceive us any longer——we know how it is; we know you are well enough, my Dear, if you would but fancy yourself so——Do but lay aside your Vapours and Imaginations, and I warrant you will have your Health for the future."

This was the first time that *Qualmsick* ever presumed to talk in this audacious Strain to his Wife; which incensed her so much, that she immediately burst out in Tears, and fell upon him with all the Bitterness of Passion. "Barbarous Monster," cried she, "how dare you insult over my Miseries, when I am just at the Point of Death? You might as well take a Knife and stab me to the Heart, you might——brutal, inhuman Wretch, thus to ridicule my Afflictions!——Get out of the Room, go, and let me never see your Face any more."

Qualmsick was so astounded at the *Premunire*[1] he had drawn himself into, that he knew not at first what to think or answer; but when he had a little recovered his Wits, which were none of the best, he endeavoured to lay the Blame on the Physician, and assured his Wife that whatever he had uttered, was by the Advice and Instigation of her Doctor. "'Tis a Lie," cried she blubbering, "'tis a horrid Lie; the Doctor has too much Humanity to contradict me, when I tell him I am at the Point of Death——No; 'tis your own Artifice, inhuman

---

1   "A difficulty; a distress. A low ungrammatical word" (Johnson).

Monster! you want to get rid of me, Barbarian! and this is the Method you have taken to murder me. I am going fast enough already, but thou wilt not suffer me to die in Peace——Get out of the Room, Cannibal, and never presume to come into my Presence any more."

With this terrible Injunction he was obliged to comply, and it was near a Fortnight before she admitted him to make his Peace; which, however, he did at length, with many Protestations of Sorrow for his past Offence, and repeated Assurances of behaving with more Humility for the future. The Physician, who gave Occasion to this Dispute, now fell a Sacrifice to it, and was immediately discarded for daring to suppose that a Lady was well, when she had made such a vehement Resolution to be ill.

CHAP. XIII

OUR HERO GOES TO THE UNIVERSITY OF CAMBRIDGE.

POMPEY had the good Fortune to bark one Day, when his Lady's Head was at the worst; whether designedly, or not, is difficult to determine; but the Sound so *pierced her Brain*, and *affected her Nerves*, that she resolved no longer to keep him in her own Apartments. And thus the same Action, which had unfortunately banished him from the Presence of *Aurora*, was now altogether as favourable in redeeming him from the sick Chamber, or rather Hospital of Mrs. *Qualmsick*.

Mrs. *Qualmsick* had a Son, who was about this Time going to the University of *Cambridge*, and as the young Gentleman had taken a Fancy to *Pompey*, he easily prevailed to carry him along with him, as a Companion to that great Seat of Learning.

Young *Qualmsick* inherited neither the hypochondriacal Disposition of his Mother, not the insipid Meekness of his Father; but, on the contrary, was blessed with a good Share of Health, and a great Flow of Animal Spirits, and a most violent Appetite for Pleasure. He received the first Part of his Education at *Westminster* School, where he had acquired what is usually called, *a very pretty Knowledge of the Town*; that is to say, he had been introduced, at the Age of Thirteen, into the most noted Bagnios,[1] knew the Names of the most celebrated Women of Pleasure, and could drink his two Bottles of Claret in an Evening, without being greatly disordered in his Understanding. At the Age of Seventeen, it was judged proper for him, merely out of Fashion, and to be like other young Gentlemen of his Acquaintance, to take Lodgings at a University; whither he went with a hearty Contempt of the Place, and a determined Resolution never to receive any Profit from it.

He was admitted under a Tutor, who knew no more of the World than if he had been bred up in a Forest, and whose sour pedantic Genius was ill-qualified to cope with the Vivacity and Spirit of a young Gentleman, warm in the Pursuit of Pleasure, and one who required much Address, and very artful Management, to make any kind of Restraint palatable and easy to him.

He was admitted in the Rank of a Fellow-commoner, which, according to the Definition given by a Member of the University in a Court of Justice, is one who sits at the same Table, and *enjoys the Conversation* of the Fellows. It differs from what is called a Gentleman-commoner at *Oxford*, not only in the Name, but also in the greater Privileges and Licenses indulged to the Members of this Order; who do not only *enjoy the Conversation of the Fellows*, but likewise a full Liberty of following their own Imaginations in every Thing. For as Tutors and Governors have usually pretty sagacious Noses after Preferment, they think it impolitic to cross the Inclinations of young Gentlemen, who are Heirs to great Estates, and from whom they expect Benefices and Dignities hereafter, as Rewards *for their Want of Care of them*, while they were under their Protection.[2] From hence it comes to pass, that Pupils of this Rank are excused from all public Exercises, and allowed to absent themselves at Pleasure from the private Lectures in their Tutor's Rooms, as often as they have made a Party for Hunting, or an Engagement at the Tennis-court, or are not well recovered from their Evening's Debauch. And whilst a poor unhappy Soph,[3] of no Fortune, is often expelled for the most trivial Offences, or merely to humour the capricious Resentment of his Tutor, who happens

---

1 Brothels.
2 See the Introduction, page 7, note 1.
3 Short form of "sophister." "At Cambridge, a student in his second or third year" (*OED*).

to dislike his Face; young Noblemen, and Heirs of great Estates, may commit any Illegalities, and, if they please, overturn a College with Impunity.

Young *Qualmsick* very early began to display his Genius, and was soon distinguished for one of the most enterprizing Spirits in the University. No-body set Order and Regularity at greater Defiance, or with more heroic Bravery than he did; which made him quickly be chosen Captain-general by his Comrades, in all their Parties of Pleasure, and Expeditions of Jollity. Many Pranks are recorded of his performing, which made the Place resound with his Name; but one of his Exploits being attended with Circumstances of a very droll Nature, we cannot forebear relating it.

There was in the same College, a young Master of Arts, *Williams* by Name, who had been elected into the Society,[1] in Preference to one of greater Genius and Learning, because he used to make a lower Bow to the Fellows, whenever he passed by them, and was not likely to disgrace any of his Seniors by the Superiority of his Parts. This Gentleman concluding now there was no farther Occasion of Study, after he had obtained a Fellowship, which had long been the Object of his Ambition, gave himself over to Pursuits more agreeable to his Temper, and spent the chief of his Time in drinking Tea with Barber's Daughters, and other young Ladies of Fashion in the University, who there take to themselves the Name of *Misses*, and receive Gownmen at their Ruelles. For nothing more is necessary to accomplish a young Lady at *Cambridge*, than a second-hand Capuchin, a white washing Gown, a Pair of dirty Silk Shoes, and long Muslin Ruffles;[2] in which Dresses they take the Air in public Walks every *Sunday*, to make their Conquests, and receive their Admirers all the rest of the Week at their Tea-tables. Now *Williams*, having a great deal of dangling Good-nature about him, was very successful in winning the Affections of these Academical Misses, and had a large Acquaintance among them. The three Miss *Higginses*, whose Mother kept the Sun Tavern; Miss

---

1   I.e., elected as a fellow or teacher in the college.
2   As being the daughters of barbers (and of the other common tradesmen later mentioned) hardly qualifies these "Misses" as fashionable gentlewomen, their apparel is cheap and dowdy.

Polly Jackson, a Baker's Daughter; the celebrated *Fanny Hill*,[1] sole Heiress of a Taylor, and Miss *Jenny* of the Coffee-house, were all great Admirers of our College-gallant; and Fame reported, that he had Admission to some of their Bed-chambers, as well as to their Tea-tables. Upon this Presumption, young *Qualmsick* laid his Head together with other young Gentlemen, his Comrades, to play him a Trick, which we now proceed to disclose.

About this Time, a Bed-maker of the College was unfortunately brought to Bed,[2] without having any Husband to father the Child; and as our Master of Arts was suspected, among others, to have had a Share in the Generation of the new-born Infant, being a Gentleman of an amorous Nature, it occurred to young *Qualmsick* to make the following Experiment upon him.

As Mr. *Williams* was coming out of his Chamber one Morning early to go to Chapel, he found a Basket standing at his Door on the top of his Stair-case, with a Direction to himself, and a Letter tied to the Handle of the Basket. He stood some little time guessing from whom such a Present could come, but as he had expected a Parcel from *London* by the Coach for a Week before, he naturally concluded this to be the same, and that it had been brought by a Porter from the Inn, and left at his Door before he was awake in the Morning. With this Thought he opened the Letter, and read to the following Effect.

Honourable Sir,
Am surprized should use me in such a manner; have never seen one Farthing of your Money, since was brought to To-bed, which is a Shame and a wicked Sin. Wherefore have sent you your own Bastard to provide for, and am your dutiful Sarvant to command tell Death——

Betty Trollop.

The Astonishment, which seized our Master of Arts at the perusal of this Letter, may easily be imagined, but not so easily de-

---

1 Coventry is recalling the name of John Cleland's prostitute heroine in his porno-graphic novel *Memoirs of a Lady of Pleasure* (1748).
2 Gave birth.

scribed: He turned pale, staggered, and looked like *Banquo's* Ghost in the Play;[1] but as his Conscience excused him from the Crime laid to his Charge, he resolved (as soon as his Confusion would suffer him to resolve) to make a public Example of the Wretch, that had dared to lay her Iniquities at his Door. To this end, as soon as Chapel was over, he desired the Master of the College to convene all the Fellows in the Common-room, for he had an Affair of great Consequence to lay before them. When the Reverend Divan[2] was met according to his Desire, he produced the Basket, and with an audible Voice read the Letter, which had been annexed to it: After which he made a long Oration on the unparalleled Impudence of the Harlot, who had attempted to scandalize him in this audacious Manner, and concluded with desiring the most exemplary Punishment might be inflicted on her; for he said, unless they discouraged such a Piece of Villainy with proper Severity, it might hereafter be their own Lots, if they were remiss in punishing the present Offender. They all heard him with great Astonishment, and many of them seemed to rejoice inwardly, that the Basket had not travelled to their Doors; as thinking, perhaps, it would have been unfatherly and unnatural to refuse it Admittance. But the Master of the College taking the thing a little more seriously, declared that if Mr. *Williams* had not been known to trespass in that Way, the Girl would never have singled him out to father her Iniquities upon him; however as the thing had happened, and he had protested himself innocent, he said he would take care the Strumpet should be punished for her Impudence. He then ordered the Basket to be unpacked; which was performed by the Butler of the College, in Presence of the whole Fraternity; when lo!——instead of a Child, puling and crying for its Father, out leaped *Pompey*, the little Hero of this little History; who had been enclosed in that Osier[3] Confinement by young *Qualmsick*, and convey'd very early in the Morning to Mr. *Williams*'s Chamber-door. The grave Assembly were astonished and enraged at the Discovery, finding themselves

---

1 See *Macbeth* 3.4.
2 "Divan," derived from a Turkish word, is defined by Johnson as "Any council assembled; used commonly in a sense of dislike." This divan is "reverend" because most
   or all of the college fellows would be in holy orders.
3 Willow-work.

convened only to be ridiculed; and all of them gazed on our Hero with the same kind of Aspect, as did the Daughters of *Cecrops* on the deformed *Erichthonius*, when their Curiosity tempted them to peep into the Basket, which *Minerva* had put into their Hands, with positive Commands to the contrary.[1]

CHAP. XIV

THE CHARACTER OF A MASTER OF ARTS AT A UNIVERSITY.

WIILIAMS, tho' much ashamed and out of Countenance, was yet in his Heart very glad to be relieved from the Apprehensions of maintaining a Bastard, which he imagined would add no great Lustre to his Reputation as a Fellow of a College. When therefore *Pompey* made his Escape out of his wicker Prison, he was in reality pleased with the Discovery, which put an end to his Fears; and feigning himself diverted with the humour of the Thing, took the little Adventurer home to his own Chambers. Thus our Hero changed his Master, which gives us an Opportunity of explaining some farther Particulars of that Gentleman's Character, being, I believe, not an uncommon one in either of our Universities.

If we were in a hurry to describe him, it might be done effectually in two or three Words, by calling him *a most egregious Trifler*; but as we have Leisure to be a little more circumstantial, the Reader is like to be troubled with a Day's Journal of his Actions.

He was in the first Place a Man of the most exact and punctilious Neatness; his Shoes were always blacked in the nicest Manner, his Wigs powdered with the most finical Delicacy, and he would scold his Laundress for a whole Morning together, if he discovered a wry Plait in the Sleeve of his Shirt, or the least Speck of Dirt on any

---

1　According to this Greek myth, which comes down to us in different versions, Erich–thonius sprang from the ground after Athena (or Minerva, in the Roman pantheon) successfully resisted an attempted rape by Hephaestus. She later gave strict orders to the daughters of Cecrops, king of Athens, not to open the box enclosing the infant Erichthonius. They disobeyed and were driven mad by his hideous appearance.

Part of his Linnen. He rose constantly to Chapel, and afterwards proceeded with great Importance to Breakfast, which moderately speaking took up to two Hours of his Morning; for when he had done sipping his Tea, he used to wash up the Cups with the most orderly Exactness, and replace them with the utmost Regularity in their Corner-cupboard. After this, he drew on his Boots, ordered his Horse, and rode out for the Air, having been told that a sedentary Life is destructive of the Constitution, and that too much Study impairs the Health. At his Return he had barely Time to wash his Hands, clean his Teeth, and put on a fresh-powdered Wig, before the College-bell summoned him to Dinner in the public Hall. When this great Affair was ended, he spent an Hour with the rest of the Fellows in the Common-room to digest his Meal, and then went to the Coffee-house to read the News-papers; where he loitered away that heavy Interval, which passed between Dinner and the Hour appointed for Afternoon Tea: But as soon as the Clock struck Three, he tucked up his Gown, and flew with all imaginable Haste to some of the young Ladies above-mentioned, who all esteemed him a prodigious Genius, and were ready to laugh at his Wit before he had opened his Mouth. In these agreeable Visits he remained till the Time of Evening Chapel; and when this was over, Supper succeeded next to find him fresh Employment; from whence he repaired again to the Coffee-House, and then to some Engagement he had made at a Friend's Room to spend the remaining Part of the Evening. By this Account of his Day's Transactions, the Reader will see how very impossible it was for him to find Leisure for Study in the midst of so many important Avocations; yet he made a shift sometimes to play half a Tune on the German Flute in the Morning, and once in a Quarter of a Year took the Pains to transcribe a Sermon out of various Authors.

Another part of his Character was a great Affectation of Politeness, which is more pretended to in Universities, where less of it is practiced, than in any other Part of the Kingdom. Thus *Williams*, like many others, was always talking of *genteel Life*, to which end he was plentifully provided with Stories by a female Cousin, who kept a Milliner's Shop in *London*, and never failed to let him know by Letters, what passed among *the Great*: Tho' she frequently mistook the Names of People, and attributed Scandal to one Lord, which was the Property of another. Her Cousin however did not find out the Mistakes, but retailed her Blunders about the Colleges with great Confidence and Security.

But nothing in the World pleased him more than shewing the University to Strangers, and especially to Ladies, which he thought gave him an Air of Acquaintance with the *genteel World*; and on such Occasions, if he could prevail on them to dine with him, he would affect to make expensive Entertainments, which neither his private Fortune or the Income of his Fellowship could afford.

[There flourished in this college, or rather was beginning to flourish, a young physician, who now stood candidate for fame and practice. He had equipped himself with a gilt-headed cane, a black suit of cloaths, a wise mysterious face, a full-bottomed flowing peruke, and all other externals of his profession: so that, if according to the inimitable *Swift*, the various members of a commonwealth are only so many different suits of cloaths,[1] this gentleman was amply qualified for the discharge of his office. But not chusing to rely totally on his dress to introduce him into business, he was willing to add to it a supplemental, and as many think, superfluous knowledge of his art.

About this time, a member of the university died in great torments of the iliac passion,[2] and some peculiarities in his case made a noise among the faculty of *Cambridge*. The theory of this terrible disorder, caused by the cessation of the peristaltic motion of the guts, our young doctor very well understood; but not contenting himself with theory only, he resolved to go a step farther, and for this purpose, cast his eyes about after some dog, intending to dissect him alive for the satisfaction of his curiosity.[3]

A dog might have been the emblematic animal of *Esculapius* or *Apollo*, with as much propriety as he was of *Mercury*;[4] for no creatures I believe have been of more eminent service to the healing tribe than dogs. Incredible is the number of these animals, who have been

---

1   See Jonathan Swift's *A Tale of a Tub* (1704), sec. 2.
2   I.e., distemper of the lower bowel.
3   Vivisection was a common practice in the eighteenth century, though widely condemned as cruel. See Appendix E.
4   Associations between dogs and the Roman god Mercury, whose counterpart in Greek mythology is Hermes, derive from this deity's traits of quickness and intelligence. The Greeks adopted Hermes from the Egyptian god Thoth, who was depicted as a dog-faced baboon.

sacrificed from time to time at the shrines of physic and surgery. Lectures of anatomy subsist by their destruction; *Ward* (says Mr. *Pope*) tried his drop on puppies and the poor;[1] and in general all new medicines and experiments of a doubtful nature are sure to be made in the first place on the bodies of these unfortunate animals. Their very ordure is one of the chief articles of the *Materia Medica*;[2] and I am persuaded, if the old *Egyptians* had any physician among them, they certainly described him by the hieroglyphic of a dog.

But to spend too much time in these conjectures, our young doctor had no sooner resolved to satisfy himself concerning the peristaltic motion of the guts, than unluckily, in an evil hour, *Pompey* presented himself to his eye. More unluckily for him still, neither his master Mr. *Williams*, nor any other of his college-friends happened to be present, or within view at this moment. *Machaon*[3] therefore very boldly seized him as a victim, and conveyed him into a little dark place near his room, which he called his cellar, and in which he kept his wine. There he shut him up three or four days in the condemned hole, while he prepared his chirurgical instruments, and invited some other young practitioners in physic of his acquaintance to be present at our hero's dissection.

The day being soon appointed for his death, the company assembled at their friend's room in the morning at breakfast, where much sapient discourse passed among them concerning the operation in hand, not material to be now related. At length cries the hero of the party, "Come gentlemen! We seem I think to have finished our breakfasts, let us now proceed to business:" after which, the tea-things were removed, the instruments of dissection placed on the table, and the doctor went to his cellar to bring forth the unhappy victim.

And here, good-natured reader, I am sure it moves thy compassion to think that poor *Pompey*, after suffering already so many misfortunes, must at last be dissected alive to satisfy a physician concerning the peristaltic motion of the guts. The case would indeed be lamen-

---

1   See *The First Epistle of the Second Book of Horace* (1737) where Alexander Pope satirizes the experimentation of Joshua Ward's (1685-1761) famous elixir on "Puppies and the Poor" (l. 182).

2   Latin: medical materials. "The remedial substances and preparations used in the practice of medicine" (*OED*).

3   Like Aesculapius, his father, Machaon was a healer and therefore his name is synonymous with those in the medical profession.

table, if it had happened: but when the doctor came to call him forth to execution, to his great surprize no dog was there to be found. He found however something else not entirely to his satisfaction, and that was his wine streaming in great profusion about his cellar. The truth is, our hero, being grown desperate with hunger, had in his struggles for liberty broke all the bottles, and at last forcibly gnawed his way thro' a deal[1] board, that composed one side of the cellar. The danger however which he had been in, made him sick of universities, and he wished earnestly for an accident, which soon happened, to relieve him from an academic life.]

CHAP. XV

ANOTHER COLLEGE-CHARACTER.

ABOUT this Time three Ladies happened to be returning out of the *North*, whither they had been to make a Summer-Visit, and were inclined to take *Cambridge* in their way Home; which Place they believed to be worthy of their Curiosity, having never seen it. For this Purpose they procured a double Recommendation to two Gentlemen of different Colleges, lest one of them should happen to be absent at the Time of their Arrival. One of these Gentlemen was the Reverend Mr. *Williams*, who received a Letter from a Friend of his, advertising him of the Arrival of three Ladies, and desiring he would assist their Curiosity in shewing them the University. At the same time came another Letter from another Gentleman to an ancient Doctor of Divinity, whose Character we shall here disclose.

This Gentleman in his Youth, when his Friend was at College, had been a Man of great Gaiety, and stands upon the Record for the first Person who introduced Tea-drinking into the University of *Cambridge*. He had good Parts, improved by much classical Reading; but it was his Misfortune very early in Life to fall in Love with an Apothecary's Daughter, with whom he maintained a Courtship

---

1   "A slice sawn from a log of timber (now always of fir or pine), and usually understood to be more than seven inches wide, and not more than three thick; a plank or board of pine or fir-wood" (*OED*).

near Twenty Years; in which Time he laboured by all means in his Power, but without Success, to obtain a Living,[1] as the Foundation of Matrimony. For tho' his Vivacity had rendered him agreeable to many young Gentlemen of Fortune, who were his Cotemporaries at College, he found himself forgotten by them, when they came into the World, and too late experienced the Difference between a Companion and a Friend. Disappointed in all his Hopes, and growing sick of a tedious Courtship, he shut himself up in his Chamber, and there abandoned himself to Melancholy: He shunned all his Friends, and became a perfect Recluse; appeared but seldom at Meals in the College-hall, and then with so wild a Face and unfashionable a Dress, that all the younger Part of the College, who knew nothing of his History, esteemed him a Madman. This was the Person recommended to conduct the Ladies about the University; for his Friend unluckily made no Allowance for the Fifty Years that had elapsed since his own leaving the College, but concluded his old Acquaintance to be the same Man of Gallantry in his Age, which he had formerly remembered him in his Youth.

When the Ladies arrived at *Cambridge*, accompanied by a Gentleman, who was their Relation, they laid their Heads together to consider what Measures they should pursue; and all agreeing that it would be proper to pay the Doctor a Visit at his Chamber, they set out in a Body for that Purpose. Being directed to his College, and having with Difficulty found out his Stair-Case, they mounted it with many wearisome Steps, and knocked at the Door for Admittance. It was a long while before the Sound pierced thro' the sevenfold Night-caps of the old Doctor, who sat dozing half-asleep in an Elbow-chair by a Fire almost extinguished. When he had opened the Door, he started back at the Sight of Ladies with as much Amazement as if he had seen a Ghost, and kept the Door half-shut in his Hand, to prevent their Entrance into his Room. Indeed his Apartment was not a Spectacle that deserved Exhibition, for it seemed not to have been swept for Twenty Years past, and lay in great Disorder, scattered over with mouldy Books and yellow Manuscripts. The Cobwebs extended themselves from one Corner of the Room to the other, and the Mice and Rats took their Pastime

---

1   I.e., an appointment as rector of a church. The Doctor's "labour" would be to obtain the favor of a nobleman or wealthy landowner, upon whom such appointments were usually dependent.

about the Floor with as much Security as if it had been uninhabited. On a Table stood a Can of stale Small Beer, and a Plate of Cheese-pairings, the Relicks of his last Night's Supper: All which Appearances created such Astonishment in his Visiters, that they began to believe themselves directed to a wrong Person, and thought it impossible for this to be the gay Gentleman, who had been recommended to them as the Perfection of Courtesy and Good-breeding.

When therefore they had suppressed their Inclination to laugh as well as they could, the Gentleman who was Spokesman of the Party, began to beg Pardon for the Disturbance they had given in consequence of a wrong Information, and desired to be directed to the Chambers of Doctor *Clouse.* "Oho," said the Doctor, "What——I warrant you are the *Folks* that I received a Letter about last Week!" The Gentleman then assured him they were the same, and begged the favour of his Assistance, if it was not too much Trouble, to shew the Ladies the University, which they would acknowledge as a very particular Favour. "A-lack-a-day!" answered he with a stammering Voice, "I should be very glad, Sir, to do the Ladies any Service in my Power; but really I protest, Sir, I have almost forgot the University. 'Tis many Years since I have ventured out of my own College, and indeed it is not often that I go out of my Room——You'll find some younger Man, Ladies, that knows more of the Matter than I do; for I suppose every Thing is altered since my Time, and I question whether I should know my Way about the Streets." After which Words he made a Motion to retire into his Chamber, which the Company observing, asked Pardon once more for the Disturbance they had given, and made haste away to laugh at this uncommon Adventure.

CHAP. XVI

A PRODIGIOUS SHORT CHAPTER.

WHEN the Gentlemen and Ladies were got back to their Inn, they diverted themselves with much Raillery at the old Doctor's Expence, and began to despair of any better Success from their second Recommendation, charitably concluding that all the Members of the

University were like the Gentleman they had seen. They resolved therefore not to be at the Trouble of visiting Mr. *Williams*, but sent a Messenger from the Inn to inform him of their Arrival, and beg the Favour of his Company at Supper; which Invitation, however, they would gladly have excused him from accepting, for they were grown sick of the Place, and determined to leave it early the next Morning.

Williams, who lived in Expectation of their coming several Days, posted away to the Inn with all imaginable Dispatch, and with many academical Compliments, welcomed them to *Cambridge*. He staid Supper, and the Evening was spent with a great deal of Mirth; for when the Ladies found they had to do with a human Being, they recounted the Adventure of the old Doctor, and *Williams*, in return, entertained them with several others of a similar Nature. Nor did he depart to his College, till he had made them promise to dine with him at his Chambers the next Day.

Early in the Morning then he rose with the Lark, and held a Consultation with the College Cook concerning the Dinner, and other Particulars of the Entertainment: For as he had never yet been honoured with Company of so high a Rank, he resolved to do what was handsome, and send them away with an Opinion of his Politeness. Among many other Devices he had *to be genteel*, one very well deserves mentioning, being of a very academical Nature indeed; for he was at the Expence of purchasing a *China Vase* of a certain Shape, which sometimes passes under a more vulgar Name, to set in his Bed-chamber; that if the Ladies should chuse to retire after Dinner, for the sake of *looking at the Pattern of his Bed*, or to *see the Prospect out of his Window*, or from any other Motive of Curiosity, they might have the Pleasure of being *served in China*.

When these Affairs were settled, he dressed himself in his best Array, and went to bid the Ladies good-morrow. As soon as they had breakfasted, he conducted them about the University, and shewed them all the Rarities of *Cambridge*. They observed, *that such a thing was very grand, another thing was very neat, and that there were a great many Books in the Libraries, which they thought it impossible for any Man to read through, tho' he was live as long as* Methuselah.[1]

---

[1]   Having died at the age of 969 (Genesis 5.27), Methuselah is the oldest person in the Bible; his name is proverbial for longevity.

When their Curiosity was satisfied, and *Williams* had indulged every Wish of Vanity, in being seen to escort Ladies about the University, and to hand them out of their Coach, they all retired to his Chambers to Dinner. Much Conversation passed, not worth recording, and when the Cloth was taken away, little *Pompey* was produced on the Table for the Ladies to admire him. They were greatly struck with his Beauty; and one of them took Courage to ask him as a Present, which the complaisant Master of Arts, in his great Civility, complied with, and immediately delivered him into the Lady's Hands. He likewise related the Story, how he came into his Possession, which another Person perhaps would have suppressed; but *Williams* was so transported with his Company, that he was half out of his Wits with Joy, and his Conversation was as ridiculous as his Behaviour.

CHAP. XVII

POMPEY RETURNS TO LONDON, AND OCCASIONS A REMARKABLE DISPUTE IN THE MALL.

ONCE more then our Hero set out for the Metropolis of *Great-Britain*, and after an easy Journey of two Days arrived at a certain Square, where his Mistresses kept their Court. To these Ladies, not improperly might be applied the Questions which *Archer* asks in the Play, *Pray which of you three is the old Lady?*[1] the Mother being full as youthful and airy as the Daughters, and the Daughters almost as ancient as the Mother.

Now as Fortune often disposes Things in the most whimsical and surprizing Manner, it so happened, that one of his Mistresses took him with her one Morning into St. *James's Park*, and set him down on his Legs almost in the very same Part of the *Mall*, from whence he had formerly made his Escape from Lady *Tempest* near eight Years before, as is recorded in the first Part of his History. Her Ladyship was walking this Morning for the Air, and happened to pass by almost at the very Instant that the little Adventurer was set on his Legs to take

---

1   *The Beaux Stratagem* (1707) 4.1., by George Farquhar (1678-1707).

his Diversion. She spied him in a Moment, with great Quickness of Discernment, and immediately recollected her old Acquaintance, caught him up in her Arms, and fell to kissing him with the highest Extravagance of Joy. His present Owner perceiving this, and thinking only that the Lady was pleased with the Beauty of her Dog, and had a mind to compliment him with a few Kisses, passed on without interrupting her: But when she saw her Ladyship preparing to carry him out of the *Mall* in her Arms, she advanced hastily towards her, and redemanded her Favourite in the following Terms: "Pray, Madam, what is your Ladyship going to do with that Dog?" Lady *Tempest* replied, "Nothing in the World, Madam, but take him home with me." "And pray, Madam, what Right has your Ladyship to take a Dog that belongs to me?" "None, my dear!" answered Lady *Tempest*; "but I take him, Child, because he belongs to me." "'Tis false," said the other Lady, "I aver it to be false; he was given me by a Gentleman of *Cambridge*, and I insist upon your Ladyship's replacing him upon his Legs, this individual Moment." To this, Lady *Tempest* replied only with a Sneer, and was walking off with our Hero; which so greatly aggravated the Rage of her Antagonist, that she now lost all Patience, and began to exert herself in a much higher Key. "Madam," said she, "I would have you to know, Madam, that I am not to be treated in this *superlative Manner.* Your Ladyship may affect to sneer, if you please, Madam, which is more due to your own Actions than to me, Madam; for thank Heaven, I have some Regard to Decency in my Actions." "Dear, Miss! don't be in a Passion," replied Lady *Tempest*; "it will spoil your Complexion Child, and perhaps ruin your Fortune——but will you be pleased to know, my Dear, that I lost this Dog eight Years ago in the *Mall*, and advertized him in all the News-papers, tho' you or your Friend at *Cambridge*, who did me the Favour to steal him, were not so obliging as to restore him?——And will you be pleased to know likewise, young Lady, that I have a Right to take my Property wherever I find it." "'Tis impossible," cried the other Lady, tossing back her Head, "'tis impossible to remember a Dog after eight Years absence; I aver it to be impossible, and nothing shall persuade me to believe it." "I protest, my Dear," answered Lady *Tempest*, "I know not what Sort of Memory you may be blest with, but really, I can remember Things of a much longer Date; and as a fresh Instance of my Memory, I think, my Dear, I remember you representing the Character of a young Lady for near these twenty Years about Town." "Madam," returned the Lady of inferior Rank, now inflamed with the highest Indignation; "you may remember yourself, Madam, representing a much worse Character, Madam, for a greater Number of Years. It would be well, Madam, if your Memory was not altogether so good, Madam, unless your Actions were better."

The War of Tongues now began to rage with the greatest Violence, and nothing was spared that Wit could suggest on the one side, or Malice on the other. The Beaux, and Belles, and Witlings, who were walking that Morning in the *Mall*, assembled round the Combatants at first, out of Curiosity, and for the sake of Entertainment; but they soon began to take Sides in the Dispute, 'till at length it became one universal Scene of Wrangle; and no Cause in *Westminster-Hall*[1] was ever more puzzled by the Multitude of Voices all contending at once for the Victory. At last, Lady *Tempest* scorning this ungenerous Altercation, told her Adversary, "Well, Madam, if you please to scold for the publick Diversion, pray continue; but for my Part, I shall no longer make myself a *Spectacle* of a Mob." And so saying, she walked courageously off with little *Pompey* under her Arm. It was impossible for her Rival to prevent her; who likewise immediately after quitted the *Mall*, and flew home, ready to burst with Shame, Spite, and Indignation.

Lady *Tempest* had not been long at her Toilette, before the following little Scroll was brought to her; and she was informed, that a Footman waited below in great Hurry for an Answer. The Note was to this Effect.

Madam,
If it was possible for me to wonder at any of your Actions, I should be astonished at your Behaviour of this Morning. Restore my Dog by the Bearer of this Letter, or by the living G—d, I will immediately commence a Prosecution against you in Chancery, and recover him by Force of Law.

---

1   A Medieval hall occupied by the courts of justice in the eighteenth century and surrounded by lively market stalls where, no doubt, the various cases would be publicly wrangled.

Yours____

Lady *Tempest*, without any Hesitation, returned the following Answer.

Madam,
I have laughed heartily at your ingenious Epistle; and am prodigiously diverted with your Menaces of a Law-Suit. *Pompey* shall be ready to put in his Answer, as soon as he hears your Bill is filed against him in Chancery.

I am, dear Miss, yours,

TEMPEST.

CHAP. XVIII

A TERRIBLE MISFORTUNE HAPPENS TO OUR HERO, WHICH BRINGS HIS HISTORY TO A CONCLUSION.

THIS Letter inflamed the Lady so much, that she immediately ordered her Coach, and drove away to *Lincoln*'s-*Inn*, to consult her Sollicitor. She found him in his Chambers, surrounded with Briefs, and haranguing to two Gentlemen, who had made him Arbitrator in a very important Controversy, concerning the Dilapidations of a Pig-stye. On the Arrival of our Lady, the Man of Law started from his Chair, and conducted her with much Civility to a Settee which stood by his Fire-side; then turning to his two Clients, whom he thought he had already treated with a proper Quantity of Eloquence, "Well, Gentlemen," said he, "when your respective Attornies have drawn up your several Cases, let them be sent to me, and I'll give Determination upon them with all possible Dispatch." This Speech had the desired Effect in driving them away, and as soon as they were gone, addressing himself with an Affectation of much Politeness to the Mistress of little *Pompey*, he began to enquire after the *good Lady her Mother*, and *the good Lady her Sister*——but our Heroine was so impatient to open her Cause, that she hardly allowed herself Time to answer his Questions, before she began in the following Manner. "Sir, I was walking this Morning in the *Mall*, when a certain extraordinary Lady, whose Actions are always of a very extraordinary Nature, was pleased, in a most peculiar Manner, to steal my Lap-dog from me." "Steal your Lap-dog from you, Madam!" said the Man of Law; "I protest, a very extraordinary Transaction indeed! And pray, Madam, what could induce her to be guilty of such a Misbehaviour?" "Induce her!" cried the Lady eagerly; "Sir, she wants no Inducement to be guilty of any thing that is audacious and impudent.——But, Sir, I desire you would immediately commence a Suit against her in Chancery, and push the Affair on with all possible Rapidity, for I am resolved to recover the Dog, if it costs me Ten Thousand Pounds." The Counsellor smiled, and commended her Resolutions; but paused a little, and seemed puzzled at the Novelty of the Case. "Madam," said he, "undoubtedly your Ladyship does right to assert your Property, for we should all soon be reduced to a State of Nature, if there were no Courts of Law; and therefore your Ladyship is highly to be applauded——but there is something very peculiar in the Nature of Dogs——There is no Question, Madam, but they are to be considered under the Denomination of Property, and not to be deemed *feræ Naturæ*, Things of no Value, as ignorant People foolishly imagine; but I say, Madam, there is something very peculiar in their Nature, Madam.——Their prodigious Attachment to Man inclines them to follow any body that calls them, and that makes it so difficult to fix a Theft.——Now, if a Man calls a Sheep, or calls a Cow, or calls a Horse, why he might call long enough before they would come, because they are not Creatures of a *following Nature*, and therefore our penal Laws have made it Felony with respect to those Animals; but Dogs, Madam, have a strange undistinguishing Proneness to run after People's Heels." "Lord bless me, Sir!" said the Lady, somewhat angry at the Orator's Declamation; "What do you mean, Sir, by following People's Heels? I do protest and asseverate, that she took him up in her Arms, and carried him away in Defiance of me, and the whole *Mall* was Witness of the Theft." "Very well, Madam, very well," replied the Counsellor, "I was only stating the Case fully on the Defendant's side, that you might have a comprehensive View of the whole Affair, before we come to unravel it all again, and shew the Advantages on the side of the Plaintiff.——Now, tho' a Dog be of *a following Nature*, as I observed, and may be sometimes tempted, and seduced, and inveigled away in such a Manner, as makes it difficult——do you observe me——makes it difficult, I say, Madam, to fix a Theft on the Person seducing; yet, wherever Property is discovered and claimed, if the Possessor refuses to restore it on Demand,——on Demand, I say, because Demand must be made——refuses to restore it, on Demand, to the proper, lawful Owner, there an Action lies, and, under this Predicament, we shall recover our Lap-dog." The Lady seeming pleased with this Harangue, the Orator continued in the following Manner; "If therefore, Madam, this Lady——whosoever she is, *A.* or *B.* or any Name serves our Purpose——if, I say, this extraordinary Lady, as your Ladyship just now described her, took your Dog before Witnesses, and refused to restore it on Demand, why then we have a lawful Action, and shall recover Damages.——Pray, Madam, do you think you can swear to the Identity of the Dog, if he should be produced in a Court of Justice?" The Lady answered, "Yes, she could swear to him amongst a Million, for there never was so remarkable a Creature." "And you first became possessed of him, you say, Madam, at the University of *Cambridge*.——Pray, Madam, will the Gentleman, who invested you with him, be ready to testify the Donation?" She answered affirmatively. "And pray, Madam, what is the Colour of your Dog?" "Black and White, Sir!" "A Male, or Female, Madam?" To this Lady replied, *She positively could not tell*; whereupon, the Counsellor, with a most sapient Aspect, declared he would search his Books for a Precedent, and wait on her, in a few Days, to receive her final Determinations; but advised her, in the mean while, to try the Effect of another Letter upon her Ladyship, and once more threaten her with a Prosecution. He then waited upon her to her Chariot, observed that *it was a very fine Day*, and promised to use his utmost Endeavours to reinstate her in the Possession of her Lap-dog.

This was the State of the Quarrel between two Ladies for a Dog, and it seemed as if all the Mouths of the Law would have opened on this important Affair (for Lady *Tempest* continued obstinate in keeping him) had not a most unlucky Accident happened to balk those honourable Gentlemen of their Fees, and disappoint them of so hopeful a Topic for shewing their Abilities. This unfortunate Stroke was nothing less than the Death of our Hero, who was seized with a violent Pthisic,[1] and after a Week's Illness, departed this Life on the Second of *June*, 1749, and was gathered to the Lapdogs of Antiquity.

From the Moment that he fell sick, his Mistress spared no Expence for his Recovery, and had him attended by the most eminent Physicians of *London*; who, I am afraid, rather hastened than delayed his Exit, according to the immemorial Custom of that right venerable Fraternity. The Chamber-maids took it by Turns to sit up with him every Night during his Illness, and her Ladyship was scarce ever away from him in the Daytime; but, alas! his Time was come, his Hour-glass was run out, and nothing could save him from paying a Visit to the *Plutonian* Regions.

It is difficult to say, whether her Ladyship's Sorrow now, or when she formerly lost him in the *Mall*, most exceeded the Bounds of Reason. He lay in State three Days after his Death, and her Ladyship, at first, took a Resolution of having him embalmed, but as her Physicians informed her the Art was lost, she was obliged to give over that chimerical Project; otherwise, our Posterity might have seem him, some Centuries hence, erected in a public Library at a University; and, perhaps, some Doctor, of great Erudition, might have undertaken to prove, with Quotations from a Thousand Authors, that he was formerly the *Egyptian Anubis*.[2]

However, tho' her Ladyship could not be gratified in her Desires of embalming him, she had him buried, with great Funeral Solemnity, in her Garden, and erected over him an elegant Marble Monument, which was inscribed with the following Epitaph, by one of the greatest Elegiac Poets of the present Age.[3]

---

1   Usually spelt "phthisic" or "phthisis," "A wasting disease, especially one involving the lungs; specifically tuberculosis" (*OED*).
2   An Egyptian god depicted as jackal-headed or dog-headed and, suitably, one of the deities of the underworld.
3   Presumably Coventry himself.

King of the Garden, blooming Rose!
Which sprang'st from Venus' *heavenly Woes,*
When weeping for Adonis *slain,*[1]
Her pearly Tears bedew'd the Plain,
Now let thy dewy Leaves bewail
A greater Beauty's greater Ill;
Ye Lillies! Hang your drooping Head,
Ye Myrtles! weep for Pompey *dead;*
Light lie the Turf upon his Breast,
Peace to his Shade, and gentle Rest.

CHAP. XIX

THE CONCLUSION.

HAVING thus traced our Hero to the Fourteenth Year of his Age, which may be reckoned the Threescore and Ten[2] of a Lap-dog, nothing now remains, but to draw his Character, for the Benefit and Information of Posterity. In so doing we imitate the greatest, and most celebrated Historians, Lord *Clarendon*, Dr. *Middleton*, and others who, when they have put a Period to a Life of an eminent Person (and such undoubtedly was our Hero) finish all with a Description of his Morals, his Religion, and private Character: Nay, many Biographers go so far, as to record the Colour of their Hero's Complexion, the Shade of his Hair, the Height of his Stature, the Manner of his Diet, when he went to Bed at Night, at what Hour he rose in the Morning, and other equally important Particulars; which cannot fail to convey the greatest Satisfaction and Improvement to their Readers. Thus a certain Painter, who obliged the World with a Life of *Milton*,[3] informs us, with an Air of great Importance, *that he was a short thick Man*, and then recollecting himself, informs us a second Time, upon maturer Deliberation, *that he was not a short thick*

---

1   Adonis, beloved by Venus, was gored to death by a boar during a hunt.
2   I.e. seventy years old.
3   *Explanatory Notes and Remarks on Milton's "Paradise Lost"* (1734) by Jonathan Richardson (1665–1745).

Man, but if he had been a little shorter, and a little thicker, he would have been a short thick Man; which prodigious Exactness, in an Affair of such Consequence, can never be sufficiently applauded.

Now as to the Description of our Hero's person, that has already been given in an Advertisement, penned by one of his Mistresses, when he had the Misfortune to be lost in *St. James's Park*, and therefore we will not trouble our reader with a needless Repetition of it, but proceed to his Religion, his Morals, his Amours, &c. in Conformity to the Practice of other Historians.

It is to be remembered, in the first Place, to his Credit, that he was a Dog of the *most courtly Manners*, ready to fetch and carry, at the Command of all his Masters, without ever considering the Service he was employed in, or the Person from whom he received his Directions: He would fawn likewise with the greatest Humility, on People who treated him with Contempt, and was always particularly officious in his Zeal, whenever he expected a new Collar, or stood Candidate for a Ribbon with other Dogs, who made up the Retinue of his Family.

Far be it from us to deny, that in the first Part of his Life he gave himself an unlimited Freedom in his Amours, and was extravagantly licentious, not to say debauched, in his Morals; but whoever considers that he was born in the House of an *Italian* Courtesan, that he made the grand Tour with a young Gentleman of Fortune, and afterwards lived near two Years with a Lady of Quality, will have more Reason to wonder that his Morals were not entirely corrupted, than that they were a little tainted by the ill Effect of such dangerous Examples: Whereas, when he became acquainted with a Philosophical Cat, who set him right in his mistaken Apprehensions of Things, he lived, afterwards, a Life of tolerable Regularity, and behaved with much Constancy to the Ladies, who were so happy as to engage his Affections.

As to Religion, we must ingeniously confess that he had none; in which Respect he had the Honour to bear an exact Resemblance of all the well-bred People of the present Age, who have long since discarded Religion, as a needless and troublesome Invention, calculated only to make People wise, virtuous, and unfashionable; and whoever will be at the Pains of perusing the Lives and Actions of the Great World, will find them, in all Points, conformable to such prodigious Principles.

In Politics, it is difficult to say whether he was Whig or Tory, for he never was heard, on any Occasion, to open his Mouth on that Subject, tho' he once served a Lady, whom Love engaged very deeply in Party, and perhaps might have been admitted to vote at a certain Election, among the Numbers that composed that stupendous Poll.

For the latter Part of his Life, his chief Amusement was to sleep before the Fire, and Indolence grew upon him so much, as he advanced in Age, that he seldom cared to be disturbed in his Slumbers, even to eat his Meals: His Eyes grew dim, his Limbs failed him, his Teeth dropped out of his Head, and, at length, a Pthisic came very seasonably to relieve him from the Pains and Calamities of long Life.

Thus perished little *Pompey*, or *Pompey the Little*, leaving his disconsolate Mistress to bemoan his Fate, and me to write his eventful History.

FINIS.

Appendix A: Omitted Section from Book II, Chapters VI–VII in The Third Edition[1]

[In the third edition of *Pompey the Little* (1752), Coventry replaced the story of Pompey's stay with Lord Danglecourt with the following story of Lord and Lady Marmazet. The possible reasons for this change are puzzling: the character of Lord Danglecourt is among the most original and interesting in the novel, and this politician's encounter with the members of a borough council is far more entertaining than the following rehearsal of Coventry's satire on the follies of the upper-ranks. He perhaps aimed to incorporate greater unity in the novel by reintroducing Lady Marmazet, who briefly appears in the Bath episodes at the end of Book one.]

This accomplished person was Lord *Marmazet*, husband to that lady, who was so familiar and intimate with the sharper at *Bath*. He was a man of consummate intrigue, a most fortunate adventurer with the fair sex, and had the reputation of uncommon success in his amours. What made this success the more extraordinary was, that in personal charms he had nothing to boast of: nature had given him neither a face or figure to strike the eyes of women; but these deficiencies were abundantly recompensed by a most happy turn of wit, a very brilliant imagination, and extensive knowledge of the world. He had the most intriguing manner of address, the readiest flow of language, and a certain art of laughing women out of their virtue, which few could imitate. It was indeed scarce possible to withstand the allurements of his conversation; and what is odd enough, the number of affairs he had been concerned in, were so far from frightening ladies from his acquaintance, that on the contrary it was fashionable and modish to cultivate an intimacy with him. They knew the danger of putting themselves in his way, and yet were ambitious of giving him opportunities.

The lady we have just now seen with him, had been his neighbour in the country, a very handsome woman under the tyranny of an

---

1   See p. 176 above for the place of this section in the third edition.

ill-natured husband. This his lordship knew, and concluding that her aversion to her husband would make her an easy prey to a lover, watched every opportunity of being alone with her. In these stolen interviews he employed all his eloquence to seduce her, and won upon her so much by his flattering representation of things, that at length she courageously eloped from her tyrant, and put herself into private lodgings under the protection of his lordship. The reader need not be told that this ended in the utter ruin of the lady, who finding her reputation lost, and her passionate lover soon growing indifferent, took refuge in citron waters, and by the help of those cordial lenitives of sorrow, soon bade adieu to the world and all its cares.

CHAP. VII.

MATRIMONIAL AMUSEMENTS.

WHEN our hero waked the next morning, and found himself in new apartments, the first thing he did was to piss on a pair of velvet breeches, which lay in a chair by his lordship's bedside; after which, the door being open, he travelled forth, and performed a much more disreputable action on a rich *Turkey* carpet in my lady's dining-room. Having thus taken possession of his new house by these two acts of *seisin*,[1] he returned to the bed-side, and reposed himself again to sleep till his lord should please to be stirring.

About ten o'clock lord *Marmazet* raised himself up in his bed, and rang his bell for servants to assist him in the fatigue of putting on his cloaths. The valet in chief immediately attended, undrew the curtain, and respectfully enquired his master's pleasure. In answer to which his lordship signifying that he would get up, *Guillaume* folded his stockings, placed his slippers by the bed-side, and was going to present him with his breeches——when lo! the crime our hero had been guilty of stared him full in the face, and gave such an air of surprize to his features, that his lordship could not

---

1   A ritual act such as handing over a piece of sod to signify the exchange of property in English feudal society.

help asking what was the matter. *Guillaume* then related the misdemeanor, at which his master was so far from being angry, that he only laughed at the astonishment of his valet, and calling the dog upon the bed, caressed him with as much tenderness as if he had performed the most meritorious action in the world. Then turning again to his servant, "what does the booby stare at," cries he, "with such amazement? I wish to G—d the dog had pissed in thy mouth. Prythee get a fresh pair of breeches, and let me rise——or am I to lie a-bed till midnight."

As soon as he was dressed in his morning dishabille, he went down stairs to breakfast; in which our hero bore him company, and had the honour of eating roll and butter in great magnificence. When breakfast was over, he recollected that it might now be time to send up compliments to his lady, which he generally performed every morning; and imagining that she would not be displeased with the present of so pretty a dog, "here *Guillaume*," said he, "take this little dog, and carry him up stairs to your lady. My compliments, and a desire to know how her ladyship does this morning. Tell her I found him——pox take him, I don't know where I found him, but he's a pretty little fellow, and am sure she must be pleased with him."

Tho' the reader must from hence conclude that lord and lady *Marmazet* reposed themselves in different beds at night, he will not, I imagine be surprised at such a circumstance in this accomplished and fashionable age. Her ladyship was a woman of great wit, pleasure and amour, as well as her husband, only with a little more reserve and caution, to save appearance with the world. Her familiarity with a sharper at *Bath*, may have already given the reader some little sketch of her character; and for the rest it will be only necessary to inform him, that she spent the greatest part of her life in *St. James's* parish.[1] Her husband had married her without the temptation of love, because she was a rich heiress of a noble family; and she had consented to the match, with an equal indifference, only because it preserved her rank and station in the world. In consequence they soon grew totally unconcerned about each other; but then, being both of easy and cheerful tempers, their

---

1   I.e., in the fashionable precincts of the royal court.

indifference did not sour into hatred; on the contrary, they made it a topic of wit, when they met, to railly one another on their mutual amours. These meetings indeed were not very frequent, once or twice a week perhaps at dinner, at which times they behaved with the utmost politeness and complaisance; or if they raillied, it was done with so much gaiety and good-humour, that they only parted with the greater spirits to their evening amusements. In short, his lordship pursued his pleasures without any domestic expostulations, and her ladyship in return was permitted to live in all respects, as *Juvenal* expresses it, *tanquam vicina mariti*, more like her husband's neighbour than his wife.[1]

Her ladyship was now just awake, and taking her morning tea in bed, when *Guillaume* ascended the stairs, and knocked at her chamber-door. The waiting gentlewoman being ordered out to see who it was, returned immediately to the bed-side with a dog in her arms, and delivered the message that accompanied him. As her ladyship had never in her life discovered any fondness for these four-footed animals, she could not conceive the meaning of such a present, and with some disdain in her countenance ordered "the fellow to carry back his puppies again to his master." But when the servant was gone down stairs, bethinking herself that there might be some joke in it, which she did not perceive, and resolving not to be out-done by her husband in wit, she asked her maid eagerly, if there was any such thing as a cat in the house. "A cat, my lady!" cries the waiting gentlewoman, "yes, my lady, I believe there is such a thing to be found." "Well then," said her ladyship, "go and catch it directly, and carry it with my compliments to his lordship. Let him know I am infinitely obliged to him for his present, and have sent him a cat in return for his dog."

The maid simpered without offering to stir, as not indeed conceiving her mistress to be in earnest; but having the orders repeated to her, she set out immediately to fulfil them. After much laughter below stairs among the servants, a cat at length was catched, and the waiting-maid went with it in her arms to his lordship's dressing room. Having rapped at the door, and being ordered to enter, with a face half-blushing and half-smiling, she delivered her message

---

1   From Juvenal, *Satires, vi*, 509.

in the following terms. "My lady desires her compliments to your lordship, and begs the favour of you to accept of THIS, in return for your dog." After which dropping the grave mouser on the floor, she was preparing to run away in all haste, being ready to burst with laughter. But his lordship, who was no less diverted, called her back, and having entertained himself with many jokes on the occasion, sent her up-stairs with a fresh message to her mistress. This was immediately returned on the part of her ladyship, and many little pieces of raillery were carried backwards and forwards, which perhaps might not be unentertaining, but as we are sensible with what contempt these little incidents will be received by the reader, if he happens to be a judge, a politician, or an alderman, we shall dwell no longer on them, and here put an end to the chapter.

Appendix B: From Anonymous, The Life and Adventures of a Cat (1760)

[Variously attributed to Henry Fielding (implausibly) and William Guthrie, *The Life and Adventures of a Cat* is a direct imitation of *Pompey the Little*. A comparison of the two works tends to illuminate Coventry's authorial abilities. The author of *The Life and Adventures of a Cat* has little of Coventry's panache for dialogue, his talent for caricature, or his ability, at his best, to make his animal "hero" an integral participant in the novel's episodes. "Tom the Cat" really is little more than a narrative device, an "it" that the narrator follows for the purpose of describing various human characters and events. Nonetheless, we find here many of the basic features of Coventry's narrative – the imitation of Fielding, the mock-biography, the pretence to learned wit, and the emphasis on human folly and degradation. Just as Coventry prefaces *Pompey the Little* with a joking defense of the importance of dogs in human history, so this novel opens with a mock-history of cats, which I have omitted.]

CHAP. IV.

TOM THE CAT IS BORN OF POOR BUT HONEST PARENTS. HIS MOTHER DIES IN CHILD-BED, HIS BROTHERS AND SISTERS, TO THE NUMBER OF NINE ARE SENT ADRIFT, AND DROWNED.

Mab, the mother of *Tom*, was left a widow by a former husband, who had left behind him no great means to support her, and therefore she wisely thought it the best expedient she could make use of to change her condition once more, and enter into the state of matrimony. We are left in the dark, as to the person who performed the ceremony, nor are we certain, whether the *Feline* gentleman who tied them together, was regularly qualified to do his office, but he discharged it to the great satisfaction of both parties; though some are malicious enough to insinuate, that he went snacks[1] with the bridegroom that very night, who not having it in his power to provide a wedding-supper, is reported by the best historians, to have left his wife in very unuxorious manner to run after a Rat, which served him for supper. Now as it is a wise child that knows his own father, so we dare not insist upon *Tom*'s being the lawful issue of *Mowser*, or the spurious child of the parson; be that as it will, he was brought into this troublesome world on the 29th day of *September*, a day memorable for the perplexity which the generality of tenants are in, to find or raise money to pay their rents.[2] On account of this day on which he was born, several of his father's friends were for having him called *Michael*, but more solid arguments, which we never heard, being offered, he was called *Tom*. His poor mother having born nine helpless children besides himself, and being exhausted in spirits, by the hard labour which she underwent, expired in the company of the mid-wife, and some other good neighbours, of the Feline species, who performed their last office, and buried her in an adjacent Dunghill. Mab's Mistress was seeking her, and having called to no purpose, found ten very fine bantlings lying under the bed, nine of which she drowned, and saved one, who happened to be our illustrious Hero, she took the care of Tom on herself, intending he should spend his days with her in regard to his mother Mab, of whom she never could get any tidings ever after; she did not care to put him out to nurse, having heard so many sad stories of those nurses daily employed to supply the foundling Hospital, and therefore she determined to nurse him herself.[3] This is the truest account we could collect from the best authors, concerning his birth; as to his genealogy, we did examine into that, and to that end ransacked several circulating libraries for Welch records, which we traced backwards even to the Cat of Whittington,[4] but found nothing that we dared advance as truth, for we scorn to impose upon our readers, with reports or facts,

---

1 I.e., to have a share.
2 St. Michael's Day (or Michaelmas), a day on which rents and debts were due.
3 I.e., to suckle him.
4 Dick Wittington was a mayor of London who, according to a popular legend, made a fortune by selling his cat to a merchant.

which we cannot vouch for. Nevertheless we make no question, but Tom's parents, by father and mother's side, could put in their claim to as high a descent, in Feline genealogy as Whittinton's[1] Cat, or the famous Cat of Montaigne, who laughed at her Master for being such a fool, as to spend his time in playing with her, and actually told him so,[2] or Montaigne himself is a liar, who very gravely reports it for truth in some of his essays.

CHAP. V.

TOM'S EDUCATION.——HIS MANNER OF LIFE WITH HIS MISTRESS, WHOSE HISTORY IS INTRODUCED HERE IN A SHORT NARRATIVE.

It was Tom's peculiar beauty, and size that saved his life, for his Mistress *had Eyes*, and chose him out of ten, so that he was a kind of *tythe Cat*,[3] and survived the unhappy fate of his brothers, and sisters by decimation,[4] proving to the disgrace of Methodists, that even among Cats, one in ten may be saved, though according to their illustrious tenets, that will not be the portion of one in ten of themselves.[5] However Tom grew up and gave earnest of being a most promising youth, having gone thro' all the gambols and feats of childhood, peculiar to those of his kind, and to the great satisfaction of all who knew him, or had the honour of his acquaintance.——His Mistress, however was inexcusable in point of tenderness, who not being sufficiently pleased with his beauty, thought the cutting off his Ears would be an abundant addition

---

1   A misprint for "Whittington's."

2   In his *Essays* (1580-92), Michel de Montaigne famously wrote, "When I play with my cat, who knows if I am not a pastime to her more than she is to me?" (Bk 2, ch. 12).

3   "Tithe," originally meaning "tenth," ordinarily refers to the proportion of income that an individual should pledge to the church.

4   "Decimation" refers here to the exemplary killing of one in ten, as practiced in Roman legions against mutineers and other offenders.

5   The author echoes common prejudices against Methodists, who were also reviled by Francis Coventry. According to some Methodists, a small proportion of people would receive spiritual assurance that they had been predestined for salvation. The author implies cynically that Methodists included all of themselves in this small number.

to that article; a barbarous instance of her love for him, but in consequence of her resolution Tom lost his Ears, for having done no crime to deserve amputation, when thousands walk the Streets with their ears on, who have a thousand times deserved to lose them.[1] His mistress, whose name was Mrs. Clotilda-Skin-Flint, began to take another more cruel thought into her head, and that was to deprive him of his manhood, by equipping him for the Opera,[2] and was advised to put this dreadful scheme into execution by a female neighbour of hers, called *Rugana*, but as this was as troublesome as it was expensive, she permitted him to keep his pebbles, as marks of that vicility,[3] which he afterwards testified to several young Cats of his acquaintance.——Whether Tom ever came to the knowledge of this sanguinary intent of his Mistress, we never could learn, if he did, he must no doubt be sensibly affected with delight to find, that by its being laid aside, he found himself in possession of that treasure which entitled him to the honourable appellation of *Ram-Cat.*[4] His mistress, after having bred him up to feed himself, and to provide for his own sustenance, left him to shift for the necessaries of life, by all those means, which most of his kind make use of to get a livelyhood, namely by *Mouseing*, and having before he was half a year old, rid not only her house, but that neighbourhood of the rats and mice which infested them, he bore the credit of being an excellent mowser, for he got no other reward, and was forced for sometime to live upon that empty saying, *Virtue is its own Reward*, verifying that fine anecdote of *Juvenal*,[5] *Ladatum Virtus et alget*, which for the sake our English Reader, we will suppose to signify, that *a good or a wise man may starve in the midst of Fleet-Market, for any thing he is likely to get from either fools or knaves.* Mrs. Clotilda-Skin-Flint, was one of those admirable ladies, who go in quest of obsolete robes, and had raised a tolerable sum by levying contributions on the necessitous, who

---

1 Ear-cropping had been punishment for criminals in the seventeenth century, particularly for sedition. The practice had been discontinued in the eighteenth century, though the author suggests that many people deserved this punishment.
2 The eighteenth century witnessed a fashion for Italian opera, which frequently included a contralto, a singer castrated at puberty to preserve a falsetto voice.
3 Evidently a misprint for "virility."
4 A colloquialism for a male cat.
5 Roman satirist who flourished in the second century CE.

where[1] glad to part with their vestments for the tenth part of their intrinsic value: she had, to make her own employment more lucrative, wedded an old taylor, whom she married purely on the account of his dexterity and skill in, or repairing the breaches of old clothes, and making them pass for new: by this profitable business she was enabled to keep a very sightly shop in the purlieus of Monmouth-Street, and was by her lending out small sums of money to the butchers, who dealt with her at an extravagant usury, in possession of five hundred pounds in money and stock.

Tom did not approve of his Mistress's niggardly temper, and though he made several attempts upon her larder, he seldom availed himself of the expedition, being glad to get off with whole bones, he being a rival in these purloinings with the old taylor, his master, who was as narrowly watched as himself in these kind of invasions, and whom his wife had starved, cudgel'd, and cuckolded into the bargain. However, one day, Tom laid a plot, and being determined to assuage the cries of hunger, he resolutely attacked two pound of beef-stakes, which were contrary to former caution left to his mercy, as the mistress had indulged herself too plentifully with the ratifai[2] of St. *Giles*'s, commonly called *Gin*. The maid had been absent by accident, at the time of this depredation, Tom prudently withdrew, when he had eat up his delicious cates, and left the blame to fall upon either the maid, or the old taylor, the former of which fasted that day for her negligence, and was discharged without payment of her wages, while old snip had like to have been destroyed by the weight of the goose,[3] with which his tender rib[4] did belabour him to his no small mortification, and of which he lay ill for three days to his wife's utter discontent, as she was forced to hire a journeyman to finish some work he had begun.

---

1   A misprint of "were."
2   A misspelling of "ratafia," a kind of liqueur.
3   An iron weight used to press clothes.
4   I.e., his wife, the reference being to "Adam's rib."

CHAP. VI.

THE MAID SERVANT TAKES OUT A WARRANT AGAINST TOM: HE IS ARRESTED, AND PUT INTO A JAIL, WHERE HE IS FORCED TO PAY GARNISH.[1]

The maid servant being thus deprived of her wages by her rapacious mistress, and knowing that ridicule would be the best method to expose her, went to a bailiff,[2] a relation of her own, and told him the case, adding, that she thought the nearest way to obtain an effectual remedy both for her wages and her private satisfaction, was to expose her mistress by some stroke of ridicule, which would be matter of laughter to all the neighbours, who hated her for her avarice and rapine, and that a comical revenge had struck into her head on a sudden, which she determined that very day, with his assistance to put into execution, he promised not only to give her the best assistance in his power, but also to be himself the instrument of her immediate revenge, whereupon she asked him if he would take upon him to arrest the Cat, who by eating the beef stakes, had been the occasion of her being deprived of her place, together with her wages; she owed that she had no particular pique of resentment against the Cat, who had been for many weeks a fellow sufferer with herself in the article of starving, and she protested that she would have done the same had she been a Cat, but as she was a Woman, and not used to eat raw beef, she therefore had never thought of stealing them; that it often happened, she used to steal a slice of bread and cheese for her poor old master, whom her barbarous mistress had also locked up the victuals from, and that she had run the risque to serve him, though his wife had privately marked the bread and cheese. Certainly said the bailiff, your cause is just, and you have sufficient reason to complain. There is no law why a Cat may or may not be taken for theft; horses are subject to be impounded, and so are cows, sheep and pigs liable to imprisonment for misdemeanors of this nature; therefore as no law exists why your fellow servant should not be arrested, I will

---

1 Money proffered to a jail-keeper in exchange for better treatment and accommodations.
2 An individual empowered by the crown to make arrests, detain those charged with crimes, and discharge legal business.

take it upon my self to make out his *Mittimus*,[1] and if his mistress thinks fit to remove him by *habeas Corpus*,[2] she may, but it shall cost her something, besides the procuring of you your wages; I don't regard, says the girl, my wages so much as my private revenge to have her exposed to her neighbours. That, answered the bailiff, shall be done, for I will have a whole posse of constables with me, and we will beset the house, and take her favourite before the whole street. They parted, she to observe the execution of her comical revenge, and he to raise the posse.

It was about the meridian hour, when the Sun is vertical over the heads of mortals, in plain English it was about twelve o'clock high noon, when the bailiff appeared with his frightful posse of scare-crows, and beset the shop, to the utter dismay and consternation of the inhabitants of the wardrobe in *Monmouth-street*. Mrs. *Clotilda Skinflint*, and her Cornutus,[3] had just sat down to a pig's foot and vinegar, (which was the portion allotted for her spouse's dinner,) two roasted pigeons, with toast and butter, being laid before herself, with a pint of that beer commonly called porter, while a pint of *Adam*'s ale,[4] was very likely thought good enough to allay the thirst of her journeyman spouse and yoke-fellow.

Tom never dreamed of any prosecution in law being carried on against him, and therefore was purring an inoffensive song, in expectation of the skeleton of the pigeons, a leg of which he was cranching[5] with sensible delight, when he was interrupted by the entrance of one of the bailiffs, who was followed by several others, who secured the person of *Tom*, and another shewed the warrant, that they might not be accused of doing any thing illegal, or contrary to form, and while some of them remained to explain the nature and legality of this seizure, he who made the caption, carried him to the first prison which came in his way, and delivered him into *Salva Custoda*,[6] under the name of *Tom Filch*, at the same time giving the gaoler and the other prisoners, a face-

---

1 "A warrant issued by a justice of the peace, etc., committing a person to custody" (*OED*).
2 "A writ issuing out of a court of justice...requiring the body of a person to be brought before the judge or into the court for the purpose specified in the writ" (*OED*).
3 "Horned one," meaning that he "wears horns" (i.e., is a cuckold).
4 I.e., water.
5 Crunching.
6 Latin: safe custody.

tious and short narrative of the whole affair, and the history of the parties concerned. When the prisoners discovered, that it was a piece of waggery, they entered hastily into the joke, and hearing that *Tom* the prisoner was the favourite particular of a substantial house-keeper, who would in all probability release him by paying his fees; they boldly and with one voice demanded garnish of *Tom*, who not being used to such questions from strangers, did not think proper to answer them. Now, if they had according to the custom of garnish, threatened to strip him, *What could they have of a Cat but his skin?* But as he made no answer to their previous question, they thought it more adviseable to lock him in a dark cell, and called for ale, which for joke's sake, was not denied them in so unprecedented a garnish, and they sat down to regale themselves, where we shall leave them in order to finish this chapter and begin another.

CHAP. VII.

A CURIOUS CONFERENCE BETWEEN SOME OF THE EMINENT PERSONAGES OF THE PRISON, DURING TOM'S CONFINEMENT. IN WHICH TOM TRAVELLER RELATES PART OF HIS OWN LIFE AND ADVENTURES.

It has been a usual, and a wise method too[1] let me tell you, with all Biographers to relax the reader's mind with somewhat[2] episodical in imitation of *Homer* and *Virgil* in their Epics, who introduce several respectable persons into the drama, beside *Achilles*, and *Æneas*,[3] so have we thought that we should oblige our readers, who would in return be obliged to us for not cramming them with the single adventures of *Tom* the *Cat* only, since we have this fair opportunity of opening a fine prison-scene to his view, and entertaining him with the most curious adventures, and interesting incidents of *Tom the Traveller*, extracted from no book, or books in the world, as his surprizing memoirs are no where to be found but in this true

---

1   A misprint for "to."

2   Something.

3   Achilles is the hero of Homer's epic the *Illiad*; Aeneas is the hero of Virgil's epic the *Aeneid*.

history, and if any of our readers should be so incredulous as to doubt the veracity of these anecdotes, we shall be bold to remind him of the more incredible travels and voyages, which are not half so well authenticated, though passed upon the world every day, as real and genuine.

While the prisoners were regaling themselves over what liquor *Tom* the *Cat*'s adventure unexpectedly afforded them, *Hugh*, known by the name of *Hugh of the Borough*, reminded one of his fellow-prisoners of telling his story, which he was going to begin, when they were interrupted by the introduction of the new prisoner the *Cat*, for, as he told him, he and the rest had just finished their narratives, and it only remained, for him to go on with his; in compliance therefore of this reasonable demand: *Tom Traveller*, so he was called, commenced his history in the following procedure.

THE LIFE OF TOM TRAVELLER

As I was begot, conceived and born in a most extraordinary manner, so it will appear in the course of my life, that my adventures, even in abstract, as I shall relate them, have been equally amazing. My mother was treacherously deluded by an opiate infused into a glass of wine, when she had the good or ill-fortune (I know not which) of being debauched in her sleep by her master, the husband of a woman of quality with whom she lived; I was the result of this piece of treachery; nor did my mother give the least intimations of her discovering this foul practice, though she on awaking, could not but perceive the alteration from that of a maid, to that of a woman. When she had got rid of me in the most private manner, (for she left her lady, when the signs of pregnancy appeared) she took me wrapt up in a basket, and going to a publick house in *Piccadilly*, she called for a gill of wine, drank it, and leaving a guinea to be changed, she went out and was seen no more, but she left me in her stead, thinking me and the guinea, a tolerable bargain for a gill of wine, nor had I remained there long, before I made my host of the tavern, sensible, that he had got a new guest; as I was a fine boy, and he had no child, he put me out to nurse, resolving to adopt me as his own, since I was a *comeby*-chance, and since he thought it cruel not to give the same reception to a human creature, as is given commonly to a Cat or a Dog, and tho' I did not come of my own accord, like a Cat, or a Dog, yet was I brought, and could not be supposed to intrude myself, as those creatures do, when they have lost their masters, so he thought me more worthy of a welcome, than either of the above animals. When I was five years old, I was brought home by the nurse, and as they saw I was a promising child of my age, being as lusty and tall, as the waiter, who was twelve, but born a dwarf, I was soon fit to be called to the bar, I improved myself in observations on men, and manners, which I made my study, till about eighteen, I became one of the knowing ones, when I left my supposed father, to join a set of gamblers, where I learnt every thing to qualify me for Bath,[1] the races, or even Ar____r's.[2] I resolved to leave this life, took the high-road, and bought a fine horse at Newmarket with what money I had won there by betting and cheating, having at one bett [sic] won a hundred guineas of the D____of ____, as was let into the secret by the riding jocky, who went halves with me for his information. Having equipt myself with every thing necessary for *collecting*, or raising contributions on the shillings, exclusive of garnish. And so ends the chapter, when the affairs of *Tom the Cat*, shall seem more desirable by the reader, than those of *Tom the Traveller*.

---

1   The spa city of Bath was a major center for gambling until this practice was banned in 1745.

2   Unidentified.

Appendix C: *Anonymous,* An Essay on the New Species of Writing Founded by Mr. Fielding *(1751)*

[The following essay, which appeared, like the first edition of *Pompey the Little*, in February 1751, has sometimes been ascribed to Coventry. The evidence for this attribution is admittedly uncertain. The *Dictionary of National Biography* rightly points out that it was published not by Coventry's usual bookseller, Robert Dodsley, but by William Owen. While this circumstance raises doubts about Coventry's authorship of this pamphlet, I would submit that the "internal" evidence for this attribution (that is, features of its style and content) are considerable. As in *Pompey the Little*, we encounter an imitation of Fielding's antiquely courteous style, right down to cap-tipping nods at the "courteous Reader"; similarly, as in Coventry's novel, the author frequently inserts long dashes at unusual points, presumably to give his writing a more conversational feeling. Most revealingly, the pamphlet's admiring advocacy of Fielding as the founder of a new kind of realistic novel, what the author calls "this new kind of Biography," is strikingly similar to Coventry's distinctive praise of Fielding in his dedication to the third edition of *Pompey the Little*. At the very least, this essay represents an interesting intervention into early debates about the novel that deserves to be read as a closely contemporaneous context for Coventry's history of a lap-dog. It is an essay that challenges the critical orthodoxies of our own day, for it places Fielding, not Defoe or Richardson, at the head of "realist" fiction.]

Though I am not blessed with the worthy Qualifications of a modern Critic, *viz.* Self-conceit, Ill-nature and Prejudice, yet am I hardy enough to offer to the Public my Thoughts on the New Species of Writing lately introduc'd by Mr. *Fielding*, by substituting (as far as lays in the Power of one who communicates his Observations to the Town under the Denomination of a Twelve-penny Author) for the First Judgment, the Second Candour, and the

Third Impartiality; which Ingredients, tho' deviating extremely from our new Receipt, were formerly look'd upon as absolutely necessary towards constituting a true Critic. And here, courteous Reader, give me leave to lament that that Title, which has at sundry Times been dignified and made venerable by the most excellent and instructive Productions of a *Longinus* and an *Horace*, a *Bossu* and an *Addison*,[1] in the different Languages of *Greek*, *Latin*, *French* and *English*; should, by our very modern Practitioners, be reduc'd to that Ignominy which was in vain attempted to be affix'd to it by the malicious Writings of a *Zoilus* and a *Dennis*.[2] For Criticism, however it may have been degraded in this Age, was, in all the preceding ones, esteem'd an useful Science; and to be thought a Critic was no mean Title in the Republic of Letters. Dr. *Newton* tells us, in the Preface of his new Edition of *Milton*, that he is next in Rank to a good Poet.[3] And it certainly must be accounted as laudable an Undertaking as it is an arduous Task, to fix the Criterion by which the most vulgar Readers may judge with Propriety of the Beauties and Blemishes of an Author. The Corruption of this useful Branch of Learning is by no means a convincing Argument of it's Non-excellence. For we are assur'd, by no less Authority than that of the famous Dr. *Tillotson*, that we shall be led into the grossest Errors if we despise every thing on Account of it's being corrupted; since it is remarkable that the best white Wines make the sharpest Vinegar.[4] Whence then does it proceed, that the Professors of a Science, which has always been accounted so useful towards the

---

1 Cassius Longinus, c.213-273 CE, Greek rhetorician and philosopher of the Neoplatonic school, and thought in the eighteenth century to be author of *On the Sublime*, though this attribution is now widely doubted; Horace, 65-8 BCE, author of *Ars Poetica*, a major source of ideas in the eighteenth century about the literary arts; René le Bossu (1631-80), author of *Traité du poème épique* (1675); Joseph Addison (1672-1719) wrote influential essays on art and beauty in the periodical *The Spectator* (1711-12), particularly the series entitled "The Pleasures of the Imagination" (nos. 411-18, 1712).

2 Zoilus, c.400-c.320 BCE, was notorious for denouncing the Homeric epics as collections of fables; John Dennis (1657-1734) gained undeserved notoriety as a bad critic largely as the result of attacks on him by Alexander Pope, who accused him of malice against himself and others.

3 I.e., *Paradise Lost : A Poem in Twelve Books / A New Edition with Notes of Various Authors by Thomas Newton, D.D.* (1749).

4 The sermons of the Anglican divine John Tillotson (1630-94) were highly popular. The reference is to his sermon "On the fifth of November, 1678, before the Honourable House of Commons," *Works*, 12 vols. (London, 1757): 1:446.

establishing true Learning, should be so generally stigmatiz'd as they at present are? 'Tis but saying of a Man,——Oh Lord, Sir! You can't possibly like him; why, he is profess'd Critic. And you comprize in that one Word, according to the present Acception of it——He is a Bundle of Folly and Ill-nature. As I find in myself some little Desire of being thought a Critic, if I take some Pains to rescue the Word from the Misapplication it now labours under: And if my Reasons should prove of any Weight, those Gentlemen who have a sincere Regard for Criticism, will be good-natur'd enough to over-look the Cause that produces so good an Effect. A true Critic then is, not a meer blustering Fellow, that knocks you down with an *ipse dixit*;[1] condemns good and bad indiscriminately; and, after having swagger'd through twenty or thirty Pages, goes off in a Flash.——No, my dear Friend, this is quite a different Creature, a meer Ass in a Lion's Skin;[2] and can with no more Propriety be stil'd a Critic, than esteemed a Man of Sense. The real Critic proceeds with Candour as well as Judgment: And tho', 'tis true indeed, he discovers the Blemishes as well as Beauties, yet he always takes more Pleasure in displaying the Excellences, than raking into the Rubbish, of an Author. The Writer of *Charlotte Summers*, which I intend (in it's Proper Place) to make some cursory Remarks on, in his last Address to his Readers, has express'd more Fear of being handled by the Critics than his Piece deserves.[3] He joins in the common Opinion, in conceiving such unjust Ideas of those valuable Persons, and looks upon them as a kind of Raw-head and Bloody-bones, which a poor Author cannot be too fearful of. But surely, if a Critic is such a Person as I have describ'd above, an Author of any Repute must be highly pleas'd with falling into his Hands, since it cannot fail of giving Credit to his Performance. It would be needless to cite many Instances of this Truth: Let it suffice to take Notice, that *Milton's Paradise Lost*, inimitable as it is, was depriv'd of near half the Reputation it now enjoys, 'till the celebrated Mr. *Addison* publish'd his excellent Remarks on

---

1   Latin: literally, "he himself said it"—an unsupported assertion.
2   A reference to one of Æsop's fables.
3   *The History of Charlotte Summers: The Fortunate Parish Girl*, 2 vols. (London, 1750). This novel was once attributed to Henry Fielding's sister, Sarah, but almost certainly wrongly. "The Author's last Address to his Readers" is the title of Book four, chapter one.

that Poem in the *Spectators*.[1] With how little Consideration then as the spurious Offspring of Mr. *Fielding,* in his poetical Generation, endeavour'd* "To make a Party among the Fair to save the Author from the merciless Persecution of the numerous Tribe of Critics. Who (says he) may find Materials sufficient in this Work, to exercise their malicious Talents of finding Fault. I have already disclaim'd their Jurisdiction, which I know must enhance their Spleen, and perhaps put it into their Heads to press me to Death for not holding up my Hand to the Bar. But if I have the Fair Sex of *Great Britain* on my Side, I shall suffer the *Pien foré dure* with heroic Constancy, and laugh at the pointless Malice of my dull Persecutors."[2] What a Torrent of Invectives has he pour'd out against us poor Critics! Dull, splenetic, malicious, and what not! Mr. *Pope* had Discernment enough to discover the Poet from the Man of Rhymes.[3] But no body will now take the Pains to distinguish the Critic from the Caviller. The Reader will be pleas'd to remember, that I propos'd in the Beginning of these Pages, to substitute Impartiality for Prejudice. But since that Qualification in a Critic, is by long Disuse almost grown obsolete, it may not be amiss to enlarge on the Expediency of reviving it; and I think it cannot be better illustrated than by an Allusion drawn from the Theatre. Whoever then has been present at the Theatre on the first Night of the Representation of a new Piece, must be very sensible how particularly essential a Quality towards making any Progress in Criticism, he proposes who is bless'd with Impartiality: They must be very well acquainted how rare, how very rare it is, to meet with an unbias'd Audience at that Juncture, neither pre-possessed in Favour of, nor prejudic'd against, the Entertainment of the Night: And that at that Time Party runs so high, that tho' it should be one of the worst Pieces that ever disgrac'd the Theatre, the

---

* See the Author of the *Parish Girl's* last Address to his Readers. [The author's note. He is referring to the subtitle of *The History of Charlotte Summers.*]

---

1 *The Spectator,* nos. 267, 273, 279, 285, 291, 297, 303, 309, 315, 321, 327, 333, 339, 345, 351, 357, 363, 369, 5 January.–3 May 1712.
2 *The History of Charlotte Summers,* Vol. 2, Bk. 4, ch. 1,152. "*Pien foré dure*" is Venetian dialect for, roughly, "full hard force." Given the context, it is significant that this expression often refers to a male erection.
3 See *Epistle to Arbuthnot* (1735), l. 13.

favourable Party would endeavour, *enixè manibus pedibusq*;[1] to save it: Or if, on the contrary, the Spirit of *Skakespear* [sic] should run thro' every Line, the other Side would endeavour to damn it *vi et armis*.[2] But I shall take the Liberty, since I am insensibly slipt into the Playhouse, to reflect with reverential Awe on that Non-pareil of modern Criticism, H____y Ch____y, Esq;[3] and bestow on that Man of Terrors, the Encomiums due to his Merit. And to do this with the more Justice, I must beg Leave to exalt the Stile above the Pitch of vulgar Pamphleteers. To begin then:

O thou tremendous Arbiter of all Representations! Whether the lofty Muse swells in the turgid Buskin, or deigns to amble in the Sock[4] more apt for Pleasantry and Humour, all hail!——Thou Terror of *Drury*, and Fear of *Covent-Garden*,[5] all hail!——Thou that really art (As Mr. *Garrick* in his *Lethe* has most feelingly express'd himself) the Dread of Poets, the Scourge of Players, and the Aversion of the Vulgar,[6] receive these sincere Pieces and Commendations from a younger Brother in the noble Art of Criticism, of which you are so noble a Professor. Receive them from one who strenuously endeavours, but alas! he fears in vain, to imitate, with Justice, so worthy, so singular an Example. Teach me, O teach thy Pupil, ardent for Instruction. Instruct him then, thou great Artist, to equal thee in those divine Emanations of the Soul, you are so particularly remarkable for, Spleen, Malice, and Inveteracy. Let him be able to cry out, with his unequalled Master, that there is not a brilliant Thought in *Shakespeare*, a smooth Line in *Rowe*,[7] nor an honest Sentiment in all *Cato*.[8]——Whilst thou remain'st

---

1 Latin: strenuously, with hands and feet.

2 Latin: by force and arms.

3 Not identified.

4 Referring to the footwear worn in classical drama, "buskin" and "sock" mean tragedy and comedy, respectively.

5 The Theatres Royal at Drury Lane and Covent Garden, the only theatres officially permitted to stage plays.

6 David Garrick, *Lethe: A Dramatic Satire* (London, 1749), 17. While he wrote many plays, Garrick (1717-79) was most famous as an actor and as manager of the theatre at Drury Lane.

7 The sentimental tragedies of Nicholas Rowe (1674-1718) were admired for their harmonious lines.

8 Joseph Addison's tragic play *Cato* (1712) famously celebrated the Stoic virtue and republicanism of Cato the Younger (95-46 BCE).

the unparalled [sic] Don *Quixote*, in this most illustrious Knight-Errantry, let me humbly attend thee in the Character of thy trusty 'Squire *Sancho Pancha*.[1] O that I were made up of Gall like thee, that my enflam'd Bosom were ready to burst with enthusiastic Venom, which I might with Pleasure vent on the first miserable Wretch that fell in my Way, who durst, with any Applause, stile himself an Author, or particularize himself, by any Degree of Merit, as an Actor.——Yes, I will follow thee, I will industriously investigate thy Foot-steps, and tread the Path thou hast beaten for me.——Yes, thou great H____y, *Sequar*, but I am afraid, *haud passibus æquis.*[*]

As in the Playhouse, so in the Press. A Piece is no sooner perform'd at *Drury-Lane* or *Covent-Garden*, than the News Papers are fill'd with Advertisements of—— This Day are publish'd, Remarks on, or a candid Examen of the new Tragedy or Comedy: In all which, the Author is either allow'd to have no Faults at all, or accus'd of having run into more Errors than a Poet could possibly be guilty of. For our *Phaetons*[2] in modern Criticism, lash on precipitately, either approve right and wrong, or abuse good and bad at random, 'till they come to the End of their Course; which, like their furious Original, 'tis a Miracle if they arrive at in Safety. This holds also, in respect to all other Pieces as well as Dramatic ones: And the partial Examen of *Tom Jones*, published about a Year ago, is a glaring Instance of the Truth of this Assertion.[3]

These certain Facts, which every Person of common Observation must be acquainted with, are stronger Proofs of the great Use of Impartiality than the most well-penn'd Arguments; and more evidently demonstrate how particularly needful it is at this Time, to restore the old true Spirit of Criticism. And as the Author of the following Sheets, by not being acquainted with the Founder of this

---

[*] This Elogium is in a Parenthesis. [The author's note. The Latin denotes "you are followed with unequal steps," which is a line from Virgil.]

---

[1] Don Quixote's low-born companion in *Don Quixote* (1604-15), by Miguel de Cervantes (1547-1616).

[2] In Greek mythology, Phaeton, son of the sun-god Helios, drove the chariot of the sun wildly off course.

[3] Evidently a reference to *An Examen of the History of Tom Jones, a Foundling* (London, 1749) by "Orbilius."

new Biography which he is now adventurous enough to make his Observations on, cannot be biass'd by Ill-nature against, or too tender a Regard for, a Person he is utterly a Stranger to, he hopes the candid Reader will be inclined to believe him, when he declares that his real Intent is to display (as far as his Judgment will permit) the Beauties and Blemishes of the Pieces under Consideration.

I shall now begin to take a critical review of these Histories in general, in performing which, if even Mr. *Fielding* himself does not confess that my Proceeding is impartial, I'll be content to send him my Name, that he may punish me *propriâ personâ*[1] in the next humorous Piece he publishes.

Sometime before this new Species of Writing appear'd, the World had been pester'd with Volumes, commonly known by the Name of Romances, or Novels, Tales, &c. fill'd with any thing which the wildest Imagination could suggest. In all these Works, Probability was not required: The more extravagant the Thought, the more exquisite the Entertainment. Diamond Palaces, flying Horses, brazen Towers, &c. were here look'd upon as proper, and in Taste. In short, the most finish'd Piece of this kind, was nothing but Chaos and Incoherency. *France* first gave Birth to this strange Monster, and *England* was proud to import it among the rest of her Neighbour's Follies. A Deluge of Impossibility overflow'd the Press. Nothing was receiv'd with any kind of Applause, that did not appear under the Title of a Romance, or Novel; and Common Sense was kick'd out of Doors to make Room for marvelous Dullness. The Stile in all these Performances was to be equal to the Subject——amazing: And may be call'd with great Propriety, "Prose run mad." This obtain'd a long Time. Every Beau was an *Orondates*, and all the Belles were *Stariras* [sic]:[2] Not a *Billet-doux* but run in Heroics, or the most common Message deliver'd but in the Sublime. The Disease became epidemical, but there were no Hopes of a Cure, 'till Mr. *Fielding* endeavour'd to show the World, that pure Nature could furnish out as agreeable Entertainment, as

---

1 Latin: in one's own proper person.
2 Orondates and Statira are names of chracters in *Cassandra* (1652), a popular romance by Gauthier de Costes, seigneur de la Calprenède (1609?-1663). This book is subsequently mentioned as exemplifying the lack of realism that Fielding sought to correct.

those airy non–entical[1] Forms they had long ador'd, and persuaded the Ladies to leave this Extravagance to their *Abigails* with their cast Cloaths.[2] Amongst which Order of People, it has ever since been observ'd to be peculiarly predominant.

His Design of Reformation was noble and public-spirited, but the Task was not quite so easy to perform, since it requir'd an uncommon Genius. For to tread the old beaten Track would be to no Purpose. Lecture would lose it's Force; and Ridicule would strive in vain to remove it. For tho' it was a Folly, it was a pleasing one: And if Sense could not yield the pretty Creatures greater Pleasure, Dear Nonsense must be ador'd.

Mr. *Fielding* therefore, who sees all the little Movements by which human Nature is actuated, found it necessary to open a new Vein of Humour, and thought the only way to make them lay down *Cassandra*, would be to compile Characters which really existed, equally entertaining with those Chimæras which were beyond Conception. This Thought produced *Joseph Andrews*,[3] which soon became a formidable Rival to the *amazing* Class of Writers; since it was not a mere dry Narrative, but a lively Representative of real Life. For chrystal Palaces and winged Horses, we find homely Cots and ambling Nags; and instead of Impossibility, what we experience every Day.

But as Mr. *Fielding* first introduc'd this new kind of Biography, he restrain'd it with Laws which should ever after be deem'd sacred by all that attempted his Manner; which I here propose to give a brief Account of. The first and grand one of all, (without which, in however regular a Manner the rest is conducted, the whole Performance must be dead and languid) is, that thro' the whole Humour must diffuse itself. But this can by no Means be perform'd without a great Genius, nay, even a particular Sort of one: for tho' Mr. *Bayes* informs us, any Man may commence Poet by his infallible Rules;[4] yet in this Kind of Writing he must be at a Stand without this grand Requisite. But to proceed.

---

1 I.e., non-existent.
2 "Abigail" was a stock name for a female servant. The author means that fine ladies would give their servants absurd romances along with their cast-off clothes.
3 Fielding's first novel (1742).
4 An allusion to the absurd and arrogant character Bayes, modeled on the poet and playwright John Dryden, in *The Rehearsal* (1672), by George Villiers, Duke of Buckingham.

The next Thing to be consider'd, is the Choice of Characters, which tho' striking and particular must be exactly copied from Nature. And who can doubt, when they see the Features of an *Abraham Adams*, or Madam *Slipslop*,[1] faithfully delineated, but that Field will afford an agreeable Variety? Every Word they speak must be entirely consonant to the Notion the Author would have his Readers entertain of them: And here it may not be amiss to remark the great Analogy there is between these Histories and Dramatic Performances, which Similitude I shall enlarge upon occasionally in the Progress of this Review. In regard to Character, after what I have mention'd as necessary, it would be the greatest Affront on the Reader's Understanding to point out the Comparison.

As this Sort of Writing was intended as a Contrast to those in which the Reader was even to suppose all the Characters ideal, and every Circumstance quite imaginary, 'twas thought necessary, to give it a greater Air of Truth, to entitle it *an History*; and the *Dramatis Personæ* (if I may venture to use the Expression) were christened not with fantastic high-sounding Names, but such as, tho' they sometimes bore some Reference to the Character, had a more modern Termination.

At the same Time Mr. *Fielding* ordain'd, that these Histories should be divided into Books, and these subdivided into Chapters; and also that the first Chapter of every Book was not to continue the Narration, but should consist of any Thing the Author chose to entertain his Readers with.[2] These if I don't forget, Mr. *Fielding* himself has nominated, the several Stages of his History, which he metaphorically calls a Journey, in which he and his Readers are Fellow-Travellers.[3] His particular Success in these preliminary Essays demonstrates (notwithstanding what the Author of *Charlotte Summers* hints on that Head) that these are not the easiest Part of his Task: Which I believe, Mr. *Fielding* somewhere says himself.

The Story should be probable, and the Characters taken from common Life, the Stile should be easy and familiar, but at the same Time sprightly and entertaining; and to enliven it the more, it is

---

1   Characters in Fielding's *Joseph Andrews*.

2   Compare these comments to Coventry's similar observations on Fielding's prelimi-
    nary essays in Book two, chapter one, of the present edition (p 131).

3   See Fielding's "Farewell to the Reader" in Book eighteen, chapter one, of *Tom Jones*.

sometimes heightened to the Mock-heroic, to ridicule the Bombast and Fustian, which obtain'd so much in the Romances. Of this Kind are his various Descriptions of the Morning, and his diverting Similes occasionally dispers'd thro' the Body of his Work. *Horace* tells us, *dulce est desipere*, but Mr. *Fielding* remember'd he added *in loco*.[1] For which Reason, he always takes care to indulge himself in these Liberties of Stile where the Story is least interesting. The last Book of *Tom Jones* is a convincing Proof, that he can comprize a great Variety of Circumstances in as small a Compass as any Author whatsoever. Besides these Descriptions, Similes, &c. there are other Licenses of Stile which it would be too tedious to be so minute as to enlarge upon. One Circumstance however, as it is a particular one, I cannot entirely pass over in Silence. Take it then as follows.———An Author of true Humour will consider, that his Book should be entertainment in the smallest Particulars, and afford Amusement.

> *Ab ovo*
> *Usque ad mala*.[2]

For which Reason Mr. *Addison* prefix'd Mottos to his Spectators, and at the Corner of each Paper added some particular Letter, which he himself imagin'd to be not the least entertaining Part of his Speculations. And nearly for the same End, Mr. *Fielding* thought proper to be facetious in the Titles to the several Chapters of his Histories, to shew the Reader he would not permit the least Occasion to slip which offer'd an Opportunity of amusing him.

As I am fallen on the Subject of the Titles to his Chapters, it will not be improper to consider them more largely, since it will only be mentioning now some Remarks I should be obliged to make by-and-by, which, for the Sake of the Connection, I rather chuse to insert here. And perhaps I may convince the Reader, these little Scraps, if rightly manag'd, conduce more to his Entertainment

---

1 Latin: "A little nonsense is pleasant" (*Carmina*, IV, 12, 27). Fielding remembered that Horace had added "in its place" ("in loco").

2 Latin: "From the egg to the apples," Horace, *Satires* 1.3, a phrase referring to Roman banquets, which began with eggs and ended with fruit—i.e., from beginning to end.

than he is at first aware of. 'Tis quite opposite to the Custom of the very best Writers in this Way, to give too full an Account of the Contents: it should be just hinted to the Reader something extraordinary is to happen in the seven or eight subsequent Pages, but what that is should be left for them to discover. Monsieur *Le Sage*, in his *Gil Blas*, (one of the best Books of the Kind extant) has always pursu'd this Method:[1] He tells us *Gil Blas* is going to such or such a Place, but does not discover the least of his Adventures there: but he is more particularly cautious when any unexpected Event is to happen. The Title to one of his Chapters of that Kind is——*Warning not to rely too much upon Prosperity.*——To another ——*Chapter the fifth, being just as long as the preceding*: With many others which it is needless to enumerate. Note, 'Tis to be wish'd this Custom had been observ'd by the Author of *Roderick Random*,[2] who tells us in his Preface, his Book is wrote in Imitation of the *Gil Blas* of Monsieur *Le Sage*. But with very little Success in my humble Opinion. As to the Titles of his Chapters, he is particularly tedious in them. This judicious Method of detaining the Reader in an agreeable Suspence, though it is right at all Times, is more particularly necessary when the History is near ended. No Writer has so strictly kept up to this as Mr. *Fielding*, in his *Tom Jones*. We are too well assured of *Gil Blas*'s Prosperity a long Time beforehand, to be surpriz'd at it. But at the Beginning of the last Book of *Tom Jones*, the Reader is apt to think it an equal Chance whether he is to be hanged or married; nor does he undeceive him by gradual Narration of Facts: And lest the Reader's Curiosity should pry too far into the Truth, what admirable Titles has he invented for his Chapters in order to keep him the longer in the Dark! such as—— *In which the History draws near to a Conclusion: In which the History draws nearer to a Conclusion,* &c. &c. which every Body will own conduces greatly to their Entertainment, and a Reader of the least Discernment will perceive how much more Consequence the clever Management of these Scraps prefix'd to each Chapter is of than [sic] he at first imagin'd. With how little Judgment has the Author of *Charlotte Summers* conducted this Particular! whose great Fault

---

1   *Gil Blas de Santillane* (1715-35), a comic novel by Alain-René Le Sage (1668-1747).
2   *The Adventures of Roderick Random* (1748) by Tobias Smollett (1721-71).

is Anticipation: That is, forestalling, by too remarkable a Title, the most remarkable Occurrences in his History. This appears even in the Title to his Book, which is, *The History of* Charlotte Summers: *or The* FORTUNATE *Parish Girl.* What Mr. *Addison* says of the Tragedies that conclude happily, may with equal Justice be apply'd here. "We see without Concern (says he) illustrious People in Distress, when we are sure they will at last be deliver'd from their Misfortunes."[1] Other Writers content themselves with entitling their Pieces, *The History of a Foundling, of Joseph Andrews, of Gil Blas, Roderick Random*, &c. without informing us as to the Event. As I find myself drawn into an unforeseen Length, I shall only subjoin one Instance from his Chapters, but at the same Time such an one, as will convince the Reader of Mr. *Fielding*'s Excellence in this Particular. The Eighth Chapter of the last Book is perhaps one of the most interesting in the whole History, and I dare say drew Tears from many Readers. For my own Part, I am not asham'd to own I have so much of the "Milk of human Nature"[2] in me, that I should have been in the greatest Concerns for the Misfortunes of the unhappy Miss *Summers*, if unluckily the Author had not assur'd me before I enter'd on these distressful Scenes, she would certainly be deliver'd from her momentarily Afflictions before I had read three Leaves further. To confess the Truth I was vastly angry with him for depriving me of such entertaining Sadness. We hope this Instance will convince all future Writers, that the Pleasure of the Reader is much more exquisite from the Reserve in the Title. These Thoughts upon the Inscriptions to the Chapters were thrown together to shew, that Mr. *Fielding* had another Intention besides making the World laugh in the Lines prefix'd to each Portion of his History. Permit me therefore, gentle Reader, upon the Authority of a Critic, to banish from all Histories above the Rank of those printed in *Black-fryars*, and sold at the small Price of one Penny, to tell us——*As how* Thomas Hickathrift *carried a Stack*

---

1 The author seems to be remembering improperly Addison's remarks on tragedy in *Spectator* No. 40 (16 April 1711): "Whatever crosses and disappointments a good man suffers in the body of the tragedy, they will make but small impression on our minds, when we know that in the last act he is to arrive at the end of his wishes and desires."

2 The author is misquoting *Macbeth* 1.5.16. The phrase is "the milk of human kindness."

of Corn. Or——Thomas Thumb *was swallow'd by a Cow,* in a Title longer than the Chapter itself.[1] After this Exertion of my Power, as a Critic, and dispersing these my Presents to all whom they may concern; let us return whence we digress'd.

No Faculty is so scarcely to be met with, tho' at the same Time there is none more frequently necessary, than that of telling a Story well. This Quality must be possess'd in an eminent Degree by a Writer of this kind. In the Progress of his Work he must adhere pretty closely to the Manners of the Drama, *viz.* In the Beginning the Plan of his Story must be clearly open'd, and the principal Characters should appear; towards the Middle his Plot should thicken, and Affairs be brought to a Crisis; and then be gradually unravell'd to the Reader 'till the Piece is concluded.

The great Critics take Notice, that Epic Poems may be call'd a kind of narrative Tragedies, since they possess Character, Plot, and every Requisite of them, except the entire Dialogue of which they consist. All the Commentators on *Homer's Iliad* observe the Affinity between that Poem and the Drama; and *Milton* is affirm'd to have originally plann'd his *Paradise lost* on the Model of a sacred Tragedy, after the Manner of his *Sampson Agonistes.*[2] Let me be permitted then, who but a low Critic after their high Example, to observe the same Relation these Performances I am now remarking on bear to Comedy. In one Respect indeed they have the Advantage of Theatrical Pieces. For tho' it is the common Business of both Writers to make as deep Researches into Nature as they can, and cull from that ample Field whatever is to their Purpose, yet the Biographer may ingraft in his Performance many Characters and Circumstances, which tho' they are entirely natural and very probable, often fall below the Dignity of the Stage. Nay it often happens that these

---

1   Thomas Hickathrift and Tom Thumb are characters in English folklore, the adventures of whom were recorded in cheap romances of the kind mocked by Fielding in Bk.1, ch.1 of *Joseph Andrews.* Blackfriars, a laboring-rank district on the Thames south of St, Paul's, was known for its shoddy booksellers. One of its most notorious booksellers, Henry Hills, reprinted a multitude of literary works and sermons in cheap editions on the pretence that he was educating the poor, and was finally curbed by the Copyright Act in 1710.
2   The *Iliad* is one of the two great epics attributed to Homer, the other being the *Odyssey.* Milton indeed originally planned his epic poem *Paradise Lost* (1667) as tragic drama such as *Samson Agonistes* (1671).

very kind of Books I am treating of fall into the Hands a [sic] Set of People who are apt to cry out, on the Sight of any Thing that gives a lively Representation of the Manners of the common People,——Oh! that's cursed low, intolerably vulgar &c. Of this the Introducer of these Pieces was aware, and has taken a great deal of Pains to obviate the Objections of these empty Cavillers: and I believe there are few Persons who have a Taste for Humour who would thank those Gentlemen for striking out the very Passages which are the Characteristics of his Excellencies as an Author ——*viz.* His thorough Insight into Low-life.[1] I shall at present take my leave of this Subject, with observing, that as the Romances it was intended to ridicule, were a kind of extravagant Landskape in which the Painter had represented purling Streams and shady Groves; or brazen Towers, and Mountains of Adamant, just as they were uppermost in his wild Imagination; so this kind of Writing is the Work of a more regular Pencil, and the exact Picture of human Life; and though a Novice in Painting may be more struck with the false Glare of the first, a Connoisseur will be more charm'd with the beautiful Plainness, and exact Similitude of the last.

The many Histories of this kind that lately have been publish'd, which undoubtedly owe their Rise to the extraordinary Success of Mr. *Fielding*'s Pieces, make it more necessary to remark on these Performances.[2]

It is very certain, that whenever any Thing new, of what kind soever, is started by one Man, and appears with great Success in the World, it quickly produces several in the same Taste. A Gentleman observ'd to me the other Day that the Applause Mr. *Garrick* had so justly acquired by his theatrical Performances, had induced more Persons to come upon the Stage since his first Playing, than for twenty Years before; and Mr. *Foote*'s giving Chocolate in the *Hay-Market*,[3] gave Birth to an hundred other Morning-Entertainments;

---

1   Again, this defense of Fielding's depictions of "low-life" should be compared with Coventry's dedication to Fielding in *Pompey the Little*.
2   If we accept Coventry's authorship of this essay, the following discussion of imitation is of particular interest in understanding his debt to Fielding in *Pompey the Little*.
3   Samuel Foote's unlicensed theatrical performances, disguised as occasions to drink coffee and hot-chocolate, are mentioned twice in *Pompey the Little* (Bk.1, chaps. 1 and 11).

the good Reception the *Tatlers*[1] and *Spectators* met with produc'd many other Papers of that sort, as the *Censor, Free-thinker, Champion*, &c. all which undoubtedly owe their Origin to those little Essays, which gain'd the respective Authors so much Credit. To descend yet lower, who can doubt but the great Reputation Mr. *Broughton* has atcheiv'd from the most noble Art of Bruising, has induc'd many a brawny Youth to aim at a Proficiency in that hardy Amusement.[2] The Reason of this is, that a Man's Talent is often unknown to himself, 'till he sees it by Reflection in another's Productions; which Correspondence of Fancy strikes out the latent Sparks of Genius within him, which would otherwise have lain neglected, by his not being conscious of his own proper Merit. This is sometimes the Case. But it more frequently happens, that when the Mind is warm'd by the Work of another Man, we are apt to mistake our Approbation for a Concurrence of Sentiment. That this is the most usual Occasion of the many profess'd Imitations that daily appear, is plain from the Instances just cited. For no Man can be partial enough to affirm that an Actor has arose equal to Mr. *Garrick*, a Mimic that can be put in Competition with Mr. Foote, or that we have read Essays equally entertaining and instructive with those of the *Tatlers* and *Spectators*.

The Author of the *Parish-Girl* professes an open avow'd Imitation of Mr. *Fielding*'s Manner:——Nay, goes so far as to call himself his poetic Issue. And in his Introduction to his History, where he describes his Sign, expresses himself thus.——"I have added (says he) at the Bottom of my Board, in large Golden Capitals, F____g's entire Humour."[3] A bold Promise, and as inviting to every Reader who is charm'd with the Humour of that *English Cervantes*, as that of his own female Republican, who gave Notice on her Sign that she sold *Welch* Ale, was to Mrs. *Margery*.[4]

---

1   The periodical *The Tatler*, founded and mostly written by Sir Richard Steele (1672-1729), ran three times a week between 1709 and 1711. Consisting largely of observations on manners and society, it was the major predecessor to *The Spectator*, which Steele co-edited and co-authored with Joseph Addison.

2   On John Broughton, who set up an amphitheatre for boxing-matches, see *Pompey the Little*, Bk.2, ch.6.

3   *History of Charlotte Summers*, 1.9.

4   The author is referring to an incident in Book one, chapter four of *The History of Charlotte Summers*, 1.53.

Imitations of what kind soever are but a servile Way of Writing, and almost as ill judg'd, as it is a difficult Foundation to build on. Nature has given every Man a Face, and Make, and Manner peculiar to himself, which however graceful and becoming in him, would sit but aukward and indecent in another to whom they were not natural. She has dealt in the same Manner in her several Distributions of Genius, Wit, and Understanding. As she has made some Men tall, some sort, she has form'd some of a grave, others of a merry Disposition: one has a Turn for Poetry; a second for Prose; a third is excellent at penning a grave Discourse; a fourth has a peculiar happy Talent at Pieces of Humour, which (Humour I mean) spreads itself into many Branches: In all which each Man has his proper Excellence, and must certainly proceed with the greatest Success in that he is most adapted to. Therefore every Man's Business, who would at the same Time write with Ease and gain Applause, is

> *To follow Nature where his Genius leads.*[1]

This Line belongs to a poem lately publish'd by Dr. *Kirkpatrick*, entitled the Sea-Piece. He is here talking of following the Bent of one's own Genius. This and the subsequent Lines are so much to my present Purpose, that I must beg leave to transcribe the whole Passage.

> *Ne'er, servile, trace the Path another treads,*
> *But follow Nature where your Genius leads.*
> *Nature, our common Dame, has well supply'd*
> *Somewhat to each, distinct from all beside,*
> *Which who pursues, discovers and obeys,*
> *Shall stoop with Prudence, or ascend with Ease.*
> *Why should I then this Spark of Nature quit,*
> *To ape, assume, and pilfer other's Wit;*
> *Which when with Care I cull, with Art dispose,*
> *No more adorns me than another's Cloaths?*
> *See the* Sea-Piece,   *pag. 35.*

---

1   James Kirkpatrick, *The Sea-Piece. A Narrative, Philosophical and Descriptive Poem* (London, 1750), canto 2, l. 182, p. 35.

The Truth of this Maxim the weakest Brain one would imagine might discover; but such is the Perverseness of Mankind, that instead of making use of those Gifts Nature has been bountiful enough to bestow on them, they rather chuse to imitate any thing that they see attempted with Success by another Hand, than submit to the Guidance of that secret Impulse they feel within them, which is sure to lead them right.

How true this is, the ill Success of almost all the Imitations that ever appear'd, plainly evinces; which, while the illustrious Original remains in as great Repute as ever, sink into Oblivion. Dr. *Swift* is very arch upon a Dramatick Performance in Imitation of the great *Shakespear,* in which the only Likeness he could find out in the whole Piece consisted in a *Go to*——*In sooth*——*in faith my good Lord,* and such ingenious Instances.[1] The *Jane Shore* of Mr. *Rowe,* whatever Merit it may have as a Tragedy, has certainly very little as an Imitation.[2] And it is very lucky for that Gentleman who has enrich'd the World with the *Black-Prince,*[3] that he thought of telling his Readers in his Title-Page, that he aim'd at the Manner of *Shakespear,* since without that Help, it would have been impossible for the most discerning Critic to discover the Similitude; though I do not doubt but the Author crampt his own Genius to adhere the closer to the Manner of his Original, throughout the elaborate Performance.

A tolerable Original is greatly preferable to the best Copy. And it shews a greater Genius in passing with some Difficulty an untrodden Path, than to go without a Slip through a broad, beaten Track. And I do not think it one of the least of *Milton*'s Excellencies, that he treats of

Things unattempted yet, in Prose, or Rhyme.[4]

But so infatuated are the modern Tribe of Imitators that they imagine all the Commendations due to their great Masters, equally the Desert of them, their Followers: and that the same Road that

1 I have not identified this citation. The author has perhaps attributed to Swift a statement by another author.
2 Nicholas Rowe, *The Tragedy of Jane Shore. Written in Imitation of Shakespear's Style* (1714).
3 William Shirley, *Edward the Black Prince; or, the Battle of Poictiers: an Historical Tragedy. Attempted after the Manner of Shakespear* (1750).
4 *Paradise Lost,* Bk. 1, l.16.

led the first to Glory will guide them also, without ever reflecting whether they are equally furnish'd for the Journey.

But not to seem too hard on this Set, it must be own'd, a good Imitation deserves it's Share of Praise. The Support of a great Writer is a Prop to a weak Genius, and many a Modern has been kept from falling by being borne up by the Wings of an Ancient.[1] And I don't know, whether their Task, if they arrive at any Perfection in it, is not more difficult than that of a good Translator. For they must write in the Manner of the copied Author, without taking his very Thoughts, and when they enter upon a Subject, must go on with it not as he has, but as would have, pursued it. It requires a great deal of Judgment, and a very intent Perusal of a Man's Works to fall into a similar Method of Stile and Sentiment with him. I say a great deal of Judgment; because I don't think an Imitator is tied down to so strict an Adherence to his Original, as to transcribe his Defects as well as his Beauties: For a good Painter will soften an ugly Feature in a Portrait, and give as favourable a Likeness as he can, with any Degree of Resemblance, to the Countenance he endeavours to represent.

As it is the Business of a Copy to avoid a Blemish, he should also endeavour to improve a Beauty, if he can do it without deviating from the Manner of the Writer he intends to imitate. For it is not allowable to indulge ever so good a Thought contrary to his avow'd Pattern. Mr. *Dryden*, in his Preface to his Miscellanies, mentions a Dislike he had conceiv'd to two Lines in his own Translation of the Episode of *Lausus* and *Mezentius*, in the Tenth Book of *Virgil*, Because (says he) tho' they are good Lines, yet I am convinc'd they are more in the Way of *Ovid* than *Virgil*.[2]

Now if so great Genius as Mr. *Dryden* found it so very difficult to keep up the Sentiments of a Writer he was even translating,

---

1 The author refers to the notorious "quarrel of the ancients and moderns." Originating in France in the late seventeenth century, this debate concerned the need for modern authors to follow the models provided by classical literature. In siding with the "ancients," the author places himself in the tradition of British authors like Swift, Pope, and Fielding.

2 Now usually known as Dryden's preface to *Sylvæ: or, the Second Part of Poetical Miscellanies* (1685). See *Essays of John Dryden*, ed. W.P. Ker (New York: Russell & Russell, 1961), 1:257. Dryden's translation of the works of Virgil (70-19 BCE) in 1697 set the standard for translations of the classics throughout the eighteenth century. Eighteenth-century readers widely thought of Ovid (43 BCE-17 CE) as a writer of exotic and often lascivious verse, quite in contrast with the formal and moralistic Virgil.

how much more so must it be to a Man who cannot boast an equal Share of Understanding, to write with Spirit in Another's Manner, without purloining his very Thoughts? But hold——while I am giving Laws to other Writers, I should consider that I am, at least *pro tempore*,[1] a Servant of the Public myself, and I am at this Minute seiz'd with a sudden Tremor of all my Limbs, occasioned by my Fancy's haunting me with a lively Representation of one of my Masters rising up in a Fury, with a D____n this Fellow, why does he not pursue the Promise of his Title-Page? Pray Sir, be seated, don't put yourself in a Passion, and I'll go on immediately.

These Remarks could hardly make a just Claim to that Impartiality, I have all long been so great a Stickler for, was I entirely to pass over in Silence the few Mistakes our Author has been guilty of in the Conduct of his several Performances. But I shall be very little inclin'd to enlarge on so disagreeable a Part of the Critic's Office. First then for *Joseph Andrews*.——We are told, that the chief End of these Pieces is the Extirpation of Vice, and the Promotion of Virtue; to say the Truth, which the general Bent of them always tends to. But we fear this grand Rule has in some Places been too much disregarded. As the Works of Mr. *Fielding* are in every Body's Hands, there ought not to be a Line in them which should cause the modestest Lady a single Blush in the Perusal. This Delicacy of Stile and Sentiment has been quite neglected in some Dialogues between the wanton Lady *Booby*[2] and most innocent *Joseph Andrews*; and more particularly so in one Chapter, which must occur to the Remembrance of every Reader conversant with these Works. We may venture to say this one Chapter has been prejudicial to the young People of both Sexes, and that more Readers have look'd upon the Innocence of *Joseph Andrews* as Stupidity, than the Wantonness of Lady *Booby* as Guilt. Lewdness is too mean a Branch of Humour (if indeed it is Branch of Humour) for a Man of Mr. *Fielding*'s Sense to have Recourse to: and we hope that he will henceforth leave it to those barren Writers of Comedy who have no other Way of pleasing, but a scandalous Coincidence with the deprav'd Taste of a vicious Audience. The next Objection we shall

---

1 Latin: for the moment.
2 In Fielding's novel, Lady Booby attempts to seduce her servant Joseph Andrews in boldly sexual language.

make to *Joseph Andrews* is a general one, which includes the whole Performance. My Reader will start perhaps at the Thoughts of so extensive an Objection, but I must beg leave to say, that tho' the Narration is conducted with great Spirit, and there are innumerable Strokes of Wit and Nature throughout, it is no small Derogation to the Merit of this Work, that the Story on which it is founded is not sufficiently interesting. The Characters indeed are equally natural and entertaining with those of *Tom Jones*, but the Parts they are allotted engage much less of our Attention. In Dramatic Pieces, where the Story must be stretch'd into Five Acts, there is some Excuse for this Inaction, and Want of Incidents, but in these Performances, where the Length of the Work is left entirely to the Discretion of the Writers, little can be alledg'd in his Defence.

We will here take our Leave of *Joseph Andrews*, and briefly observe what deserves Reproof in Mr. *Fielding*'s last Piece, *viz. Tom Jones*; a Performance which on the whole perhaps is the most lively Book ever publish'd, but our Author has here and there put in his Claim to that Privilege of being dull, which the Critics have indulg'd to the Writers of Books of any Length.

———*Opere in longo fas est obrepere somnum.*[1]
  HOR.
—————Sleep
O'er Works of Length allowably may creep.
FRANCIS.[2]

The most glaring Instance of this kind in all this Author's Works is the long unenliven'd Story of *the Man of the Hill*; which makes up so great a Part of a Volume.[3] A Narration which neither interests or entertains the Reader, and is of no more Service than in filling up so many Pages. The Substance of the Story is such as (to make use of Mr. *Shirley*'s Phrase)

  "*almost staggers Credibility.*"[4]

---

1   Horace, *Ars Poetica*, l. 360.
2   Rev. Philip Francis (1708–73), author of *A Poetical Translation of the Works of Horace* (1742–46).
3   This story occurs in *Tom Jones*, Bk. 8, chs. 10–15.
4   Shirley, *Edward the Black Prince*, 1.2.4.

For though I have heard it affirm'd that there is such a Character as the *Man of the Hill*; yet I believe the Generality of Readers concurr'd with me thinking it chimerical and unnaturally singular. I am very sorry Mr. *Fielding* should have introduc'd so improbable a Story, because there is no kind of Writing where the Rule of *Horace*, concerning Probability, should so strictly be observed, as in these Works.

Ficta voluptatis causâ sint proxima veris;
Nec quodcunque volet, poscat sibi fabula credi.[1]

Of which be pleas'd, my courteous *English* Reader, to accept the following free Translation.

The Life-wrought Tale should ne'er advance
A Line that favours of Romance.

I am now most heartily tired of cavilling, for which Reason I shall take no Notice of the other few Blemishes in the Works of this Author, which may have arose from Heedlessness; or the Frailty of human Nature may have given Birth to. And which are more conspicuous in Writings so lively in general, as Freckles are more remarkable in those of Fair Complexions. Praise is Insolence where the Man that praises dares not discommend: on which Account I trust that our *English Cervantes* will not be offended at the Freedom I have taken in censuring some Parts of his Works. I have all along endeavour'd to act according to the laudable Resolution I took at my first setting out; that is, to proceed without Prejudice, or Partiality, like a candid, honest Critic, who will, (according to *Shakespear* in his *Othello*)

"*Nothing extenuate,*
Nor set down aught in Malice."[2]

FINIS.

---

1   Horace, *Ars Poetica*, ll. 338-39.
2   *Othello*, 5.2.342-43.

Appendix D: Poems by Francis Coventry

1. *Penshurst* (1750)

[Penshurst, about thirty miles from London, is the family estate of
the Sidneys, whose most famous ancestor is the Elizabethan poet and
soldier Sir Philip Sidney (1554–86). Ben Jonson visited there, and his
"To Penshurst" (1616) is an early contribution to the genre of the
"country house" poem to which Coventry's *Penshurst* belongs. By
the time Coventry was invited to Penshurst, it had fallen into the
hands of William Perry, who had married Elizabeth Sidney, and who
set about modernizing the estate before he died in a lunatic asylum,
in 1757. Coventry certainly knew Jonson's "To Penshurst," to which
he alludes in the penultimate line of *Penshurst*. But he wrote a very
different kind of "country house" poem. Jonson had celebrated the
harmony of this noble estate with the natural world and with the local
peasantry. Coventry uses his tribute to lionize the poetic and military
history associated with Penshurst and, by extension, all of England.
In the author's use of the estate as an epitome of English history, this
poem more resembles Pope's highly influential *Windsor Forest* (1713).
As a background to *Pompey the Little*, *Penshurst* is significant for its
contrast between the heroic past of the estate and the corruption and
decadence of the modern age, particularly in London, the main setting for his novel. Coventry is unabashedly proud of his friendship
with the Sidney family, an indication of his social and literary ambition. Moreover, the evidence of the poem tends to contradict Robert
Adams Day's opinion that Coventry was a "Tory" on the evidence of
his literary debts to Tory writers like Pope and Swift. The Tories were
sympathetic to the claim that the Stuart royal family, ousted from the
throne in 1688, were the legitimate rulers of Britain, even if they increasingly conceded that overturning the present Hanoverian regime
would be political disruptive. In this poem, however, Coventry
calls the ousted Stuart monarchy "England's worst disgrace," lauds
the republican Algernon Sidney as a "patriot," and laments the loss
of England's ancient "Liberty." This is very much the language
typical of Whigs, who strongly supported the Hanoverian monarchy and condemned the Stuarts as threats to popular freedom.]

Genius of Penshurst old!
Who saws't the birth of each immortal oak,
Here sacred from the stroke;
And all thy tenants of yon turrets bold,
Inspir'ist to arts or arms;
Where Sidney* his Arcadian landscape drew,
Genuine from thy Doric View; [1]
And patriot Algernon[2] unshaken rose
Above insulting foes;
And Saccarissa[3] nurs'd her angel charms:
O suffer me with sober tread
To enter on thy holy shade;
Bid smoothly-sliding Medway[4] stand,
And wave his sedgy tresses bland,
A stranger let him kindly greet,
And pour his urn beneath my feet.
And see where Perry opes his door,
To land me on the social floor;
Not does the heiress of these shades deny
To bend her bright majestic eye,
Where beauty shines, and friendship warm,
And honor in a female form.
With them in aged groves to walk,
And lose my thoughts in artless talk,
I shun the voice of Party loud,
I shun loose Pleasure's idle crowd,

---

*   Sir Philip Sidney [Coventry's note].

---

1   Arcadia, a real province in Greece, was the traditional setting of pastoral literature,
     including Sir Philip Sidney's prose fiction *The Countess of Pembroke's Arcadia*
     (1593). The reference to "Doric" here is confusing. This term usually refers to a
     form of classical architecture, but Penshurst House is without classical influence,
     as observed by Ben Jonson in *To Penshurst*: "No Doric nor Corinthian pillars
     grace / With imagery this structure's naked face" (ll. 29–30). Coventry might be
     using "Doric" to suggest Sidney's general debt to classical culture (including the
     pastoral).
2   Politician and writer Algernon Sidney (1622–83), who was born at Penshurst, favored
     republican government and was executed for an alleged plot against King Charles II.
3   The seventeenth-century poet Edmund Waller's poetical name for Lady Dorothy
     Sidney.
4   The River Medway is adjacent to the Penshurst estate.

And monkish Academic cell,
Where science only feigns to dwell,
And court, where speckled vanity
Apes her tricks in tawdry dye,
And shifts each hour her tinsel hue,
Still furbelow'd[1] in follies new.
Here nature no distortion wears,
Old Truth retains his silver hairs,
And Chastity her matron step,
And purple health his rosy lip.
Ah! on the virgin's gentle brow
How innocence delights to glow?
Unlike the town-dame's haughty air,
The scornful eye and harlot's stare;
But bending mild the bashful front
As modest fear is ever wont:
Shepherdesses such of old
Doric bards enamor'd told,
Where the pleas'd Arcadian vale
Eccho'd the enchanting tale.
          But chief of virtue's lovely train,
A pensive exile of the plain,
No longer active now to wield
Th'avenging sword, protecting shield,
Here thoughtful-walking Liberty
Remembers Britons once were free.
And her would Nobles old converse,
And learn her dictates to rehearse,
Ere yet they grew refin'd to hate
The hospitable rural seat,
The spacious hall with tenants stor'd;
Where mirth and plenty crown'd the board;
Ere yet their *Lares*[2] they forsook,
And lost the genuine British look,
The conscious brow of inward merit,

---

1 Decorated with "showy ornaments or trimming, especially in a lady's dress" (*OED*).
2 In Roman religion, guardian spirits of the household.

The rough, unbending, martial spirit,
To clink the chain of thraldom gay,
And court-idolatry pay;
To live in city smoaks obscure,
Where morn ne'er wakes her breezes pure,
Where darkest midnight reigns at noon,
And fogs eternal blot the sun.

But come, the minutes flit away,
And eager fancy longs to stray;
Come, friendly Genius! lead me round
Thy Sylvan haunts and magic ground;
Point ev'ry spot of hill or dale,
And tell me, as we tread the vale,
"Here mighty Dudly[1] once wou'd rove,
To plan his triumphs in the grove;
There looser Waller,[2] ever gay,
With Sacchariss in dalliance lay;
And Philip, side-long yonder spring,
His lavish carols wont to sing."
Hark! I hear the echoes call,
Hark! The rushing waters fall;
Lead me to the green retreats,
Guide me to the Muses seats,
Where ancient bards retirement chose,
Or ancient Lovers wept their woes.
What Genius points to yonder oak*?
What rapture does my soul provoke?
There let me hang a garland high,
There let my muse her accents try;
Be there my earliest homage paid,
Be there my latest vigils made;
For thou wast planted in the earth

---

* An oak in Penshurst park, planted the day Sir Philip Sidney was born, of which Ben.
   Johnson speaks in the following manner. "That taller tree, which of a Nut was set. /
   At his great birth, where all the Muses met" [Coventry's note].

---

1 Robert Dudley (1532-88), Earl of Leicester, best known as the favorite of Queen
   Elizabeth I.
2 The poet Edmund Waller (1606-87).

The day that shone on Sidney's birth.
That happy time, that glorious day
The Muses came in concert gay;
With harps in tune, and ready song,
The jolly Chorus tript along;
In honour of th'auspicious morn,
To hail an infant genius born:
Next came the Fauns in order meet,
The Satyrs next with cloven feet,
The Dryads swift that roam the woods;
The Naiads[1] green that swim the floods;
Sylvanus[2] note left his silent cave,
Medway came dropping from the wave;
Vertumnus[3] led his blushing spouse,
And Ceres[4] shook her wheaten brows,
And Mars[5] with milder look was there,
And laughing Venus[6] grac'd the rear.
They join'd their hands in festive dance,
And bade the smiling babe advance;
Each gave a gift; Sylvanus last
Ordain'd, when all the pomp was past,
Memorial meet, a tree to grow,
Which might to future ages shew,
That on select occasion rare,
A troop of Gods assembled there:
The Naiads water'd well the ground,
And Flora[7] twin'd a wood-bine[8] round:
The tree sprung fast in hallow'd earth,
Co-æval with th'illustrious birth.

　　　　Thus let my feet unwearied stray;
Nor satisfied with one survey,

---

1 River nymphs.
2 Roman god of forests, groves, and fields.
3 Roman deity of the seasons.
4 Roman goddess of agriculture, particularly cereals.
5 Roman god of war.
6 Roman goddess of beauty.
7 Roman goddess of flowers and the spring.
8 A climbing plant, particularly honeysuckle.

When morn returns with doubtful light,
And Phebe[1] pales her lamp of night,
Still let me wander forth anew,
And print my footsteps in the dew,
What time the swain with ruddy cheek
Prepares to yoke his oxen meek,
And early drest in neat array
The milk-maid chanting shrill her lay,
Comes abroad with morning pail;
And the sound of distant flail
Gives the ear a rough good-morrow,
And the lark from out his furrow
Soars upright on matin[2] wings,
And at the gate of heaven sings.
        But when the sun with fervid ray
Drives upward to his noon of day,
And couching oxen lay them down
Beneath the beachen umbrage brown;
Then let me wander in the hall,
Round whose antique-visag'd wall
Hangs the armour Britons wore,
Rudely cast in days of yore.
Yon sword some hero's arm might wield,
Red the ranks of *Chalgrave* field,
Where ever-glorious Hampden bled,[3]
And Freedom tears of sorrow shed:
Or in the gallery let me walk,
Where living pictures seem to talk,
Where beauty smiles serenely fair,
And courage frowns with martial air;
Tho' whiskers quaint the face disguise,
And habits odd to modern eyes.

---

1 The moon. In Greek mythology, "Phoebe" (meaning "bright moon") is a Titan, or
   one of the original fourteen deities.
2 Morning.
3 In the English Civil Wars (1642–49), which pitted the Parliament against King Charles
   I, John Hampden died fighting for the Parliamentary forces at the Battle of Chalgrave
   Hill (1643).

Behold what kings in Britain reign'd,
Plantagenets with blood distain'd,
And valiant Tudor's haughty race,
And Stuarts, England's worst disgrace.
The Norman first, with cruel frown,
Proud of his new-usurped crown,
Begins the list;[1] and many more,
Stern Heroes form'd of roughest ore.
See victor Henry[2] there advance,
Ev'n in his look he conquers France;
And murtherer Richard, justly slain
By Richmond's steel on Bosworth plain;[3]
See the tyrant of his wives,
Prodigal of fairest lives,
And laureat Edward nurs'd in arts,
Minerva school'd his kingly parts:
But ah! the melancholy Jane,[4]
A soul too tender for a queen!
She sinks beneath the imperial sway,
The dear-bought scepter of a day!
And must she mount the scaffold drear?
Hard-hearted Mary learn to spare!
Eliza[5] next salutes the eye;

---

1   Coventry recites the names of the royal families who had ruled England since the
    Norman Invasion in 1066, when William the Conqueror overthrew the Anglo-Saxon
    King Harold II. Following William and his heirs, England was ruled by the Planta-
    genets (1133-1400). The English throne was contested until the accession of the first
    Tudor king, Henry VII, in 1485. Coventry's disdain for the Stuart royal family, which
    came to the throne in 1603, indicates his agreement with those who maintained that
    the Stuarts had been rightly excluded from the throne in 1714 as the result of their
    Roman Catholicism. The heirs of the royal family installed on the throne in 1714, the
    House of Hanover, have remained the British monarchs to this day.
2   Henry V (reigned 1413-22).
3   Coventry is following Shakespeare's inaccurate account of the death of Richard III at
    the hand of the Earl of Richmond at the Battle of Bosworth Field (1485).
4   Edward VI (reigned 1547-53), who was considered learned despite his youth, hence
    the allusion to Minerva, Greek goddess of wisdom. Edward was briefly succeeded
    after his death by his cousin Lady Jane Grey, who was executed by nobles loyal to the
    Catholic Mary Tudor ("Bloody Mary").
5   The reign of Elizabeth I, from 1558 to 1603, was widely admired as an era of English
    greatness. It also accorded with the zenith of the Sidney family's accomplishments.

Exalt the song to liberty,
The Muse repeats the sacred name,
Eliza fills the voice of fame.
From thence a baser age began,
The royal ore polluted ran,
Till foreign Nassau's valiant hand
Chac'd the holy Tyrants from the land:[1]
Downward from hence descend apace
To Brunswick's high, illustrious race;[2]
And see the canvass speaks them brave,
An injur'd nation born to save,
Active in freedom's righteous cause,
And conscious of a just applause.
      But chiefly pleas'd, the curious eye,
With nice discernment loves to try
The labour'd wonders, passing thought,
Which warm Italian pencils wrought;
Fables of love, and stories old,
By Greek and Latian[3] poets told;
How Jove committed many a rape,[4]
How young Acteon lost his shape;[5]
Or what celestial Pen-men writ,
Or what the painter's genuine wit
From fancy's store-house could devise;
Where Raphael claims the highest prize.[6]
Madonas here decline the head,
With fond maternal pleasure fed,
Or lift their lucid eyes above,
Where more is seen than holy love.

---

1   With his Protestant wife Mary Stuart, William III, who belonged to the Dutch House of Orange-Nassau, succeeded Mary's deposed Catholic father, James II, to the English throne in 1688.
2   The Hanover dynasty of Coventry's time, also known as the House of Brunswick.
3   A variant spelling of "Latin."
4   Jove, the Roman counterpart of Zeus, king of the gods, coupled with mortal women in many myths.
5   In the myth told by Ovid, Acteon accidentally spied the goddess Diana bathing. Diana turned him into a stag, and he was killed by his own hunting party.
6   The Renaissance painter Raphael (1483-1520) enjoyed a high reputation in the eighteenth century. He was particularly admired for his naturalistic Madonnas.

There temples stand display'd within,
And pillars in long order seen,
And roofs rush forward to the sight,
And lamps affect a living light,
Or landscapes tire the trav'ling eye,
The clouds in azure volumes fly,
The distant trees distinguish'd rise,
And hills look little in the skies.
    When day declines, and ev'ning cool
Begins her gentle, silent rule,
Again, as fancy points the way,
Benignant leader, let me stray:
And wilt thou, Genius, bring along
(So shall my Muse exalt her song)
The Lord who rules this ample scene,
His consort too with gracious mien,
Her little offspring prattling round,
While Eccho lisps their infant sound.
And let good-nature, born to please,
Wait on our steps, and graceful ease;
Nor mirth be wanting as we walk,
Nor wit to season sober talk;
Let gay description too attend,
And fable told with moral end,
And satire quick that comes by stealth,
And flowing laughter, friend to health.
Meanwhile attention loves to mark
The deer that crop the shaven park,
The steep-brow'd hill, or forest wild,
The sloping lawns, and zephyrs[1] mild,
The clouds that blush with ev'ning red,
Or meads with silver fountains fed,
The fragrance of the new-mown hay,
And black-bird chanting on the spray;
The calm farewel of parting light,
And ev'ning sad'ning into night.

---

1   Literally, west-winds, but a conventional poetic word for any gentle breezes.

Nor wearied yet my roving feet,
Tho' night comes on amain, retreat;
But still abroad I walk unseen
Along the star-enlighten'd green;
Superior joys my soul invite,
Lift, lift to heav'n the dazzled sight;
Lo, where the moon enthron'd on high,
Sits steady empress of the sky,
Enticing nations to revere,
And proudly vain of Pagan fear;
Or where thro' clouds she travels fast,
And seems on journey bent in haste,
While thousand hand-maid stars await,
Attendant on their queen of state.
'Tis now that in her high controul,
Ambitious of a foreign rule,
She stirs the ocean to rebel,
And factious waters fond to swell
Guides to battle in her carr,
'Gainst her sister earth to war.
Thus let me muse on things sublime,
Above the flight of modern rhyme,
And call the soul of Newton down,[1]
Where it sits high on starry throne,
Inventing laws for worlds to come,
Or teaching comets how to roam:
With him I'd learn of every star,
But four-ey'd pedantry be far,
And ignorance in garb of sense,
With terms of art to make pretence.
Hail happy soil! illustrious earth!
Which gav'st so many heroes birth;
Where never wand'ring poet trod,
But felt within th'inspiring God!
In these transporting, solemn shades

---

1   Sir Isaac Newton (1643-1727), whose revolutionary theories on gravitation and plan-
etary motions had been widely disseminated in a simplified form.

First I salute th'Aonian maids.[1]
Ah lead me, Genius, to thy haunts,
Where Philomel at ev'ning chants,[2]
And as my oaten pipe resounds,
Give musick to the forming sounds.
A simple shepherd, yet unknown,
Aspires to snatch an ivy crown,
On daring pinions bold to soar,
Tho' here thy Waller sung before,
And Johnson[3] dipt his learned pen,
And Sidney pour'd his fancy-flowing strain.

FINIS.

2. "To the Hon. Wilmot Vaughan, Esq. in Wales" (1755)

[Coventry's last published literary production is this poetical epistle to Wilmot Vaughan, first Earl of Lisburne (1730-1800), who lived at that time in northern Wales. First published in Robert Dodsley's *Collection of Poems* (1755) not long after Coventry's death, it is a poem remarkable chiefly for signs of the author's final despair and loneliness. The rugged Welsh landscape, presented as bleak and sickly rather than sublime, seems hardly better than the corrupt world of London, which Coventry treats with his usual distaste. The poet addresses Vaughan almost only in interrogatives, suggesting that he really does not know his friend's thoughts concerning the long geographical and emotional distance that separates them. Despite Coventry's longing to see his friend again, the poem's conclusion suggests that Vaughan is probably better off in Wales.]

Ye distant realms that hold my friend
Beneath a cold ungenial sky,

---

1   The nine Muses, whose mythological home was Mount Helicon in the Greek region of Aonia.
2   In a version of an old myth told by Ovid, the Athenian princess Philomel was transformed by the gods into a nightingale.
3   Ben Jonson.

Where lab'ring groves with weight of vapours bend,
Or raving winds o'er barren mountains fly;
Restore him quick to London's social clime,
Restore him quick to friendship, love and joy;
      Be swift, ye lazy steeds of Time,
      Ye moments, all your speed employ.
      Behold November's glooms arise,
      Pale suns with fainter glory shine,
Dark gathering tempests blacken in the skies,
And shiv'ring woods their sickly leaves resign.
Is this a time on Cambrian[1] hills to roam,
To court disease in Winter's baleful reign,
      To listen to th' Atlantic foam,
      While rocks repel the roaring main,
      While horror fills the region vast,
      Rheumatic tortures Eurus[2] brings,
Pregnant with agues flies the northern blast,
And clouds drop quartans[3] from their flagging wings:
Dost thou explore Sabrina's[4] fountful source.
Where huge Plinlimmon's[5] hoary height ascends:
      Then downward mark her vagrant course,
      Till mix'd with clouds the landscape ends?
      Dost thou revere the hallow'd soil
      Where Druids[6] old sepulchered lie;
Or up cold Snowden's[7] craggy summits toil.
And muse on ancient savage liberty?
Ill suit such walks with bleak autumnal air,
Say, can November yield the joys of May?
      When Jove deforms the blasted year,
      Can Wallia[8] boast a chearful day?
      The town expects thee.——Hark, around,

---

1 Welsh.
2 God of the east wind.
3 Agues and quartans: fevers.
4 The Roman name for the River Severn.
5 A mountain in Wales.
6 The priests of the ancient Welsh.
7 The highest and most famous Welsh mountain.
8 A barbarian king and warrior against the Romans in the fifth century CE.

Thro' every street of gay resort,
New chariots rattle with awak'ning sound,
And crowd the levees,[1] and besiege the court.
The patriot, kindling as his wars ensue,
Now fires his soul with liberty and fame,
     Marshals his threat'ning tropes anew,
     And gives his hoarded thunders aim.
     Now seats their absent lords deplore,
     Neglected villas empty stand,
Capacious Gro'venor gathers all its store,
And mighty London swallows up the land.[2]
See sportive Vanity her flights begin,
See new-blown Folly's plenteous harvest rise,
     See mimick beauties dye their skin,
     And harlots roll their venal eyes.
     Fashions are set, and fops return,
     And young coquettes in arms appear;
Dreaming of conquest, how their bosoms burn,
Trick'd in the new fantastry of the year.
Fly then away, nor scorn to bear a part
In this gay scene of folly amply spread:
     Follies well us'd refine the heart,
     And pleasures clear the studious head;
     By grateful interchange of mirth
     And toils of study sweeter grow,
As varying seasons recommend the earth,
Nor does Apollo[3] always bend his bow.

---

1   A levee (from the French *se lever*) was an audience granted to especially favored people upon the rising of a monarch or some other dignitary from bed.

2   Coventry is referring to the exodus of England's aristocracy and landed gentry each winter from their estates in the country to houses in fashionable parts of London such as Grosvenor Square, in Mayfair.

3   The Greek god of truth and learning, traditionally portrayed as carrying a bow and arrows.

Appendix E: Eighteenth-Century Discussions of Animals

1. Pierre Bayle, "Rorarius," from *The Dictionary Historical and Critical* (1696)

[Pierre Bayle (1647-1706) exerted a major influence on the development of free-thinking, skeptical ideas during the French Enlightenment. Besides casting doubt on the reality of Christ's miracles, and more generally on the supposed superiority of Christianity to other religions or to atheism, Bayle gave a sympathetic hearing to the heterodox opinion that beasts are as rational as human beings. Largely due to Bayle's fame as a free-thinker, both French and British authors widely cited the following article on Rorarius, an obscure philosopher of the sixteenth century. Excerpting here from the 1734 English translation of *Dictionnaire historique et critique*, I have omitted the lengthy footnotes in which Bayle quotes the writers he mentions.]

RORARIUS (Hierôme), Nuncio of Clement VII at the court of Ferdinand king of Hungary, has composed a book which is worth the reading. He undertakes to show, not only that brute beasts have reason, but that they make better use of it than man. The occasion which moved him to write that book is curious, and very singular. He happened to be in a company, where a learned man affirmed that Charles V did not equal the Otho's, nor Frederic Barbarossa. There needed no more to make Rorarius conclude that beasts are more reasonable than men, and he set himself immediately about the composing a treatise upon this subject. It was at the time that Charles V made war against the league of Smalcalde.¹ This book is not ill wrote, and it contains a great many singular facts concerning

---

1   Bayle is being anti-Catholic: Charles V was a great Catholic hero who suppressed Protestantism during the Thirty Years War. Yet someone's suggestion that Charles V was not a great hero drove the exasperated Rorarius, a high-ranking Catholic, to write a tract claiming that men are stupider than beasts. As official Catholic belief strongly upheld the superiority of humans over beasts, Rorarius's enthusiastic piety led him to offend the dogma of his own church, much to Bayle's amusement.

the ingenuity of beasts, and the malice of man. Those which concern the capacity of beasts, put under great difficulties both the followers of Mr. Des Cartes and those of Aristotle.[1] The first deny that beasts have any soul; the latter maintain that they are endowed with sense, with memory, and with passions, but not at all with reason. It is a pity that the opinion of Des Cartes should be so hard to maintain, and so improbable; for it is otherwise very advantageous to religion, and this is the only reason which hinders some people from quitting it. It is not liable to the most dangerous consequences of the common opinion. It is a long time since it has been maintained that the souls of beasts are rational. The Philosophers of the schools[2] are very much mistaken, if, by rejecting that, they persuade themselves, that they shall avoid the ill consequences of the opinion that gives beasts a sensitive soul. These gentlemen want neither distinctions, nor exceptions, nor assurance to decide, that the acts of this soul do not exceed certain bounds, which they prescribe to them: but all this idle and unintelligible discourse signifies nothing towards the establishing a specific difference between the souls of men and those of beasts; and it is not likely, that they can ever invent a better explication, than that which they have already given. The author, who has best confuted the opinion of Des Cartes concerning the souls of beasts, would have done us a singular favour, if he could have cleared the common opinion from the great difficulties that attend it. Mr. Leibniz, one of the greatest wits of Europe, being sensible of these difficulties, has given us some insights, which deserve to be improved[3]... But to return to Rorarius, I do not believe I am mistaken when I think he was born at Pordenone in Italy. I wish I

---

1   The writings of Aristotle (384-322 BCE) dominated European philosophy until the seventeenth century, when the French writer René Descartes (1596-1650) became a principal figure in the foundation of new philosophical theories and methodologies. Aristotle argued that animals have "sensitive" souls whereas humans have "rational" souls. Descartes, on the other hand, maintained that animals were merely machines without souls.

2   The Medieval universities, where Aristotle's philosophy was virtually unchallenged.

3   The German philosopher Gottfried Wilhelm Leibniz (1646-1716) maintained that all things, including animals and inanimate objects, are truly individual souls, or what he called "monads." Different monads possess differing levels of awareness, very high in the case of humans and somewhat lower in the case of animals. Leibniz therefore avoided the problems attendant on the "common" opinion of Aristotle, that humans and animals have different *kinds* of souls.

had read the plea, which he composed for Rats. It was printed in the country of the Grisons in the year 1548. There is something like it in the works of President Chassaneus. I shall here give the remainder of the collection, whereof you have seen the principal part in the article of Pereira.

2. Samuel Johnson, *The Idler*, No. 24, 30 September 1758

[This essay in Samuel Johnson's journal *The Idler* is comparable to *Pompey the Little* in its satirical ruminations on the similarity between animals and humans. Taking up the philosophical question of whether animals "think," Johnson muses that most people seem hardly more rational than beasts.]

When man sees one of the inferior creatures perched upon a tree, or basking in the sunshine, without any apparent endeavour or pursuit, he often asks himself, or his companion, "on what that animal can be supposed to be thinking?"

Of this question, since neither bird nor beast can answer it, we must be content to live without the resolution. We know not how much the brutes recollect of the past, or anticipate of the future; what power they have of comparing and preferring; or whether their faculties may not rest in motionless indifference, till they are moved by the presence of their proper object or stimulated to act by corporal sensations.

I am the less inclined to these superfluous inquiries, because I have always been able to find sufficient matter for curiosity in my own species. It is useless to go far in quest of that which may be found at home; a very narrow circle of observation will supply a sufficient number of men and women, who might be asked with equal propriety, "on what they can be thinking?"

It is reasonable to believe, that thought, like every thing else, has its causes and effects; that it must proceed from something known, done, or suffered; and must produce some action or event. Yet how great is the number of those in whose minds no source of thought has ever been opened, in whose life no consequence of thought is ever discovered; who have learned nothing upon which they can reflect; who have neither seen nor felt any thing which could leave traces on the memory; who neither foresee nor desire any change of their condition, and have therefore neither fear, hope, nor design, and yet are supposed to be thinking beings.

To every act a subject is required. He that thinks, must think upon something. But tell me, ye that pierce deepest into nature, ye that take the widest surveys of life, inform me, kind shades of Malebranche and Locke,[1] what that something can be, which excites and continues thought in maiden aunts with small fortunes; in younger brothers that live upon annuities; in traders retired from business; in soldiers absent from their regiments, or in widows that have no children?

Life is commonly considered as either active or contemplative; but surely this division, how long soever it has been received, is inadequate and fallacious. There are mortals whose life is certainly not active, for they do neither good nor evil, and whose life cannot be properly called contemplative; for they never attend either to the conduct of men, or the works of nature, but rise in the morning, look round them till night in careless stupidity, go to bed and sleep, and rise again in the morning.

3. From Anonymous, *A Dissertation on Mr. Hogarth's ... The Four Stages of Cruelty* (1751)

[Campaigns for animal rights evolved slowly, and did not exist in the time of Francis Coventry. In 1824, the first Society for the Prevention of Cruelty Animals was formed, partly through the efforts of William Wilberforce, best known for his tireless campaign against the slave trade. Coventry's disgust with cruelty to animals therefore precedes such movements, though he was not entirely without fellow sympathizers. The artist William Hogarth had depicted cruelty to animals in his engravings "The Four Stages of Cruelty," his message being that such abuses led naturally to cruelty to humans. Appearing during the same year as *Pompey the Little*, the following excerpt from

---

1 Nicolas Malebranche (1638-1715) and John Locke (1632-1704) had little in common besides being eminent modern philosophers.

an anonymous dissertation on Hogarth's engravings indicates the increased value for sympathy and benevolence in the mid-century. Like Coventry, the author links such cruelty particularly to the young and to the uneducated social underclass. Unlike Coventry, the author is particularly concerned to exonerate the British of their continental reputation as the cruelest nation in Europe.]

The First Stage of CRUELTY.

Here Mr. *Hogarth* has displayed his Ingenuity, in describing various Acts of Cruelty, as practised by our Youth in their Wantonness upon the Brute Creation; and many more he might have added, to shew the Depravity of the Mind before it is corrected by the fuller Exercise of Reason. This, however, has given Foreigners an Occasion to remark, that the Inhabitants of this Island are naturally savage, and in their Temper and Disposition more inhuman and tyrannical than any other People on Earth. The many Instances that are daily seen among us of this Kind, it must be granted, leave but too much Room for this Observation: However, they who make it are desired at the same Time to take Notice, that the Offenders are generally such as are too young to reflect on the Pains the poor Animal suffers under their torturing Hands; or else they are poor, ignorant, uneducated Wretches, who have scarce any Thing more of the Man about them than his Figure and Shape. That Cruelty is the national Character of *Britons*, I may appeal to their general Behaviour and Actions on all Occasions. Whenever we have been engaged in War with any of our Neighbours, whoever charged the *English* with treating their prostrate Foes cruelly and inhumanly? On the contrary, is it not known to all the World, that our Generals and Soldiers have been remarkably kind and generous to a conquered Enemy? We always fought fairly in the Field, and when we conquered, it was by the mere Dint of our Courage and Bravery, and never thought that the insulting an Enemy, after he had submitted, or was fallen into our Hands, added any Thing to the Triumph we had gained. Can this be said of the *French*? Ask the poor Soldiers that fell into their Hands at the Battle of *Fontenoy*,[1] that were wounded, not with Bullets, but with Bits of old Iron, broken Glass, jagged Flints, &c. a Parcel of which, extracted from the torn Flesh of the miserable Soldiers, our young General sent as a Specimen of their Humanity to the *French* Court.

Were I to enter deeper into the Subject, and give a full Scope to the Argument, I believe I could make it evidently appear, that there is not a Nation in the World where Acts of Generosity,

---

1   Won by the French, this battle took place in 1745 during the War of the Austrian Succession.

Charity, Benevolence, Compassion and Mercy, and all the social Virtues, have been so universally practised as in this Kingdom. But when I say this, I must at the same Time condemn the Barbarities exercised by our Youth on brute Animals.

I must therefore inform my young and uninformed Pupils, and it's highly proper they should know, that Animals are as sensible of Pain, Torture and Misery, as themselves; that they have as much Right to Life and the Comforts of Being as their Masters; and that although some of them are destined to be the Food, and others for the Pleasure or Service of Mankind, yet Providence has not given us a Liberty to sport with their Lives, or wanton in their cruel Usage. Remember the Fable of the Frogs, and some unlucky Boys that were throwing Stones at them: *Pray, Gentlemen,* said the Frogs, *forbear; for though this may be Sport to you, it is Death to us*; so may the poor Bird say, and says as much in its sad Outcries, when a wanton Boy is burning out its Eyes with a hot Knitting-needle; a Cock, when his Legs and Limbs are broken to Pieces with heavy Libbets[1] for the Diversion of rude brutish Spectators; the Dog, when a barbed Arrow is stuck into his Fundament to make a Parcel of Oafs laugh at his Outcries; a Couple of Cats thrown over a Signpost to divert a Company of young Urchins, in seeing the furious Animals tearing one another to pieces with their Claws; or a poor Cat worried to Death by a huge Mastiff, to make Sport for Porters and Carmen, those greater Brutes of the two. But how amiable is it to see a School-boy, with a Satchel at his Back, pleading for a tortured Animal roaring with the Extremity of its Misery? How lovely is it to see him exerting his Benevolence, and striving with all his Might, and offering his sweet Morsel of a Tart, perhaps his whole Breakfast, to prevail on the Cruel Tormentors to leave off their Barbarity? Dear Youth! If I presage rightly, thou wilt one Day be a Blessing to thy Country, thy Friends, and thy Neighbours. The Poor shall accumulate Blessings on thy Head for thy Charity; the Prayers of the Prisoner shall be thine for the Liberty he shall enjoy by thy Bounty; the Orphan shall esteem thee as a Father, and the Widow as her Husband, and the Distressed of every Kind shall feel the gracious Influence of thy extensive Benevolence.

---

1   Sticks.

Select Bibliography

[The reader may also wish to consult the introduction to Robert Adam Day's edition of *The History of Pompey the Little; or the Life and Adventures of a Lap-Dog* (London: Oxford UP, 1974). Besides this, there is currently scant scholarship on either *Pompey the Little* or "it-narratives."]

Blackwell, Mark, ed. *The Secret Life of Things: Animals, Objects, and It-Narratives.* Lewisburg: Bucknell UP, 2007.

Brown, Bill. "Reification, Reanimation, and the American Uncanny." *Critical Inquiry* 32:2 (Winter 2006): 175-207.

Cottegnies, Line. "Les traductions de *Pompey the Little* de Francis Coventry (Londres, 1751) ou la réception du roman domestique anglais en France." *La traduction romanesque au XVIIIe siècle.* Annie Cointre, Alain Lautel, and Annie Rivara, eds. Arras, France: Artois PU, 2003: 295-315.

Douglas, Aileen. "Britannia's Rule and the It-Narrator." *Eighteenth-Century Fiction* 6 (1993): 65-82.

Ellis, Markman. *The Politics of Sensibility: Race, Gender and Commerce in the Sentimental Novel.* Cambridge: Cambridge UP, 1996.

Flint, Christopher. "Speaking Objects: The Circulation Stories in Eighteenth-Century Prose Fiction." *PMLA* 113 (March 1998): 212-26.

Haywood, Ian. "Chatterton's Lady Tempest." *Notes and Queries* 30 (1983): 63-64.

Lamb, Jonathan. "Modern Metamorphoses and Disgraceful Tales." *Critical Inquiry* 28 (Autumn 2001): 133-66.

——. "The Crying of Lost Things." *ELH* 71 (2004): 949-67.

Olshin, Toby A. "Form and Theme in Novels about Non-Human Objects, a Neglected Genre." *Genre* 2 (1969): 43-56.

——. "*Pompey the Little*: A Study of Fielding's Influence." *Revue des langues vivantes* 36 (1970): 117-24.

Wheatcraft, N. Dean. "Francis Coventry's *Pompey the Little*: An Historical, Textual, and Critical Study." Diss, Ohio State University, 1974.